BLAZE ME
A SUN

A NOVEL ABOUT A CRIME

CHRISTOFFER
CARLSSON

Translated by
RACHEL WILLSON-BROYLES

LONDON/NEW YORK

Translation copyright © 2023 by Rachel Willson-Broyles

Published in the United States by Hogarth, an imprint of the Random House Publishing Group, a division of Penguin Random House LLC, New York.

HOGARTH is a trademark of the Random House Group Limited, and the H colophon is a trademark of Penguin Random House LLC.

Originally published in Sweden in Swedish as *Brinn mig en sol* by Albert Bonniers Förlag in Stockholm, Sweden. Copyright © 2021 by Christoffer Carlsson. Published by arrangement with Ahlander Agency, Stockholm, Sweden.

LIBRARY OF CONGRESS CATALOGING-IN-PUBLICATION DATA
Names: Carlsson, Christoffer, author. | Willson-Broyles, Rachel, translator.
Title: Blaze me a sun : a novel about a crime / Christoffer Carlsson ; translated by Rachel Willson-Broyles.
Other titles: Brinn mig en sol. English
Description: London ; New York : Hogarth, [2023] | "Originally published in Sweden as Brinn mig en sol by Albert Bonniers Förlag in Stockholm, Sweden."
Identifiers: LCCN 2021053543 (print) | LCCN 2021053544 (ebook) |
ISBN 9780593449356 (hardcover ; acid-free paper) |
ISBN 9780593449363 (ebook)
Subjects: LCGFT: Detective and mystery fiction. | Novels.
Classification: LCC PT9877.13.A75 B7513 2023 (print) |
LCC PT9877.13.A75 (ebook) | DDC 839.73/8—dc23/eng/20211105
LC record available at https://lccn.loc.gov/2021053543
LC ebook record available at https://lccn.loc.gov/2021053544

Printed in The United States of America

randomhousebooks.com

First Edition

Book design by Susan Turner

For Ida

Everything has its own place.
Everything has its own time.

A time to live and a time to die.
For summer and for winter.
To plant, to harvest.
To dream, to wake,
To leave home and return.

The coldest of winters has its time,
the summer and the heat
and the greatest of romances
and love all have a time of their own.

So blaze me a sun tonight,
you who shall bring me the dark.

—ELSA GRAVE

I

THE RETURN

———

Halland County, southern Sweden, 2019

1

It was the summer Evy Carlén got very sick, realized she didn't have long to live, and confided in me that she knew what had happened to Sven Jörgensson and his son, Vidar, up in Tiarp.

We hadn't known each other very long. I knew Evy had been a police officer and had moved to the house near Tofta a few years after retiring. Her husband, Ronnie, had died, and in her widowhood she devoted her days to the beautiful garden surrounding their house. It was situated a few kilometers up in the woods. That was how we met.

Ever since my return, I've lived a relatively quiet life. That's how I like it. I'm over forty now, and my days don't include any children, women, or other distractions. I spend my time writing or reading. Once or twice a week I take the car and go grocery shopping, drop by the bookstore, or visit my parents. They're in their seventies now. On occasion I drive down to Lund, where my brother works and where my editor spends half his time. I don't do much else. If I like I can walk down to the bus stop on Växjövägen and ride into town to see an old friend over a cup of coffee or a beer. Those trips are increasingly scarce now.

The only truly regular facet of my existence, beyond writing and reading, is taking walks. I hardly ever took walks during my years in Stockholm, unless I had some destination in mind, but down here I walk a few kilometers almost every day. I don't know quite why I need it, but I do. Alongside the treat of a glass of whiskey a few times a week, after an especially productive workday, my walks are one of the few rewards I allow myself.

The first time I met her was in late June. The old woman was in her garden next to an open bag of potting soil. The quiet nature of her surroundings meant that she noticed me right away as I came walking by. She looked up, spotted me, nodded, and smiled.

"Aren't you the one who moved in down by the road? Into the yellow house?"

"Yes, that's me, I moved here recently," I said.

"Where did you live before?"

"Stockholm. But I'm from here originally."

"I've seen you on walks in the neighborhood."

"It's become a habit. This is a beautiful stretch."

"Oh. Maybe it is. It's like I don't see it myself anymore." She strode over to the fence and put out her hand. "I'm Evy."

Once I'd introduced myself, she said, "That's right. You're the one who writes books. Aren't you?"

"Yes," I said, even though I hadn't been able to write a word since I came back. "I suppose I am."

"I haven't read any of them, I have to confess."

"There's no need to. Have you lived here long?"

"For almost fifteen years. My husband and I bought the house. Now it's just me. I've thought about selling it, of course," she went on, as if anticipating a question she heard often, "but I don't know, where would I go? I'm eighty years old. I guess I'll just keep living."

The next time we met, a week or so later, she invited me in for a cup of coffee and we exchanged phone numbers. We sat in her kitchen. Evy had a new cellphone, which she'd received from one of her grandchildren, and I showed her how the alarm clock worked.

She visited me sometimes. We drank wine, chatted, played cards, and kept each other company. She told me stories from her life as a police officer, hilarious and tragic stories of criminals and addicts, victims and next of kin. How it had been different, being a woman on the force at the time, and yet not. She showed me pictures from a photo album and spoke about her late husband, Ronnie, about her children and grandchildren, about her brother, Einar. I told her I'd moved back to my childhood home, that I was trying to get it in order but didn't know how, that I hadn't been able to write, and hadn't even had anything to write about, in ages.

"That sounds lonely. You, I mean. You sound lonely."

"So do you," I said.

She chuckled. "It's not the same."

Her eyes were alert and disarming in a way I wasn't used to, as if her gaze were an art she had perfected and used to great advantage during years' worth of encounters with those who found themselves in the clutches of law enforcement. It would take time for me to realize that, despite her austere background, there were years when she'd relied on cigarettes and gin to calm her nerves and make it through.

Then one day in early August, something went wrong. Evy had gotten up early that morning and felt strange. Her equilibrium was off; she felt dizzy as she brewed her morning coffee, and when she walked into her front hall she had to grab the wall for support because everything was tilting weirdly. Her stomach began to churn. Standing before the mirror, she straightened up and tried to smile, even though she didn't feel like smiling. One side of her mouth didn't move. She looked off-kilter. She raised her arms and began to count to ten, but stopped when she saw her left arm fall back down. She made her way to an easy chair and called the emergency number.

"My name is Evy Carlén. It's a lovely morning. Can you hear what I'm saying?"

"I'm sorry," said the operator on the other end. "Can you repeat that? I didn't hear you. What's your name?"

"My name is Evy Carlén, and I said: *It's a lovely morning.* Can you hear what I'm saying?"

"I see you're calling from Norteforsen near Tofta. Is it Norteforsen 195? What's your name? I'm having trouble hearing you."

"Okay," Evy said with a sigh. "I understand. Well, I suppose you'd better come over here, then."

She struggled to walk to the front door, phone in hand, and turned the lock so they could get in. She collapsed on the floor, because the living room was too far away. By the time the ambulance arrived, she was unconscious.

I heard that she'd had a stroke. And when she woke up in the hospital bed she seemed to have lost her speech. All she did was burst into tears. Days went by before she could say much of anything, and when she did, what she said was a name. But it wasn't the name of her late husband or the friend she sometimes met at Kupan; it wasn't her brother, Einar, or her children or grandchildren. She said: "Sven Jörgensson."

And burst into tears again.

By that point, she'd probably realized that I hadn't been completely honest with her, that in fact I had basically deceived her. But what was I supposed to do? In the time leading up to Evy's stroke, my life had slowly begun to revolve around what happened up in Tiarp, in that early spring long ago.

Moral suffering is strange. It can strike the strong as easily as the weak, and no surgery, painkillers, or artificial respirations can help. Moral pain is a different beast. The only solution is to let yourself be slowly consumed, or to resort to drastic measures to free yourself.

That was what she would come to teach me.

2

When I grew up, I used to see Sven Jörgensson several times a week. That's the way of it, when you come from a place like Tofta, you learn an awful lot about everyone without even trying.

I lived with my brother, Rasmus, and my parents near Lake Tofta, along the highway that goes to Simlångsdalen. The year I turned ten, 1986, I started riding the school bus to Snöstorp School. Each morning, I walked down to the mailboxes at the side of the road and waited for the old orange-and-white bus to appear over at the bend in the road over toward Skedala. I don't remember the bus driver's name, but it was always the same thin-haired and quiet man. He came from town, stopped for us, and then headed up to Marbäck until the bus turned around at Tofta Art Center, came back down the highway, and turned off at Snöstorp.

My brother is three years younger than me, and when he started school we waited by the mailboxes together. Never had I felt so grown up as when I stood next to him in the early mornings, keeping an eye on the road and making sure he didn't get too close, making sure that the reflective accents on his coat were visible in the autumn and winter, when the mornings were dark, and that he had brought everything with him. You can never be sure, with little seven-year-olds.

That's when we would see Sven Jörgensson. He came driving by from Marbäck, wearing his uniform, looking tired, a cigarette in the corner of his mouth and the window rolled down just a little, squinting at the morning as if he were in the middle of some great trial of which we kids were still unaware. Sometimes he was in a patrol car, but most of the time he was driving his own vehicle, a red Volvo station wagon. Those times, it was a little harder to pick him out at a distance, but it was still possible.

One morning, as the Volvo passed, we gasped. A thick red sludge had run down from the roof of Sven's car, onto the rear windows and the fenders, and congealed there.

My brother and I were thoroughly intrigued. All the way to school we tried to guess what might have happened, whispering imagined events and exchanging scenarios, each more thrilling than the last. Maybe he'd caught a robber and beat him up. Maybe he even shot him. We knew Sven carried a handgun—all cops did. Or maybe he'd had to fight someone on the roof of the car, someone who obviously lost, maybe a man who had stolen something expensive from a store and tried to flee. Sven might have beaten the robber half to death with his baton.

When we told Dad about it that evening, he—a man who, even back then, had a good sense of humor—was as taken aback as we were.

"To think that such criminal drama took place so close to us. Maybe that's what I heard. The shot, that is."

"The shot?" I looked at my brother. "What shot?"

"I woke up around three this morning. You know how sometimes you're dreaming, and real life creeps into your dream?"

"Yeah," said my brother, his eyes wide.

"Yeah. So, I remember I was dreaming about a door slamming really hard, and it made a hell of a bang." Dad squinted and lowered his voice. "Maybe that was actually Sven, shooting the robber."

We were entranced and listened intently until Mom cocked her head pointedly and gave a wry smile. Then he laughed and, in a voice that was suddenly drained of imagination and excitement, making way for boring fatherly reality, he said, well, there was no ruling out that it had been a robber. Or that a rooftop fistfight had ended poorly, or any of the other events we'd dreamed up. But, he added, once upon a time, Sven had been a hunter. He didn't hunt anymore, he'd turned in his firearms and all that, but he was still friends with Lennart Börjesson, Göran Lundgren, and the other hunters up in the village. Sometimes he helped them with the animals they shot. Recently they'd got a moose, and Sven had had to transport it on the roof, because it didn't fit anywhere else, and the tarp they'd wrapped it in had leaked.

We were disappointed, obviously. But when you stopped to think about it, it would be really out of character for Sven to shoot another person out of the blue, even if it was a robber. Or even to hit someone. Sven was Sven. We liked to wave at him when he drove by each morning. Sometimes he waved back. You could catch a hint of a smile, not a big one, because he'd drop his cigarette, but a smile nonetheless.

Back then, two car mechanics lived in the area surrounding Marbäck and Tofta. One was Peter Nyqvist on Svanåsvägen, up in the village. The other was my father. He worked at Rejmes in Halmstad, behind Sannarp High School and across from the fire station. When the cars of the Marbäck area broke down, people turned to him or Peter for an initial assessment of the problem, especially in the summer or on weekends. Getting your car into a shop was a project in and of itself—better to let Dad or Peter have a look first. Cheaper, too. On any number of days I woke up to the phone ringing and heard Dad get up, answer sleepily, say, *Oh, hello there, Göran* and *Damn, that's too bad* and *Yes, I'm home, that's fine, can you drive it over?*

We got used to seeing cars that didn't belong to us in the driveway, propped up by a jack, their hoods open, Dad on his back on a worn rubber mat that had once been yellow but was now stained dark brown with oil and dirt. I recall that car being Sven Jörgensson's on two occasions. I don't remember what the weather was like, what was wrong with the car, whether Dad could fix it in the driveway or whether he had to call Kenneth's Towing. What stuck with me was Sven.

Sven's chin was wide and chiseled like a steam shovel, and his hands were the size of sledgehammers. He had broad shoulders and thinning hair and a slight potbelly thanks to poor cop fare and the beer he liked to drink at night; he really looked more like a farmer than a police officer. But everyone knew he was a cop. It defined him. My brother and I stood by the window or sat on the steps, carefully studying how he moved, how he talked, how he held a cigarette in one hand and rested the other on his belt, as if he missed his holster, as if his world was a little skewed when it wasn't there. While Dad took a look at the car, they talked about houses, what needed doing and what had been done, vacations, soccer, the Breared-Snöstorp match, which had ended 1–2, what was going on up in Marbäck and here in Tofta, and about us. The kids.

Sven and his wife, Bibbi, had one son, Vidar. He was just like his dad, big and strong and tenderhearted. Vidar was in high school, played offense for Breared's soccer team, already chopped wood like a man, and was well-liked by all. We'd seen him in the village now and then, and often heard his name. *Not even Vidar Jörgensson could chop that one down, no sir, we had to call the company in the city,* Farmer Andersson said once, nodding at an unusually massive spruce at the edge of his cow pasture. *Wow, look at that, you're getting close to Vidar Jörgensson's old record,* our gym teacher exclaimed as he solemnly raised the high-jump bar to an astonishing one meter and sixty-six centimeters. Vidar did odd jobs for the farmers sometimes, mostly because he thought it was fun. Even then, as I recall, he appeared to be one with his environment, his life, and his dreams, whatever they might have been.

Let me know if there's anything you need, or if I can lend a hand. So said Sven sometimes, and his words seemed to fill you up as he looked down at you with his clear, green eyes, placed a big, meaty hand on your shoulder, and said *Take care of yourself, kiddo, and be good to your parents.* I took those words seriously, because they had come from him. He called me kiddo but looked at me almost like I was an adult.

It wasn't that we wanted to be like Sven. It was just that we were so drawn in by the world we could sense in his presence, the illusion that it was possible to create around ourselves, around Marbäck and Tofta and their people and life. He made our world seem safe and secure, made us feel that even our tiny steps on earth were full of meaning and purpose, that we could make a difference, that we could trust we would never be overlooked. That someone would always be watching over us.

Sven must have been sick even then. It just wasn't noticeable. Or, I suppose it was; we just didn't want to see it. There are many things that exist and yet we don't see, because it would be too painful.

3

The idea that I should write about Sven and Vidar now, so many years later, is almost unreal. At times our orbits have come quite close to one another's, even very close now and then—I picture lifelines that cross for an instant and are about to twine together, but for one reason or another they veer away at the last second.

It could have ended differently. I've thought a lot about them, these two men and the tooth of time, everything that went on without anyone noticing.

One evening in May of 2019, a few months after my return, I found myself in Halmstad. More precisely, I was sitting at a bar. My marriage to Sara had fallen apart and the papers were signed, the division of property completed, the chapter finished, and a fresh page turned. I was recently divorced and had no desire to do anything at all, least of all write. That was about the size of it.

I had deliberately chosen a bar that was a little out-of-the-way, close to Lilla Torg. Most of the other patrons were sitting on the patio in the evening light, so I chose a table indoors, in the corner closest to the bar, with the hope that I wouldn't have to get up to order more rounds. The bartender seemed amenable to my plan.

My return home wasn't turning out as I'd imagined. I was

surprised at how little had changed in almost thirty years. Surprised and, I realized, disappointed—and for reasons I couldn't quite understand. Did I want to see a change? Me, the guy who'd come back specifically to live in the past?

That's the dilemma of the homecomer. It really isn't possible to return, and those who try only end up confused. Maybe that's where the real change happens—not in what one returns home to, but in the one who returns home.

I sat there feeling melancholy as I drank a beer, listening to the anonymous lounge music pouring endlessly from the stereo system and staring out the window. Now and then someone walked by on the street. The women looked beautiful, but the men seemed haggard somehow.

Consumed by old ideas is how I spent that spring, by thoughts of the past, by the way things had been a long time ago and in recent days, thoughts of my childhood and the role models I'd had, the dreams. About men and women who had promised each other more than they could make good on.

A large, worn-out figure stepped in and approached the bar. He leaned against it as if he needed the support, ordered a beer, and gazed around with bottle in hand.

He stared straight at me. Then I realized who it was.

"Vidar?"

The large man took a few steps toward me, squinting.

"Moth? Shit, is that you?"

I rose from my chair and put out my hand. Vidar offered a palm that was already cold and damp from the beer. His hands were dirty— black rinds under his nails, as if he had just been pulling potatoes out of the field.

"Haven't seen you in what, thirty years? Are you visiting?"

"Actually, I moved back," I said.

"Since when?"

"February. What's that, like three months?"

"I'll be damned. So what are you going to do here?"

"Oh, you know." I laughed. "Write, is the plan. Work. Live."

He opened his mouth to say something else, but he must have remembered why he'd come in the first place, because he looked around again at all the empty chairs.

"It's okay," I said. "I'm not here to socialize either."

Vidar took in my half-empty beer glass. He drank from his bottle, and half its contents vanished. His dull voice rumbled from his chest.

"We can talk for the first beer. We'll drink the second in silence."

He pulled out a chair and sat down.

Moth. It had been a long time since I'd heard that name, but it was what they used to call me. There had been two of us in my class with the same first name, and I liked books. My name twin didn't—his first love was hockey. Imaginations don't always go much further than that, but then again, why should they? I don't know who bestowed my nickname upon me, but it had started out as "Book moth" back in the dawn of time on the Snöstorp schoolyard. Eventually it was shortened to "Moth." I didn't have it so bad; there was one guy we called Bean because someone said he looked like Mr. Bean, and worst of all was the kid called Wank. No need to be an author to imagine the origins of that one.

It was weird to hear my nickname again. Remarkable that Vidar even remembered it.

Only now did I notice that his clothes, too, were covered in dirt, that the dark spots on his face weren't just stubble but filth as well. He carried a heavy odor of nature and sweat, and had aged considerably.

For me, having once admired him, it was unexpectedly hard to witness. I could sense him in my memories, hurtling across a soccer pitch on his way to leading Breared to victory in an important match and making us all throw our hands up in the air. I saw him dancing with some beautiful young woman the rest of us wished we were man enough to touch, and I recalled how amazed we were, as fifteen-year-olds, that it was possible to conduct oneself so gently but decisively, that it was actually possible, and visibly easy, to master the complex art of leading a woman in a dance without steering her. How he seemed so self-confident as he walked through the village. In my mind he was enveloped in a shimmering light, but I couldn't quite make out that shimmer here in the bar.

"Did you just come from work, or something?"

Vidar looked confused.

"What?"

I nodded to indicate his clothes.

"Oh. No, I came from home, was just doing some yard work. I needed to get away for a bit and didn't feel like showering. How come you moved back?"

"I'm no longer married, for starters."

"You were married?"

"For forty-seven months." My eyes fell on the ring finger of his left hand. "You too, I see. I mean, you're married."

"Twenty-three years in August. I don't even know how many months that is."

We drank. He ran a finger over his wedding ring, as if to rub some dirt away.

"So where do you live now?" he asked.

"Where I always lived, down here." I smiled. "By Lake Tofta. The yellow house, you know."

"What, in the same house? You moved back to your childhood home?"

My parents had decided to sell it, and I guess I couldn't let it be lost. That's often how big decisions are made: because otherwise things slip through your fingers.

To Vidar I said, "I took it over, or whatever. Mom and Dad were going to sell it. They moved to a two-bedroom place in Tegelbruket."

"Those new buildings up on Slottsmöllan? The high-rises?"

I nodded. "So all I ever do these days is sulk and brood and try to call handypeople, consider their offers, search for new furniture. Turns out it's not really my forte."

"I can imagine."

"You know, my parents wanted to sell for a reason."

The house needed new insulation, the floor had to be torn up and replaced, and the foundation had moisture damage. It could use a new roof, and the wiring in the bathroom had aged poorly; most of the appliances were ancient, and the lot, over two thousand square meters of the typical lush, unruly Marbäck foliage, was starting to get overgrown. These problems were all mine now, and had resulted in the sense that I was caught up in something I couldn't quite handle.

I had spent my whole life keeping the everyday, manual labor that made the world go 'round at arm's length. I came from a family of craftspeople and had grown up with an image of work as something you did with your hands, not your head. On occasion, standing or lying in the house, I felt a sudden burst of happiness and pride at doing physical work, at feeling the ache in my body and the sweat on my back.

I shouldn't exaggerate. Those moments were few and far between.

So few, in fact, that I had begun to regret all my choices and was feeling even more alone than I had during the worst parts of the divorce. That was probably why I was sitting there at the bar.

"So how are they doing up on Slottsmöllan?" Vidar asked.

"Pretty damn great, surprisingly enough. They've started going to museums every week. They like to try out new cafés. Dad has started *reading books.* He reads more than I do."

Vidar laughed. "That's great."

"I hear you aren't with the police anymore?"

"Haven't been there for fifteen years. No, I work out at the airfield."

"Do you like it?"

"I actually got an offer to come back to the police earlier this spring, but I said no." He gave a wan smile. "So I suppose I'm happy where I am."

Of course he was. How could Vidar, who had always been perfectly at ease with himself, be anything but happy right where he was? But he said it as if it weren't quite that simple. He raised his bottle with a hint of gloom in his eyes. It would soon be empty. I reluctantly finished my beer, suddenly wishing the conversation didn't have to end.

Vidar drank the last of his bottle and turned to the bartender to order another. The power of attraction I'd felt toward him as a child was still there. And now silence would reign. Were we just going to sit across from each other and drink? One of us would have to move. Wouldn't it be too awkward otherwise?

But the conversation didn't end. It was as if he'd forgotten. Or had changed his mind. Instead we continued to chat: Hey, whatever happened to that guy? Oh, she married *him*? I never would have guessed. No, that bastard drank away everything he owned; it was tragic. Did you hear about the farm they tore up over in Frösakull? They found three dead horses in the stable and a red 1960 MG in the barn. Mint condition. What the fuck are people thinking? I saw her and her husband at a book signing in Falkenberg about a year ago—it was like the two of us were strangers and yet not. We're from the same soil. Sometimes that's enough.

He laughed quite a bit; I did too. It was nice. The dark clouds around him didn't scatter completely, though. When I came back from a trip to the bathroom, I found him deep in thought, staring down at the table.

"It must be nice to be an author," he said. "Because as an author, you can never be wrong, can you?"

This sudden declaration surprised me. It was a thought that seemed to have come from someone other than Vidar.

"As an author you're always wrong," I said.

"Oh. Okay. Sure, maybe." He didn't understand what I meant. "Hey, can I ask you something?"

"I expect so." Then I chuckled, because I was starting to feel tipsy from the beer and didn't quite know what to say. "Depends what it is."

"Why did you get divorced? You and . . ."

"Sara." I considered the question. "She said I was empty."

Vidar raised one substantial eyebrow. "What does that mean?"

"I don't really know. But it felt accurate."

"So she was the one who wanted a divorce?"

"Not the only one."

Vidar appeared to be trying to understand this too, without much success.

"I don't think it's really . . ." I began, taking a drink of my beer. "I mean, I don't know. But I think it might have something to do with why I'm sitting here now. You know, it's like there are different ways to find meaning in life. I'm sure one is the way you feel as a parent. I don't have kids, but I imagine there's a sense of meaning to parenthood, like you have a duty. A purpose. Right?"

"Yeah, sure."

"Or, you know, when you renovate your house. When you build the home you want to have, sort of, or try to care for and manage your childhood home. But the only true meaning I know, the only time I feel grounded in my everyday life, is when I'm writing. When I imagine that I'm living other people's lives. That's what you do as an author. I feel like I'm doing what I was put on earth to do, and that's how I find a sort of purpose. And I guess it probably made me a pretty absent partner. What was left over wasn't enough for her. She wanted both of us to find meaning in *us*. I couldn't do that."

Vidar nodded thoughtfully.

"That does sound empty. And a little sad. But maybe that's just what it's like, being an author. That you live other people's lives. I don't think I've ever looked at it that way, but then again, I haven't thought about it much. Speaking of." He put down his beer bottle. "This has been nice, Moth, but I have to be getting home. I need to do some thinking."

"About what?"

"About my dad, actually."

"Sven? What about him?"

In response, Vidar merely gazed at me vacantly, his mouth half-open, as if he had revealed too much. He suddenly seemed embarrassed.

"Oh, you know . . . you should just be glad your parents are still alive. Once they're gone, it's too late to ask questions. No matter how much you might want to. You think you know who they were, but you don't."

"That's true," I agreed, rather unsure of what he was trying to say.

Only then did I see it. His face was ravaged in that way faces get only when someone is caught up in a great tragedy and can't see any way out. And he had lied to me. Wherever the dirt on his face and clothes and hands had come from, I suspected he hadn't been at home doing yard work. I didn't blame him, but on that spring evening the expression on his face was easy for me to identify, because I had seen it so often in my own reflection, in Sara's face as she sat across from me during our unbearable conversations and fights. Something foundational in Vidar Jörgensson's life was amiss.

"It was nice to see you, Moth."

"Same to you."

Once he'd left the bar, I remained seated, gazing after him. I happened to recall my image of Sven by the car in the driveway as Dad bent over the hood, how friendly and stable that large man seemed, how calm and sensible he appeared. How Vidar moved through the village with the little world that belonged to him resting safely on his shoulders, convinced that it would never fall to pieces.

But there are cracks in everything. That's no secret. That spring, I came to understand this truth better than many others, but I still had trouble seeing them in Vidar; I couldn't imagine what must have befallen him and those close to him.

4

The news broke about two weeks later, on June 12, 2019.

33 YEARS LATER: TIARP MAN IDENTIFIED

The subject was the three homicides and one attempted homicide that had occurred in the area over thirty years ago but were only now solved. It was a thrilling read, and it was a long time before I put down the newspaper. Then I snatched it up again. I realized it contained a clue of sorts.

In the days that followed, the Tiarp Man was, once again, the only thing anyone wrote or talked about, and almost, it seemed, the only thing anyone was thinking about. I tried to work on the house and deal with everyday chores, but my mind kept returning to them: to Vidar and his father and the murders in Tiarp.

The first murder had taken place in March 1986, when Stina Franzén's body was found in a car near Tiarp Farm. Sven Jörgensson had been in charge of the investigation, and it wasn't until now, thirty years after his death, that the perpetrator had come to light. His son had put the puzzle pieces together to show the true picture. But what kind of picture was it?

When I met Vidar in the bar, I was almost disappointed. Disappointed. But why? Maybe because something seemed to have broken in the man who had always seemed unbreakable.

Sixty minutes, no more, no less. I once read that if you're facing a problem, and you spend an hour trying and failing to solve it, you might as well turn your mind to something else. I don't remember what book it was, or if it even was a book, or maybe an article, but each day I sat in front of the computer for exactly sixty minutes, as if this were a duty I refused to relinquish, in the hopes that something would happen and prompt me to write a sentence I didn't delete straight away.

As a child, I would see Sven Jörgensson several times a week.

Outside my window, a streak of sky peeked between the treetops like a thin pale-blue throat. I thought about Sven and his son, leaned back, and closed my eyes. By the time I opened them, fifty-three minutes had passed. I sat there for another seven minutes before I deleted the sentence and left the room, terribly confused although I didn't quite know why.

Each time I finished working on a book, I felt oddly untethered, as though I had been unplugged somehow. As if the book had had me in its grips, and I had finally been set free. I had been free for a long time now. Was this what it felt like? Being unattached. Words like *free* are fragile and delicate, flimsy as paper. They can't hold up to scrutiny.

The next morning, it happened again.

As a child, I would see Sven Jörgensson several times a week.

I stared at the sentence. Clearly I was returning to that time. After a while, I happened to think about the school bus. The autumn chill as I stood by the highway, waiting with my brother, the morning commuters heading into town. Sometimes he drove by, Sven did. I jotted down the surprisingly few memories I had of him and Vidar. I recalled a soccer match from March 1986. Breared had been playing a city team, was it HBK? No, it couldn't have been. I don't recall who we were playing, but I did remember that we won and that it had been important. Vidar wasn't the one who made the crucial goal, I was sure of that, but what was that guy's name who . . .

I sifted through my memories. And I persevered. Everything I could recall, I noted. Somehow, I realized after a few days, I was trying to square my memories of the two men with what happened later, after I left Tofta. After I went to Stockholm and started university, after I became an author and almost a different person, and they kept living their lives down here.

In the end, I hit a wall, but it was already too late. Something was waking up inside of me; as I sat in the yellow house by Lake Tofta I had increasingly begun searching for something, or maybe someone, to get lost in.

5

Soon I was sitting in other people's houses, paging through their photo albums, asking questions and recording their stories on a small Dictaphone. I visited the area around Vapnö and went to the city library to look through old newspaper clippings. I collected articles about the Tiarp Man, took notes and collated information, joined the groups *Old Halmstad* and *Halmstad Then and Now* on Facebook. Thus far I had avoided trying to talk to Vidar. The thought scared me, maybe because I had an idea of what the consequences might be.

I still didn't quite know what sort of narrative I was in the process of researching, but you never know that sort of thing at first; only when the story is collected and finished can you look back and understand it. I hadn't written about crimes before, but there was something about the Tiarp Man that captured my interest. I think I wanted to understand what he'd done to the people who, in one way or another, had been forced to confront him and his misdeeds. That's what I told people, at least, and as we sat there discussing Vidar and his father, there was one name that kept popping up: Evy Carlén.

She had worked in close proximity to Sven for years. I learned that she used to live near Söndrum, and then out toward Kärleken, until she moved elsewhere late in life. I didn't know where to. When I searched for her current address, I had to laugh. Norteforsen 195 was just a few kilometers from where I was sitting at that very moment, at the kitchen table in my half-renovated childhood home.

I decided to head over the same day, to find out what kind of house it was, how she lived. Whether it was possible to catch a glimpse of her. I hadn't planned to do any more than that, I want to make that clear. When she turned out to be in her garden, and we said hello and struck up a conversation, I was amazed how easy it was to get close to her. During our encounters over the next few weeks, I began to share events from my own life and confided in her about things few others knew: why I had left the area when I was young, what it was like to return; I even talked about my divorce.

It was actually really nice to talk to someone, but that wasn't why I did it. I did it because the author in me was greedy; I did it because I wanted Evy to trust me. I had begun to suspect that there was something she wasn't telling me about them, about Sven and Vidar. There were hints, small signs—an odd gesture, a look, or a silence that lasted too long when I brought them up. I was waiting for her to reveal what she knew.

"How well do you know Vidar?" I asked one evening.

"You know, not very well, I'd say. We're no more than acquaintances, him and me. But I did know his father. Sven Jörgensson. Now there was a good man. Such a loss, that he got sick and died so young."

When we spoke about Sven, she often came back to his death.

"But, you know," she continued. "Everything has its time. A time to live, a time to die."

Everything has its time. She liked to say that, sometimes. "But, listen," she went on. "Forgive this tired old dolly so late in the day. But what is it you're actually after?"

"Me? What do you mean, after?"

"You're asking about Sven and Vidar."

"I guess I'm just trying to wrap my head around it," I said, "all the stuff I read about in the paper this summer. About Tiarp and the

Tiarp Man. And how it fits with my image of them. I can't quite make it all mesh. Especially Vidar, I mean, he . . . There was something special about him. At least, that's how I remember him. Like nothing could quite touch him."

She cocked her head and smiled faintly. "Is someone lying to me?"

All of a sudden my palms were damp and slick. I cleared my throat. "Why would I do that?"

But Evy didn't respond. Instead she looked at me with that peculiar gaze that made me suspect she knew what I was really doing there, and I realized she would never tell me.

And then she had her stroke.

6

At first, all she could say was *yes*. That was her response to everything, while her brain tried to rediscover the space where the rest of the words were waiting: *Yes, yes, yes*. Evy had other visitors, people from the neighborhood and old friends, children and grandchildren, but I visited her now and then to make sure she was doing okay.

"How are you?" I asked one day.

"Yes."

Evy was a stout woman with broad shoulders and strong wrists, but her stroke and her time in the hospital had made her unnaturally pale and gaunt. I could see her cheekbones. She was sitting at a table, the radio feeding out news at low volume. The last time I visited, I'd offered her pen and paper, but she could no longer write. The small notepad and the pen lay untouched on the tabletop.

"Should we take a little walk?"

"Yes."

Evy rose with great effort and grabbed on to her rollator. I started to help her with her shoes, but she waved off my attempts, annoyed, and put them on by herself.

It had been drizzling that morning, and the smell of wet asphalt lingered. It was still August. We didn't see many cars. It was still vacation season; everything was slumbering. We found ourselves surrounded by a great Swedish stillness.

At that moment, Evy stiffened.

"Sven."

"What?"

"Sven Jörgensson."

"You just happened to think of him now?"

"Singing in the rain."

"What was that?"

She repeated the words, but I was mystified. The rest of our walk was taken in silence.

After that, her speech slowly began to return, and it seemed something had changed. She began to tell me the story, maybe because she didn't have much time left and knew it.

"I think I'm going to die soon," she said one afternoon when autumn was approaching. "Things can't just go on like this."

"I bet you're going to live at least another twenty years."

"It was all thanks to Sven," she said. "Without him, it never would have happened."

"What do you mean?"

"You know, Tiarp."

"That the murders were solved? That was thanks to Sven?"

"Yes, yes."

I didn't understand. Sven Jörgensson had been dead for almost thirty years. The Tiarp murders hadn't been solved until about a month ago.

"Everything has its time."

I waited.

"Yes. Everything has its time."

"A time to remember. A time to forget. I've been thinking about that, how sooner or later I suppose I'll forget. But I've never been able to forget it."

"What's that?"

"That night up in the forest."

"What night?"

I had to wait a long time for her answer.

I guess I thought she would recover, but after a while I understood I had it backward. During the autumn and winter, Evy's mind became clearer and her thoughts somewhat more cohesive, but her body broke down and got worse, a slow but inexorable process. Medicines were strewn about the house; they were supposed to help her get up, sleep, avoid blood clots, prevent another stroke. Soon she was unable to take walks. Her memory was unreliable, her appetite gone, and her nights grew long and sleepless. Each time I visited, she threw up her hands and smiled absently.

"Not dead yet, apparently," she said. "Still here. But soon."

I suspected she was right.

One evening she got out her photo albums and showed them to me again, pointing out people I now recognized from her stories.

"Even Sven is here," she said, pointing at a grainy photograph. "I think this was the spring of 1986."

I don't quite know why she did it. Maybe it was just to show me, but possibly it was a piece of her preparation, as if she wanted to see them one last time, the people who had surrounded her in life, people she'd cared about, before it was all over. The thought made me feel dejected.

"Where was this taken? Is it by the police station?"

"I'm not sure," she said. "Don't remember. Do you want it?"

The question took me by surprise. "You want to give it to me?"

She pulled the photo from its plastic sleeve and I studied it carefully. Sven was leaning against the wall of a building, holding a cigarette. He looked tired. I turned the picture over.

"It looks like it was the autumn of '85," I said. "At least that's what it says on the back. Is this your handwriting?"

"Yes, it is. See what I mean? My memory isn't so good."

As I write this, the photograph of Sven is at the top of my pile of work materials, along with another picture.

"You can have this one too," she said. "I have so many of them."

Evy had turned the page of the album and pulled out another photograph. It was a family photo, taken indoors. In the background was a Christmas tree, covered in colorful ornaments.

"That's me," she said. "There's my brother, Einar. There's Ronnie and his mother, back before she died. And those are our kids in front of me and Ronnie. I don't know which Christmas this was." She squinted. "I wasn't too bad looking in those days. Look at that. Young and beautiful. These days, I'm only *and*."

"You are not."

Evy chuckled. I accepted the photograph with a certain amount of hesitation.

"Christmas, 1987," I read on the back. "You really want me to have this?"

She nodded.

"Something to remember me by when I'm gone."

I didn't quite know what to say, so I just put the two photos in my pocket and excused myself, heading for the bathroom with a lump in my throat.

As they had for so many other kids in the neighborhood, Sven and Vidar Jörgensson had awoken in me the greatest fantasy imaginable: the idea that you can feel entirely at home and at peace right where you are. But that, on its own, wasn't much of a story; it was just an image, beautiful from a distance.

I began to think about the questions that must have bedeviled Sven, and maybe his son as well, until the day he died: Why had he, *Sven*, such a fair-minded man, been faced with a perpetrator who seemed to stand for the very opposite of all Sven knew? Why was *Sven*, a man who always strove to uncover the truth on behalf of others, cast into a series of events for which the solution remained elusive? And then there was his son. What was it all like for his son?

I know my portrait of them can never be complete. There's still so much I don't know about Sven, about Vidar, about Evy and all the others. We do it all the time—assign to people opinions and motives, intentions. But are we ever sure? What can we actually know about another person?

The author's power rests in the ability to bring people onto a stage, one he himself controls, in order to fill in the gaps, the empty spaces, to try to understand what might have happened. Onto this stage I brought people who not only lived and worked in Sweden, but in some sense *were* Sweden, the way it appeared to those of us who were children in 1986, the year that would turn out to be, above anything else, a year of dread.

Now it begins.

II

DEATH ON NYÅRSÅSEN

1986

7

Out of all the birds, we loved the white wagtails the best. The winter had been so long, and the days so short, that when the little bird finally appeared it was hard not to get carried away with excitement.

As spring arrived, the village came to life. Everything seemed to shimmer, and the colors grew so vivid. Sweet days awaited.

The first white wagtail sighting also brought a moment of uncertainty. We learned to be very cautious. If you saw the bird from the back, which you almost always did, it meant happiness and good fortune. But on those rare instances in which you first happened to catch sight of it from the front, and got a good look at the black spot on its tiny breast, it was a bad omen: Misfortune and sorrow lay ahead.

That was the thing about life: It was sweet, but precarious.

Surely it was just superstition, but people took it very seriously. Maybe there was a reason. Old man Nilsson up in Torvsjön saw the black breast spot of a white wagtail, and suddenly things went south for his business, and just a week or so later his wife fell down the stairs and broke her hip. Soon she was addicted to painkillers. It all turned out okay in the end; his wife made it through, she could just take the pills, and the old man could sell the business. But it sure was a run of bad luck, and one piece of bad luck is seldom the last of it. It had all started with the bird.

:::

Carl Jörgensson, son of a Jörgen, was born in Marbäck in May 1860. Carl had seven children, the youngest of whom was called Ludvig. On a March morning in 1902 he emerged, this Ludvig, a strong and healthy baby boy who unfortunately demanded more than his mother, Elfrid, could handle. She fell very ill and died in the infirmary before the sun came up the next day. She would have been thirty-eight the next week. No information to be had about any white wagtails, even though it was springtime.

Ludvig met Märta at school. Life was simple. It was his work at the mill and his service as a constable, it was taking care of the house and the property, participating in the village council meetings, and power struggles within the new workers' union. But what didn't happen was a baby. They were thirty-five before Märta's belly began to grow round and she had trouble sleeping. Then they both realized what it meant. This was in the autumn. Sven Jörgensson was born on May 20, 1937.

He grew up, met Bibbi, got married, and eventually became a police officer; he had been part of city law enforcement for twenty-five years when it all started. The man we saw heading into town in his car in the mornings was a workhorse, raised in Marbäck with that village's morals and worldview. He seemed taciturn and introverted yet warm and kind, and he conducted himself like someone who's trying to be everything life demands: a kind spouse, a decent father, a good neighbor, a dependable colleague. Sven, too, had loved white wagtails as a child. When he spotted one again in the early spring of 1986, his blood ran cold. Dread sank its claws into him; surely he hadn't gotten it wrong. It was true, right? Hadn't he loved them once?

When I close my eyes and picture the man on the stage, that's where I find him. That morning, when Sven had gotten ready for work as usual, and his son, Vidar, nearly grown, sat at the kitchen table with a glass of milk and his military enrollment papers in front of him, and Bibbi stood at the stove in her robe, stirring her tea.

Nothing was out of the ordinary: his coat on and the little black notebook he always used at work in its spot in his breast pocket, a pen in his back pocket, and his car keys in hand. He said goodbye and walked out the door, but returned almost immediately.

"What's wrong?" Bibbi wondered, her back to him. "Wouldn't the car start?"

"No, no." He cleared his throat. "It was the wagtail."

Bibbi was a person who tended not to take on many things. But what she did set out to do, she did properly: She performed her job impeccably, prepared meals as if for a feast; when she got around to cleaning she cleaned as if her mother-in-law were about to visit, and she raised their son with conviction and persistence, as if he was a chance to set to rights something that had gone wrong long ago. And her love for Sven was like the last love on earth. Now she turned to face him.

"What did you say?"

"I saw the wagtail."

"In February? You must have seen wrong."

"It was a wagtail. She was perching on the fence over there, by Jansson's place."

"Surely spring can't come that early this year."

"From the front. Its breast spot was . . . I saw it from the front."

Bibbi didn't say anything for a moment, with all the strength that a woman like her could muster in something as simple as not speaking. Vidar rose from his chair and went to the window, squinting at Jansson's place. No bird.

He sighed wearily, full of a disappointment Sven would have preferred he keep to himself.

"It couldn't have been a wagtail, Sven. You must have seen wrong. It's still way too cold." Bibbi looked at him again. "Was that all?"

"Yes."

She pressed her lips to his cheek.

"See you tonight."

"I know that's what I saw." He opened the door again. "I know it."

8

When Sven arrived at the station, a colleague asked if he would be willing to take an extra shift and stay late. This colleague had three children and two of them had come down with chicken pox overnight. He needed to be home to help their mother.

It was common to switch shifts and duty time to make sure there was enough coverage each day. Everyone had to do their part. Sven called the reception desk at Scandic, the hotel where Bibbi worked, to ask if his wife had come in yet. She had.

"Hi, Bibbi. It's me. I just wanted to let you know I'll be home late tonight. Around midnight, maybe."

"Okay," she said breezily, already busy with something at work. "That's fine. And hey."

"Yeah?"

"Sorry about this morning. Was it really a wagtail?"

It was. He was sure. But he said, "Maybe I was wrong. See you tonight."

The Halmstad police personnel file documents the day: Sven responded to a traffic accident at ten, wrote a speeding ticket after lunch, was called in for a suspected assault in the afternoon, and then had a few hours' rest before he was back on the job at eight. At eight-thirty he was dispatched to a presumed burglary at a summer cottage in Tylösand. That took some time, and it was ten-thirty before he returned to headquarters to do paperwork. He would be late getting home. He considered calling Bibbi again, but instead he just kept pecking at the typewriter and trying to decipher his own notes from the burglary.

Sven liked working at night. The world was calm and quiet; all the offices were silent and dark, and he had time to catch up on tasks he would otherwise fall behind in. From his window he had a view of the small city that spread out like a carpet of lights. It was peaceful.

And he got to work with Evy Carlén. What more could you ask for? She had been born Evy Bengtsson and took Carlén when she married. She was forty-six, with a shot-putter's body and the brain of a true detective; she was sharp and likeable and had a gruff, masculine sort of laugh that poured forth when she heard a bad joke.

It was almost twelve-thirty at night when they heard the bulletin. They looked up from their typewriters. Sven set his smoking cigarette in the ashtray and listened to the radio as the rest of the news reached police forces across the nation.

Sven and Evy exchanged glances. She seemed surprised, almost nonplussed. Once the voice stopped speaking, there were several seconds of static before a call came from one of the patrol cars.

"Sixty-three ten. Is this some kind of joke? Over."

The radio sputtered and crackled. The center operator responded. "Negative, it is serious."

Sven stared at the radio. It was simply unthinkable. Not here. Not in Sweden.

He tried to go back to the page in his typewriter, his half-finished incident report. He picked up the cigarette from the ashtray, took one last drag, and coughed. His chest felt hot and thick inside.

Phones began to ring. Sven and Evy did their best, their minds clouded with shock. People were nervous, and when they got nervous they turned to the police for information, and for some reason the switchboard was transferring all incoming calls to them. The lines lit up red. Evy shrugged her broad shoulders and shook her head, making her curly hair bounce.

When they weren't at the phones, they gathered around the radio. They were waiting for information, just like everyone else. Sven went into another room, picked up the receiver, found an open line, dialed home.

"Hello?"

"It's me," said Sven. "Have you heard?"

"Heard what?" Bibbi yawned. "I was sleeping, what time is it?"

"They shot Palme."

"What?"

"The prime minister has been shot."

"Wait, what? What's going on?"

He told her again.

"Oh my God. But he's still alive, right?"

"No." Sven stared out the window, at the black sky hanging over them out there. "No, he's dead."

That's when the call came in.

At four minutes to one, about an hour and a half after shots were fired up in Stockholm, the switchboard at the Halland Police received a phone call. The caller was a man.

I raped a woman in a car. It's near Tiarp Farm. A brief silence followed. Then: *I'm going to do it again. Bye.*

That's what he said. Then he hung up.

9

What if it was a joke, a prank call from a nut who wanted to see some lights and sirens? It was a Friday night, a payday weekend, and someone had just shot the prime minister, how the hell was anyone supposed to know? Chaos reigned. Turn on the police radio and it was a cacophony of voices.

"The both of us can go," Evy suggested.

"One of us better stay here." Sven nodded at the phones. "Maybe it's nothing."

So he went alone. His route took him through a shadowy landscape, barren and blue-gray, almost moonlike. It was cold and icy out, but the sky was clear. Sven saw the stars, brilliant and motionless in the heavens. They calmed him.

His journey took him along narrow, winding county roads where traffic accidents claimed a number of lives each year. Sven had seen it himself. Delivering the news of death was one of the worst parts of his job. Someone has to do it, though, he told himself. Everything in this life has to be done by someone. Even when it's difficult to do.

In the distance ahead of him rose the blue hulk of Nyårsåsen; tiny villages like Tiarp, Risarp, and Björkebo perched atop the ridge. It was a primeval rock formation sparsely populated with farms and homesteads where the people worked vast areas of land. If you looked closely, you could see remnants of the paths taken by ice-age glaciers.

The terrain shifted from caves to bogs to deep ravines. In summertime, the rare bog asphodel blossomed in crevices. On the north side, streams plunged down the slope, foaming with water that was, in the past, said to be a source of miracles.

No miracles on this night. Only thoughts. *My son—why don't I understand him anymore? What happened? Bibbi—I should spend more time with her. I wish she were here right now. Why have I had such a terrible cough recently? What will the neighbors think? Palme. Jesus Christ, Palme. What the fuck is going to happen now?*

The straight stretch at Tiarp ran between two fields, the road there a kilometer long and black as night. He passed dark farms where people lay in their beds, dreaming in a different era.

Sven had never voted for Olof Palme. The prime minister for him was Thorbjörn Fälldin: folksy, plainspoken, simple. A steady man. Palme was too crafty, too rich, too smart, had read too many books. When he spoke, you could sense movement in the shadows.

Sven squinted into the blackness. His stomach clenched when he saw it. A car, a ten-year-old Opel Rekord, was sitting on the side of a forest road not far from Tiarp Farm, all its lights off.

Sven reached for his radio and hailed the station.

"There's a car here. It might be the one."

He took the flashlight from the passenger seat and stepped into the night. The forest road was uneven and slick with dirty patches of ice. The cone of light darted here and there ahead of him. He could see his breath in the cold.

The light slipped across the grille, the hood, the windshield. He took note of the license plate. Some cars, the ones that were often illegally parked or investigated in connection with home burglaries and such, you recognized. Halmstad was growing, but it was still a small city. This Opel, though, wasn't familiar.

He took off a glove and felt the hood. Cool, not cold.

The forest road was narrow and the fir trees tall. Sven aimed the flashlight into the car and recoiled.

She was lying on her side in the back seat, very still. Her pants were crumpled on the floor behind the driver's seat. She looked young. Sven tried the door. Unlocked. A heavy smell, like that of iron and meat, struck him as he leaned into the car, took off his glove, and felt for a pulse at the woman's throat.

He grabbed her and called out. The notebook in his breast pocket fell to the floor. Nothing else happened. She had dark hair and was wearing a white shirt with the top two buttons undone. She looked very proper. *Work*, he thought. *She was at work.* Blood was flowing profusely from her head, but he couldn't tell quite where it was coming from.

Sven was breathing hard. He got blood on his hands, and, damn it all to hell, he wished he'd never come here, shit, he should have said *No, I'm sorry, I can't take that shift today. I have to get home.*

The key was in the ignition. The car was evidence, but saving lives came first. He reached across the inert body again and buckled a seatbelt around it.

Sven started the car and revved the engine. He drove onto the forest road and headed back down to the Tiarp stretch. The car skidded, fighting the slick road. He didn't dare glance at the woman in the back seat.

Once inside the emergency room, he shouted for help. His voice cracked. Two nurses came to his rescue and followed him out to the car. He was short of breath, gasping and coughing. His chest burned. The nurses asked questions, the kind of questions emergency room nurses always ask, but between his harsh, rasping breaths, Sven just repeated the same thing over and over, told them what he wished was true: "I felt a pulse. I think she's alive."

But she wasn't. Not anymore.

Multiple blows to the head with a blunt object meant she was beyond saving. Death had come for her somewhere between the damp darkness of Tiarp and the cold, pale light outside the emergency room entrance. The doctor who was soon called in to examine the body estimated the time of death at 1:45 A.M. on March 1.

Sven walked out through the heavy sliding doors of the emergency room and took out his pack of Princes, lit one, and smoked it in silence, longing for his porch back home in Marbäck. Tiny snowflakes floated to the ground. He had felt her pulse.

Then he remembered: the notebook.

Sven went over to the Opel and crouched down, cautiously groping around the back seat floor until he found it and put it back in his breast pocket.

10

A shaken voice on the radio did its best not to fall apart as it conveyed a message.

Olof Palme, prime minister of Sweden, is dead. He was shot in downtown Stockholm tonight. Olof Palme was shot at the intersection of Tunnelgatan and Sveavägen and later died at Sabbatsberg Hospital. The government has been informed. Finance Minister Kjell-Olof Feldt and Deputy Prime Minister Ingvar Carlsson have been informed and both confirm that Olof Palme has died.

The police are searching for a man between the ages of thirty-five and forty with dark hair and a long, dark coat.

Up to this point the voice sounded rather straightforward and mechanical, despite a couple of repetitions and unusual aspects that didn't match the usual streamlined, anonymous prose of Radio Sweden. Now, the rest, more meandering and uncertain, the voice much more breathless and thick:

The government has been . . . has convened for a special session. Ingvar Carlsson, the deputy prime minister, is chairing the meeting. His only comment when he arrived at Rosenbad tonight was that "It is terrible," he said . . . to the TT wire service, when he arrived at Rosenbad.

There was a crackling sound and a second of dead air.

Then, back to music.

Sven heard the radio broadcast in his colleagues' car. They were driving him back to Tiarp; his car was still there, in the dark. He opened his notebook and took a few preliminary notes. His writing was messy, uneven, and cramped. He needed to keep his hands busy. As soon as they stilled, he could feel the dead woman and the blood, his grip on the wheel, the fear that had overtaken him in the blackness of Nyårsåsen.

His colleagues couldn't find their way. He had to direct them. This patrol was made up of two young men, one short and one tall; neither of them had been to Nyårsåsen before, and both of them were in deep shock over Palme.

They stopped at a distance. He directed them to set up a perimeter. They looked around in the darkness, wide-eyed, apparently wishing they were anywhere else.

"What the hell kind of place is this—have you been here before?" said the short one.

"No, have you?"

The short one shook his head.

Sven had removed his bloody outerwear at the hospital but hadn't had a chance to go back to the station for a clean set, so his arms were bare as he stepped into the cold. He made his way to the spot where the Opel had sat, carefully, the way you'd approach a wounded animal. There was something on the ground. His flashlight. Had he dropped it? He must have. He turned it on, and the bright beam played over the gravel road.

He saw a set of tire tracks, obviously from a second vehicle, next to those of the Opel. He went to his own car, called the station, and requested a team of technicians to come make a cast of the tracks.

Silence on the line, then someone asking in a hesitant tone: "You know they just shot Palme, right?"

"Yes. So?"

"We're kind of busy here. The phones are ringing nonstop."

"Well, tell people to listen to the radio. Send me a tech."

He brusquely hung the microphone back on the dashboard. His hands. Had to keep them busy, all the time.

Sven was so cold he was shaking.

He wondered who she was, the woman in the Opel. He hailed the station again and asked if any news had come in from the hospital yet.

The same operator. Sounding testier this time: Nothing. But the clothes had been sent over, were on their way to the station, so they ought to arrive soon. Apparently there was a wallet in one of the pockets.

"Didn't anyone write it down? Her name?"

"I'm sure they did. But I can't reach anyone right now; it's a little chaotic here."

This time, he slammed the microphone home so hard that it bounced out of its cradle and ended up dangling from its cord.

He leaned against the car, waiting and trying not to think about how cold he was.

"Hey, Sven."

He turned around. The patrol officers had cordoned off the area and were walking his way.

"You're going to freeze to death if you stay here. We'll hold down the fort. You go ahead and go."

11

"Sven. What are you doing?"

Evy had just downed another cup of coffee-machine coffee and was holding a white plastic bag in her hand as she cracked the door to one of the offices at the liaison center.

Sven was leaning over the silent tape recorder, his hands flat on the desk, as if he were struggling against a weight only he could see.

He turned around. His eyes flared red with exhaustion. She wanted to touch him. It looked like he needed it.

"Listening to him."

Evy looked at the empty chair next to the desk.

"Don't you want to sit down?"

"No, I'm fine."

His gaze fell on the bag in Evy's hand.

"Her clothes." She placed the bag on the table beside him. "They just arrived."

"Good."

He turned back to the tape recorder and rewound it. No one had had time to trace the call yet; everyone was too busy. A national alert had been sent out. Palme's killer was sought from Kiruna to Trelleborg.

"We . . ." Evy began, then cleared her throat. "We're all sitting around listening to the radio out there. Things are pretty quiet in town right now, everyone's asleep. Would you like . . ."

"I'll be there in a bit."

"But . . ."

"Evy." Sven looked at his colleague. "I'll be there in a bit."

He heard her close the door, and once again he was alone.

He rewound. Played it again. The voice was agitated; the words came out in a clear Halland accent, but it wasn't the variety spoken by the farmers or the older generation. Was he putting it on? Sven took his notepad from his breast pocket and jotted down: *City-dweller? 40, tops.*

I raped a woman in a car. It's near Tiarp Farm. I'm going to do it again. Bye.

He hadn't said "I killed." Didn't he know? Sven pictured the woman's head, her hair and all the blood; he saw his own hands stained dark up there in Tiarp. He must have realized.

Sven turned to the white bag and cautiously opened it. He put on a pair of gloves and examined the clothing. The wallet, thin and double-folded and black, was on top. The hospital staff had searched it.

Her name was Stina Franzén. Born in September 1965.

Twenty years old. Her whole life ahead of her. He wondered if she had done well in school, had lots of friends, whether she'd kept a diary, listed her dreams and crushes in it. Who they had been. Maybe their man was one of them, a love interest; that was often the case. In his notebook, he jotted down: *Boyfriends, exes?*

Sven went to the bathroom and sat there for a while. He wanted to call them, to hear Bibbi's and Vidar's voices. Instead he thought about the darkness in Tiarp, the car and the solitude up there, tried to picture the perpetrator.

Was he able to sleep, despite what he'd done? Did he have siblings? Maybe he planned to visit his parents on Saturday. He might decide to go shopping at Domus, buy coffee filters, bakery treats, and new shampoo, like anyone else. Monstrousness was always sleeping right beneath the surface, just out of sight.

Someone had shot the prime minister last night. Did their man know about that? Had he listened to the radio? Or perhaps he was too high on his own crime to notice that the country he lived in had been shaken up, just as if there had been a coup.

I'm going to do it again.

He might be searching for his next victim.

Sven looked at his hands. Blood. Blood under his nails. He had grabbed her and tried to rouse her to life. He had failed. Sven hunched over the sink and scrubbed his fingers until his skin was stinging and red and he sank back onto the toilet, just sat there breathing.

The wagtail. He'd heard the doubt in his wife's voice, he'd felt Vidar's disdainful teenage eyes on his back, but he was sure. He'd seen it.

This must be why it had come back so early.

As an omen.

12

Gisela was known as a kind person. It probably wasn't because she had survived, but maybe that helped. A daughter who dies during childbirth and isn't far from taking her mother with her is seldom considered kind. That was the story for her big sister.

But Gisela, the little one? There wasn't a mean bone in that girl's body. That was the consensus at home in Harplinge.

She grew up in a brown house near the clearing in the forest where the roads joined up, with her mother and father and a picture of her sister. It had been taken after her sister died. Mom was the one who had wanted it. In the photo, which still hung in her parents' living room, the tiny bundle looked like she was sleeping. It was a black-and-white photograph, possibly so the abnormally pale skin wouldn't be noticeable. But wasn't it noticeable anyway, if you looked closely? Gisela had always noticed.

That was life. You became someone's *instead of*, in one way or another. She wasn't the only one. Robert was the man she met instead of Christian. This was after she moved to the shack in Risarp.

She had loved Christian; maybe she still did. He'd hurt her badly, in a way that made her doubt, even though she was only nineteen, that she would ever be able to trust someone again.

She met Robert at a friend's house party in Holm. Now, less than six months later, he spent more time at Gisela's place than at his apartment in town. He took care of her, was kind and thoughtful even as he allowed her the space she needed. He drove a truck for a carrier and was away several nights each week.

Robert was the one who woke her up. He had come straight from Malmö in his truck and parked behind the shack. The clanky diesel engine gave a few pops before it settled into silence and he closed the driver's door. His keys scraped the front door, which creaked as it swung open.

"Gis?" came his voice from the entryway. "Gis, are you awake?"

"No," she grunted, wishing she hadn't given him a key.

"I think something's going on," he said.

"What is it?"

"There's lights and sirens over at Tiarp Farm. They were cordoning it off as I drove by."

Gisela heard him undressing in the hall and going to the bathroom. She stretched and looked out the window. It was so dark. She could just make out the sharp contours of the treetops against the sky, their branches making silhouettes.

He was right. Something was going on. Far, far away, on the other side of the ridge, she could see faint pulses of blue.

"Do you know what happened?"

"Must be an accident," Robert said. "It's too fucking dark on the roads now."

He flushed the toilet. The pipes rattled. He was just removing his shirt as he came in, and she took in the ropy, slender muscles of his chest, the delicate chain with its pendant that dangled at the hollow of his throat.

"Hi," she said with a faint smile. "I missed you."

He crawled into bed and kissed her. He tasted like toothpaste and sweat, and he grabbed her waist. Cold hands chilled her skin through the flimsy nightgown. This was one of the things she liked best about Robert, how he touched her. Properly, firmly, as if she belonged to him.

"Don't you want to sleep?" he asked. "It's so late."

"Soon," she said, her voice thick, and pulled him on top of her.

13

The morning light was pale and thin. Robert was standing at the stove, shirtless, his bare feet on the cold hardwood floor, wearing only faded blue jeans that slipped down his hips. In one hand was a saucepan of boiling water; in the other, a large mug with a tea bag.

"How can you be awake already?" she mumbled, wrapping herself in her robe.

"It's seven o'clock," Robert said. "The question is, how can you have slept in so late?"

"Someone really tired me out last night."

He laughed. She put her arms around him from behind, stroked his belly, rested her cheek against the rough skin between his shoulder blades.

"Maybe we should turn on the radio." Robert twisted the knobs of the old transistor in the window, and there was a crackle before the local radio station came to life. "They might say something about what was up last night."

But when they heard the voice on the radio, Gisela whipped her head around in surprise.

"What? What did he say? Palme?"

Robert had stopped in his tracks. He listened.

"Oh my God," he said softly.

"Last night," said Gisela. "But they didn't say anything on the radio when you were driving home?"

"I didn't have the radio on."

Gisela turned her head, gazed out the window, and noticed a boy sitting in the field.

"Good lord. What's he doing?"

"Who?"

"That's Wille."

He was sitting on a boulder the size of a tractor tire, dangling his legs. His winter clothes were worn at the elbows and knees, and he wasn't wearing a hat. His big ears were bright red. In his hands was a matte black pistol. He weighed it, turning it over with first one hand and then both, as if he were trying to figure out a way to hold it properly.

Gisela let go of Robert.

"I'm going to go talk to him."

"Should I come with you?"

"No, you wait here. If both of us go it might scare him."

Gisela put on her winter coat and stepped out into the field. *Palme,* she thought. *My God.* And now this. She called the boy's name, and he froze.

Wilhelm Skog lived in one of the houses up in Tiarp. He was a good kid, withdrawn, liked to roam around the neighborhood quietly, on his own, deeply absorbed in his own thoughts, as if he had been snipped out of a world he didn't think much of, even at the tender age of six.

"Hi, Wille. What are you doing with that?"

"It's my dad's. I borrowed it."

Gisela approached him with caution.

"Does he know you borrowed it?"

The boy lowered his gaze, biting his lip. He shook his head.

"Can I have a look?"

He hesitated, but handed the pistol over.

"Wow, it's heavy. You must have gotten really strong over the winter, to be able to hold it up the way you were."

He swelled with pride. Gisela weighed the gun in her hand and squeezed the grip, felt the warmth left by the boy's hand. "It's an air gun, right?"

Wille nodded.

"I just wanted it to protect myself."

"From what?"

His eyes went wide. "Something happened last night. Something awful. Didn't you see?"

At first, Gisela thought of Palme. Then she remembered the blue flashes she'd glimpsed between the trees when Robert woke her up. She turned to glance back at the shack. There he was in the window, Robert, still shirtless, his face tense with worry.

"Yes, I saw. But," she added, turning back to the boy, "did *you*? Were you still up that late?"

Wille gave a sly smile. His bright blue eyes sparkled. "I snuck out after Mom fell asleep on the sofa. I saw it happen, too. How horrible he was. But I was scared to do anything, so I hid. Then I ran up on the ridge." He looked at the air gun, resting in Gisela's hands. "Can I have it? I want it in case he comes back."

"In case who comes back?"

"The man I saw."

"What? What did you see?"

"Down by Tiarp Farm, kind of. That's where it was. I saw him hit her in the car. But that's all. I . . ." He started to say something more, but trailed off.

The boy clenched his jaw to keep from crying. Gisela placed a gentle hand on his shoulder and spoke quietly; she helped him down from the boulder and felt his small hand in her own as they walked across the field together.

14

A sudden pounding at the door.

"Hello?" came a voice from the other side. "Hello, Sven? Everything okay in there?"

He was stiff. He had a headache, and his eyes felt like they were full of grit. Unsteadily, he rose from the toilet and came out, saw his colleague's surprised face.

"What time is it?"

His colleague, a young man whose name Sven didn't recall, consulted his watch.

"Eight-thirty. In the morning," he added, to be safe. "There's . . . there's a woman on the phone. It's about the thing in Tiarp. Her name is Gisela Mellberg. She said it was important."

Sven cursed and walked past him, into the corridor, coughing. He'd been asleep on the toilet for over four hours.

15

The boy sat on the edge of the chair, small and stiff. The kitchen had a musty smell of old coffee grounds and dirty dishes. He gripped his juice glass and gulped down its contents.

"I love juice," he said, putting the empty glass back.

Sven looked at the boy's parents. He'd dealt with the father once before. He was a plumber and had driven an American car back in the seventies, had been a frequent patron of Fridhem Grill in town. Sometimes fights broke out. He hadn't been any worse than the others, nor any better. Later he met his wife, traded the Camaro in for a Saab, and Wilhelm arrived a few years after that.

"You aren't the ones he told first. Isn't that so?"

The parents exchanged glances. The boy's mother shook her head reluctantly.

"Yeah, that's right. He wanders off across the ridge sometimes. There's a couple he likes over there, they're nice to him. Gisela and Robert. There's a big boulder near them that he likes to play on."

Sven coughed. A radio was on in the living room, doling out news about Palme.

"Do you think we could turn that off?"

The father left the kitchen and turned the radio down to a low hum. Sven took a seat at the table, across from the boy. He should have brought Evy, or maybe that youngster who woke him up in the bathroom. Presumably they were better at talking to kids.

"Listen, Wille."

The boy looked up.

"Yeah?"

"I thought we could have a little chat. I'm sure your mom and dad told you what I want to talk about, right?"

Wille nodded grimly and gazed longingly at his glass.

"Can I have some more juice, Mom?"

"After you're done talking to Sven."

"Actually," Sven said calmly, "I think it's fine for Wille to have more juice. And if we could talk just the two of us . . ."

Once Wille's glass was refilled and his mother, too, had left the kitchen, Sven placed his notepad on the table and clicked a pen.

"I'm going to write down what we talk about," he said, tapping his temple. "So I don't forget. Look, don't drink that all at once. Save some."

Wille put down the glass and wiped his mouth.

"I saw a guy in the forest. I know that's what you want to talk about."

"I'll probably want to ask a bunch of questions about that. I know you might think it's a pain, but it's just so I can understand. It's not always easy. Is that okay?"

Wille nodded.

"Where did you see him, this guy?"

"On the gravel road."

"What gravel road is that? I mean," Sven clarified, "can you name something nearby?"

The boy frowned.

"Oh, well . . . . Jonasson's field is there. And it's not far to Bengan's place. And the farm, that's close. I go there a lot."

"You mean Tiarp Farm?"

"Yeah, with the horses. You can write that down. They have horses there."

Sven absently scribbled *there are horses*. He really should have brought Evy along.

"Can you tell me what you saw? What was on the road?"

"They were in a car. A pretty small one, I don't know what it's called. It was hard to see in the dark."

"Was there someone in the car, you said?"

"Yes, a girl and a guy. The girl was lying in the back seat."

"And where was the guy?"

"He was there too, but he wasn't lying down. He was . . ." Wille's eyes roved from wall to wall in the room. "I don't know what it's called. But he was sort of lying on top of her. He was hitting really hard. Then that was all I saw."

Sven took notes. "How come? How come that was all you saw, I mean."

The boy didn't say anything for a long moment. He reached for his glass of juice again and took a small sip.

"You're not supposed to be scared," he whispered, as if this was something he'd been taught. "Only wussies get scared. But I . . . it was so awful. So I ran away. That's why I didn't see more."

Sven regarded him gravely.

"That was smart of you, Wille. Sometimes it's a really good thing to get scared. Sometimes being scared is how you survive."

These words rearranged something inside the kid, Sven could tell. He wanted to take back what he'd said, and replace it with something that would bring solace. But the words wouldn't come.

"Can you describe the guy you saw? I have a pretty good idea what the girl looked like, but I need some help with the guy."

Wille looked down at his hands.

"He was . . . I think he had a hat. It's cold out and all."

"Did you see his face?"

"No. It was dark."

"I understand. I'm going to keep asking questions, okay? So I don't miss anything. Was he tall or short?"

Wille aimed a bewildered look at Sven.

"Well, he was taller than me."

Sven stood up and took a few steps back.

"Would you say he was taller or shorter than I am?"

Wille squinted. "Shorter."

"What was he wearing besides a hat?"

"He had gloves. And a jacket. And pants."

Sven jotted this down. He was burning with exhaustion inside, and the back of his neck ached. He looked at the words he'd written and didn't understand them. *Pants: yes,* he had written.

"It's pretty far from Tiarp to Risarp, by car," Sven said. "And far if you walk, too."

"Not if you go over the ridge."

"You know the way around there?"

The boy nodded, suddenly proud. "I know exactly where to go. I can show you, but you'll have to be careful. The old quarry and marl holes. Mom says they're deep. The marl children live there."

Sven had heard of those. Marl holes were a result of excavating done around the region in the late 1800s, so that the poor Halland soil could be fertilized with rich marlstone. This had been attempted up on the ridge too, to get it to flourish. But their ancestors had been greedy, had dug too deep. The soil and bedrock opened up. Many people had fallen to their deaths or been drowned. The story went that they had been taken by the marl children, a cautionary tale meant to keep little ones in the area from getting too close and falling in. The holes were still there.

Sven considered the boy. There was a lonely air about him. His fingernails were dirty, his clothing threadbare. He tried to picture who Wilhelm Skog would be as an adult, whether he would have a job and a family, be married, whether he would end up in lockup at the station. Whether life would eat into his bones, the way it did to just about everyone, sooner or later.

"There was another car there too."

"What was that?"

"There was another car there."

"There was?"

"Yeah, and it was bigger."

"What, like a cargo truck?"

"No, no," said the boy. "No, a regular car. Like the other one, but different. It was bigger. But had a bed like a truck."

"And where was that?"

"Right behind it."

Sven waited.

"Behind what? Behind the other car?"

Wille nodded and looked at Sven's pen. Sven handed it to him, and he took it between his fingers with great focus and pulled over Sven's notepad. With his tongue poking from the corner of his mouth, the boy began to draw two lines on the page.

"Here's the road."

He drew two cars in a row, as if they had parallel parked along the road.

"This is how they were. This one," he pointed at the first car, "was the one they were in. The other one was the bigger one. It was empty."

Sven nodded slowly. "Now I see. Thanks, Wille. Well done."

The boy leaned back in his chair and drank his juice, clearly relieved at having succeeded in the tricky art of making oneself understood by an adult.

16

Drifting apart—it must be almost unavoidable, something that happened simply by virtue of being human. It wasn't only families; it could happen to friends, spouses. By the time Vidar and his father realized it had happened to them, it was impossible to remedy the distance between them. So they just let it be.

It was almost pleasant, when he wasn't home. Not that Vidar had anything against his father, not really, but he was gone so much that it had started to feel kind of unusual to move in his orbit, to share a kitchen and living room and bathroom cabinet. Like strangers. Vidar couldn't wait to leave home and do his military service, to embark upon a life of his own.

On the TV in the living room were images of central Stockholm. A book of condolences had been placed at the entry to the government building. Everyone in the endless line to reach it was wearing black; the camera flew high above them through a brilliant and beautiful March day; bright sunshine and blue sky. Citizens were interviewed. A woman who sold newspapers stood in her shop next to a stack of dailies, *Dagens Nyheter* and *Svenska Dagbladet*. Her fingers were black with ink, and she said *It's impossible to think at all. Everyone's speechless. Totally speechless.*

Stockholm was far away. Vidar had watched for a while before going outside and moving his car into the driveway, opening the hood, placing a blanket on the cold ground, and lying down with a flashlight between his teeth to inspect the engine compartment from below.

He was lying there in the cold when he heard his father coming down the street in his patrol car.

"Hello," his father said, observing the nearly grown Vidar. "How's it going?"

"The fuel injection is weak when it starts cold." Vidar crawled up off the ground. "I'm not sure why."

"You can take it to Peter up here. Or the guy in Tofta. He's good."

His dad tried to smile, but his face was almost gray. His wrinkles were deeper, his eyes full of shadows, and his posture slumped.

He went into the garage and took out a few mismatched boards, lay them over two old paint-spattered wooden sawhorses, and began to saw. Then he nailed them together into what looked like a rough, uneven frame. When he was finished, he reached for one of the shelves full of buckets, plastic containers, paint cans, and other stuff and pulled down a can. His uniform strained. The can was big, heavy as a bucket of water. Reluctantly, Vidar walked into the garage.

"Want some help?"

"No, I'm fine."

His father's voice betrayed his effort, and he tried to hold on to the wooden frame with his other hand, but dropped it. Vidar grabbed the contraption an instant before it hit the floor.

"Can you put that in the car?" his dad said hoarsely. "And do me a favor and grab a dough scraper from the kitchen."

"A dough scraper?"

"Yes."

Vidar went inside and pulled out drawers until he found the dough scraper, which he put in the back seat of the patrol car along with the wooden frame. It smelled odd in there, a surprising metallic odor mixed with the stink of old cigarettes and cleaning products. That was where the drunks and junkies rode. So no wonder accidents happened now and then.

"What is that?"

The can his dad had set in the front seat looked like paint.

"Plaster. Listen, Vidar, I'm probably going to be gone for a while, so I . . ." He stopped. Then he said, with great effort, "It actually takes two people to do this. Do you want . . . Will you come with me?"

"No, that's okay."

"It won't take long."

"You just said you'd be gone for a while."

"We can . . . It takes two, and I have . . . It'll be quick."

It almost seemed like his dad was in pain.

"Where are you going?"

"Out by Vapnö and Tiarp."

"But that's all the way on the other side of town. Is it about Palme?"

"No, no."

"Did they catch him?"

His dad looked oddly perplexed. "Catch who?"

"You know, the guy who shot him?"

"I doubt it." He looked at his watch, suddenly impatient. "You don't have to come with me, Vidar. It's fine. But I have to get this done before dark."

Vidar looked at his beloved car, sitting there waiting for him with its hood open.

"Just let me lock up the car," he mumbled.

17

When Vidar was little, his dad used to keep his duty belt way up high so the boy couldn't reach it, but sometimes he forgot and tossed it on the bed or on the bench in the front hall. Mom had to remind him: *Sven, he's got your flashlight again. Watch out so he doesn't get the belt. Sven, he's got your baton. Sven!*

When Vidar got a little older, his dad began to explain how it all worked. This was like getting access to an almost mystical shard of reality, the one where his father spent all his time when he was away from home. The person his father was when Vidar couldn't see.

"Hear that siren, Vidar? That's how our patrol cars sound. But that one—that's not a police car, that's a fire truck. Can you hear the difference? The signals aren't the same. This here, this is our communications radio, or comm radio, as we call it. If you press there, you can speak. They can hear me at the station. No, we don't need to test it out now, I'll show you later. Vidar, give me that. Exactly, when you're finished you let go, no, not there, *here*. And if I push this button here, I can talk to my coworkers out in their patrol cars. I can ask if they need help or anything. A warning shot? Where'd you hear that? No, they're two different things. You always fire a warning shot first, as long as no one's life is in immediate danger. *Effective fire* is different. That's when we're allowed to shoot someone straight away. It's not fun. Sometimes you have to do it, but most of the time you don't.

Sam, one of my colleagues, he's been a police officer since 1950 and he's never had to turn to effective fire. So don't worry. What was that? Yes. Yes, I have. Twice."

And so on. Hard to say why he did it, shared all of this. Maybe because Vidar wanted to know. Or because it was the only thing his dad really knew how to talk about. It was the part of life that made sense to him. It gave him a purpose and a context, an answer to the toughest question of all: who he was.

Children learn about the world as they observe the actions of others, and Vidar formed his notion of the world and how it functioned by watching his parents. Perhaps his most formative moment had begun with a phone call. It must have been the summer of 1979, when Vidar was still a child. The call came from a woman in Skärkered, who had been told that there was supposedly a moose buried on her property. She'd heard that the moose had been poached years ago, and to hide the evidence it had been put in the ground on the lot that now belonged to her. She found the whole thing unsettling and very much wanted to find out if it was true. Most of all, she wanted whoever had shot and buried the moose to be found and held responsible. His dad, who had heard the rumors about the moose, said it would probably be difficult to find the guilty party, but it wasn't out of the question that they could find the moose. He did wonder, though, whether it was really worth the trouble. She insisted; it was creepy, the thought of having a poached animal hidden on her own property; couldn't Sven please come by?

His dad had been talking on the phone in the kitchen, where the sound from the receiver was so loud that Vidar usually held it away from his ear to keep from getting a headache. Since he was sitting at the kitchen table, he heard the whole conversation.

"How does it work, Dad?"

"How does what work?"

"How can you find something that's buried in the ground? Do you have to dig everything up?"

"There's another way. I'm not positive it will work, but with a little luck it might. I can take a look this weekend, so she can calm her nerves up there. Want to come with me?"

When Saturday rolled around, they went out to the garage, and his dad dug through his boxes while Vidar stood nearby with a small bag in hand.

"Let's see here," Sven said. "It's a good thing you're coming along, see, because I'm starting to get a little scatterbrained, I forget things."

Vidar felt very important, even though it seemed to him like his dad never forgot anything.

"We need filter papers." His dad pulled out a drawer of the workbench and took out a small bundle of strips. "Little ones like this."

He handed the bundle to Vidar, who carefully put it in the bag.

"And then we need citric acid. That's here." He brought down the container, which was small but heavy, like the bottle of cough medicine Vidar was given spoonfuls of when he was sick. "And we need some ammonium molybdate."

"What?"

"Ammonium molybdate. It's not easy to say." He pulled out another drawer. "Here it is."

Vidar carefully examined the small bottle before adding it to the bag.

"Then we need a pad and pen, but I've got those in the car. Let's go."

When they arrived in Skärkered, the air was crisp and clear. It smelled like autumn. The house was the gray one with the reddish-brown roof that Vidar and Mom biked past sometimes. The lot was large, its edges lined by unruly bushes. The woman who came out to greet them was named Elsa; she had white hair and a wrinkly face, and was only a little taller than Vidar, who was starting to shoot up like a weed. She had kind eyes and was very grateful that they both had come to help her. *Both*, she said, as if in that moment he was his father's equal, although that was impossible. Vidar swelled with the magnitude of this moment.

"Let's get started," Sven said. "First we need to draw a grid on the paper here. This is the property. Here's the house, there's Elsa's garage.

This square here, up on the left-hand side, signifies the corner down there, see? I'd say it's about one square meter, maybe a little more. We'll set the pad on the steps for the time being. Now we go up here, do you have the bag? First we take out a filter paper. I'll do it the first time and show you, and you can try later. We start by taking a sample of the soil. Now, it's grass here, so we have to dig down a little. There, that's good. Just a pinch, that's all, right on the paper. Then we mix it with the acid and ammonium molybdate—if you hold this, I can pour. Make sure not to get it on your shoes, it smells awful. Just a tiny little bit is all we need. And now we wait for a few seconds. Look. See that? Now we go back to the notepad and glue this paper in the square at the top left-hand corner. Then we do the same with all the rest."

"With all the squares?"

"Yes, every one."

"But why did the paper turn purple?"

"That's a good question." They went back out in the yard. "It shows changes in the soil. When waste, like a dead animal, for instance, ends up in the ground and breaks down, it affects the vegetation there. Sometimes in a very particular way. So if there's an animal buried anywhere around here, the paper might turn a little darker in that spot. The phosphate values, as they're called, will vary everywhere, since they spread through the soil. But not in equal amounts. Where the color is darkest, that's where the animal could be."

Sampling and testing took forever, so long that Vidar got bored, excited, and then bored again, several times over. The sun moved across the sky and Sven insisted that they keep going, so they would finish before darkness fell.

The grid they'd drawn slowly filled in with purple filter papers. At first it was difficult work, and Vidar got citric acid on his shoes. It stank. It was impossible to see any differences in the shades of color on the papers while they worked; they all just looked purple. He was beginning to lose heart.

"There," Sven said when they were done with the final filter paper and the page was full. They got into the car and Sven took out a flashlight. "It can be helpful to use a flashlight when it's time to look, because the light is a little colder and sharper, see? It's easier to make out different shades than if you just look under a regular light. We sure ended up with a lot of samples, didn't we?"

"Yeah."

They inspected the color chart in a tense, heavy silence.

"What do you say, Vidar?"

He knew this was an important moment. With one finger hovering in the air—his dad had made it clear they must not touch the strips—Vidar circled cautiously around four of the samples that had been taken from the very back corner of the lot, right next to the garage.

"There." He looked at his father with expectation and nerviness in his chest. "Right?" He lowered his hand, already feeling almost ashamed. "Is that wrong?"

His father smiled. "I couldn't agree more. If there's a cadaver on the lot, it's there."

The next day, Elsa's two sons paid a visit. They lived and worked in town these days, but had been summoned out to Skärkered to find two shovels leaning against the garage wall and waiting for them. They started digging in the spot Vidar had marked with Sven, and after a morning's work they found the first bone: a vertebra.

That's the way it is, Vidar thought. Everything could be uncovered. Everything could be brought to light. As long as you were stubborn enough and didn't give up.

18

Vidar had felt so filled with purpose and insight back then. The more he thought about it now, the sadder he felt.

"I'm thinking about becoming a pilot," said the nearly grown Vidar into the silence of the car, and saw out of the corner of his eye how his dad turned his head.

"A pilot?"

"Or a firefighter. I was also thinking about the military. Or maybe engineering."

"Well, those would certainly all be good money. But lots of training."

"Not for the military, though?"

"I suppose it depends."

That was all he said. They turned off onto a narrow forest road near Tiarp Farm. Not far ahead of them, police tape ran from tree to tree. Sven parked and asked Vidar to bring out the wooden frame and the dough scraper.

"What are we going to do?" Vidar asked, sounding more uncertain than he would have liked.

Sven took the can of plaster from the back seat and closed the door.

"Make a cast."

: : :

And soon Vidar was standing alongside his father, shivering, with the frame and the scraper in his hands. Sven inspected the frozen ground meticulously.

"See the tire tracks here?"

"Yes."

"Put down the frame so the tracks are in the middle."

"Shouldn't you do that?"

"No, it's fine, just do it."

Vidar looked around. "But . . ."

"Vidar."

He sighed and crouched down, slowly lowering the frame.

"A little farther. It needs to kind of sink in. More."

"I'm trying," Vidar snapped. "But the ground is frozen."

"You have to press harder."

"It's going."

"This is important, Vidar," his father said, his voice louder, "that's not good enough, you have to—"

"I know!"

In the same instant as Vidar's firm pressure on the frame caused the ground to give way, he realized why he was here. The realization probably would have frightened him if only his father hadn't just made him feel like a child again.

His dad was no longer capable of doing this on his own.

His father opened the large can of plaster in silence. Its contents were starting to set. There was a stirring stick inside.

"You're actually supposed to mix it right before you use it," he said, stirring the plaster. "But this time, we couldn't. It's important to use just the right amount of water and powder, and you have to feel your way there and make sure there aren't any air bubbles." He picked up the can and tilted it above the tire tracks. "Now, place one hand on either side of the frame, but don't push down, just keep it in place."

A thin stream of plaster ran onto the ground beside the track.

"Really the technicians should do this, but they don't have time. So I have to do it myself. Look here, how I'm not pouring it directly into the track. That would spoil it. You always start by pouring some out on either side, carefully, nice and slow so it flows in and fills up the frame. You should never pour it right on the impression, and you should never pour it too fast. You might ruin it, especially if it's a soft track. That goes for footprints, too. A tiny, tiny bit at a time. Like this. Now, the air is cold today, as you can tell, but in here it's still pretty shadowy and damp, so the ground might crumble much easier than you'd expect."

Vidar wasn't listening. When the can of plaster was empty and the frame full of thick, white goo, Sven took the dough scraper and made a few careful passes back and forth.

"You have to just barely touch it. Especially if you aren't using very much plaster, because it can be shallow. If you get the scraper in too deep, you might reach the print and destroy it. Then you're screwed. So smooth carefully. See? Just until it's even. Want to try?"

"No."

When Sven was finished, he stood up and straightened his back. His spine cracked. He lit a cigarette and coughed.

"You should quit."

"Thanks for your help, Vidar. Well done. That went great."

Vidar rolled his eyes. "So now what?"

"Now we get in the car and wait for it to dry. Half an hour, more or less."

The smoke from his father's cigarette stung his eyes. Vidar looked around. You could feel it: Something terrible had happened here.

The chilly air crept into the car and the minutes passed slowly. Neither of them said anything. In recent years, they'd had a lot of practice being quiet together. They needed more.

At last Vidar asked his father a question and received no response. When he turned his head, he saw that his dad's chin was propped on his chest and his heavy eyelids were closed.

"Dad."

When Vidar placed a hand on his father's arm, he startled and looked around in confusion, staring at his son with wide red eyes.

"What did you say?"

Vidar looked at him, a sudden feeling of uncertainty in his body. "Nothing. It was nothing."

"I'm sorry, I . . ."

"It's okay."

Vidar looked straight ahead instead, at the police tape and the white cast in the ground. Everything was very still. "We've got a match tomorrow."

His father turned his head. "Do you? Up at home?"

"Yeah, against Alet."

"Are you playing? It's supposed to rain."

"What does it matter if it rains?"

Sven didn't say anything for a moment.

"I'll try to make it."

It didn't matter. Vidar wondered if Linus would show up, the forward. He was a crucial player in front of the goal; they needed him. Alet was a strong team. Their coach was really good.

"You know, they do casts in the military too."

"I don't know if I want to join the military."

"Being a pilot would be great too. Or a firefighter. But, what was it, the last thing you said?"

"Engineer."

"I hardly even know what that is. It's good to have a straight-forward job. I . . ."

Sven stopped speaking and went stiff. Something had fluttered in the rearview mirror.

"What was that?" Vidar asked.

"A bird, I think." His father squinted at the glimpses of sky among the treetops, way up high. "Just a bird taking off."

: : :

We try to emulate them, those whose affirmation we seek but have trouble attaining. It would be strange if we didn't. It's how we struggle to be seen, hope to get what we yearn for and wish for from others. There's no other means available, neither as a child nor as an adult.

For Vidar Jörgensson this realization would be a long time coming, and once it did come to him he would think about this day, up here at the very edges of Tiarp, the day he sat in the car with his father, cold and clueless.

And he would wish he had understood earlier.

19

Stina Franzén had no boyfriend and just a few brief high school flings behind her. She worked in the restaurant at Grand Hotel over by the train station. Her shift had ended at eleven and she had left the restaurant fifteen minutes later. According to witnesses, she was heading home. Everything was as usual. She seemed tired but cheerful. She said goodbye to her colleagues and left through the staff entrance, which faced the parking lot where her Opel was parked.

Someone was waiting for her outside.

The colleague who had seen her last of all had just taken out the garbage. She ran into Stina at the door and held it for her. When the colleague turned her head, she heard movement, as if someone was walking toward Stina. The colleague thought she'd heard Stina say something like "Oh, hi," the way you might when you unexpectedly encounter someone you know.

The door closed. The colleague went back to work and Stina's "Oh, hi" was the last anyone ever heard from her. There was someone out there, the colleague was sure of it. Someone in the shadows, close by.

The call came in less than two hours later. By then it was all over and the car had been abandoned alongside a forest road near Tiarp Farm.

Her apartment in the Vallås neighborhood was untouched. None of the neighbors saw her come home. She never got that far.

Sven stood in the parking lot outside Grand Hotel in the cold and looked around. Cars pulled in and out. There was something about everyone's faces. The city seemed anxious in a way he had never experienced before.

Or maybe it was him.

Who had been waiting out here in the shadows? Ex-boyfriends and other logical candidates all seemed to have alibis. He looked at the empty space where the Opel had been parked. No clues.

Oh, hi, thought Sven.

Someone you know. She knew him.

Her parents were in shock, almost unreachable. He didn't know what to say to them, so he said very little. Responded to the few questions they managed to ask. They were getting psychiatric support, although the clinic had been full up last night because they had to care for all the poor souls who were having a hard time dealing with the death of the prime minister.

There were few thoughts he didn't dare to think, but one of them was what would happen if his own son, nearly grown Vidar, were taken from him. How could anyone go on?

Sven couldn't imagine.

Making the cast of the tire tracks in the forest had stuck with Sven and filled him with a strange warmth. He had explained how it worked to Vidar, just like when Vidar was little. For a brief moment it had almost felt like before. He'd done a good job with the casting, the boy had.

He walked over to a phone booth and called home to hear Bibbi's voice.

"What are you doing?" he asked.

"Watering the flowers."

He was nonplussed. Didn't she understand?

No, she never understood anything; for her the world was nothing but flowers and the guests at Scandic, her friends up in Simlångsdalen and all the chores at home, laundry and flower beds and the dishes, a few new mugs from the old ceramics works in Oskarström, the morning paper with a crossword in the back pages. Such a sheltered world she lived in, the woman who had been by his side for so many years. She didn't see what he was forced to see and what he didn't dare to tell her about.

He saw all the ugliness and how pointless it was. Every store had money, so any one of them could be hit by some high and desperate bastard, a store where his wife or son was standing in one of the aisles holding a carton of milk or a loaf of bread, it could go wrong and that bastard could open fire; there were drunk and high drivers on every road and you could encounter them at any moment, it could be Vidar or Bibbi or any of his dear neighbors up in Marbäck who lay crushed in a smoking wreck in the ditch. People would beat each other to death in a fight over a parking spot or a quick kiss on Midsummer. Nothing was forever; everything could be lost. He witnessed this fact every day. He could lose the ones he loved most at any moment.

Sven struggled with this fact every day, as if he had been assigned a duty early in life: Don't lose faith.

20

As Gisela walked home after dropping Wille off with his parents, she noticed the cordon tape from the night before and saw police cars parked along the edge of the road. She wondered what had happened; the boy had been hesitant to say more than that it was about a man who had done something awful, who had hit someone.

A truck came chugging and rumbling along the gravel road. She jumped out of the way and saw it was old Carl-Henrik Håkansson. He pulled up alongside her and rolled down the window.

"Hi, Gisela. How're things?"

"Oh, fine."

"Just out for a walk, then?"

"Yup."

Most of the folks around here were still farmers, farmworkers, or tradespeople. Carl-Henrik was pleasant enough, but a little nosy and forward at times. He'd celebrated his sixtieth birthday a few years ago, but still supported himself by collecting scrap metal from the farms on the ridge and taking it to the junkyard in town, even on the weekends. He would accept most items; the bed of his truck already held a dead lawnmower and an old cement mixer.

"I see you're hard at work today."

"Arvid Carlsson's old junk. Evidently he tried to fix this mixer last night, got help from Linder's boy. It's heavy as shit, so it takes two. But when Arvid tried to start it up this morning it still didn't work. So I'm taking it now, and I've got Olsson's lawnmower too. I'm on my way to pick up a boat motor in Fammarp before I head to the junkyard."

There was a hint of worry in Carl-Henrik's old gray eyes. His engine was idling and the odor of exhaust rose around the truck. "Strange times we're living in."

"Yeah."

"Can I give you a ride?"

"No thanks, I'm fine." She glanced at the cordon. "Anyone know what happened over there?"

"Apparently someone was murdered. A girl. Or, you know, a woman. Young, but not a child."

"Whoa." Gisela's stomach turned to knots. "Who was it? Someone from up here?"

"No word yet, I guess. Could be. But evidently . . . Well, I don't know. But I heard it involved rape, too." He gave her a significant look. "That's why I was thinking . . . if you wanted a ride."

"Oh, thanks, but that's okay."

Carl-Henrik thoughtfully tapped his finger against the wheel. Then he nodded and sighed. "And you've heard about Palme, I assume?"

"Yes."

"Damn. Hell of a night. I never liked him, but that didn't mean I wanted him dead. Oh well, guess it's about time I get going here. Still got junk to deal with today. Are you sure you don't want to ride with me?"

"Yes, I'm sure," said Gisela, who didn't feel sure at all.

She watched the truck drive off. A young woman. Carl-Henrik was worried about Gisela, but not about himself. It was always the way: Half the population never had to worry about being taken with violence. At least not like that. She looked around. The forest was deep and full of shadows.

As she walked on, she moved faster, and not just because she wanted to get home and call everyone she knew, check in to make sure they were all okay.

Robert had left to drop the truck off at the carrier, then pick up his own car and get groceries. He wouldn't be home for a while yet, but as she walked she kept an eye on the road in the hopes that his beat-up old Saab would appear.

Someone was waiting for Gisela when she got home. It was a young police officer who wanted to take her statement about Wille. He apologized; they hadn't quite had time for her with so much else to do. He was steady and upright but looked a little modest and almost shy, as if he were carefully weighing his options each time he elected to look at her. She recognized him but had a hard time remembering from where, until he introduced himself as David and said he lived up here, not far away.

"Oh, it's you," she said. "I *have* seen you around."

"Yes, I thought you looked familiar too."

He stood there in his uniform, regarding her quietly; he seemed safe and calm, and that was just what she needed. Once he'd taken Gisela's information, thanked her for her time, and stepped out of the shack, she felt lonely once more.

Gisela herself was the one who referred to the house in Risarp as a shack. It made Robert laugh.

"Funny," he said.

"Accurate," she maintained, and of course it was.

Everything about it was old: the wiring, the washing machine, the toilet, the lights, the radiators that no longer put out heat but just stood there clanking. The doors were flimsy, the walls and the floors creaky and in poor condition. But there was no mold. That was enough for Gisela. She hadn't had to pay much. Just beyond the property was a large field that led up to the sharp, dark tree line of Nyårsåsen. The field probably had an owner, but, as was so often the case up here, no one quite knew who it might be.

She'd lived here for almost a year now. Christian had been by a few times at first and didn't seem to be comfortable at all. Maybe that was why he'd left her; that was what she had originally told herself when she made mental lists of the potential reasons for their breakup. *Well,* she thought, *maybe it was the fault of this damn shack.* She supposed it was a way to try to understand and move on. She and Christian had never even slept together here.

Then Robert came into her life, looked at the shack with warmth in his eyes, and expressed the opinion that it had a certain charm after all.

She liked Robert, the way he looked at her and touched her, listened to her when they sat opposite each other at the kitchen table or talked on the phone on nights when he had to sleep away from home. She liked how even-keeled and considerate he was, how he listened to most of the same music she did, how he didn't seem to be scared of her being the person she was. She felt secure with him, just as she felt secure in the shack in Risarp.

Darkness fell early that afternoon. She was on the phone for hours. Everyone was fine but anxious. No one knew who the young woman was yet. Gisela stared out at the black night beyond the window.

21

"I need someone else."

Sven's boss, Reidar Björkman, was a gruff man in his fifties who looked more like an auditor than a policeman, with his mustache, close-cropped curly hair, and big glasses. He had a reputation for being a bad person but a decent police officer. Sven had tried to strike up a conversation with the fellow a few times, but Björkman's only personal interest was the horses he kept on his farm in Veinge. Considering that Sven's only real interests in life were hunting and sitting alone in silence, they had a hard time getting on.

Björkman looked as if Sven had just insulted him. "And who might that be?"

"Anyone. I can't handle this on my own. Carlén? She's good. She was there last night too."

"She's busy with other things."

"Like what?"

"The Sibylla robbery."

Björkman's office smelled sour and musty. In one corner stood the riding boots he insisted, for some reason, on arriving to work in. Maybe he didn't notice the smell anymore.

Björkman lowered his gaze to the top of his desk. "Jörgensson, they shot the prime minister not even thirty-six hours ago."

"But that's Stockholm."

"And down here, we're full up with shit as it is."

"But," Sven attempted, "I mean, we can't keep going like this much longer. The newspaper will run the news tomorrow; they've already been in touch. The hospital just called me to confirm the injuries. Not only did he kill her, he raped her first. It's horrific, Reidar. We're going to look bad if we don't devote more resources to this."

Björkman's face was tense and grim, the skin behind his glasses gray and purple. He grabbed a plastic cup that was half full of coffee and drank it with a grimace. "Damn, that's cold."

The door to the corridor was open. Sven could hear movement outside. He turned his head and saw a young blond man passing by.

"Well, then again, you could have him," Björkman said, as if this would mean one less problem on his plate.

"Who's that?"

"He's new. But I think he went up to Tiarp to talk to someone."

"He did? Who'd he talk to?"

"That Mellberg woman, what the hell is her name? Gunnel? I sent him there while you were talking to the kid." Björkman walked around his desk and toward the door. "Hey." He raised his voice. "Hey, you there. Stop. What's your name again?"

"David," came an uncertain voice from out in the corridor.

"Come here."

The young man came slinking over with his hands in his pockets, looking like he'd just been called to the principal's office to be given what-for.

Sven eyed the youngster in the doorway with skepticism.

It was him. The one who had discovered Sven in the bathroom.

22

David Linder was a newly minted police officer from up near Tiarp; he'd grown up on a farm a stone's throw from the lovely old church in Vapnö. He was tall and blond with the shoulders and hands of the farmworker his parents might have hoped he'd become.

"Shit, it's plain awful." He dropped the investigation notes on the table and shook his head. "I was up there talking to Gisela Mellberg about Wille, but I had no idea how bad it was. Right around the corner, too. I used to play in that forest. I thought maybe my kids would run around there someday. And boom, there's a car with a raped and murdered woman inside. On the same night someone shoots the prime minister. What the hell kind of country is this? Ugh."

They were in one of the offices. Sven took a photograph of the casting he'd made from a plastic sleeve.

"It's not from Franzén's car. I think it might be from the perpetrator's. We have a witness who reports he saw two vehicles. The other one had some sort of flatbed, he says. A pickup, maybe?"

Sven showed him the little drawing in his notepad.

"But Wille's only six," said David.

"Six-year-olds notice more than you'd expect."

David didn't respond. Instead he went back to the photograph.

"Have they been up there, then? The techs?"

"I did that myself. Yesterday."

With my son, Sven almost said, full of pride. But he couldn't, so he said nothing. David thumbed the photograph.

"There are quite a few utility vehicles and pickups around up there. Not all of them are registered, either, although people still use them when they need them. We even have one of those ourselves, on the farm. What about the car we actually brought in, what was it, an Opel?"

"What about it?"

David stared at Sven with bright blue eyes. "Has anyone taken a look at it yet?"

"No one's had time. It's in storage."

Sven could have asked someone in the technical division for a favor. That probably would have solved the matter. But anyone who knew him knew that it would be like his asking someone else to paint his house or chop wood for the autumn. You didn't solve problems by putting yourself in debt to another person. That never ended well.

"We should do as much as we can before the papers start writing about this." Up to this point, ironically enough, they'd been overshadowed by the shooting up in Stockholm, which protected them from any media coverage. That time would soon be past. "I could have done it myself, but I . . ."

It happened again. He was sitting in the driver's seat of the car with his hands on the wheel and Franzén's body just visible in the rearview mirror, revving the engine along the Tiarp stretch on his way to the hospital. The lonely Vapnö Church steeple reached for the sky in the black of night, that strange smell in the car, his solitude. Anxiety grasped for his throat, burned behind his eyes, made his hands shake—what the hell?

"I was thinking," the young officer said gently, as if to catch Sven as he fell, "that maybe we could both go down and take a good look at it. If that's okay with you, I mean."

:::

The Opel was waiting in a dim corner of the massive hall. Sven stared into the passenger compartment as if an apparition were moving around inside. He wanted to light a cigarette but resisted the urge.

The car was dark blue and in good condition. They documented traces of what they believed was saliva, and also blood. Lots of blood; the dried spots on the upholstery were black, the size of platters. Here and there were some smaller sprays and drips, which prompted contemplation in David.

"I'm no blood expert, but I think these are in weird spots. These ones on the headrest, for instance. This spatter could have come from another person."

On the floor mat in the back seat, Sven identified a print from a size 44 boot, which likely belonged to the perpetrator given that it would likely have been quite fresh at the time the crime was committed, and that the victim herself wore a size 37. David lifted an identical print from the passenger-side floor mat up front.

"And that one?"

David pointed at a partial print on the mat under the driver's seat.

"That's probably mine," Sven said faintly, sitting in the seat.

Nausea rose in his belly. He glanced at the passenger seat. The perpetrator had sat there. She had driven him. Sven swallowed. The car was getting claustrophobic.

"What have we actually got here?" David said. "Just possible blood evidence?"

"And probably saliva."

"No semen?"

"Doesn't seem like it. Not in . . ." Sven said, hesitating, "you know, not inside her either, according to the initial reports from the hospital. And no sign of a condom or anything."

"So he didn't ejaculate," David said.

"At least not there and then."

"He took care of that later, you mean?"

"Some do, I guess."

"What do you think it means?"

Sven cautiously touched the wheel.

"I don't know. That it's not actually about the sex, maybe."

"Even though it was a rape?"

Sven nodded but didn't say anything, so it was impossible to know what was on his mind. David pulled a narrow strip of paper from the glove compartment and studied it, frowning.

"A receipt." He held it up to the light. "I think we might have fingerprints here. Looks like it, anyway."

David carefully placed the receipt in a small plastic bag. When he was finished, he held it up to the dim roof light again.

"The print must be hers. Twenty minutes past eleven on Friday night, she gets gas at the OK station on Slottsgatan. She gets half a tank, even though she's only going home."

"To avoid having to stop there again the next day, when she leaves?"

"But if she's heading home, why go in that direction? She lives the other way, in Vallås. And there's a station there too."

"So you don't think that was it?"

David hesitated.

"You said someone was waiting for her outside, right? Someone she knew?"

"Someone she recognized, anyway."

David looked at the gas receipt.

"Maybe she was going to drive him home."

23

The silence between them was oddly companionable. David observed the world outside, lost in thought, as Sven drove, wishing it felt like this when his own son was in the passenger seat.

A light rain was falling. Sting's latest single was on the radio. Sven looked at the console with distaste.

"You can't even tell what he's singing."

"'I hope the Russians love their children, too,' I think," David said. "Which means . . ."

"I know English, thanks."

But he still didn't understand what it meant. They parked at the gas station. Behind the register was a gangly teenager with brown hair and a concerned expression. When they asked, it turned out that yes, he was the one who'd been working that night.

Sven took a photograph from his jacket pocket. The young man took it between long fingers and gazed at it. He had a serious overbite; his front teeth seemed permanently on display. Now he scratched his pimply cheek.

"She filled up here on Friday."

"What time?"

"Well, uh, I'm not quite sure, sometime after I took my break at nine, but quite a while before we heard about Palme on the radio. After eleven, maybe."

She hadn't seemed particularly frightened or nervous. Hadn't done a lot of looking around or anything. She was just there, he said. And she had been on her own. He couldn't remember if anyone else had been in the store at the time; there could have been a customer or two among the shelves, but no one who was there with her.

"I don't think so, anyway, but, I mean, I wasn't watching that closely."

"You don't have any security cameras here?"

His eyes got big and round. "No, we don't."

"Or outside?"

The teenager looked anxiously from Sven to David. "Hey, what's going on? Did something happen?"

"Yes," said Sven. "What about at the pumps? Was anyone out there?"

"No. But there was someone in the car."

"Which car?"

"You know, her car. In the front seat. I mean," the teenager tried to explain nervously, "there was no one out by the pumps, but there was someone in the car."

"How did you know which car was hers?" David asked.

"She pointed it out when she came inside. She was at pump two, she said. So I glanced out to make sure she had the right number, because sometimes people think they're using pump two when really they're at one. And so then I saw there was a man in the car."

"Are you sure it was a man?" Sven asked.

"Yeah. That kind of thing, you can tell."

Sven was satisfied with that. "So there was a man in her car. Can you describe him?"

"I mean . . . It was pretty dark. I couldn't see him very well. Mostly a, what's it called, when you see the outline, a . . ."

"A silhouette?"

"Exactly. But I'm sure he was there."

"How about his hair?" David asked.

"Short. Maybe blond, but I don't know. Or else he was wearing a hat."

"You're saying he was wearing a hat?" Sven asked.

"Yeah, maybe. I don't know. But, short hair or a hat."

"Not a cap?"

"No, it didn't have a brim."

Sven nodded, jotted down *hat?* When it came to that detail, perhaps little Wille had been sure of what he'd seen after all. That was encouraging.

"Could you tell if he was wearing glasses?"

"No."

"No, meaning . . . ?"

The youngster blinked. "What?"

Frustration welled up inside Sven. "No as in he wasn't wearing glasses, or no as in you couldn't tell?"

"I . . ." he stammered. "I didn't see any glasses."

"Okay. Thanks."

"How was he sitting?" David asked. "Leaning forward, straight up, what was he looking at?"

"I think . . ." He hesitated. "Yeah, I think he was sitting straight up. And I had the sense he was staring right at her."

24

They were waiting for him when he returned, two shadows in dark clothing, a man and a woman outside the entrance in the damp March day. Sven was deep in conversation with David and was taken by surprise when the father held out his hand to stop him.

"Can you . . . can we talk? About Stina?"

Dark circles under his bloodshot eyes, his extended hand trembling as if from withdrawal. The mother stood beside him, stiff and grim.

"Certainly. See if you can get hold of the analysts at Televerket," Sven said softly to David, who quickly strode off with his eyes on the ground, as if it were forbidden to look Stina's parents in the eye.

The pale sky was sinking toward Sven. He could hardly breathe. They stood there alone, looking at each other, Sven and the parents of the daughter he hadn't managed to save.

Once he'd taken a seat behind his desk at headquarters, he began to cough violently, the sort of cough you couldn't hold in, the kind that made other people lean in and ask if you needed a glass of water. The coughs echoed between the walls, loud and sharp.

The couple in front of him didn't react. They just sat there.

"Please excuse me," he managed. "I'm sorry."

"Well," the mother said, tentatively, "I don't really remember what we said yesterday, it's such a blur. We thought it would be best to meet with you again, if you could, it's just . . . It's so incomprehensible."

"I understand. I can . . . We're putting all our efforts into trying to catch him."

"Are you?" The mother resembled her daughter, the common features concentrated around the eyes and mouth, and in the shape of her chin. "I mean, clearly no one cares about us. All they can think about is Palme."

"I care about you."

"We haven't even gotten to see her," she continued. "Since we were at the hospital. Where is she?"

"Do you want to? See her again?"

"Yes."

"I'll help you with that."

Sven took his notepad from his pocket. He told them he was glad they'd come, and if they were up to it he wanted to double-check a few details with them.

"We think," he said slowly, "that it happened like this. She leaves Grand Hotel just after eleven, when her shift is over. Someone is waiting for her outside the staff entrance. Shortly thereafter she gets gas at the station on Slottsgatan." He lowered his voice, even though they were the only ones in the room. "Someone is sitting in the passenger seat. A man, presumably someone she knows. We believe it's the same man who was waiting for her outside her work. A witness observes part of what happens, we think, up in the forest a little while later. But he doesn't see much, because it's dark." He cleared his throat. "Do you know if this had ever happened before, that someone was waiting for her when she was done with work?"

The parents exchanged glances and shook their heads.

"But," the mother said, "this witness. The one who, what did you call it, observed? You're saying that he was watching as he . . . . He was watching when Stina . . . ."

"Yes. We believe so."

"Then why, I mean, why didn't he do anything? How could he just let it happen?"

"Exactly," the father said, his voice cold as ice. "Who the hell would just stand there and watch?"

"Because he's six years old. He was frightened."

The mother's hand flew to her mouth. The father lowered his eyes.

"In any case, that's where we stand right now. I promise I will keep you up to date."

"I . . ." the mother began, again with her eyes on her husband. "I mean." She turned to Sven. "We told you before that we have a good relationship with Stina, and we do, a lovely one. But this past year, we maybe haven't talked all that much. We live in Mickedala, and she's out in Vallås. Across town. She's an adult now, and we don't want to interfere too much; we wanted her to be able to live her own life. She was so eager to move out. She was so happy. And we had a good relationship."

She waited, as if expecting confirmation from her husband. He just looked perplexed.

"But I had gotten this idea that something was up. Recently, maybe in the last month or so. I thought maybe she had met someone."

"You don't know that," the father contradicted, with a stern look at his wife.

"No, but I . . ." The mother wrung her hands. "Maybe it wasn't even that, but I just felt like something was going on. And there were calls, I know."

"Calls?"

"Calls, to her telephone. Someone who would hang up."

Sven clicked his pen, jotted down notes.

"Did she describe them at all?"

"No, just that someone would call and hang up. We assumed they had the wrong number, but after it happened a few times we started to wonder."

"You said 'they,' do you think it was more than one person?'"

"No, I don't know. I think it was just one person."

"And the caller never said anything?"

The mother shook her head. "No, whoever was calling just hung up."

"How long had this been going on?"

"For maybe the past two weeks. But, I mean, she didn't seem worried or scared or anything like that. Just angry, really."

Sven nodded and considered his notes, trying to determine what question he should ask next.

"You said you got the idea that something was up. With this person she might have been seeing, I mean. Do you think it was the same person making the calls?'"

"No idea. It was mostly just a feeling, that something was going on."

"What made you feel that way?"

"You know, as a parent— Do you have kids? So you know, sometimes you can just tell, with your children. That something is up."

A brief silence. Then she collapsed into sobs. Her husband put his arm around her and rocked her gently.

There was a knock at the door. Sven excused himself and left the room with a lump in his throat.

25

There he found David, waiting with a document in his hands.

"How's it going?"

"What do you want?"

He handed the paper to Sven.

"The phone call. We got a response from Televerket."

The perpetrator had placed his call from the old phone booth in Söndrum, about ten minutes from the scene of the crime in Tiarp.

Everything revealed something. The only question was what that was.

"If we start from where the car was found," David said, "is there a phone booth closer than the one on Söndrum?"

"Maybe the one in Gullbrandstorp. But I don't know, that's also pretty far. I don't think so."

"So . . ."

"Familiarity with the local area. He knows his way around. He knows where to go."

And ten minutes wasn't long at all. He wanted to announce himself right away. That, too, meant something.

"I called the hospital as well. They found scrapings of skin under her nails."

"And?"

"We'll see what the medical examiner says, but unfortunately there wasn't enough good material for an analysis. We'll just have to cope. The blood evidence on the headrest might have come from the perpetrator, at least. Should I . . ." David began, glancing anxiously at the door, as if he'd done something wrong. "How's it going? Should I have waited?"

Sven placed a hand on his shoulder and patted it awkwardly.

"Go check out the phone booth. Take a tech with you."

"It was you," the mother said slowly once Sven had shut the door and returned to the chair behind his desk. "Wasn't it?"

"Who drove her to the hospital," the father added.

Sven nodded quietly. The father leaned forward.

"Was she still alive?"

"Yes. But not by the time we arrived."

"Did she say anything?" the mother asked.

"She wasn't conscious. I tried to rouse her. But I . . ."

"How did you try? I mean, did you touch her, or . . ."

"I took her by the shoulders. Tried to wake her up. I shouted too, I think. Yes, I did. But she didn't react, so I started driving instead. I went as fast as I could in the dark, the roads up there are in bad shape, and I . . ."

"But you must have noticed that she was bleeding from the head," the father interrupted.

"Yes."

Silence descended over the room. The mother glanced at the father. Sven could hear his own breaths, the cars passing out on Patrikshillsvägen.

The father clasped his hands so hard they went white. "And you shook her anyway."

Perhaps Sven should have realized this earlier, but sometimes you don't fully understand something until it's over, and by then it's too late to make any difference. He sat very still.

"I'm sorry," he said, "but if you'd like to file a complaint I'll have to direct you to my boss."

"A complaint?" The father stood up swiftly. "A *complaint?*"

Saliva sprayed Sven's face. Only now did he notice the smell of alcohol on the man's breath. The mother placed a hand on her husband's chest.

"Sit down," she said softly. "Honey." She squeezed his hand. "Please, sit down."

The father remained standing.

"Maybe you . . . You could have . . ." He made a terrible face and collapsed back into his chair. "A complaint? A complaint that our daughter is dead?"

"I'm sorry. That was . . . I shouldn't have said that. I was just so flustered."

"A complaint," the father repeated vacantly, shaking his head.

His rage had dissolved as quickly as it had welled up. In its wake it left nothing but exhaustion.

Sven lit a cigarette, lingered in front of the police station, and watched the two figures vanish into the dim light, leaning in shoulder to shoulder as if they needed each other's support to keep from toppling over.

A sudden fury blossomed in his chest. No wonder he was jittery! They had confronted him out of the blue. He was completely unprepared. Not only that, it felt as if a film had settled over their small city, a massive, trembling membrane. It was only a matter of time. Someone was waiting for the right moment. *I'm going to do it again.* Sven believed him.

When he finally left the station that Sunday evening, the rain was still falling. *If you'd like to file a complaint I'll have to direct you to my boss.*

As if they were dealing with a defective coffeemaker or kitchen light.

Sitting in his car, he smacked his palms against the wheel as hard as he could stand, again and again, until his joints ached.

26

The crowd was larger than usual, despite the rain. Perhaps it had something to do with the circumstances. Everyone was looking for something that could bring hope and a feeling of camaraderie.

On Sunday, March 2, almost the whole village was huddled under umbrellas on the low bleachers of the sporting field behind the school in Breared. Everyone was there to watch the annual opening match between Breared and Alet, a team of middle-class boys from the city.

It was really too early in the year. No one could remember a time when this match had been played under a blue sky. Nor would it be this year, although the rain was melting the snow and eroding the ice. Hagge Söderman's mother had sold coffee, hot dogs, cookies, and juice from the little kiosk before the match. Everyone was talking about Palme and the gunman on Sveavägen. They felt that the guilty party might as well be shot himself. An eye for an eye, a tooth for a tooth, a life for a life. Order must be restored. Those were the sentiments of these men, who were otherwise such peaceful workers of the land, such taciturn foresters, dutiful craftsmen, and placid mechanics who spent their days keeping the world turning, their efforts often going unnoticed. In the evenings they sat at the dining table and ate, read the newspaper headlines, watched the news on TV, and drank beer until they dozed off on the sofa, then got up and did it all over again the next day. Regular, decent folks who were now giving voice to words and desires their children had never heard before.

That must do something to you, to hear those sorts of sentiments as a child.

They talked about the unsettling finds that were rumored to have been discovered in Tiarp. What a hell of a world they lived in— apparently Sven Jörgensson had been one of the cops on the scene. And the parents, what on earth would happen to them now? How could anyone survive such a loss? Damn. And Palme!

Then the match began, and after almost ninety minutes of play Linus Sjöö got so dizzy he didn't know which way the goal was. That was how Breared won. Then he took another blow to the head.

It's a little tricky to explain how it happened, but just before the Breared boys' team got a corner kick against Alet, Linus had jumped in for a header wrong, battling against one of Alet's strikers, and happened to butt the striker's shoulder. It was bad enough to split his forehead. The crowd gasped.

A little bit of tape and the wound was closed, but his dizziness was a different story. That couldn't just be fixed on the spot.

The score was 1–1 with under a minute left on the clock, and Linus could hardly get up, much less stand steady. With his face a mess of blood and mud, he was a sorry sight. Some red was still trickling from his forehead. Breared's relief players had stayed home, one because he had the flu and was puking, and one because he thought the weather was too nasty. To have a full roster and a chance to win, Linus had to at least be present on the pitch. One of the strikers was Vidar Jörgensson, who came up to Linus and put an arm around his shoulders, bending down in the rain. You could tell he was talking to Linus, but no one could make out what he was saying even though a hush fell over the field. Vidar gave him a pat and trotted back to the penalty area.

Alet's coach was a slim blond man who couldn't be more than twenty-five; he had neatly combed hair and sharp features. He seemed like an encouraging and thoughtful coach; he appeared to take good care of his players. Vidar looked at him with a bit of longing in his eyes. Their own coach was a fat carpenter named Bosse who often reeked of alcohol.

"Just stand there," Bosse roared as he placed the dazed Linus directly in front of Alet's frightened goalie, a city boy with a tidy hairstyle and expensive gloves. "For Christ sake, just stand there. It's *one* corner kick. You can handle it."

Just before the ref blew his whistle, Vidar swept his gaze across the bleachers, searching for someone.

The corner kick was made by Breared's notorious left winger Hagge Söderman. Over in the kiosk, his mother clasped her hands as if in prayer. The ball traveled in a beautiful, neatly bent curve. Linus stood in the middle of the penalty area, facing the wrong direction, a wide strip of duct tape on his forehead.

Vidar, who was way too far away, called his name.

Linus turned around, confused. At that moment, the ball struck him in the back of the neck. In some ways, this was a good thing. He avoided being hit in the forehead.

The Alet goalie had anticipated the ball's path and was already heading for it with a fist. However, he hadn't expected Linus's sudden turn. When the ball hit his neck and changed direction, it went past the goalie and into the dingy white net, and a split second later the goalie's fist hit Linus's nape instead.

First a shoulder to the forehead. Then a ball to the neck and, finally, a fist. And yet Vidar, Hagge, and the rest of the team roared. It was unbelievable. The village had leapt to their feet in the bleachers and thrown their hands in the air, cheering with the sort of relief and joy that only emerges when its true purpose is to repress something else entirely.

Linus had no idea what was going on. On the dirty, cold pitch of Breared sporting fields, his dizziness overcame him and he collapsed.

Alet's coach hugged his players, patted their shoulders, shook them gently. His lips moved: *Well done, good effort, bad luck.* One of the players gave some short response; the coach answered with a joke, you could tell by his face and movements, the way he was gesturing. He made the player laugh; it was a tired and dejected one but a laugh nonetheless.

Across the field, the celebration was in full swing. Coach Bosse was jubilant, bellowing in the midst of his players. They joined hands and raised them to the sky, jumping and bouncing, all smiles.

Once that too had ebbed out, Vidar Jörgensson remained on the pitch, squinting at the bleachers. He waved at his mother, who was on her feet and clapping, before his search resumed. He saw his teammates hugging their parents.

When Vidar understood that his dad wasn't there, he headed for the locker room, head hanging.

27

Owing to the circumstances, the news about the murder in Tiarp was relegated to a relatively out-of-the-way part of the paper. Not even there did Stina Franzén's death stand on its own: The fact that it happened within the same time frame as the shots in Stockholm was mentioned more than once, first by the reporter and then by the police officer who most commonly handled media inquiries. It was probably unavoidable. But that didn't make it any better.

Sven read the paper in the morning before he left for work. Bibbi was sitting across from him, quietly munching on a sandwich with sliced egg and caviar and drinking her tea.

"*You* work at Scandic."

Bibbi looked up, bewildered.

"Yeah . . . ?"

"Is it typical for your colleagues to meet up with someone after work? That is, when they have a car of their own?"

"Oh, I suppose it happens. I don't know. Why?"

He shook his head. "Never mind."

"Vidar won yesterday. Did you hear? They beat Alet."

"Did they? Great."

As ever, when he responded with this sort of absent reply, Bibbi pursed her lips.

He loved her dearly, the way you love someone you've grown

enmeshed with, someone who's almost become part of you. They had one kid and he suspected she secretly wanted more. Now it was too late, and he hoped she had come to terms with just *one* labor, *one* pair of tiny feet, *one* spell with her breasts heavy with milk, *one* first day of school. When you know you'll experience something only once, it turns out to be exactly what you end up missing most of all.

She had been waiting up for him when he got home late the night before. *Do you need me?* she had whispered into the darkness of the bedroom, as if her body were an aid she could offer him, or maybe more like a crutch. After all, wasn't that what sex was, more than anything else: a comfort? What he needed was simply to help someone he loved and cared about, someone he wanted to care for and protect, feel good—and to help himself feel something beyond the incomprehensible shadow that had settled over life in the last forty-eight hours. Soon enough, as he silently and gently emptied himself into Bibbi, he stroked her hair, kissed her forehead, and touched the only female face he'd ever loved touching.

"Is that what you're working on?" she asked now, looking at the open newspaper.

"Yeah."

"Ugh. I don't know how you manage."

He'd had a deep, dark sleep and now, in the morning, the events of the previous day seemed almost unreal, swept in a dreamlike fog. *If you'd like to file a complaint, I'll have to direct you to my boss.*

Had he really said that? No, it must have gone wrong in his mind. But the words were too deeply etched in his memory to be anything but real.

The article in the paper was perhaps not all bad. When he arrived at the station that morning, he was met by his younger colleague, who looked surprisingly elated.

"Two things have happened," he said.

28

Gisela had heard the rumor on Sunday night. It was still the weekend, which felt odd. The days had been so eventful, so full of emotions and thoughts that they'd stretched out to an unnatural length.

She and Robert had spent that time by the TV or the radio, but all the news there revolved around Palme. Almost no one was talking about what had happened here at Nyårsåsen. It made you wonder. Maybe it hadn't happened after all; it could be that the whole thing was a terrible dream. Even though you knew. But it made you feel—it was hard to come up with the right word, but eventually she figured it out—invisible.

She said so to Robert, who pointed out that some people were more valued than others even in death.

"Did you vote for Palme?"

"No, never." He was quiet for a moment, then added, in a softer tone, as if overnight it had become a terrible taboo to admit: "I actually never liked him."

"Why not?"

"I don't know. I mean, it's totally nuts that he was shot on the street. Or that he was shot at all, that it can happen in Sweden. I haven't quite taken it in, I don't think. If I seem like I'm being insensitive, that's probably why, I can't understand it. But I . . . It's hard to say, I just couldn't trust him. Even if I'm sure he did plenty of good for Sweden too. How about you?"

"He was okay, I thought."

"Yeah," Robert said thoughtfully. "Maybe he was."

Gisela appreciated that she could talk to him about serious matters, and that they could have different opinions without getting upset about it. And how Robert listened to her when she said something, how he wasn't just waiting for his chance to talk. When he didn't understand what she meant, he asked. She liked the way he looked when he was paying close attention, when the smooth skin of his forehead creased a little, and his head cocked slightly as if he wanted to make sure his ears wouldn't miss anything she said.

She liked his warm eyes, how alert and curious they were when they looked at her, and there was a sudden, unexpected vibration in her belly, and then they were in the bedroom and she was gripped with a lustful desire for control she'd only ever fantasized about before. She pressed Robert to the bed with both hands on his chest, began to move above him so slowly that he emitted noises of frustration and she had to lean forward, put one hand over his mouth and one on the back of his neck to keep him quiet, and she smiled, enjoying his warm breath against her palm and seeing his eyes flash in the dark.

This wasn't their usual style. She had told him that she preferred a submissive role, being taken rather than taking, being held down rather than holding down. There was something about it that spoke to her. But not this time.

Afterward they lay naked and glistening with heat on the bed, the bedspread and sheets in a tangle.

"Wow," said Robert.

"Did you like that?" she wondered, drowsy.

"Mm-hmm."

He squeezed her hand.

"Me too."

"But where did it come from?"

"I don't know."

∷

Robert had to leave soon, to pick up the truck. Tomorrow was Monday, which almost felt nice. Maybe everything would start getting back to normal. He kissed her hungrily, then walked out into the evening chill, saying he would be back in a bit.

Gisela got ready for her shift at the hospital tomorrow, even calling in to hear how the weekend had gone. Then she put a load in the old washing machine, washed the dishes, and turned on the radio. It was strange to be home alone; she almost wanted to stay away from the windows.

Just then, the doorbell rang. She went to the front hall and approached the door, peering through its little window.

Micke Håkansson was standing out there, breathless and jittery. He was old man Håkansson's son. He'd been twenty-five a year or so ago, but still worked for his father sometimes. She and Micke had had sex once at a party in Söndrum, and the next morning he had confessed that he was in love with her. This was after her breakup with Christian and before she'd met Robert. She hadn't been prepared to do anything but go home. So go home she did, but she knew his feelings had been deeply hurt.

She wished Robert would come back and watched as Micke leaned against the door again, pounding it several times.

When she opened the door, a chilly draft blew into the house.

"Oh, Micke, what's up? Is everything okay?"

"I thought . . . I just wanted to check. I chased him this way. I lost him somewhere around here." He bent double and propped his hands against his thighs, breathing hard. "Sorry if I scared you."

"Who were you chasing?"

Micke stood up again, ran a hand through his hair. His forehead was shiny.

"I was up on the ridge having evening coffee with Frans and Evy. Then I was heading home, but I didn't get very far before my fucking car died and wouldn't start again. Shit, I thought, guess I'll have to go borrow some tools from Dad, he's got everything. So I left the car on the forest path and started walking, and that's when I saw him, creeping around one of the farms down by the road. I snuck after him, you know, so I could get close enough to see who it was. But then he went over a fence and I thought, shit, what'll happen if I don't make it in time, what if he does something? And I was just standing here watching him? Hell no. So then I shouted at the bastard to stop. And he took off. Christ, he ran fast. Right up here, and I lost him at the road." Micke was talking fast and frenetically, as if he were still chasing the man. "So I wanted to make sure he didn't come up this way. That you were okay. I know you live up here but then I saw that he, what's his name, the guy you're dating . . ."

"Robert."

"Right, Robert." Micke said his name like it was an unappetizing dish. "His truck wasn't here. So I just wanted to make sure he didn't . . . Well." He lowered his gaze. "You never know. Apparently he's been lurking around outside a bunch of houses . . . I heard Jonasson spotted some guy over at his place too."

"Oh my God. What, so you're saying he came by here?"

"By the road," Micke said, pointing into the darkness. "I'm glad you're okay, anyway. Are . . . are you going to be alone tonight?"

"No." She crossed her arms. Micke looked at her breasts. "Robert's on his way," she said, making him jump. "He's picking up the truck ahead of tomorrow."

"Should I wait?"

"Maybe you should call the police," she said. "Did you see what he looked like?"

Micke shook his head.

"Not more than from a distance, in the dark. Can I borrow your phone? Or your car, so I can get to Dad's? I still need to get the tools for my car from him."

Gisela hesitated. She had mentioned Micke to Robert but didn't want anything to seem suspicious when he got home. Then she shook off the thought. Robert would understand.

She stepped aside and let him in.

29

There hadn't been fresh coffee in the break room since yesterday. Sven began to make a new pot, pouring in water and tracking down a filter while David spoke.

"So," he said. "Two things. I was thinking—after work yesterday I was sitting around having coffee with Mom and Dad. They asked if I knew anything more about what happened over by the farm. Apparently one of their neighbors spotted a prowler around there. And, you know, considering what the perpetrator said on the call, I was thinking it might be worth checking out."

The young officer took a notepad from his pocket and flipped through it as Sven put grounds in the filter and stuck it in the basket.

"From what I understand, there were a number of sightings. He's been seen prowling around farms up there, and I've made a map of their locations in relation to the site where you found Franzén's car. All of this happened within about three hours yesterday evening. Near identical descriptions and more or less identical behavior as well. You can see right here."

"Young, pretty broad shoulders, wearing dark clothing," Sven read, taking two mugs from the cabinet. "Moving slowly around the farmyard, making a number of laps. Spying in toward the farm."

"As if he was searching it. And I know the folks who live there— the parents have kids around my age. Daughters. Of course this is your case, I mean, I'm only a rookie, after all. And everyone on the farms back home is rattled by what happened. This weekend really kind of got into people's heads. They're all saying anything could happen now. So it could just be people's brains messing with them, too. One of them, though, Micke Håkansson, he even pursued him, but he lost him around Risarp."

Sven looked surprised. "Pursued him?"

"I noted it down here." David turned the page. "Here. The man was jumping a fence, heading for another farm. What do you think?"

He sounded almost nervous, as if this thought were an assignment he had to hand in to be graded.

"Good. That's good. We'll have to question him, what's his name, Håkansson. And we'll send an unmarked car up there, let it circle around a few times, for starters. Maybe a marked one too, to scare him off, especially in the evening. What was the second thing?"

"What?"

"You said two things had happened."

"Right." From his back pocket David produced a piece of paper. "A call came in this morning from a man who saw the article in the paper. He's got a view of the staff entrance at Grand Hotel from his bedroom window, and he saw a man loitering out there just before eleven P.M. on the night of the crime. He saw a woman come out, and this man met up with her, and then they went to her car."

Enough coffee for the two of them had dripped into the carafe. He poured it into the two mugs and gave one to David, took the paper from him, and read it.

"'Young, broad-shouldered. Wearing light-colored jeans and boots. They seemed friendly.'" Sven looked up. "*Friendly?* What does that mean, who wrote this?"

"The call came in to reception. I don't know. I take it to mean they knew each other."

They drank the coffee. Out in the corridor, the fax machine coughed to life and began to spit out a message. Sven looked at the wall clock.

It had been fifty-eight hours since the murder. They were losing the scent.

"Who lives on the farm where he jumped the fence?"

"I don't know. I'll check."

"Good."

"We could use more help," David said.

"Right. So I guess I'll be going."

"Where to?"

"To Tiarp."

"Now?"

"I'll take first shift. You can take second." Sven thought for a moment. "Several farms. As though he was searching them. That complicates things."

"Yes, it tells us something," David said. "But I don't quite know what."

"That maybe he didn't know Stina Franzén."

David looked surprised. "No?"

"If he's searching the farms up there, it's probably to identify his most suitable victim. He doesn't choose them because he knows them. He chooses them because he can take what he wants and still get away."

David nodded slowly. "That, or he knows them all."

On his way to the car, Sven ran into Evy, who was walking toward him with her arms full of pastries.

"Nothing arrived this morning," she huffed in response to Sven's raised eyebrows. "So I had to go pick this up myself."

Sven rolled his eyes.

"I know," Evy said, her voice labored, gesturing with her head for Sven to open the door for her. "I really feel like I've found my calling. All this police work, someone else can handle that. I'm going to be a bakery messenger. Hey, by the way, it seems congratulations are in order."

"What for?"

Evy stopped in the doorway. "You know, the match. You won. Doesn't your boy play for Breared?"

"Yes," said Sven, who initially found himself swelling with pride. "Yes, right. He's a hell of a player."

Dammit. They had a match yesterday. Shit. Had Bibbi mentioned it this morning? He wasn't sure. He deflated again. Evy didn't seem to notice, just smiled and nodded.

"My brother, you know, he subs in as coach for Alet sometimes. So I hear things. Okay then, see you. Bye."

Sven let go of the door. It closed behind Evy, who vanished into the station.

30

To the east along Växjövägen, between Sannarp and Snöstorp, was a fast-food joint called Mack Inn. Sometimes Sven and Bibbi liked to stop in on weekends for lunch. The place wasn't what you'd call attractive, but the staff was friendly and they made a mean meatball platter; there were always tables available and on sunny days you could sit outside. Today, a cool rain was falling outside the window.

A radio inside the restaurant was playing music, and in a booth nearby sat four men in their thirties, chatting in low voices with half-finished plates in front of them. Sven thought he recognized two of them and tried to recall where he'd seen them before.

He and Bibbi had selected a spot by a window and were looking out at Växjövägen and the cars streaming by on the highway. Bibbi complained that they were going way too fast and that sooner or later there would be an accident, especially if the traffic lights crapped out, which of course they often did.

"Yeah," said Sven. "And then we'll have to respond."

He glanced at the men. Rolf and Mats? Were those their names?

He was having a schnitzel platter; she had a hot dog with mashed potatoes. They talked about Vidar and about the weather, whether they would try to travel during the summer, maybe buy some new patio furniture. Bibbi did most of the talking; Sven preferred to listen and think. It was pleasant, spending time with her. He didn't have to be anything but a spouse. It had taken many years, but these days he felt a kind of freedom in that.

On the radio, the music gave way to news. The four men in the nearby booth fell silent to listen. Yes, Rolf and Mats, that was right. They worked at the vehicle inspection site.

Sven heard the name of the prime minister, police investigation, a short clip of Hans Holmér's familiar bass voice. It sounded steady, a befitting tone for the Stockholm County police commissioner.

"Shit." Rolf had been sitting with a piece of french fry between his fingers. Now he dropped it gloomily on his plate. "What a god-damn disaster."

"What?" Mats asked.

"Didn't you hear?"

The other two at the table chuckled and shook their heads ruefully.

"You mean Holmér?"

"What a fucking typical Stockholmer. Loves to be seen, loves to be the center of attention. But does he actually know a damn thing? It's not like someone poisoned some John Doe out in the forest. That might have been a challenge, what the hell do I know, but at least I would have understood the problem. But here they shoot the prime minister on a Friday night, after payday, on one of the biggest streets in the capital city. It's been almost a week, why haven't the police gotten any further? I'll tell you why: Holmér. I've never heard of a more incompetent bastard than him."

"Then he's the perfect front man for the Swedish police," said a third member of the group.

"Yeah." Rolf laughed, but there was no humor in it. "Yeah, he fits right in in that sense, if nothing else. Did you hear about Janne's car? It was stolen over by Fridhem last week. Do you think the police showed up when Janne called? The hell they did."

Bibbi turned her head to look at them, then turned back to Sven and watched him, her eyes full of worry. She put down her fork and reached for his hand. He pulled it away.

"You shouldn't listen to . . ."

"Yeah, I should."

He cleared his throat and looked out the window again, at the rain and the emptiness, at Växjövägen and the cars and everything that was just as it had always been, and he thought about Palme, about Stina Franzén, about her parents.

"Maybe they're right."

That was how people saw them now. That was the image of the police. When he pictured himself in his uniform he felt, for the first time, something that resembled shame.

31

With March came spring, and the sun warmed the cold ground of Marbäck. Sven sometimes took the route through town in the morning, and suddenly there were birds sitting by the fountain on the square; the stores began to unfurl their awnings, and the streets were clean.

He'd been on stakeout up in Tiarp. So far, the hours in his car had resulted in nothing beyond a worsening cough. It was the cigarettes. Maybe he should quit. Some nights it got so bad that Bibbi woke up and told him to go sleep on the sofa.

His eyes swept over the dark asphalt of the Tiarp straightaway, the farmland, the vast fields, the almost brutal landscape. He rolled down the window and lit a cigarette. Hours might pass in which he saw no one but the farmers on their tractors and the birds way up high on the black electrical wires.

Sven smoked and thought about a time long past. As a child, Vidar never stayed with Bibbi in the kitchen; he was always out in the yard or in the garage with Sven. In old home movies, you could see them together the few times Bibbi held the camera. Those movies had no sound, but if you looked closely you could see how the boy went so far as to repeat Sven's words. *My, what have we here?* Sven had said once when he came into the kitchen and put his hands on his hips in front of Bibbi, who was filming. In that clip, the pint-sized boy stepped up beside his father and put his tiny hands on his skinny waist. When his lips moved in the same way, saying the same words, Sven lost his serious composure and laughed. *My little echo,* Sven had sometimes called him, tousling his hair. *Vidar is my little echo.*

When he thought back and tried to put into words what had happened between them in recent years, none came to him. It was something, of course, but he didn't know what to call it.

What should he do? Did he even need to do anything? Really, things were going very well for Vidar. But an *engineer?* No way in hell you can trust an engineer.

He smoked and listened to the radio to pass the time, reading the notes from his little black book. *Someone calls her phone and hangs up. A man is waiting for her when she gets off work. She met someone.*

The little boy witnessed the crime alone in the dark. Sven wondered what Wilhelm Skog was doing now, what he was thinking about, whether he had been able to forget what he saw, whether what he witnessed would mark him for life.

If you'd like to file a complaint . . .

It cut him to the quick. How could he?

People in the village were friendly. They nodded at him in passing, asked if he wanted a cup of coffee there in the car. He declined. One time he let himself be talked into visiting one of the farmers' homes. He drank coffee and heard all about the history, cultural significance, and farm ways of the area. He was given a book of poetry by a local author. He kept it, even though he didn't read books. Who had the time?

On the radio: An avalanche in Norway had claimed the lives of more than ten people. Palme. This week lead investigator Hans Holmér had announced a reward of half a million kronor to anyone with information that could lead to solving the crime. In addition, there was a composite sketch now, based on witness descriptions of a man who had run down Snickarbacken. In other news: The funeral for the deceased prime minister was planned for March 15. Now to AIDS, a brief report on Rock Hudson, the first Hollywood star to publicly disclose that he was a victim of the gay cancer. He had died just a few weeks before his sixtieth birthday. To hide his homosexuality, he had entered a sham marriage. When he died, and all this became known, it was something of a turning point. If Rock Hudson had AIDS, anyone might get it. They were trying to send the message that it was an illness, not a moral failure. And now to the local news: Still no leads in the case of a man suspected of raping and murdering a woman in Tiarp outside of Halm—

Sven coughed and turned off the radio.

Half a million kronor. That was an enormous amount of money. He pictured the flood of information that must be drowning the police department up in the capital city. Hans Holmér. That fucking clown. Rewards. Composite sketches? What the hell kind of good do those do? They needed to be focusing on police work, not the media circus. If Sven could give his son just one piece of advice in this life, if he would listen, it would be to watch out for people like Holmér, no matter what line of work he ended up in. Surely charlatans like Holmér were a common type among engineers.

They took turns sitting up there, him and David. One day, the comm radio crackled to life. Sven reached for the little microphone.

"David here," the staticky voice said. "How's it going up there today?"

"It's not going at all."

"Want me to relieve you?"

"No, I'm fine. And we'll give it another couple days. What did you want?"

"Right, it's the casting. The one you made at the scene of the crime, I mean, of the tire tracks. Not very good news on that front either, I'm afraid."

The track had been made by a maintenance vehicle that had been in the forest to inspect the power lines up there. In addition, the driver had a solid alibi: At the time the crime was committed, he had been at the hospital along with his girlfriend, who was in the middle of giving birth.

Sven leaned back against the headrest and closed his eyes.

"Was there anything more?"

"The fingerprint on the gas station receipt was hers, of course. And I checked with Televerket to see if they can retrieve the records of calls made to her number. The person who allegedly called and hung up. But they can't."

"Why not?"

"The logs are too old."

Sven sighed.

"But," David continued, "blood type B-positive."

"What about it?"

"That's the perpetrator's blood type. We got the results of the analysis of the blood found in Franzén's car. Lots of it was hers, but not all of it. It was deposited there at the same time as hers, though. She had type A blood. He doesn't. That might not help us much right now, but it's something, at least."

Sven considered this. Unfortunately, B-positive was one of the three most common blood types in the country.

"So he hurt himself in the process. Given that he was bleeding, I mean."

"Well, there wasn't that much blood. Just some spatter on the headrest. I expect she managed to scratch him or something, considering the scrapings of skin under her nails."

"Anything else?"

"Not at the moment, no."

When Sven closed his eyes, everything went still and quiet and he felt nothing, thought nothing, almost *was* nothing.

And then it appeared again.

It came to him like a gray silhouette in all that black, wings spread, tiny head lowered, claws sharp, as if it were ready to attack. The wagtail.

He opened his eyes.

Nothing had changed.

Then he remembered. There was a story about Aron, son of one Per-Olov, a farmhand from Marbäck who went west to serve at one of the farms there. It was a story of horses.

Aron went to work for Farmer Jönsson down by Gränstorpet. One spring evening he was in the wagon, driving a pair of horses across Nyårsåsen back down to Tiarp after having sold some potatoes for the Gränstorp farmer. The moon was clear and white up in the sky, and the farmhand was relaxing after a long day's work.

And then, supposedly, an eerie chill surrounded him there on the wagon seat. All of a sudden, the horses reared so violently that Aron had to haul on the reins to keep the wagon from overturning. Then, as if a great power had touched their minds, the horses were perfectly calm again.

Aron squinted into the deep forest and saw a snakelike creature of smoke, black as soot, emerging from the dark shadows. He was at his wits' end up there on Nyårsåsen and, terrified, burst into tears. He thought of his old father back home in Marbäck, his mother who had died too soon, and his brothers who had gone to America to seek their fortunes. They had carried Christ in their hearts, but not him. He was twenty-two years old and had never feared God.

Is that why? he's said to have asked the massive darkness that towered before him. *In that case, I pray! I pray! I pray for forgiveness!*

There was no reply. It was probably too late.

Who are you? he cried, his voice shrill and trembling. *Who has come for me? Tell me!*

This was, perhaps, the worst part. To see a ghastly hand reaching for your throat, with no idea who it belonged to. It was said, of course, that in your final moments there would be clarity. But no.

It wasn't until dawn that the pair of horses came pelting down the ridge, where the Gränstorp farmer had just gotten up to milk his cows. He had to leap into the gravel road to stop them. Aron was gone. It was still plain to see in the horses' eyes what had happened, and thus Aron's fate could be recorded.

It was the summer of 1886, and they said the forest could take those who had strayed from God.

Sven, who had always carried his faith in his heart, stared into the trees.

32

Then, one day, a sudden triumph, like a shimmer in the dark. Not on Nyårsåsen, but in Stockholm. Sven turned up the radio.

They had apprehended a thirty-three-year-old man who was now a suspect in the murder of the prime minister. He had been in the vicinity of the crime scene shortly before the shots were fired. He had expressed a hatred of Palme to others. What's more, anti-Palme pamphlets and a parka-style jacket like the one worn by the man witnesses saw on the night of the murder were found in a search of his home. There were traces of gunpowder on the parka.

He wasn't a lone madman, which was a relief. The thirty-three-year-old may have been acting alone on the scene, but he was likely there on assignment—possibly from the CIA or the Indian Intelligence Bureau. He was part of a larger movement.

After the loud attention-getter that was the arrest and remanding of the thirty-three-year-old came something remarkable: silence.

Sven's colleagues weren't worried, though. Instead they put their trust in the belief that the wheels of justice would turn with their usual precision and systematic approach—that a very high-resolution image of the events before, during, and after the shots on Sveavägen was being developed within the four walls that already went by the name "the Palme Room," and it would bolster the country for a very long time.

Some questions require an answer; some crimes demand to be solved. Otherwise, it will all fall apart. Sven knew this better than most.

When he closed his eyes, he was sitting in the car cruising into the darkness, and the ancient forest enveloped him. The light was sucked away and nature crept through the vents, filling his lungs with a heavy, earthy scent that felt eternal.

Some nights, he went to the shore. He liked the sea. Maybe that was because he had grown up in, and was deeply rooted in, the dense forests of Halland. There was something about the open vista of the sea that spoke to him. Or was it the feeling of standing at a border? He could take off his shoes and walk down to the water, place his bare feet at the point where his country, the kingdom that was Sweden, began.

A few times, Evy joined him. They didn't exchange many words, but she sat there next to him and, for a brief moment, everything that rested on Sven's shoulders felt remarkably light.

One cool spring day in April, just over a month later, the thirty-three-year-old was released. It wasn't him.

By that point, Sven and David had stopped patrolling the area around Tiarp. There had been no results, and when it came to Stina Franzén's killer, the trail had gone cold.

Everything was at a standstill. Sven, David, and Evy really knew no more about what had happened than they did on that strange night when Sven failed to save Stina's life.

Then it happened again.

33

Something happened inside Vidar that spring. A transformation took place, and no one saw it, not even Vidar himself, not at first. Nor were its origins clear, but maybe it had to do with that Saturday in Tiarp, when he and his father tried to talk while the casting was done.

That spring, he began to return to a memory. That wasn't where the change came from, but it probably wasn't unrelated either. It was a memory from long ago, almost twelve years before.

It was late summer down by Lake Tofta. Vidar was six years old. The sun was high in a warm, blue August sky, and he and Sven were changing clothes in the car. When Vidar set his feet on the gravel parking lot, the heat rose through his legs, and for a brief moment he felt as though time stood still. It had been summer for so long now, and Vidar wished it could remain summer forever.

He loved Lake Tofta. It lay perfectly smooth and still and was wrapped in the natural landscape around it, almost like a secret. A narrow, uneven gravel road led down to a small swimming beach. For folks passing by on the highway, the glittering water was only visible in one tiny spot where the trees gave way just a bit. If you didn't look at exactly the right second, you would miss it. Tadpoles and small fish swam through the water, sometimes so close to the grassy edge that Vidar could stand in the water and feel them tickling his shins.

Sven ran down to the water's edge, turned to Vidar, and waved with a big smile on his rugged face. Then he stepped into the water and dove under. He always did that when they went swimming, because according to him it was the only way to take on the lake: dive into it and feel the water enveloping you, cooling your head and your soul, before you returned to the surface, almost a new person.

Vidar watched the water, which slowly stilled once his father's large body was submerged. He waited for Sven to come up again in a fountain of water and foam, for him to shake his head and send sheets and droplets in every direction. Long seconds ticked by. It was perfectly quiet.

"Dad?"

Nothing happened.

Vidar's knees began to tremble as fear overtook him. It latched on to him like a snake, and he cried out: "Dad!"

Vidar heard the rustle of the trees and smelled the scent of the earth and the grass rising from the ground.

He cried out again, so loudly that it hurt his throat. But the water didn't move.

"Dad . . ." Vidar began, his voice weaker.

A big, black hole had opened up in his torso. The trembling that had begun in his knees had reached his chest now, it was too hard to breathe, he couldn't do it anymore. Everything came out in stutters and starts.

What should he do? He didn't know what to do.

Vidar turned his back to the lake and shivered in the warm air. He didn't want to see it anymore, didn't want to acknowledge it; he wanted to get back in the car and squeeze his eyes shut so hard they might burst. The world went grainy and the tears came. They ran hot down his cheeks.

A splash in the water. Vidar turned around.

Way out on the lake there was a floating wooden raft. It was simply part of the lake, had been there so long that even Sven couldn't say when and how it had appeared.

"No one ever swims out to it, it's too far," he'd said.

Now the raft bobbed as if an invisible hand had given it a shove. The boy didn't understand how, but a big, burly man was standing out there, his tanned skin gleaming in the sun that reflected off the water. He raised a hand and waved, and Vidar heard his name.

His relief was so great that Vidar burst into laughter, laughter that grew from his belly and spread all the way out to his cheeks, and he raised his hand to wave back.

It was incredible. Not just that his father could swim so far, farther than anyone else swam in that lake. But of course, if anyone could do it, it would be his dad.

But the time he had spent there in the depths of the lake, missing and invisible, had been so terrible—as if his father were already dead. And now he had returned, as if he had risen from the kingdom of the dead.

A resurrection, almost. Was his father immortal? Maybe. How could you tell? If he was, Dad sure kept it quiet. In fact, when you stopped to think about it, he was pretty secretive sometimes.

That was the day Sven almost cheated death, and Vidar realized there might be things he still didn't know about his father, important things. The person Vidar knew better than anyone else, the one he loved most of all, had secrets.

34

In 1986, Walpurgis Eve fell on a Wednesday. She disappeared the day before, twenty-three years old. On the whole, it was a remarkable day; the air had been smoky since dawn. Something new had begun to rise into the sky, and it soon made the entire northern hemisphere, not least the backwater that was Sweden, gasp in horror.

Something had happened at the nuclear reactor called Chernobyl in Ukraine. Because it happened on the other side of freedom, no one knew, yet, how dire the situation was, but recent information indicated a complete meltdown of the reactor. Which would explain why the instruments up at the Forsmark nuclear plant were acting, as someone put it, totally insane.

If the end was near, it was very near indeed.

So they said in Marbäck and gazed at the sky, fearing a lethal rain. But there were no signs of one. The evening was warm, and an emergency call with much greater consequences for this tale came in just before ten P.M.

Ninety thousand, what's your emergency?

A brief silence. Then:

I did it again.

Pardon? What is your emergency?

I did it again. Ringenäs.

I don't understand, what did you do in Ringenäs?

You could hear him breathing. He sounded out of breath.

You'll never find her.

And the call ended.

There was no doubt that it was the same perpetrator. He had begun to visit Sven in his dreams.

Her name was Frida Östmark and she lived not in Ringenäs but in Villshärad, a few kilometers away. Her friend Lotta was the one who lived in Ringenäs. Frida and Lotta had eaten dinner and made plans for their Walpurgis celebrations the next night. Then, around nine, Frida headed homeward on her bicycle. She was wearing a dark red dress, black tights, and a denim jacket with the sleeves rolled up; she had a backpack on.

Ringenäs and Villshärad were connected by a small strip of road called Kungsvägen—King's Way. It was said that long ago, on a journey through Halland, the king of Sweden veered from the path recommended by his subjects and chose this passage instead. It had a view of the sea, and the king was one for aesthetics. He had found the stretch very beautiful. By 1986, the trees and buildings had grown too tall for a clear view of the sea, but you could still hear it. This was to the perpetrator's advantage: The working hypothesis that emerged was that the rush of the waves had allowed him to approach his victim unheard while the dusk light left him unseen.

They found the bicycle in the grass on the shoulder of the road: a woman's Monark, maroon. Her backpack was nearby. Sven stood in the dark with Evy, looking down at what had been left behind, and he felt oddly alone as he listened to the constant rush of the sea, almost unsafe. He felt strange vibrations in his hands, as if his body already knew what was going on.

His watch showed eleven o'clock. It would be a long night.

Sven lifted his eyes to the sky. He heard news on the radio. For a God-fearing man, the thought of a damning rain from above was probably not without significance. Not even if it was a human hand that had set the disaster in motion.

But no rain fell.

Maybe that wasn't without significance, either.

They didn't find much, and that was almost the worst part. They had the emergency call. Maybe that was enough: A technical comparison with the call from the phone booth in Söndrum from two months previously showed that it was the same man. He was even calling from the same phone. They examined the phone booth for evidence, prints, detritus. Nothing.

They began to search for a link between Frida and Stina. They certainly had clear similarities when it came to appearance, lifestyle, and demography, and Halmstad was a small city. Perhaps a common acquaintance? Had they had the same boyfriend, the same guy friend at some point? The same colleague or classmate? But no. They had gone to different schools, frequented different parts of the city. Frida had been studying at the college and wanted to become a dietitian.

"Well," said Sven to Björkman. "Stina Franzén played soccer when she was younger, and so did Frida Östmark's brother, Sören."

"Her *brother*? What about Frida herself?"

"No, she never played. She liked to draw."

Björkman stared at him. "Is that the link?"

"No, it's no kind of link."

"No." Frustrated, Björkman threw his pen to the table. It bounced off and fell to the floor. "It damn sure isn't."

If there was any link, it was buried too deep to be seen.

This time, too, phone calls came before the crime was committed. Someone who had called and hung up over the past weeks. This was what her friend Lotta told them. But beyond that, no clues, just that click on the other end. Both victims had heard it.

But where was she?

They checked around the county, telephone trees from station to station. They wondered why he hadn't just killed her and let her be found. Was he keeping her captive?

Blood type B-positive. If only they had something to compare it to, a body from which to take a tiny sample of blood. All Sven had was an image of him, like a spirit. The man in Tiarp was a figure backlit in the cold gleam of the streetlights. No body full of blood, no face, just lines and shadows and a voice. Strained, exhilarated in a way that felt obscene.

Sven sometimes wondered what drove the killer. Power, maybe. Perversions. A terrible monster. Yes, he probably was. It was impossible to imagine otherwise.

They had the media after them now. Worst was Inger Nilsson with *Hallandsposten*, who was dependable in the sense that you could always expect her call just when you least wanted it. She was a savage bastard who never let herself be fooled, and she got into Sven's head; he had the strange feeling of being observed each morning and began to eye his surroundings like a runaway inmate.

The murder of Stina Franzén had taken place in the shadow of the Palme assassination, and the newspapers never really quite got a handle on it. Once they realized what had happened, it was too late. Like police work, effective journalism is in many ways dependent upon time. You have to be quick on your feet to grab all the pieces that together solve the puzzle. As time passes, police and loved ones close themselves off, witnesses forget; it's harder to cause people to slip up and reveal things they'd prefer to keep to themselves. That was the case with Stina Franzén, but Frida Östmark's disappearance breathed new life into everything. The rumor was that the two cases were being investigated within the framework of one big preliminary investigation, and when that tidbit was published in *Hallandsposten*, the reader understood that a killer was on the loose, a man who would strike again under cover of darkness.

"But don't you see that people are scared?" said Inger Nilsson, who had finally managed to get Sven to answer her call after days of trying.

"Of course I do."

"What leads do you have on the Tiarp Man?"

"The Tiarp Man? Who's calling him that?"

"That's how we're referring to him here at the news desk. What are you calling him?"

"Nothing."

"What steps are the police taking to find Frida Östmark? People are upset; they haven't even heard a helicopter in the air. Don't you have one?"

"Yes, we do. We're collaborating with the armed forces on that matter, and they—"

"We've heard that the general public is organizing foot searches up there, will you comment on that?"

"Sure, it can only be a good thing, right? We'll try to provide them information to the extent we're able."

"What are you doing to respond to the public's fears? Stina and Frida looked quite a lot alike, and women who resemble the victims are terrified they'll be next."

"We don't know that he intends to continue. We don't even know what happened to Frida Östmark."

"But surely you must be operating on the assumption that he's going to act again? You can't just assume he's—"

"Listen," Sven interrupted. "I have things to do here."

"You should hold a press conference so we can ask questions," Inger Nilsson said. "Just like they do in Stockholm." She gave a laugh. "No, but seriously."

Sven slammed the receiver home.

35

They gathered at ten this time too. Fewer of them now than last time, which was probably to be expected, but there was still quite a big group assembling in the field near Kungsvägen. Gisela tried to count them, but she got mixed up, had to start over, and eventually gave up. About forty people. Somewhere around there. A man in a safety jacket was waiting for them with a blue plastic folder in hand. The journalists' cars waited at a distance. Photographers stood in their own group.

When Gisela looked up, she saw the sky reaching out to sea, torn and haggard as though it were trying to recover after a storm.

The first time they'd done this, a week ago, she and Robert had come together. This time it was just her; he had to go to Jönköping on a job and wouldn't be home before evening.

Every one of them was from the area. She nodded at Carl-Henrik Håkansson and the elderly Carlsson couple in recognition. The man in the safety jacket opened his folder and took out a photograph of Frida Östmark. He described her appearance, the clothes she was supposedly wearing, and her last known whereabouts, ending with a run-through of the chain search they were about to perform.

They would head west along this path, he said, toward the sea. The police had a theory that the perpetrator might have gone that way to increase his chances of escaping unseen.

Gisela thought of the shadow that must have been lurking so close to her home in Risarp, the man Micke had chased up on Nyårsåsen. When Micke asked to come in and call his father, she had hesitated. She'd kept an eye on his hands, his movements. You couldn't trust anyone. Not anymore. But he had only done what he'd said he would; he was, after all, the man he was. Why would he have done anything else? There wasn't an evil bone in his body. He'd made the call, lingered for a bit, and when she sent signals that she wanted to be alone, he'd left.

Afterward, she had a guilty conscience.

They began to walk. The wind bit her cheeks. They moved slowly, their eyes on the ground, keeping a meter's distance between themselves, heading straight for the sea.

"I told Anders," she heard a nearby woman say, "time to load the shotgun and keep it at the ready. I won't even go out to get the newspaper, that's up to him. It's getting lighter out in the morning now, so soon I can go out on my own. But I still want to have the shotgun with me."

"I hardly go anywhere without the dog," said her friend. "I was supposed to go down to Bjällbo on Tuesday, to check in on Mom, and it's only a fifteen-minute walk, but no way in hell was I doing that."

It was nice, not to be alone in your feelings. They turned to a discussion of the police, how useless they were. They didn't even seem to be able to catch the man who shot the prime minister. So what could you expect? Gisela listened without saying anything.

They crossed the road. Traffic stopped as if it understood the gravity of the situation. For a moment, she felt very important.

Soon she saw a vague streak of darker gray at the horizon, melting into the sky. There was the sea.

"Well now," said the man beside her, and only now did she realize it was old Carl-Henrik. "Well, I'm sure I dunno who could do such a horrid thing."

People stood along the side of the road, watching their search.

They looked worried. When she turned her head, she saw a man raising a hand in her direction; he looked young and friendly. He took a few steps their way.

"I think he wants to talk to us," said Carl-Henrik. "Maybe he saw something."

Gisela left the chain and approached the man. His face was open and his eyes warm; he was wearing blue jeans and a stylish lightweight jacket, but his hands were dirty, with black rinds under the nails, as if he worked at a mechanic shop.

"What's going on?" he asked.

"We're looking for Frida Östmark. The missing girl."

The man raised his eyebrows. "She's the one in the newspaper."

"We're hoping to find her."

"I live right nearby. There's a couple of us, over there," he said, moving his head to indicate the cluster, "we were wondering if there's some way to help."

"Sure. Just get in touch with the lead organizer; I'll give you his contact info. Tell him Gisela sent you."

"Thanks, I'll do that."

She was happy he wanted to help; he looked like he appreciated the fact that she already was. She went back to her spot in the chain.

Gisela kept her eyes on the ground. She wondered how she would react if she suddenly spotted an arm, a leg, Frida's hair. She imagined it as filthy with dirt and muck, her skin unnaturally pale and her veins like the pattern in a slab of marble. The fear she would feel in her own body when she saw the lifelessness of Frida's. Would it be worse than the fear that would come creeping in if they never found her?

It wasn't easy to decide which would be worse: finding her or not.

36

They were cruising toward Tiarp again, Sven, David, and Evy.

They didn't have a specific errand in mind, other than to see if they ran across anything that might bring them closer to the Tiarp Man. While Evy drove, Sven watched the shoulder of the road and tried to peer into the kitchens and bedrooms of the old farmhouses. A search party was crossing the field over yonder, looking for Frida Öst-mark. Evy slowed down and surveyed the area.

"What did you say?" Sven turned his head and looked at Evy. "Sorry, I wasn't listening."

"I just said it's so quiet here."

Every crime spree had a center point; every perpetrator a view-point from which he surveyed his world. Sven was close to it, he was sure. The Tiarp Man. They were calling him that too now.

They made small talk in the car. Evy said she was going to attend a soccer match over the weekend, Alet against Halmia. Her brother would be there.

"Speaking of, Sven, you don't have any siblings, do you?" David asked.

"Unfortunately, no. When I was a kid I wanted a little brother."

"Mine is one of those, you know, oops babies," Evy said. "Einar showed up late. I loved him like he was my own child." She turned to David. "How about you, David?"

"An only child, like Sven. No siblings. I think my parents felt like they didn't have time for more kids." He laughed. "They had to take care of the farm. But I would have loved a little sister."

"Why a sister?" Sven asked.

"I don't know. Someone to take care of, I guess. Someone to protect. I think I would have liked that."

"Did you like growing up out here?"

"Sure, I suppose so. I just had a lot of extra time. Later on I had to help out on the farm. But I don't know, I think that's probably why I would have liked a sibling, too. I wouldn't have been as lonely."

"Has it affected you?" Evy asked.

"Don't ask me. I'm sure it has. A therapist would probably say so, anyway."

"Do you go to therapy?" Sven said, surprised. "Or did you used to?"

David shook his head. "I was just joking," he said. "All I mean is that I'm sure it has affected me, but it's a little hard for me to say exactly how."

"More men should go to therapy," said Evy. "I think it would do you all good."

"Yeah," said David, as if this were something he'd put a lot of thought into. "Yeah, maybe."

Sven glanced his way. What an unusual young man. Not quite a police officer, not quite a farmer, and there was something deeper about him that you didn't notice at first. But what it was called, what it was about his young colleague, he had no words for.

"Oh, that's right." David cleared his throat from the back seat. "The phone calls to both Franzén and Östmark. That he seems to call them. I was talking to Björkman yesterday, and he wondered if we shouldn't go public with that."

Sven turned his head. "Why would we do that?"

"Well," David said cautiously, "to warn people, I suppose. The general public, women. So they can contact us if they start getting calls."

"People prank call each other all the time," Evy said dryly. "We can't let that become general knowledge in this case; people wouldn't be able to handle it. Some folks would panic the minute the phone rang, and others would start making prank calls because they're idiots and would think it was funny."

David looked curiously at Sven.

"Evy's right," Sven said, and began to cough.

Evy gazed at him, worried. "Listen, Sven."

"Yeah?"

"Is everything okay with you?"

The question caught him off guard as much as if she'd made a pass at him. They had never spoken to each other this way.

"I'm fine," he said. "Why?"

Evy didn't respond. They drove on and watched the chain of searchers from a distance.

"Who would do something like this?" David said at last.

"I don't know," Sven said, feeling a wave of hatred, no, *contempt*, for the perpetrator spread through his body like poison. He clenched his teeth. "But whatever it is that's wrong with him, it's wrong through and through."

37

Bibbi was asleep, and Sven was alone in the kitchen when the phone rang. He thought it would be Vidar calling to say he would be late getting home, but when Sven picked up the receiver and stated his name, he heard a strange sound.

"Sven," a man repeated. "That's right. It's you. It is you, right? Who's looking for me?"

He sounded almost curious, as if he were examining something that had caught his interest. He was holding something to the mouthpiece, a thick rag or towel, to disguise his voice. It made him sound strangely dull, but there was something familiar about that voice.

"Who is this?" Sven said.

"I've seen you in the paper. In the articles about me."

"About you? Who are you, then?"

"I call them beforehand. More than once."

Silence ensued; it felt electric. Sven's chest felt icy inside. *That's why he sounds familiar. I've listened to him. Heard him call in about Stina and Frida.*

Sven pressed the receiver firmly to his ear. "Where is Frida?"

A ruckus on the line, suddenly, as if the man were adjusting the rag or towel.

Sven listened for clues behind the voice, for background noises. The tiniest detail might be a lead, a signal. He heard nothing.

"They say I'm sick. They're writing in the papers that I have to be. Do you think I am?"

Got to keep him on the line, Sven thought. *Got to try to force him out of the shadows.*

"A sick person can become healthy again. Something's wrong inside you, I know that much. But whether it's something you can recover from, I don't know."

"But," the voice said, "aren't you curious why I took those particular girls? Why I didn't take whores or junkies or some other poor soul no one cares about?"

The receiver began to tremble in Sven's hand. "I just want to know where Frida is. Is she alive?"

The voice returned: "I've always had it inside me, I think. Deep down inside. I don't know what it is."

He said it as if this were something he'd been pondering for a long time. Sven waited. For a moment, they simply listened to each other breathe. It was remarkably intimate.

"Are you afraid of me, Sven?"

"No. Why did you call me?"

"I feel it sometimes. The thing inside me. But not right now."

"Is that why you called? Because you wanted to know if I think you're sick?"

"I just wanted to know what you think of me. Since you're looking for me, who you think you're looking for. What kind of person. How it feels to hunt for someone the way you're hunting for me."

"Does that matter to you? What I think of you?"

"Yes."

"And now that you know what I think, how does it feel?"

The man sighed. As if he hadn't heard Sven's question, he said, "I just left Stina in the car. It wasn't planned. She didn't do what I wanted."

"Did you get angry with her?"

"Yes."

"Was that why you killed her?"

"Frida, I took with me. It was simpler."

The man's voice was emotionless, expressionless. But he didn't say the victims' names as though they were objects. He said "Stina" and "Frida" as if he knew they had been young women, humans made of flesh and blood, who had lives and dreams. He just didn't care. That frightened Sven.

"It couldn't have been that simple," he tried. "Taking Frida with you, I mean. Did you have a car to use?"

"Frida is alive."

"Is she?"

The voice laughed. "What do you think?"

Sven's fear turned into a sincere red fury. It blazed up in him.

"Listen, you bastard," he said, through clenched teeth, "do you want to know how it feels to hunt you down? It doesn't feel like anything. You're a job for me, okay? A job. A piece of paper that needs copying, a car that needs washing, trash that needs taking out. That's all you are. I'll get you, and when I find you I will—"

"Goodbye."

The man on the other end sounded oddly pleased, as if he had Sven right where he wanted him.

Click.

1988

38

On the surface, everything looked identical. The trees were the same, as were the colors, sounds, the roads and shops, the meatball platter you ate at Mack Inn after a visit to the beach, the tourists and the crowds. But something was off.

Maybe it was just the weather. After all, this summer was so hot and stifling. The lawns of Marbäck were yellow by Midsummer. One of Backlund's cows, old Greta, got so hot that she ran away. The village was out looking all day before they found her on toward evening, lying in the shade of the oak in Johansson's yard, slurping cool water from the little pond he kept there.

Strange stories came across television sets that summer. Two Finnish youngsters, a boy and his girlfriend, had killed three people at a cemetery somewhere up north, in a village called Åmsele. That was a shock. The newspapers devoted a lot of ink to the Finnish boy's charm, his radiance and warm smile, the youthful gleam in his eyes. He didn't look like a monster.

This wasn't the only story that washed over the country that summer. There were the robberies and the refugees, the drugs and violence; there was the trial for the stabbing homicide and hearings about the Committee on the Constitution, all during a sweltering heat wave that made everything feel almost like it was rotting.

It was as though this was a different life than everyone had grown

142 | CHRISTOFFER CARLSSON

up with and was familiar with, just beneath the surface of Volvos and summer camping and backyard grilling. It was hard to make sense of, and in the house up in Marbäck, where the Jörgensson family lived, Sven sat on the sofa watching Anders Björck interrogate Carl Lidbom:

You allowed your wife to read confidential documents?

I will not respond, because this hearing is a total sham.

It does not fall to you, Carl Lidbom, to make such a remark. You shall act with decorum while you are here. Period.

All of that, the Finnish boy who was in the end probably not unlike many Swedes—it was unsettling—and the dismemberment case with the general practitioner and pathologist who somehow had something to do with a prostitute, and the prime minister's death and the collapse of the judicial system from within, *From within! How is that possible! God damn it!*, the goddamn terrible heat, tourism in full swing, and the constantly growing piles of violent cases at police departments all across the country, and the media reporting on it all as though there would be no tomorrow. No wonder folks were fed up. It was like everyone was being forced to take a look in the mirror, and no one recognized the image they saw there.

That's what Sven thought, on occasion, during that summer: *Is this us? Is this Sweden?*

When the prime minister was shot and the shooter was never more than a shadow heading up the stairs into the dim light of David Bagares Gata, it unleashed something. Distaste. A rage that no one could quite control.

From opinion pages and kitchen tables came an indignant clamor over police and politics, criminality and immigrants, the wretched creature that had become Sweden and one's own reflection in the mirror. It was clear now. The country could have come through anything unscathed—anything but this. The youthful boy with his smiling eyes, a mother-in-law's dream who turned out to be a murdering monster up there in the north: Maybe that's us.

Of course this sort of thing leaves its mark on you. Of course it marks a country. How could it not?

In the spring of 1987, reinforcements arrived from Stockholm and took on the case of the Tiarp Man. It was of such high caliber, was the idea, that the National Criminal Investigation Department probably needed to be sent down to show the country bumpkins in Halland how to properly handle a crime investigation. In any case, that's how Sven and his colleagues experienced it.

The NCID investigators arrived in April, stayed for a month and a half, and went out to Tiarp a few times, where they smoked cigarettes and performed a visual inspection of the area. A few weeks after they headed north again, relieved; they sent a report to Björkman. In it they summarized their findings: *Given the current state of intelligence work, esp. a clear lack of forensic evidence, the likelihood of further progress in this investigation must be considered negligible.*

"NCID." Björkman tore the report to shreds. "What a great contribution to policing in Sweden." He tossed the shreds into the wastebasket. "Truly."

And thus time passed. In August 1988, Frida Östmark's father hanged himself in the garage. He wanted to be reunited with Frida, he wrote to his wife in a letter he left on the workbench.

Her mother landed in the psych ward. *I refuse to die. I just don't know how to keep on living.* That was all she would say.

39

It cannot be ruled out.

So it said in the police report filed against Sven Jörgensson that arrived one hot Thursday evening in August and was registered the next day.

> It cannot be ruled out that the actions of this individual police officer, while honorable in intent and performed in a moment of great stress, contributed to a severe degradation of the victim's condition and hastened her death. In such situations it is reasonable to try the individual officer in a court of law, as it meets the necessary threshold for negligence. See appendices for supporting evidence incl. cited paragraphs.

The paragraphs in question were those pertaining to *manslaughter by negligence.*

The appendices consisted of, among other things, a medical assessment that had been prepared at the request of Stina Franzén's parents. It was based on information that had come to light on the night of the murder—not least from Sven himself—and in conjunction with the autopsy. According to this assessment, it could not be ruled out that Sven's actions had aggravated the victim's injuries.

The complainants were Hans-Martin and Gun Franzén, two

parents who had lost their daughter to a perpetrator he never apprehended.

Never apprehended. That's how he felt. As though it was over, a lost battle, even though he told himself he hadn't given up yet.

He read the brief, matter-of-fact communiqué at the station. The paper trembled in his hands.

Something was off about his colleagues' eyes. They moved past him the way cars on the highway pass an accident. Did they already know? How was it possible? Maybe copies had been sent around.

His chest felt heavy. A police report, against him. Suddenly it was hard to breathe, and he headed for the bathroom. His lungs were burning.

If you'd like to file a complaint, I'll have to direct you to my boss, he thought.

It cannot be ruled out.

He began to sob, but no tears came. Instead, he coughed. A twisting sensation in his chest; it ripped and tugged, pain sharp as a scalpel sliced through his airways and lungs. He was sweating now; the coughing fit came in waves but refused to let up. He brought his hand to his lips as the retching began, and squeezed his eyes shut.

By the time the fit finally began to ebb out, his palm was wet and red with blood.

He washed his hands. A few blood vessels in his eyes had burst. He looked ill.

Blood. I coughed up blood.

But there were no words. Only fear.

He had to hurry. The café in town had patio seating and Vidar was already there, waiting at one of the many tables, when he arrived.

"Hi," said Sven. "Sorry I'm late, I . . ."

"It's fine." Vidar nodded at the register inside. "There's no line right now, go ahead."

Sven went in and bought a cup of coffee. His chest was still burning from the coughing fit. Blood. What the hell. The report waited in his shirt pocket, folded up. He didn't dare to leave it at work, in case someone else saw it, but nor could he destroy it. Sven wished he could fold and fold and fold that damn piece of paper until it disappeared.

He hated all of it, the cough and the blood and the parents and the report, so fervently just then.

"We should do this more often," he said once he'd steeled himself and returned to his son. "It's so pleasant to meet up in town."

"Sure, maybe."

"Do you want anything else?"

"You were just at the counter." Then, as if Vidar had decided to make an effort, he said, "No thanks, I'm fine."

Sven drank his coffee. It was good, and strong. As always, they spoke quietly, calmly, with each other, almost slowly—as though each was afraid something might come out wrong.

"I'm thinking about whether I should apply," Vidar said at last.

"I see." Sven put down his mug. "For what?"

"Well, you know, the police. What . . . I mean, what would you think of that?"

"Of you becoming a cop?"

"Yeah."

The sun shone down on them. A bus coughed to life nearby.

"Why would you be a cop?"

Vidar laughed. "Well, that's what happens if you go through the training."

"But why would you *want* to?"

"I just feel like I want to do something meaningful, I suppose." He looked at his father, his eyes full of an honest curiosity. "Isn't what you do meaningful?"

"But," Sven said, "isn't there meaning to be found in plenty of other jobs? The military, firefighters, pilots, woodworkers, there's tons of options. Hell, why would you want to turn into your old dad?"

"Why not?" Vidar's question was so frank and forthright that Sven couldn't respond. His son took a deep breath. "Yeah, no, you're right. Maybe it's stupid. I don't know." He stood up. "I'm going to the bathroom."

Sven looked at his son and wanted to touch him, but whether it was to give Vidar a hug or a slap he couldn't decide. Instead he was left alone with an empty, buzzing head. He drank some coffee. It had gone cold. His hand wandered toward his shirt pocket and the report. The report against him. He couldn't leave it alone; why couldn't he leave it alone if what he wanted most of all was to forget it? He didn't understand himself.

Also: meaningful? What kind of foolish notions had they put into his son's head, that he thought a job had to be meaningful? *Did* we *do that? Me and Bibbi? No way in hell would we be that irresponsible.*

Nothing made any sense.

40

Why now, and not back then, in 1986? Why two years later? That must have been the question he asked himself once the worst of the shock died down and he tried to make sense of it. What had happened during those two years to make her parents resort to something so drastic and brutal, something so *devastating,* as filing a police report? Did they understand what they were doing? Did they appreciate the magnitude of what they were doing to him, a man who had wanted nothing more than to find their daughter's killer?

Nothing. Nothing had happened. That was the most likely answer. Maybe, at some point during summer vacation, they had decided to clean the attic. To make space in the living room for their new sofa, they had to put the old one in the attic, and to cram it in there they had to do some purging. That's how it tends to go with summer projects—you start with one thing and end up doing something totally different. So they went up and found the boxes of Stina's childhood clothes, the old things they could never toss, in the hopes they would one day be grandparents. Gun and Hans-Martin found themselves going through all of them, all the boxes of little shirts and pants, skirts and dresses, all the toys, picture books, baby utensils and baby plates and cups and glasses, and her first skis, the bike helmets, the cassette player with bedtime stories and music, her little radio with its accompanying microphone and recording function. There was a tape in it, Hans-Martin noticed, and once he'd gone down to get some fresh batteries for it, and got the red light to turn on in the dim attic light, he pressed *rewind*. It worked, the tape squealed and hissed as it spun back, and when he pushed *play* they heard Stina, heard her for the first time in a long time, it was their daughter and her classmate Lisa. The two children sang and talked and laughed, and Hans-Martin looked at his wife and that was all it took. The loss had turned them into two empty husks lying side by side in bed at night, two husks that were merely the remains of a couple who had once been parents and humans.

What could she have been, eight? Nine? That was Lisa on the tape, and hadn't they started playing outside of school when Stina was eight? Oh God, the fact that they couldn't remember, it was horrible, how could they forget such a thing?

She had been their only child. They listened to Stina's voice and thought about how little she sounded, remembered how she sounded at twenty, and imagined how she would have sounded at thirty, forty, fifty. It hurt, it all hurt, it would never end, never be over, and the police couldn't find the person who had taken her away from them, couldn't even explain what had happened. No one had been held accountable, even though two years had gone by. Two years! Dear God, how had they managed to survive for so long without any answers? The police had stopped sharing news of the investigation over a year ago, maybe because there wasn't any news to share. To the police, it was over. They could move on.

It wasn't fair. Someone had to be held accountable. Even the police should be held accountable, not least the officer they'd spoken with, the one who'd insulted them and referred them to his boss if they had any complaints. Complaints! If it wasn't for his actions, Stina might have made it to the hospital, they would still have their daughter with them, and she would have been able to experience everything life had in store for her, and he called that a complaint! They shouldn't have let it go at the time, but they didn't have it in them to act. There was too much going on. They were in pain. It was too demanding. They still had hope that they would get to look the killer in the eye.

They never got the chance. But, standing in the dim light of the attic, to the sound of their daughter simply saying and doing the things a little daughter said and did when she was playing with her friend after school one day at the very beginning of a life that seemed it would go on forever, they reached a breaking point.

Just a summer project. That was all it was supposed to be. A new sofa they bought from Severin Furniture on Ryttarevägen and had delivered to their home. Instead, a complete breakdown in a world that had been distorted down to every last constituent part, leaving behind two husks that were once people.

41

It was the details that revealed that Gisela had grown used to him. She no longer noticed the second toothbrush in the medicine cabinet, the jackets hanging in the front hall that didn't belong to her, the shoes that were way too big for her on the floor; the smells; the fact that she automatically cut extra slices of breakfast bread in the morning when she woke up first. It was a bizarre feeling, that the everyday life that had always been hers alone now so deeply included another person whose body she sometimes turned over in her sleep and reached for. The nights and days he worked and slept elsewhere had become the exception. When she talked to her mother on the phone, she always heard: *And Robert? How's Robert?*

She had come to realize that she lived with him, and that she didn't want it any other way. Robert, a truck driver from Gullbrandstorp. She never would have guessed.

Halmstad was a small city, but it was still big enough that you could avoid people you didn't want to see, as long as you stayed away from certain locations or circles. But then she saw him one day in early summer, just a coincidence; she was on her way out of the store and he was on his way in, Gisela with two bags of groceries and Christian, the man she had once loved, pushing a baby carriage. In it lay a bundle, a squishy, quiet baby sleeping with a lightweight little cap on its head and a bright red pacifier in its mouth, secure in the safe cocoon that comes only from the love of two parents.

"Hi," she said.

"Hi," he replied.

Gisela noted the baby carriage and managed to produce a smile. "Congratulations."

"Thanks." He looked at her groceries. "How are you?"

"Good," she said, still smiling, hard to say if it was a real smile or just a grimace, and once they went back to their lives that day, he on his way into the store and she walking toward the car with bags in hand, she was struck by how unfamiliar Christian seemed, how surreal it was to think that they had ever been each other's allies, lovers, loves.

She had thought she loved him. She probably had. But not in the way she had come to love Robert.

"But what's going to happen?" her mother said now. "Aren't you going to . . . I mean, haven't you and Robert been together for quite some time now?"

At her parents' house in Harplinge, the photograph of her dead sister was still on the wall.

"You still have that up?"

"Yes. Are you sure you don't want any dinner? You look too skinny."

Gisela shook her head. The teacup was burning hot and felt good in her hands. "I have to go soon. I just wanted to say hi. Do you know when Dad will be back?"

"He's at Gösse's." Mom pronounced the neighbor's name as though it were a curse word. "So I suppose he'll be back when the liquor's gone. Why, where are you going?"

Mom was in her usual easy chair, with the same blanket across her legs, the same small glasses and frizzy brown hair. Gisela supposed she had thought she would always be there. But, of course, she wouldn't.

Love can look like a lot of things. She met her mother's eyes.

Gisela had gotten her father's brown eyes, not her mom's blue ones, but still, they were so alike. A sudden warmth rose in her chest.

"I have to go to work."

"I thought you would have a little one by now, at least." Mom drank her tea. "That you'd bring a grandbaby home for Rolf and me."

"I'm only twenty-seven, Mom."

"And believe me, all of a sudden you'll be sixty-seven and wonder what happened. If you even get so old. You might not."

"Oh, Mom."

Her mother cackled.

"Did you read the paper, by the way? They wrote about the Tiarp murders this week."

"Did they?"

Mom stood up. "I saved it for you, I assumed you wouldn't have time to read it, since you hardly ever have time to read anything now that you're working so much, so I . . ."

Her mother chattered on as she went to the kitchen. Gisela stayed put and stopped listening.

The Tiarp murders. That's what people called them, even though they had never found Frida Östmark. When Gisela thought of those long, cold spring days in 1986, they seemed unreal, almost dreamlike. How she and other people from the area had done a foot search toward the sea, with an uneasy sense of foreboding in her chest.

People had watched them from a distance, looking on; some had asked what they were doing, and who to turn to if they wanted to help. She appreciated that they had prompted such reactions in the onlookers, that they were a force that encouraged others to act. She made new friends, Fanny and Olivia and a few others. Sometimes they met up and had coffee, went into town, went to the movies.

Everyone was somewhere. It was impossible to disappear. Sooner or later they would find Frida; that was the prevailing sentiment. But time passed, warmth returned, people traveled away when the city filled with summer tourists, and the calls for fresh search parties became more sporadic. People forgot and moved on.

Including Gisela. It was probably to be expected.

But it still didn't feel right, somehow.

"Here, look at this."

Mom had returned with a page of the newspaper. THE SEARCH FOR FRIDA, 794 DAYS LATER read the headline.

They had elected to count the days rather than the years. It probably sounded more drastic that way. She thought of the parents. To spend 794 days, evenings, and nights without your child. She'd heard rumors that the father took his own life. What happened to the mother, she didn't know.

A large photograph to accompany a very short article. They had interviewed a man who was described as in charge of the search effort following Frida Östmark's disappearance. Gisela recognized the spot, a shrubby area in Villshärad.

She shook her head. "We looked there. We didn't find anything."

"But maybe it's worth looking again."

Gisela looked at her dead sister on the wall.

"Or maybe they're just desperate."

"Took them long enough," her mother muttered, going back to her chair. "Listen, Gis."

"Yeah?"

"Are you happy with him? Robert, I mean."

She was surprised at the question, but maybe even more surprised at her answer.

"Yeah. It feels like my life is starting now, somehow."

42

"I applied."

It was a warm night. The dull hum of late-summer insects made a pleasant backdrop. Sven, who was sitting on the porch with a cigarette in one hand and a bottle of beer in the other, turned his head to look at the door. There he stood, so tall, Sven's only son, who in recent times had begun to look a lot like Sven himself. He looked uncertain.

"You mean . . ."

"To the police academy. I'm giving it a shot."

Sven blinked. His eyelids felt heavy. Vidar cautiously stepped out and took a seat in the other chair. In the distance was the rising, sputtering sound of a moped.

"You really want to do it?"

"I mostly want to see if I get in."

"I'm sure you will."

"I guess we'll see." Vidar took a breath. "But I thought you might want to know." When his father didn't say anything, the son sighed. "Okay. Fine. I'm leaving soon, just have to help Mom with the dishes."

Sven nodded; he didn't respond, just took a drag from his cigarette.

Vidar had moved out last fall, to a little house on the other side of Marbäck. Old man Hedensjö had lived there once, until he got too old and ended up at the home up in Simlångsdalen instead. The house had been sold for cheap, and Vidar had been able to purchase it himself with the money he'd saved.

Sven felt proud about that, that *his* son didn't need anyone else's money to get a place of his own.

He felt other things too. It was hard to put into words, but it was kind of like loss. As if something had been taken from him the day Vidar moved out.

And now this: *I applied.*

Sven had always endeavored to do the right thing. That's what you're taught: A person's worth is determined by their efforts to do what is good. No one can succeed all the time; it's only human to fail sometimes, but you have to try.

Sven thought of the nicknames he'd heard around town, all the times people—kids, drunks, old people, sick people—had thrown up on his uniform, the globs of spittle and the obscene gestures, the threats and blows, taunts, all the blood he'd seen, the open wounds, cracked skulls, stab wounds and bruises and tears. All the very things a parent most wants to shield their child from seeing, and now that child was voluntarily walking straight into the fray.

Sven didn't understand. He must have done something wrong.

Sitting on the porch in the quiet Marbäck night, he was surprised at how great the distance between them had become. An important process had been ticking away inside his son, and he hadn't even noticed. How could he miss something so pivotal?

He thought of the report and tried to picture the Franzéns' faces, as they'd looked when they were waiting for him outside the station on that day over two years ago.

I'm sorry, but if you'd like to file a complaint, I'll have to refer you to my boss.

That's what he'd said. That much, he remembered.

But he no longer remembered the complainants' faces.

He had time to think about all of this during the silence between him and his son on the porch, and he couldn't manage to say a word.

43

Early the next morning, coughing all the while, he spread his old map of Halmstad across the desk. His exhaustion was making him dizzy, and as he studied the map, the letters of the place names floated into one another. He blinked a few times, took a sip of coffee, and tried to concentrate.

There were his old notations. The *X* marks he'd made on Tiarp and Ringenäs, and even Söndrum, later on; small squares for Villshärad and Vallås, the neighborhoods where the victims had lived.

He hadn't seen these marks in almost two years and observed them with chagrin. In want of a pattern you try to create one, any one at all, as long as you can make it make sense.

Sven had made these notations on the morning after the Tiarp Man called him. He'd thought about it many times. *I just left Stina in the car. Frida, I took with me. It was simpler.*

Sven had been shaken.

The whole west side of the city was surrounded by a thicker, black line drawn with a marker: from where the Nissan flowed into the city to Åled ten kilometers away; northwest from there up to Kvibille, then sharply to the southwest all the way to Haverdal, until the final line ran east to close the black box at Tylösand.

Somewhere in here. About ten thousand people lived in that area, half of them men, and of those it was statistically likely that around 8 percent had blood type B-positive. Which meant just over 400 candidates—around 390 too many to be able to get anywhere with them. One of them was, in all likelihood, the man guilty of the crimes in Tiarp and Ringenäs, but they hadn't made any progress beyond this since 1986.

He studied the old notations as if they were puzzle pieces that could be arranged into a picture, if only you arranged them correctly.

And how difficult it was to assemble them the right way. He brought one hand to the map, ran a finger across Tiarp, and moved it toward Ringenäs via Fammarp.

Are you afraid of me, Sven?

You were nearby. I don't think you lived north of Nyårsåsen. People up there are too scattered, too on guard. Have to remember the old adage: Not even a ghost can escape notice by the old farmers and farmwives. That means something here.

Tiarp. Ringenäs. The phone booth in Söndrum. It all felt familiar, yet still strangely new, as if the time that had passed made the case appear stronger, purer.

Maybe if you . . .

"Jörgensson."

He looked up. Björkman stood in the doorway, one hand on his hip, the other holding a piece of paper, and his belly bulging over his belt, still wearing riding boots. They stank.

"Yes?"

"What the hell kind of foolishness is this? Manslaughter by negligence?"

Sven deflated. It was unavoidable. But that didn't make it feel any better.

"Well, it's a police report."

Björkman squinted. "But it's bullshit."

Sven straightened his back and looked at his boss. "I don't know."

"What do you mean, you don't know? You know what you did, right?"

"I tried to save her life."

"Exactly. And that's how everyone here sees it, too. I want you to know that."

"I tried. But I failed."

"We've all been there."

"What do you want me to say, Reidar?"

"That this isn't going to keep you up at night, no reason for that. You did exactly what you should have done—more, even. No one here thinks otherwise."

With his gaze lowered, Sven said, "I just don't know."

"Don't know what?"

"What to do."

"About what?"

"The report." His mouth dry. Pain in his chest. When he spoke, his voice was weak and brittle. He looked at the desk, the map. "I tried and I failed. She died. Isn't that enough, Reidar? Isn't that enough! Isn't it punishment enough? It's been two years, and I'm still trying to find that bastard."

Sven stood with his palms against the surface of the desk, leaning forward as if he might throw himself onto it, trembling. His throat felt strange and his ears were ringing. He must have shouted.

Björkman took a few steps back; he brought a hand to the door and closed it gently.

Such a terrible burning in his chest. Sven looked at the map again and couldn't understand how it turned out like this. Was this the sort of thing his own son would one day get caught up in? He'd talked about joining the military, becoming a pilot, maybe a firefighter, what the hell had happened?

If only Sven could find him. If only he could find the Tiarp Man.

"Sven. This sort of thing happens sometimes. It's awful, but that's how it is. This isn't at all out of the ordinary." Björkman took a deep breath. "But even so, I'll have to ask you to write down your version of what happened, just as you remember it. You can write the same thing you did in the report from that night. It's nothing but a formality."

"My *version*?"

"Yes . . . ? Your version."

Björkman looked almost sad, as if it were a downright shame that they would have to refer to it this way from now on.

44

It wasn't easy to find, but eventually Sven located the farm, surrounded by a low fence with flaking paint. Everything looked old-fashioned, all red wooden buildings and white doors, mossy roofs. A tractor stood in repose next to a large utility vehicle whose bed was full of wood and bags full of sand or soil. At the edges of the farmyard were small groves of trees and bushes.

The house looked inviting with its two stories and big windows; it had white trim and a low, wide set of wooden stairs leading up to the front door. It was on these stairs he sat, with a thermos mug and newspaper in hand under the late-summer sun. At first he squinted in puzzlement at his visitor, but he smiled when he saw who it was.

"I'll be damned." David Linder stood up and came toward Sven, brusquely took his hand and shook it heartily. "What an unexpected visit!" he rumbled.

"What a beautiful farm."

"Thanks, but it's seen better days. I'm mostly trying to keep it going. It was easier when Dad was still around. Are you thirsty? I don't have much in the kitchen, but the coffee in the thermos is probably still hot, if you'd like some."

"That sounds great."

David went into the house and returned with a mug, which he filled from the thermos. The coffee steamed, giving off an agreeable scent.

"How are y'all doing down there?"

Sven took a first hot sip. "Same old. For the most part."

David gazed out at the farmyard. "At first I missed it like hell. I was only there for just over two years, but that was enough for it to, you know, get its claws into me. It's a very special kind of job. But now I'm glad I left after all. This suits me better."

In later days, David had withdrawn. His father was too sick and David had taken long periods of leave before he returned home for good. His time on the farm had aged the young man. He looked tired and gaunt, with gray circles under his eyes and a dull tone in his voice.

"I was sorry to hear about your father, by the way. But your mother is still around?"

"Thanks. Yes, she's still with us. She doesn't live here anymore, but she comes to visit sometimes. Or, I go pick her up and drive her out so she can spend some time here. She likes it here. Sometimes, when I don't have time, the farmhand has to do it."

That sounded nice. Sven wondered if Vidar would do the same for him. Maybe not. It sure as hell wasn't easy, being a father. Then again, it wasn't easy to be a son either. Especially not when you were an only child.

"I've actually been thinking about moving," David said. "Selling the farm, or at least the livestock." He nodded at the tractor and the truck. "And the machinery and vehicles. There's this guy I was in training with, he moved home to Sundsvall for work when we were done. But he left the force too, and now he runs a firm up there. He said he could use some help. It's kind of tempting. But I could never sell this place; it belongs to my family. Or, well, I *could*, but my mom would never speak to me again."

"But you have to do what makes you happy. It doesn't sound like you're happy here."

"No. No, I guess that's true. Not anymore."

"Would you rather come back and work for us?"

David laughed.

"Not right now, no."

They drank their coffee. The heat lingered over Halland. The sun was strong and bright. Something was weighing on David. Maybe that was just what happened in this city, Sven thought. The factories and the mine, the stonemasonry and the farms, the police station: They gobbled up their men and spat out what was left.

"I've been reported."

"What? What for?"

"Manslaughter by negligence. By Gun and Hans-Martin Franzén." He blinked. "Her parents."

David looked bewildered. "What, Stina's parents? But . . . how? Why?"

Sven swallowed.

"They say I shook her."

"Did you?"

"I don't remember. They say I said I did, at the hospital. But I have no recollection of it."

David looked like he wanted to touch Sven. Sven was grateful that he elected not to.

"I suppose it's understandable that you don't remember. And even if you did shake her, that would also be extremely understandable, given the circumstances. I'm sure they just need to . . . I mean, they probably need someone to blame. If you put yourself in their shoes, they lost their daughter, and they don't know who did it. They just want someone to punish, because . . ."

"Because we failed."

David opened his mouth to protest, but there was nothing to say. It was true.

"You did the best you could," he said at last. "We all did."

"He called me once. Did you know that?"

"Who, him? The Tiarp Man?"

Sven nodded. "The call was too short to trace."

"So, what? What did he say?"

David listened as Sven told him.

"Crazy. And he never called again?"

"No," Sven said. "I wonder if it's happened again. Or if it happened before. If Stina Franzén wasn't the first. If we just missed it."

"Yeah," David said contemplatively. "Yeah, sure, maybe. But we checked. Didn't we?"

"If you take a closer look at the victims, there's as many similarities between them as there are differences. He's not consistent that way, he . . . There's something else."

"Yeah, now that you mention it. I never thought of it that way."

"But what it means, I have no idea."

"Wouldn't he have called us? To alert us, like he did with Stina and Frida?"

"Maybe not. We don't know if he does that every time."

David glanced at Sven's cigarette. "Can I have a drag?"

Sven gave him the cigarette. David smoked, and when he exhaled Sven could smell alcohol on his breath. Just behind David, on the ground, was an empty whiskey bottle. A truck went by on the road, wheezing and heavy, heading for town or over to Vapnö farm. David slowly twirled the cigarette between his fingers, apparently lost in thought. He didn't seem drunk, just gloomy.

"You can keep that," Sven said. "I'll light another. I wonder if he . . . I don't think it's happened again but we missed it. We haven't had that many rapes of that type. I've been keeping my eyes peeled. So why would he stop?"

"Because he got caught for something else? That's often the case."

"Blood type B-positive, shoe size forty-four, a pickup. Haven't seen anything like that."

"But you're only looking here in town." David took a drag of the cigarette. He looked like he was out of practice but eager. As he exhaled, he closed his eyes. "He might be in jail somewhere else."

"Sure, maybe."

David could tell Sven didn't believe it was so. "Or else I guess he's dead. Or very sick. Who the hell knows."

"So you don't think he could have stopped of his own volition either?"

David shook his head. "No. I don't think so. He wasn't the type."

It was good to hear someone else say it.

"But," Sven said, "there aren't all that many men under forty who wear size forty-four shoes and have that blood type who have died here in town in the past two years either."

David gave a wan smile. "How many?"

"Two."

"And you've ruled them out?"

"Yes."

Sven lit another cigarette.

"I remember when we were circling around up here. There were witness reports about someone prowling around the farms. Did anything ever come of that? I mean, was it something people kept talking about up here? Did it happen again?"

David hesitated. "Is it really such a good idea for you to keep working on this? With the report against you, I mean."

Sven lowered his eyes.

"No, I know. It's just hard to . . . I don't know . . . hard to let it go, you know."

David gazed at him for a long time and nodded slowly.

"No," he eventually said, "no, as far as I know it didn't happen again. I don't think people talked about it either, for that very reason. It was probably something else they saw. Maybe a junkie from town who wandered out here by accident and was looking for someplace to sleep or something to eat. Who the hell knows? But it had nothing to do with the Tiarp Man, anyway."

They talked about the summer: the hearings in parliament, the Åmsele murders, the da Costa dismemberment trial. David asked how everyone was doing, how Björkman and Carlén were, what was going on with that rascal down in the archives whose name he could never remember.

"They're good," Sven said. "They're all good."

David took one last drag from the cigarette butt and dropped it to the ground, stamped it out.

"I have to go see to the cows soon. My farmhand usually does it, but he's not back yet. Listen, though, this was nice, we should . . ."

"Definitely." Sven stood up from the stairs. His knees and spine creaked; his lungs burned. "I'll head back. Bibbi will be home in an hour or so. By the way, do you live here alone?"

"Just me and the animals." David looked up at him, squinting into the sun. "But there's a woman I see sometimes. We meet up down at her place in Genevad now and then."

There was something about him. David was a man who, at first glance, appeared stable and reliable, calm and content. But beneath that was something more; Sven had seen it in his last days on the force, when he was grappling with the emotions that arose around his father's illness, leaving the force, and returning to the farm. A blackness.

"But you're doing all right?" Sven tried.

"It's not always easy. But I survive."

"You know I'm always here if there's anything I can do for you."

David smiled weakly.

"It was nice to see you."

"Same here. And if there's anything I can do . . ."

"Thanks."

As Sven was walking toward the car, his thoughts nagged at him and formed an uneasy knot in his stomach. In the car, he coughed up more blood.

45

Her eyes, unaccustomed to the sudden darkness, fooled Gisela when she turned out the kitchen light and looked out the window. The silhouettes of trees and branches had, in time, become as familiar as the artwork on the hall wall. That was why she'd noticed it—a sudden deviation in the darkness, a shadow that reacted to the sudden change inside the house. It had been in motion, and now it froze, melting into its surroundings and becoming invisible once again. A tremor ran through her chest.

She took one cautious step toward the window and peered out, her face so close that fog appeared on the glass.

Then she slowly backed away.

"Robert."

He didn't hear her. She turned around and hurried out of the kitchen and to the bedroom, where he was lying in bed bathed in the cool, flickering light of the television.

She said it as collectedly, as naturally as she could: "I think there's someone outside."

"What?"

"I think there's someone—"

Robert was already up. He stepped into a pair of jeans and headed for the front door, grabbing the wooden bat that was leaning against the wall beside the shoe rack. He didn't usually react like this, but her face must have betrayed her fear.

"Where?"

"Outside the kitchen. Here, honey."

Gisela handed him the flashlight. She waited as he went outside. She could see the long beam of light revealing the dense foliage out there.

She stood in the kitchen with her arms crossed and watched Robert inspect the surroundings with the bat in hand.

When she tried turning the light on and off it happened again; it looked like a shadow suddenly emerged from the background for an instant.

When Robert came back inside, she felt ashamed and wanted to apologize, but she couldn't do it.

"I don't think anyone's there," he said.

"I know." She felt ridiculous. So incredibly ridiculous. "I'm sorry, I thought . . . It was . . ."

"Let's go get in bed," he said simply, pressing his lips to her forehead and giving her a firm hug.

She lived with him now. She had become his next of kin. When he came home with new medical paperwork from work a few weeks ago, she was supposed to give her contact information. She got warm fuzzies as she filled it in, elated at the feeling of belonging. Of being someone's person. How she had longed to feel this way.

It was a small packet of papers. His sight, hearing, blood pressure—it was all there. The carriers required this information now, for insurance purposes. She noticed his blood type.

"Whoa, we've got the same one. That's funny, I didn't know that." He smiled.

"Then we can give each other blood if we need to. Although I guess we should hope we never have to." He put his arm around her.

"Then again, I would be more than happy to save your life. It would be good for me, give me an ace up my sleeve. *Honey, can't you clean up? No, I'm too tired, can't you do it? After all, I'm the one who saved your life.*"

She laughed and whacked him on the arm. He kissed her hair. She liked it when he inhaled the scent of her hair.

46

September arrived. The leaves began to turn yellow. There was something timeless about the change; each year you knew it would happen sooner or later. It was comforting. Sven's cough was ever worse; he wasn't sleeping well and worked way too much. He was in the process of losing himself.

"Couldn't you . . ." Evy began, leaning over him. She pointed at the document to follow the words. "You could say this, couldn't you? *I acted to the best of my ability, in accordance with the guidelines to which we are previously bound.* It's true."

Bibbi didn't know. Nor did Vidar. Sven kept it so close to the vest that it hurt. Maybe because he was ashamed but mostly, he told himself, because it was wrong, all wrong. He wasn't trying to protect himself but those he loved most.

Björkman had forced him to sit down at the typewriter, but Sven didn't know which words to use. Evy had come in to fetch something, and she took one look at him and asked what the matter was. When she finally managed to get it out of him, she offered to help.

"If you . . ." He had to clear his throat in order to continue. "If you could avoid mentioning this to anyone."

Evy placed a hand on Sven's shoulder, and it had been so long since anyone touched him he didn't know how to react.

So here they were.

"To the best of my ability," Sven said. "But how good is *the best of one's ability*? If you're useless, the result will be crap. It doesn't mean anything. I didn't take the wrong action. I did the right thing." He said it with conviction. As time passed, he had become nearly sure of it. "Yes, I did touch her. Of course I did. I was trying to save her life." Trying to save her goddamn life! What else was he supposed to do, leave her there? "But for what I did to have hurt her . . ."

"*Aggravated* her injuries," Evy corrected. "That's another matter."

"I'm risking . . ." he began, and coughed. "I don't even know what I'm risking here. Losing my job, I suppose. They'll probably give me a suspension."

"Sven," Evy said gently, cocking her head. "What is it?"

He blinked.

"My son is going to be a cop."

She just stood there, obviously confused.

"Okay? That's not so bad, is it?"

"Why would he . . . like, this." He gestured at something—maybe the paper in the typewriter or Stina Franzén and Frida Östmark; maybe what you put yourself through just by going to this job every day, life, maybe everything. "My only child is going to . . . it's just . . . I don't understand why."

"Listen," she said, softly placing her hand on his forearm again. "In this case, following in your father's footsteps certainly isn't something to be ashamed of. Quite the opposite, in fact. Remember that."

She looked him in the eye and kept her hand where it was. That hand gave him a light squeeze. He looked at her fingers and found them, in the moment, really beautiful. Strong and fine. She pressed herself to him and brought her lips to his own. Evy let out a heavy breath through her nose, as if she were giving in to something she'd imagined for a long time and had tried to resist. Her breath was warm against Sven's upper lip, and his hands reached for her in a newfound need to touch Evy, hold her.

Had there always been something between them, unspoken? No, but it was there now. It was all that mattered. He was surprised to find he'd forgotten what desire felt like, how suddenly it could flare to life, that it could still be evoked inside of him.

Evy's eyes were wide open, sparking in a way he'd never seen before. Her hand moved to the back of his neck. Her touch was tender but firm. Sven shuddered. It had been a long time since anyone touched him with anything but habit. A new sort of hunger grew inside of him and he was about to stand up when Evy took his hand and whispered: "Yes. Come on. Let's go somewhere."

It was her voice that made him turn back, Evy's voice, familiar and strange at the same time.

"Evy." He pushed her away. "I can't."

She stared at him, her face falling, her arms still full of the hollow feeling that lingered after Sven pulled back.

"No," she said, taking a deep breath. "I know. Me neither."

47

To keep from thinking, he wrote. It didn't work.

Sven rose from his chair and shoved the typewriter aside as though it were an annoying pet that didn't belong at his workplace. For a moment he wished he could hurl it against the wall with all his might.

Then he pulled it back again. What was he going to do?

At last he tore the paper from the typewriter, signed it without reading it, and put the damn thing in Björkman's mailbox. It was no more than half a page long, but he didn't want to look at it.

He stood out back, smoking his cigarette and trying to recall the words he and Evy had formulated, which ones had been his and which had been hers, which had been edited out and which were still there. He focused on this because no matter how horrible the report against him felt, it was easier to think about the report than about Evy's lips, her body, how close he had come to touching her. He felt the heat going to his crotch and he grew hard thinking of her, regretted pushing her away, and felt confused about that regret.

He thought of how drops of rain sink into the earth. Days sucked up by time, memories slipping into oblivion. He wondered how this would happen for him later in life, whether it would fade away like the rain and the days, or displace something permanently, never to be undone. If this was how the future was rewritten.

What had gotten into him? How could he? He thought of Bibbi

and Evy, how Evy was feeling, whether he had hurt her. What would happen now?

He went to the café in town to meet Vidar again. He arrived early and was reading the paper when the door jingled and someone stepped in, approached the counter.

"I think I'll have a coffee. A coffee and an almond tart, please."

A jolt of tension went through Sven, from his stomach to his heart and on up the back of his neck, until he was sitting ramrod straight in his chair.

This was a slim man of around thirty, tops, wearing blue jeans and a jacket. He took his tray with the coffee and the small pastry and passed Sven, who tried but failed to make eye contact. The hands holding the tray were rough and veiny; Sven could see a hint of pale fuzz on their backs. He smelled faintly of cologne. *A tradesman,* Sven thought. *But he's got the day off.*

That voice. Wasn't it familiar? Sven had heard it before. He turned around. The man took a seat at a table in the corner, pulled over a newspaper someone had left behind, and paged through it absent-mindedly.

I think I'll have a coffee. A coffee and an almond tart, please.

Are you afraid of me, Sven?

His chest began to burn and Sven realized he was holding his breath. He inhaled deeply. A wheeze escaped his throat.

He rose from his chair and turned around. He stared at the man sitting there with his newspaper and almond tart, his cup of coffee. He had light blond hair and a strong jaw, sharp cheekbones. The door jingled again, but in Sven's head it sounded dull and distant. A fog had encircled him.

Without being fully aware of it, he kept moving toward the man's table. Now he was so close he could put out his hand and pull out the chair from under the table. That was what he should do, he thought, just pull out that chair and sit down, cross one leg over the other, and see how the young man reacted. He'll know it's me when he looks up at me. That I'm the one who's been chasing him, and it's over now. His hands began to tingle; it felt faint and agreeable, as though they were getting ready.

"Hi," he heard from behind him. "Sorry I'm late. I got stuck at work, I . . ."

A woman swept past Sven and took his spot at the table, causing the man to startle and look up.

"That's okay," the man said, smiling. He put down the newspaper and leaned across the table; they kissed. "I didn't know what you wanted, so I just ordered for myself."

"I'll go grab something."

As the woman hung her coat on the chair and headed for the counter, she gave Sven an anxious look; he was staring at her at close range.

The man raised an eyebrow. "Can I help you?"

Now he heard it. Far too bright, high. A totally different melody in his voice. Sven gazed down at the man's shoes. Too small.

He shook his head.

"No, sorry, I thought you were someone else. I'm waiting for my son."

What the hell? What was he doing? He looked at his hands; the sensation lingered—what it would have felt like to grab the man by the throat. What he had almost done.

48

The prosecutor was a woman by the name of Selvin. Nora Selvin. Her contact information was included in the report. When he got back to the station he went to the phone and stared down at it for what must have been the jillionth time.

He picked up the receiver and dialed the number.

She answered with her name and "Prosecution Authority of Halmstad." When he didn't say anything, she added: "Hello?"

He cleared his throat.

"Hello, this is Sven Jörgensson. With the Halmstad police. We have a meeting scheduled for Friday. I'm calling about Gun and Hans-Martin. Franzén, that is," he clarified.

"Okay?"

"I don't know if you're the right person to talk to, but is there any way I could speak to them before Friday?"

"Unfortunately I don't think that would be a good idea."

Selvin spoke a flat, nasal Småland dialect. She sounded cool, neutral, as if this were a customer service call.

"But . . ."

"We need to handle this smoothly, Sven. Properly. So the answer is no. Was that all?"

He swallowed.

"Yes."

"Then I'll see you on Friday."

Click.

49

On the inside, everything was falling apart, but on the outside life went on as usual. He didn't want to worry anyone and was surprised to find that it seemed to be working.

The pain when he looked at Bibbi was almost physical; it made him chafe and ache. He told himself he had done the right thing. Evy was the one who approached him, and he'd pushed her away. That was that. It didn't matter so much how he felt; the important part was what he had done.

Bibbi wondered what was up, of course, he could tell by looking at her, but she didn't say anything. Nor did the boy, those times when he came for a visit.

"Dad," he said, the evening before the interrogation, when he stopped by for a cup of coffee.

"Yes?"

"Is everything okay?"

"Everything is okay."

The boy drank his coffee. Sven wanted to light a cigarette to give his hands something to do, but he was afraid he'd start coughing.

"I got in," Vidar said suddenly.

"You mean . . ."

"To the academy."

Sven didn't say anything for a long time. Then he heard the words coming out and recognized them as his own, but it surprised him that he was actually saying them. As though they were coming from a stranger's mouth.

"Vidar, I . . . I know you want to do this. But I'd really prefer to see you do something else with your life."

"Why?"

"Why not? Why would you want to turn into your father? I mean, look at me. Do I look healthy? Do I look happy?"

"I don't see what the problem is," Vidar said, his voice louder. "And I don't see how you can be so surprised, either. All we ever did together when I was little was stuff that had to do with your work. And no, I'm not saying," Vidar continued when Sven opened his mouth, "that that's why I want to do this, it's not that. You always going on about it when I was little has nothing to do with it. But how can you be so surprised?"

Sven took a deep breath.

"I did all of that because I was so sure you would become something else. No way in hell would you be so stupid as to go and turn out like your father. I thought you were curious about your dad's job. It's natural, all kids are."

Vidar stared at him. "I know why you did all that. It was the only thing you knew how to be. A police officer. That was all you could do then, and it's all you can do now. You have no idea how to be a dad."

Sven's eyes felt hot and wet. He blinked.

"Vidar, I would really prefer to see you do something else."

"I know. But that's not what's going to happen."

Okay then. Was that all? Surprised at his son's resolve, Sven drank his coffee. It was cold. A biting autumn gale blew outside.

Once Vidar had left his childhood home and gone back to his own place, and Bibbi was in bed for the night, lights out, Sven lingered by himself at the kitchen table, listening to the wind. He thought horrible thoughts about love. About being a father, about Evy, about the Tiarp

Man and Stina Franzén's Opel Rekord, blood, blood and coughing, violence and death and the life he'd ended up living, the life that might become his son's, why would he go and do that? What the hell had gotten into him, saying such terrible things to his own father? Wasn't it about time for Vidar to meet someone? Someone good for him, right, exactly, that was what he needed, a woman who could make him take a good, sober look at his life and realize that he should not go off and become a cop, dammit. The way he had Bibbi. Bibbi, who had always stood by his side. Who had never betrayed him.

Do I look healthy? Do I look happy?

Vidar hadn't even seemed to hear him. Maybe if he had, he would have realized something was wrong, but Vidar saw only himself.

When Sven closed his eyes, he saw the green fields and the deep forests of Nyårsåsen, the car that had been left up in Tiarp and the violence that had befallen the woman in the back seat. Hardly a day went by that he didn't do this—close his eyes and meander through these scenes he'd once experienced, perhaps in the hopes of noticing something he'd overlooked before. In the grass, at the edge of the road, or hastily tossed a ways into the forest, he saw an unfinished notebook, Frida Östmark's backpack, a size 44 footprint, a phone receiver dangling in its booth. This was how he approached his perpetrator, by way of the clues he'd left behind, to try to make him into a physical being, visible and apparent, with skin and a pulse, shoulders and arms and legs, a face.

When Sven closed his eyes, he sometimes came walking by there, at the very edge of the scene: the man he was chasing after.

A face. That's all I ask. I want to see your face, you bastard.

He thought of the man at the café. It wasn't him, but the worst part was that it could have been. Maybe Sven had already encountered the Tiarp Man on his way into or out of a store, standing at the counter at the gas station, or waiting in line for help at the home improvement warehouse. Few things in this world can drive you to madness as well as uncertainty can. It was like being in a dark room and knowing he wasn't alone.

Madness. A report had been filed against him. He'd only wanted to do the right thing, and for it he'd been reported. Blood, blood, and death right next door. Evy. Horses reared before evil in the darkness on Nyårsåsen. He coughed. Evy. Bibbi. Vidar. Death. It was all madness.

50

Nora Selvin's appearance matched her speaking voice. She wore a gray suit and had a ponytail that was tight and black as coal. Her suit coat sloped down her skinny shoulders. She had a pointy nose and small, angular glasses; she looked like a business analyst.

"Glad you could come. You didn't bring anyone?"

"I didn't think it was necessary."

Selvin invited Sven to sit down on the other side of the imposing desk and put aside a collection of documents. She took out a tape recorder and inserted a cassette.

"Let's see here . . ." she muttered, fiddling with the buttons. "There." When she found the right one and pressed it, the machine began to emit a dull hum. "Now then. I'd like—" she began, but then she pressed *pause*. "Before we begin, I want you to know that I'm not trying to cause you any harm. I want the best for you. What happened, I understand it's tough. And we're going to figure this out. We're on the same side, you know that. But I have to be meticulous and do as my position demands. Which means this interrogation is unavoidable. Do you understand what I'm telling you?"

She was the doctor, and he the clueless patient who had to be subjected to more pain before it got better. What should he do, what could he say—nothing. He simply gave a stiff nod and wondered if she too had once kissed a colleague, maybe a young, well-dressed lawyer who had been there for her when she was having a rough time. If a woman like Selvin could have a rough time in the first place, that is. He doubted it. She didn't look like she'd suffered any of life's torments yet. Maybe some people never did? Maybe some people were spared. He wasn't sure.

She turned on the tape recorder and it began to hum again.

He was asked to tell what had happened in his own words. When he pointed out that he'd already turned in a written testimony, Selvin nodded dismissively, muttered a *Yes, right* with her eyes on her documents, and asked him to tell her anyway.

The tape recorder hummed. It was cool in the room.

"Can I just ask, how are her parents? How are they doing?"

"Why do you ask?"

"Just out of . . . well, out of consideration. Or whatever I should call it. I did meet them a number of times."

"Please go ahead and tell me what happened now."

He did the best he could. When he fell silent, Selvin looked surprised, as though she had been expecting a much lengthier account.

"Okay."

"Well, that's about it."

The thin woman cocked her head. Her tightly bound hair looked stiff and hard, like a helmet.

"I appreciate that this is difficult, Sven. But it's difficult for her parents too. Do you regret the way you expressed yourself?"

"When do you mean?"

Selvin looked down at her papers. Sven saw the medical report, typewritten. He saw the police report, the write-in response, and her finger searching the page:

"I'm sorry, but if you'd like to file a complaint I'll have to direct you to my boss."

"Oh. Yes. Of course."

"Sven, her parents don't wish any harm. They've been very clear about their wishes. They don't want to go to the media, don't want to seek damages, nothing. And I don't represent them. All they want is to understand what happened—just as I do. As you know, this is a question of negligence. So I have to ask you again, can you take me through what you did when you arrived on the scene one more time? You stop the car and get out. Then what?"

"I . . ." He cleared his throat. "I went over to the car and shone the flashlight into the passenger compartment. That's when I saw her lying there, in the back seat. On her side. She had . . . I'm pretty sure she didn't have any pants on. I—"

"But she did have pants on."

"I didn't see them at first. They were scrunched down at her ankles, I think."

"Okay. Then what?"

"I tried the door and realized it wasn't locked, so I got in and touched her. She—"

"Where?"

Sven paused again. Selvin rearranged her documents, placing the medical report on top.

"Where?"

"Where did you touch her?"

"Her throat."

"How did you touch her?"

"The way you're supposed to."

"And what way is that?"

Sven held up his hand and showed her, explained what he had done. Selvin followed the movements of his hand intently.

"Thank you. Please go on."

"She had . . . well, it was hard to feel, but she had a very, very faint pulse. And . . . well, in accordance with paragraph two, item four of the police statutes, I considered it my duty to try to determine her condition and render first aid in an attempt to save her life."

"And what did you do?"

"I touched her. I called out."

"One thing at a time. Where did you touch her?"

"Her shoulder."

"In what manner?"

"I put my hand there. My hands. Both of them."

"Did you shake her?"

"I wouldn't say that."

"What would you say?"

"After I tried to take her pulse, I placed one hand on her shoulder. Then the other. I called out to her and tried to rouse her kind of gently."

"Kind of gently? You stated that you shook her. The perpetrator had already caused brain damage and a broken neck."

"That was hard to see, since it was dark."

"So you didn't notice she was injured?"

Sven stared at the tape recorder, humming endlessly between them. He clasped his hands under the desk. His pulse began to pound at his temples.

"I hardly touched her," he said, his voice strained, as he tried to control his breathing. "I had one hand on her shoulder. Then the other. It was only a few seconds, tops. I shouted something, I don't remember what, but I think it was *Hello, hello*, something like that. That's when I realized how dire it was."

"What made you realize that?"

"The blood. Her pulse." He swallowed. "The fact that she didn't react. That she was so pale. But it all happened so fast. It wasn't like I was slowly putting two and two together. The whole thing, from the moment I got into the car until I drove off, took maybe ten seconds. Or fifteen."

"But you had blood on your hands. Right?"

"Yes."

"How did that happen, if you only touched her shoulder?"

"I don't know. Maybe I put my hand on the seat, and there must have been blood there."

"You're speculating." Selvin looked apologetic.

"Well, yes—I don't know. You wouldn't know either, if it'd been you. No one would. Like I said, when you're there, it all goes so incredibly fast, all of it."

"Sven." Selvin put down her pen and paused the tape recorder. The humming noise stopped. "You misunderstand me. I have only your best interests in mind. No one, least of all me, is out to get you. But in order for me to protect you, in order for me to help you, I need to know what happened. Only then will I know what I need to do to cushion the blow for everyone."

He felt so helpless. "Okay."

She started the recording again. The humming resumed. She studied the medical report once more.

"Isn't it true that you touched her head? That you turned it?" Selvin looked up and held out her hands, demonstrating as she spoke. "You get into the car. You place one hand on her shoulder. Then the other. Nothing happens. You shake her a little bit. You place your hands on her cheeks and turn her head so you can see her face. Isn't that what happened?"

For an instant the floor swayed like the trampoline he'd built in the yard one summer when the boy was little.

"No. It wasn't."

"But you—"

"No."

She had raised doubts inside him. How could this be having his best interests in mind? Did he even want this—for her to, how had she put it, *protect* him? He didn't want to be protected; he wanted to explain. Set things to rights.

He tried to picture his hands in the darkness out there in the forest, the open car door and the woman dying inside.

"On her cheeks, if you'll recall, there was smeared blood, you had your hands—"

"No, dammit, I didn't!"

"Sven," Selvin requested, "please sit back down."

"No! Christ, you're not listening!" Rage throbbed in his blood, hot and hard. Each breath squeaked and rasped in his chest. "What the hell do you think you're doing? I've been a cop for thirty years. *Thirty years*. It's not as simple as you try to make it seem with your questions. Did I do *this* or did I do *that*, was it like *this* or like *that*, it's impossible to say. You don't know what it was like, being up in the forest, right after the prime minister was shot, the *prime minister,* for God's sake! And there's a car there and it's dark and awful, cold as shit and you can't see a thing, and then you realize there's blood. You have seconds to react, you don't even think—you just do. And everything I did, *everything,* was to try to save her life. Hell, I drove her to the emergency room! I . . ."

As though a plug had been pulled, all his energy drained from his muscles. Everything began to sway, and it was hard to stand upright. He placed his palms on the desk and leaned over the small woman, panting.

"I did everything I could. But she was dead when I arrived. There was no time."

Selvin blinked. She straightened her papers.

"I think I've got all I need."

A pale, bony index finger pressed a different button on the tape recorder and it went quiet. As if this was only a matter of finding the truth and only the truth, as if it had nothing to do with Sven and his career, his identity, or his existence on the most basic level.

"What . . ." he began, but he couldn't go on.

"No, this will be fine." She gave a stiff nod. Her voice was toneless. "Thank you."

51

He started carrying a handkerchief in his pocket, something to bring to his lips when the worst coughing fits came over him. He had to switch it out halfway through the workday. The red bled through.

"Hey, Sven."

He trembled. Evy was standing at the door to the copy room, where Sven was in the process of producing a stack of terrain maps of the area around Tiarp.

"Yes?"

"I was thinking . . . you wouldn't want to go grab something to eat tonight, would you? I mean," she quickly added when, perhaps, she realized how this sounded, "not like *that*. That's not what I meant. It was dumb, what happened, I don't know what got into me."

"Me neither."

"No, let's forget it ever happened."

In that moment, he could sense how she would have felt in his hands. Remarkably small. He ached with longing. Her cheeks flushed.

"But maybe it's a good idea to debrief outside these four walls."

"What about?"

"Well," Evy said hesitantly, "about Selvin."

"I don't know if I have the time." Sven began to gather up his copies. "I was thinking I might go up to Tiarp."

"Why?"

"I want to run something by a land surveyor who lives there."

"Why?"

"I need his advice."

Evy studied the paper copies. Maps.

"What kind of advice?"

"There might be a new rise or hollow in the ground somewhere. The farmers and foresters know their land. They might have noticed something. I'm sure she's buried up there."

Evy pushed: "Coffee, then? In the car on the way up to Tiarp? I'll drive."

It was warm and quiet in Evy's car. He drank coffee from a paper mug while she slowly guided them out of the city.

"How'd it go with Selvin?"

"Fine." That was all he said. He didn't want to talk about it. "Did they talk to you too? About me, I mean. That night."

"Me? No, why would they?" When Sven didn't respond, she continued: "My dad had a good doctor. She's a heart and lung specialist. Her name is Eva-Britt Simonsson."

"Okay?"

"You could give her a call."

"Why?"

"I've seen your handkerchiefs. Coughing up blood—that's serious."

Women. You bet your ass they would see everything, hear everything, meddle in everything. Did Bibbi have her suspicions too? He'd kissed Evy. That was that. It was hard to think of anything else.

"It's just a virus. There's nothing wrong with me."

As far back as he could remember, this city's traffic had been choked by all the railroad crossings. Tourism ads for Halmstad often had soundtracks of children laughing in summertime, the rush of the sea and shrieking gulls, but the most accurate sound would have been the clanging of the railroad crossing arms as they lowered. The cars idled. Exhaust seeped into Evy's car, sharp and acrid. Sven turned off the fan.

"Does Bibbi know?"

Sven froze. "Does Ronnie know?"

"I meant your cough, Sven. The blood."

"Oh. Yes, Bibbi knows."

"And what does she have to say about it?"

"That it's a virus. She's not worried."

He didn't understand why she would bring up Bibbi. It made him feel embarrassed and almost angry—she had some nerve, after what she'd done. What *they'd* done. Evy worked a small scrap of paper from her pants pocket.

"Just take this anyway. Eva-Britt's name and phone number. She'll know what it's about, if you give her a call."

"Wait, what did you tell her?"

"That you're coughing up blood and have trouble breathing sometimes."

Sven didn't say anything. No snow yet. Everything was gray and brown.

"And no," she added. "Ronnie doesn't know."

She blushed. She looked at his left hand, holding the folder of documents for the land surveyor, saw the thin strands of hair on the back of his hand, his rough skin. Her own hand was smooth and soft. Sven kept wanting to touch it. It was a struggle not to.

"I don't know why I'm meddling," she said cautiously, as though she were searching for an explanation that would sound plausible. "I think maybe it's just part of me, something I got from my family. I guess I just try to help people."

The freight train came rumbling by.

"I don't need any help," Sven said loudly, to make himself heard. "I feel fine."

She rolled her eyes at his grouchiness.

Hans-Martin and Gun Franzén. Their daughter was dead; he was under investigation. Selvin's eyes, cold and expressionless. The forest deep and unfathomable, the air stale with something rotten. Once again, the Tiarp Man had descended over Sven like a shadow. The realization hit him almost violently. This time it wasn't just the victims on the line. It was Sven himself, too.

A song came on the radio.

"Hey, Sven."

"Yeah?"

She knew he liked this song, so she turned up the volume. It was an oldie, about singing in the rain. In the song, dark clouds moved across the sky. Evy sang along, her voice dramatic and loud, goofy. Eventually Sven began to laugh. Sometimes there was nothing else you could do.

Soon they were singing together.

52

The land surveyor had nothing to say, other than he thought it was terrible, just a travesty, that someone like the Tiarp Man hadn't been apprehended yet. Sven could only agree. When he asked about changes in the landscape, whether anything had stuck out or seemed out of the ordinary to his surveyor's eyes, he shook his head and said that you can't tell with the naked eye—he would have to perform a careful examination to make any sort of pronouncement. But no, everything was same old, same old up here. Sven believed him.

It was December, but autumn had yet to make way for winter. Advent candelabras glowed in windows. Someone rolled out a red runner on the table in the break room. An undecorated Christmas tree waited down in the lobby. They tried to make the station look cozy and festive. It was necessary, ahead of the long winter they now faced.

One day, a call came in from Vapnödalen. Someone on one of the farms there had observed a prowler lurking along the property lines of the farm next door, a dark figure wearing a hood and what the caller had identified as a backpack of some sort. The caller had neither Stina Franzén nor Frida Östmark in mind when he got in touch; he was more concerned with the burglary he'd experienced two months previously. Someone had broken into his garage and emptied the diesel fuel out of both tractors there. He thought it might be one of those goddamn foreigners who were pouring in and destroying the country for honest farmers and workers. He wanted to nip this behavior in the bud on behalf of his neighbor, and advised the police that he also intended to loan his neighbor the use of one of his two shotguns, just to be safe.

"Wait, you can't just do that," protested the dispatcher who took the call.

"I don't give a shit."

Björkman considered assigning this matter to Sven. Then he thought about everything that had happened recently and gave it to Evy. But of course she consulted Sven. When Sven saw her, his stomach tied itself in knots again. To think that such a small action, just a momentary weakness, would send ripples so far. And when she came to his office, he was once again struck by the impulse to touch her, place a hand on hers.

The only thing they could really discuss without feeling awkward was their cases, work, everyday life inside the walls of the station. Anything else felt like it would go sideways if he didn't pick his way through with the utmost caution.

"Hey, have you seen this?"

Sven looked at the initial report.

"Why, that's in Tiarp."

"That's why, I was thinking . . . didn't we receive information about a similar incident a few years back?"

"Yes." He looked at her. "How long can this go on, Evy?"

She looked almost breathless. "What do you mean? Which, I mean, what—"

"The investigation. Selvin."

"Oh." Something clicked in her eyes. "I don't know. Haven't you heard anything yet?"

He shook his head.

It was shredding his nerves. In his worst nightmares, the Tiarp Man was still chasing him, even if he seldom actually saw him. It was like he was lurking just off-screen. Sven could feel him there, like a spirit.

He stood up and grabbed his coat.

"Great. Let's go."

53

Sven sank into his seat. Darkness had fallen over Vapnödalen. He sat in the car behind a grove of trees. Through the branches he had a view of the farm. Once every two hours he carefully got out and took a silent lap around the area.

This was his fifth evening here. He sat in the car again, smoking a cigarette, taking in the shadowy landscape, the silhouettes of the farmhouses and outbuildings. Nyårsåsen rested in a deep slumber.

It was probably just a fuel thief. Or a foreigner somehow gone astray around here. Who the hell knew anymore. But he doubted it was the Tiarp Man. There were women living on the farm, a mother and daughter, forty-seven and twenty-two years old. Sven had met with them and explained why a patrol car would be hanging around the farm for a bit. They were shaken, but despite his urgings they refused to seek alternative lodging for the time being. No one listened to the police anymore. People wanted to handle everything on their own.

An hour passed. Two. It was that time again. He got out of the car and stuck a cigarette between his lips, took out his lighter. The cold nipped at his cheeks. But then he went stiff. He stood perfectly still, one hand cupped around the lighter. He moved nothing but his eyes, as if even the tiniest movement would ruin everything.

He was hard to see. If Sven hadn't been familiar with every last detail of this landscape, he would have mistaken him for a shadow in the yard. The figure was like a piece of the darkness. Sven slowly lowered his hand and put back the lighter. Took the cigarette from his mouth.

The man was wearing dark clothes with the hood up; he had a backpack. His attention was on the farmhouse, where a single lamp was lit in one of the windows. It was the bedroom. He was waiting for the light to go out, Sven imagined.

They were a stone's throw apart. Too far. Sven moved closer. The wind, rustling through the dead fields and the bare trees, hid the sound of his movements. His hand edged toward his service weapon.

He took another step. One too many. It was as though a wave of electricity went through the figure—he straightened his back and turned his head. They looked right at each other; Sven could feel it even though he couldn't see the man's face, and he knew it was him.

He drew his weapon and aimed it at the man.

"Police! Stop!"

The man took off. Sven pulled the trigger. The shot split the night in two and a sudden muzzle flash turned everything white.

Sven ran, his steps heavy, while the Tiarp Man's were much lighter, the gait of a young body. The tall grass brushed his legs and arms. The description was accurate, he seemed slender, with broad shoulders and a narrow waist. Sven tried and failed to find his flashlight. Fuck, it was still in the car. *Fuck.*

The man was running toward Nyårsåsen. He appeared smaller as he left Sven behind. When he reached the trees, Sven realized he would have to try to head him off. Otherwise it was all over.

He went as fast as his body would allow, but it was like being in a tunnel despite the bare, open landscape. Nothing really mattered anymore. All that existed in the world was that figure way up ahead, and the backpack jouncing lightly in time with his steps.

Into the forest, among tightly clustered tree trunks, tall and straight like the masts of a ship. Sven couldn't see him anymore. Branches tore at his arms. He put his head down and kept on going. Just forest, moss, branches, trees, rocks, rocks, more moss. Sven stopped. Panting turned into coughing, and he bent double from the pain. *Not now,* he thought. *Not now.* He powered through the fire in his lungs and held his breath until he could stand up straight again.

He jogged a few fruitless steps forward, back the other way, in one direction, then the next. He listened for movement but knew it was pointless.

It was as though the man had dissolved into the woods, or become one with it.

Sven felt the loss in his knees, his lungs, down into his fingertips. He wanted to holler, but he wasn't a hollering sort of man.

You're not dead, he thought in despair. *You're not locked up. You've just been biding your time. It's not over.*

1991

54

The call from Snapparp came in as a routine vehicle check on a dark green Volkswagen work van. It had been parked at the rest stop for two days when one of the workers out there called, annoyed, and said it would be great if someone could come tow it away. Before the tow company could be called, someone needed to run a vehicle lookup. This kind of grunt work fell to the faithful patrol officers, and on this particular day that meant Vidar Jörgensson and Markus Danielsson, each of them with just over two months' experience in a patrol car.

Markus Danielsson was a dependable man from Laholm, a small town just ten minutes from the rest stop they were now heading to. He and Vidar had grown close during their time at the academy. Vidar appreciated that Markus was talkative and cheerful when the situation allowed, even as they were still comfortable sitting in companionable silence for hours when there was nothing to say.

"It's almost pleasant to spend time in a car with you," Vidar said over beer once.

"It's hard to imagine a finer compliment, from a man from Marbäck," Markus replied, raising his glass for a toast. "And, same to you."

They left it at that; anything more would have been too sappy.

As Markus turned off the highway, the fields stretched before them in billowing waves. It was all so beautiful—at least as long as you only looked eastward. Snapparp had not one but two rest stops, one on each side of the highway. You might have thought it didn't make much of a difference, but in the summer Snapparp East was cleaned three times a day; twice a day in the winter. There was a good restaurant and clean bathrooms. It was big and spacious and had been named Halland's best travel plaza more than once.

The dark green van, a five-year-old Volkswagen, was parked in a corner of the other rest stop: Snapparp West. Snapparp West was small, filthy, and shady. No distinctions, not even of the negative variety. If you were coming from the north and needed to take a leak, it was best to hold it.

The van appeared abandoned. Markus slowly turned off at the rest stop and passed a family trying to secure a canoe onto the roof of their car.

He squinted at the van.

"It looks drivable, at least. From a distance, anyway."

They climbed out of the car. March in Halland looked nicer than it felt, and a chilly, damp wind came in off the sea. The children from the canoe family had turned around and were pointing at them. Markus smiled and waved back. The canoe tipped as the mother let go.

"Not totally roadworthy, though," Vidar said, pointing.

The van didn't have any license plates. That was a familiar sight. Sometimes homeless people in the area would steal a car—often a van in particular—remove the plates, and park in a grove of trees or a clearing somewhere and stay there until someone, typically the landowner, discovered them and chased them off or called the police.

The van was dusty and shabby and didn't smell very good. Vidar turned on his flashlight and aimed it inside. A plastic cup of coffee in the cup holder, a newspaper and an empty bottle in the passenger seat. A pair of work gloves peeked from one door compartment.

"Can you see the VIN from there?" Markus asked from the other side of the van.

"No. We'll have to open it up."

The children were standing nearby, watching.

Markus brought a knuckle to the van and rapped loudly.

"Hello." He switched to his palm, striking it so hard that the metal exterior vibrated. "Police. Anybody home?"

Vidar studied the rear door. It was locked, but the hinges were a little loose. He got a crowbar from their car, a seizure from a burglary case a month or so ago, and inserted it into the crack, then began to pry. The metal protested, creaking. The hinges whined.

"Vidar."

"What?"

Then he noticed it too. The stench.

"Did you touch the handle?" Markus asked.

Vidar shook his head.

"Good."

Marcus grabbed the crowbar and together they pried at the door. The stench got worse. The door whined and moaned like an injured animal.

The handle gave way with a bang. Vidar and Markus staggered backward as the door swung open.

The van had been reported missing a few days ago. But sometimes things get overlooked, typically due to the most banal of factors. In this case: The van was missing its license plates and had been ditched in an out-of-the-way corner down at Snapparp West.

The dispatcher who took the call about the van at the rest stop was from way up north in Umeå and had just moved to Halland because he'd met a woman from the area who had attended a conference in Umeå. He didn't yet know that you'd pass by Snapparp if you were traveling from Malmö to Halmstad. If he had known, things wouldn't have turned out as they did for Vidar and Markus that day, which is probably small comfort given the situation.

::::

Everything fell perfectly silent at the rest stop. At least it did in Vidar's head. Sometimes you just know. With Markus by his side, he stepped forward and peered into the van. He could feel the eyes of the canoe family on his back. Their attention was no longer on their canoe.

There was a man inside. He was wearing boots, jeans, and a long-sleeved, collared navy shirt, and the blood had drained from his head like someone had opened a faucet. In a manner of speaking, that is. There wasn't actually much of a head left. When Vidar squinted, he could make out splinters of the destroyed skull; they looked like shards of very thin plastic on the floor.

It was later determined that the cause of death was repeated blows to the head with a wooden bat.

According to the medical examiner, it was impossible to say exactly how many blows. Forty was probably a low estimate; fifty at most. So maybe forty-five.

Vidar was far too inexperienced to participate in the investigation. The case had been sent up the chain to people who were better earn-ers and better thinkers and could understand why this sort of senseless violence happened. But when he'd compiled the report from Snap-parp and was about to add it to the files, he found some old docu-ments and papers. He paged through them and saw his father's name, saw 1986, Dad's colleague Evy Carlén, a collection of terrain maps with notes made in the autumn of 1988.

This was as close they would ever get, as colleagues. This unex-pected closeness to his father, suddenly seeing these physical artifacts he'd left behind, it still burned his fingertips.

At first it was as though Vidar had landed in a context that didn't belong to him. At the police station he remained "Sven's boy," just like all the times he'd been there with his father as a child. It was as though the old man was still in the building somewhere, had only run to the fax machine or the bathroom, or maybe up to the mess for a cup of coffee.

They probably wanted to make him feel at home: One Jörgensson retires, another comes in. That's wonderful. How's that father of yours? Some things are just in the blood. We need fresh faces around in these times. Is everything okay at home, with Sven? What is he up to these days? I heard he was too sick to keep working, that he preferred to be home rather than be stuck on desk duty. Is that true?

It was true. It wasn't good for his disability pension, but he couldn't stand it.

It was probably for the best. True cops are restless souls, and that Sven, now he was a true cop. You're so alike, you two. Just say the word if you need anything, and I'll do what I can. We sure do miss him around here, you know.

Vidar never asked for help. Not like that. He wanted to make it on his own. He didn't mention any of this to his father—what could he have said? It would only have made him sad.

Eventually it fell away, that sense that he became, in some strange manner, a version of his own father whenever he was at the station. But it took a van in Snapparp. It was like a rite of passage. After that he was his own person, his own self.

His own self. Well, if you could say that.

55

There was no pattern. That was the worst part. If only it were possible to be prepared, Gisela sometimes thought. Then it would be so much simpler.

Not simple, but simpler.

She had no forewarning when it happened. In those instances when it was almost to be expected, it didn't happen. As though, on those occasions, he had the feeling he would fail, and so he decided not to show himself, instead waiting and biding his time.

She could have been just anyone, standing in line at the store to buy a new dish scrubber, a green one. Her whole body still ached; everything was tender but also remarkably dull, as though her very life had been taken out of commission. That's when he got into her head. She didn't know how. A shadow in dark clothing chased her past the table in the kitchen where she and Robert usually ate breakfast. She rushed to the front door and had time to grab the handle but not to turn it, open it. He grabbed her, yanked her violently backward. She fell against him, a firm body. He smelled cold like the early spring outside.

The headlines about her and Robert didn't affect her. They were just words about someone else. The phone ringing at her parents' house could be unplugged when it got to be too much, and if the reporters knocked on the door, she could hide in the bathroom, close the door, and sit down next to the toilet. She could protect herself.

But standing in the store with the green dish scrubber in hand, she couldn't breathe. She saw her hand and noticed, to her surprise, that she had grabbed hold of the shelf. *Why?* she thought. *That's weird,* and then she let go but realized she was about to fall over and had to grab on again.

Gisela staggered out of the store. She had taken the scrubber with her by mistake. No one noticed. That was the worst thing she could imagine: Someone might think she had stolen it. She tossed it in a trash can and hurried off.

She had never thought it would happen to her, but it did. Stina Franzén, Frida Östmark, and then her, her name beside theirs in the paper. And yet there was something different about Gisela—she was the one whose house he broke into. The others had been spared—that's how she thought of it, *spared*—being taken in their own homes. He'd been generous to them. Not her. Why? She couldn't understand. She didn't go out that much, of course. So maybe he couldn't have done what he did with the others?

And also she had survived. She thought of her dead sister. Now Gisela had survived not once but twice.

But why Gisela? What had she done? She felt shame, even though she knew it was wrong. That thought, too, made her feel ashamed, because she knew she shouldn't be. There was no way out.

Who was he? In her thoughts—when the police questioned her, first at the hospital, then at home, later at the hospital again, at the emergency mental health clinic where she went after her first breakdown, after the dish scrubber incident—there was nothing. When she struggled to remember, fighting so hard that she tensed herself into an arc, a vague swinging motion rose in the back of her neck, like sudden dizziness. She remembered everything, every protracted moment of fear and confusion, pain and panic—and still, nothing.

Something must have surprised him. That was all Gisela had to say about the man who had broken into her house. She couldn't say how long it had gone on, maybe minutes? An hour, maybe.

Four words had come back to her, suddenly, restrained and wet, as though he had been drunk. Like drops in the darkness they had fallen from his mouth, rained over her.

Lie still now, dolly.

That's what he'd said. She remembered that.

And then he froze on top of her, suddenly, like an animal when it senses danger.

Something he didn't expect had happened. Then he turned to Gisela again and struck her unconscious.

The phone had rung. This was earlier that evening. Gisela didn't have caller ID, so she didn't know who was on the other end. She picked up the phone but all she heard was someone hanging up.

This wasn't the first time it had happened. Recently she'd been getting prank calls. She thought it was an older man she'd encountered at work, at the hospital, someone who had been awfully pushy a time or two.

The police asked so many questions, over and over again. What surprised her was that so many of them were about Robert. That was the first thing she'd asked when she woke up, whether Robert was there. She needed him, needed his body close, and his voice. She wanted to hear him. But she hurt all over; every time Gisela moved it felt like someone was pulling on a saw that was embedded deep in her stomach, and her head was throbbing and pounding angrily. She was too weak to call Malmö and asked one of the nurses to do it. When the nurse walked away, Gisela looked at the clock.

They didn't wake her up until two hours later. Sleep had taken her. How was that possible? She could hardly breathe, and yet she had slept.

The nurse at her side wasn't alone. She had two cops with her. They asked about Robert.

"Haven't you talked to him?"

"When did you last speak to him?" one of the officers asked gently.

"This . . . I . . ." She blinked. Her temples flashed pain. "I don't remember. This morning. He called this morning."

"What did you talk about?"

She looked from the officer to the nurse, to the other officer.

"What's wrong?" she whispered.

"We haven't," one of the officers said slowly, "gotten hold of him yet."

"But he's in Malmö . . . ? Just call the carrier."

"He left Malmö."

"But he was supposed to come back tomorrow."

"He finished early." The officer cleared her throat. "So he left."

"We think your husband might have reached the Halmstad area around the time . . ." the second officer began, but didn't continue.

Her husband. They had gotten married on a Saturday in August last year. She felt so beautiful that day, and Robert was so stylish. She was supposed to ovulate within the next week, their third month of trying.

"He was driving a green Volkswagen van," the officer said. "We've put out a bulletin on the vehicle."

Lie still now, dolly. That was all. The police took down the words but weren't sure what to do with them.

"We thought," one of them said, "we would try to produce a picture of him. A composite sketch, you know."

"But I didn't see him."

"It could still be valuable to have."

She sat for hours with an artist, a young woman, and one of the officers—also a woman.

What did his chin look like? How would she describe his nose? His eyes? How far apart were they, like this? More or less? His eyebrows. The bridge of his nose. Let's go back to the chin, I know he was wearing a mask, but . . .

When the artist turned the sketchpad around and showed Gisela the image, she was surprised to find she didn't have much of a reaction. It was just an image. Maybe that was what he looked like. Maybe not.

How had he moved? Did he touch the nightstand? Did she remember where he had set his feet? When did he bind her hands, was it before or after they entered the bedroom? What did he use to penetrate her?

They had brought accessories, things that were supposed to make this easier on her; she wouldn't have to say everything out loud. She was given a list and a pen: *Penis. Finger/fingers.* She read down the list. It was long. *Dildo. Bottle. Screwdriver.* She stopped at this last word, surprised, and wondered why it was on the list. Then she realized: There was always someone who had it worse.

"You think in those terms," her psychologist said, as a question.

"What? *Worse?*"

"Yes. And *spared.*"

"Yes." She blinked. "Yes, I guess I do."

Three days later, Robert Mellberg was found in a green van in Snapparp.

Also in the van was the wooden bat that usually stood next to the door in his and Gisela's home. The bat was full of gray matter and hair that had gotten caught in the blood and dried there.

56

Somewhere beyond the verdant foliage of Vapnödalen, in the dense forest of Nyårsåsen, was an unmarked grave. There lay a truth that could only be discovered by someone willing to search long enough, someone obsessed enough never to give up.

I'd love to give up, Sven thought. But he couldn't.

They existed in some strange symbiosis, those two winter murders. One up in Stockholm, which had drawn eyes from all over, and one down here that had passed almost unnoticed. They seemed to be connected and unrelated at the same time. A thin thread of fate linked them. That was how he thought of it.

A shadow played around Stina Franzén's body, around the car up there in the forest, along the road between Villshärad and Ringenäs where Frida Östmark rode home. Sven had heard this man's voice in his ear, had listened to this man breathe. He had pursued him across the ridge once upon a time, through bushes and icy winter thickets. They had seen each other, Sven and the shadow. Sven had lost.

He'd been so close. It consumed him. He thought of the composite sketch he'd seen in the paper. It was an ordinary sort of face, a man who could be anyone. He could be a cashier at ICA, he could be a letter carrier or a plumber, or maybe an administrator at the Tax Agency; he could even work for the police.

No matter how hard Sven tried, he couldn't shake the thought of reaching out his hand in the dark and simply touching him.

He was sitting on the porch. Cold tonight. The cigarettes there, bottle of beer right next to them. Tractors. Magpies in the evening sky. He thought about the harvest. Lights glowed through the forest, the little village in the distance. People here just kept living their regular old lives, and so did he.

There was so much you gave, and for so little. Everything stood where it stood, was where it was. Life had its difficult moments, but often that was about it. You could manage. It would all turn out okay.

Sven had quit the force by now; the farewell ceremony had taken place a few days before Christmas. On December 29, 1990, he completed his last day of work. For good. Game over. His son had taken over where he left off.

Just a few days ago, someone had broken into Gisela and Robert Mellberg's house up in Tiarp. He read about the incident in the paper.

The table on the porch was small and round. It tilted when he set down his beer bottle. He and Bibbi should have gone to Copenhagen. She had wanted to go back in the summer of, what was it, '85? She'd hardly talked about anything else. It never happened. Which was probably on account of Sven, or maybe it was her job; he didn't remember.

She would make a new life for herself here, once he was gone. Women were good at that sort of thing. New routines, relationships, new plates and sheets and new things to hope for, dream about; maybe she would get to see Copenhagen. He believed she would.

Sometimes he wanted to say something to her, but the words broke apart in his throat.

Sven opened his notebook. Old voices crawled through his head like worms. *Tiarp.*

After several years, a return.

57

The old albums were black and brown, leather-bound. There were his paternal grandparents, his maternal grandmother too, and there was his own father, who must have been fifty-something then, the same age he was now.

Such an odd thing. You have way too much spare time after retirement, but your body is worn out. So what are you supposed to do? He should start prepping the garden for the summer season, remove the mold from the bathroom, call Ove up in Simlångsdalen and see if he could come over to replace the floor.

Instead he looked back to the good old days. There was a picture of him in uniform. He was very young and stood with his back ramrod straight. He was smiling. He recalled the moment the photo was snapped: It was the morning before his second day of work. The previous day had ended with his being covered in the vomit of a drunk outside Fridhem Grill. The man, intoxicated beyond reason, had been trying to get into his car, and Sven had stopped him.

Still, he smiled at the picture. It meant something.

He had washed his uniform, scrubbed it and hung it to dry overnight.

That was a long time ago. It was his son's turn now. Strange.

: : :

In Sven's mind was an image of death. It had been there for so long that it must have come to him as a child, perhaps through the stories and tales he'd heard from the old folks around the dinner table. You were standing at the edge of a forest and gazing across a field, waiting. You had been wandering for so long, living through triumph and sorrow, moments great and small had come and gone, and at last you had approached a sort of border, where everything was finished and put to rights. On the other side was a complete lull.

Then someone moved, suddenly, a figure emerging from the stillness and coming to greet him as he took his first step into the field, to cross over.

That was death, and he thought about it often.

Appointments at the clinic, running errands to the pharmacy, car inspections, buying new potted plants for the kitchen window, shopping at the store, visiting the ag co-op to bring home soil, purchasing a new hose for the garden, raking the gravel driveway, reading the paper in the kitchen with a cup of coffee in hand. Ove in Simlångsdalen, who never picked up the phone. That was everyday life, gray and raw and also strangely full of fog. Almost every morning it settled across Marbäck like a curtain. When Bibbi left for work each day, he stood by the kitchen window and watched the car vanish into the whiteness even before it passed Jansson's place. Sometimes the fog lingered until lunch.

He came to appreciate having a regular routine, the predictable, placid nature of his existence. Maybe this was what happened when your son's work involved battling something risky and unpredictable by nature, and your own health was a source of fear.

More than once he found himself with phone in hand, about to call Gun and Hans-Martin Franzén. In the early spring of 1989, the decision came down, and he hadn't known whether to laugh or cry.

"It's being dismissed." He'd been sitting in the room where he always sat, on the chair that was his, and had held the document up to show Evy. "I'm not at fault."

For a brief, brief instant she looked like she wanted to launch herself across the table and throw her arms around him. But she just said: "I know you aren't. You knew that too."

Sven nodded silently. He dropped the paper back onto the desk and took it in. He didn't know what to say or do, how to feel.

"What if . . ." he began. "What if it was me? I mean, if she was right—Selvin. Maybe she just couldn't prove it. Or didn't want to. She told me—"

"That's bullshit, Sven."

Then life just rushed on, during the last year of his career. Exonerated. As though that were possible. He hadn't spoken with her parents, and he felt, well, what? Shame? He wanted to say something to them, give them an answer, but he didn't have one. He always hung up the phone. When the new phone book arrived he opened it to search for their names, to make sure that they still lived there, that they were still alive, that they had the same phone number in case he did make up his mind to call after all.

One day he went out to get the paper with his coffee cup in hand, as usual, and was greeted by the front-page headline: WOMAN RAPED, MAN MISSING.

The journalists went at the story so hard that the walls of the *Hallandsposten* offices must have been quaking. The evening papers caught wind of the story and descended. They knew it had to be the Tiarp Man. They spotlighted Stina Franzén and Frida Östmark, obtained aerial images of the ridge, interviewed folks who lived nearby, and described the horror anew. When the van was discovered out at the Snapparp rest stop, all hell broke loose. Three murders and one attempted homicide was a sensation, a mystery, and high drama.

Snapparp. His boy, Vidar, had made the discovery.

Goddamn. There always has to be a first time, but that it had to be his son in particular who . . .

Sven really ought to call Vidar and see how he was doing. He went outside. Fog. It was perfectly silent. He smoked a cigarette. The heat in his chest grew stronger. He coughed up phlegm.

Each time Sven thought about the Tiarp Man, his innate moderate and restrained manner began to crumble. When he tried to call up an image of the man it grew too vast, too powerful, a massive shadow beyond all proportion. Sven felt his heart beat faster.

"That's enough now," he told himself harshly as he stood there on the lawn.

The edge of the forest. The field. Vidar. Bibbi. Evy. The figure stepping forth with its hand outstretched. He recoiled at the thought.

Two young men passed by on the street. They were Backlund's boys. They must be twenty by now. Their backs straight, shoulders broad, smiling and laughing. *So young*, he thought. *So strong, and armed to the teeth with time.*

In the mornings, more and more often, blood cough.

58

Gisela no longer recalled how many times she'd wished Robert hadn't finished early. That he'd stayed in Malmö. If he hadn't come home, everything would have turned out differently. But he did come home. He put the key in the lock and turned it, and that was what the Tiarp Man heard. That was why he reacted the way he did, ears pricking like a dog's.

Her mother and father, the police, the psychologists, everyone explained that she *couldn't look at it that way, that it wasn't fair to herself.* But how else could she look at it? It stung like a burn, but the pain was inside, impossible to ward off. She missed his hands, his hair, his voice, the sounds he made when he rummaged through utensils in the kitchen. The sun rose over Nyårsåsen; the men and women drove to work in their cars; the animals plodded languidly across the fields in Vapnödalen. The combines roared. The newspaper arrived. Everything was the same. It was incredible, how everything could just go on.

"But, Gis, do you really want to stay in this house?"

It was her mother asking, one week after they found Robert. She'd returned home from the hospital and they were sitting in the kitchen where it all started. The crime scene technicians had spent a great deal of time there, performing their investigations. They'd done their best to disguise the signs of their work, but they were still visible. Dishes were in the wrong spot; the sofa had ended up too close to the living room wall; there was a metallic smell in the bedroom, left behind by some forensic solution; and here and there she found some strange dust that she only later realized was fingerprint powder.

"Yeah," she said. "I do."

Mom looked bewildered.

"But why?"

"It's . . ." she began, glancing toward the front hall and the hat rack, its hooks for jackets and coats, with Robert's still there. "It's all I have left."

"But . . ."

"Mom, no."

Gisela spoke dull words in a toneless voice. It was a common symptom of shock. Okay, so she was probably in shock. That didn't change anything.

"Does it look like him, by the way?" Mom asked cautiously.

"What?"

"You know, in the paper. The sketch of the man."

"Of course it looks like him, I'm the one who described him."

"Everyone's talking about it. It was even on *Rapport*." The national news. "Did you see? I was just thinking, you know, he was wearing a mask. It must be hard to . . . I don't know. I was just thinking out loud."

Gisela didn't respond. Mom was right, but Gisela didn't care about the sketch. What did it matter now? To her?

Nothing got worse in the house, but she had a hard time taking care of herself in there. She stopped showering, stopped eating, didn't take the pills she'd been prescribed. They called from work and when she didn't pick up, they left a message on her answering machine. They wondered when she could come back.

She quit. She could hardly ever work anyway, and the few times she did it only reminded her of that night and what a turning point it had been, what life could have become and what it had been reduced to.

It was like living in terror. That was why, one evening—this was after the funeral—she found herself standing in the rain outside her childhood home in Harplinge and asking if she could come in.

Mom embraced her.

In hindsight, it seemed like madness that she stuck it out for so long. She would never visit the house again.

And her father. It was as though he hadn't been able to protect what was his. At night he got in his car and cruised the roads in search of a shadow. He was convinced he would find the Tiarp Man sooner or later. It was only a matter of time. In the passenger seat was his sawed-off shotgun.

She wished she possessed his rage, his bitterness, his strong will and stubbornness, or Mom's warmth, her friends' tenderness. Everyone around her had something she wanted. What did she have? Nothing. She had nothing, was no one.

If there was anything that moved her, that caused vibrations inside of her, aside from the attacks of memory, it was what she learned about how much a person can withstand and still be able to open her eyes each morning. She got up, went to the bathroom, and began her day. As though there was no rock bottom, just an infinite hole to fall through. That was the lot that fell to humanity.

Or to her, anyway. To Gisela, who had survived twice, when perhaps it would have been best not to, either time.

That was what she thought.

Or was she, perhaps, already dead? After all, it's impossible to live without feeling anything. The more she thought about it, the more convinced she became. It was a logical conclusion: She felt nothing, therefore she must be dead. This was what separated her from everyone else. They were alive, and she had been annihilated.

59

The composite sketch. It changed a lot of things. The Tiarp Man was a cashier at Åhléns, a plumber who lived in Åled, one of the agents at the real estate firm on Stora Torg. He stood at the meat counter at ICA, worked as a high school counselor, and sold Volkswagens at a recently opened dealership at Stenalyckan.

"As far as I can tell, it's hopeless," said Evy. "Everyone thinks they've seen him. The problem is, no one has seen him. I'm doing other stuff now."

Evy had called Sven to see how he was doing at home in Marbäck. She was no longer working on the Tiarp Man cases. They'd been handed over to younger minds who could view the series of crimes through fresh eyes.

Sven didn't understand. Fresh eyes? Ones that had no idea what they were looking at, because they hadn't been there from the start? Idiocy.

"Do you remember Micke Håkansson?" Evy asked.

"Of course," said Sven, as though any other answer was out of the question. "Old man Håkansson's son. He claimed to have spotted the Tiarp Man once, and chased him."

"Apparently he slept with Gisela Mellberg a few years ago."

Sven perked up.

"He did?"

"One night together, at least. But it never turned into anything.

Apparently Gisela wasn't interested. He was, though, and I guess he felt pretty burned by her."

"Are they looking at him?"

"I think so. He does look quite a bit like the man in the picture."

Sven thought back. "As I recall, he was pretty puny and a timid kind of guy. I don't think he would have had it in him. And anyway, didn't we get an alibi for him?"

"No," said Evy. "Turns out we never did. And," she added emphatically, "it's tough to know what other people do or do not have in them."

Sven tried to picture the young man and closed his eyes as he combed through his memories. No, no way in hell it was him. Way too weak-minded, that one.

They spoke for a while, about everyday life and their plans for spring, and Sven mentioned the mold in the bathroom.

"Haven't you gotten rid of that yet?"

"Haven't gotten around to it," Sven muttered.

"I miss when we used to go to the beach and look at the sea," she said. "Do you remember that?"

"Yes."

"Those were peaceful times for me."

"Me too."

"Now everything is all so . . . I don't know, chaotic. It was more fun with you."

"Yeah," Sven said slowly, because that was all he could think of to say, and as he stood at the window in his beloved house it felt as if he were gazing out at all the free time he still had at his disposal and which he had no idea how to fill.

And he had reconsidered. Made a few calls and tried, one last time, to put it all together. He suspected he was close and that it was possible he would have a breakthrough. But in order to do that, to be certain of success, he needed help.

"I've got . . ." he began slowly, opening his notebook, which he had scribbled almost full in recent days. "I've got something I want to ask, Evy. If you could do something for me."

60

Gisela saw the man from the apartment window. She often stood by that window. From the sixth floor, she could tolerate the world. The cars and the people, the roads, the buildings and lives were remarkably small and inconsequential. It made her feel secure to know that. From a distance, she could withstand anything.

He closed the car door and looked around. He was wearing clothes that looked too big, and the wind ruffled his sparse, thin hair. As he walked to the front door of her building, she wondered who he was coming to visit. She hadn't yet lived here a week, and she didn't know the routines, didn't know her neighbors, didn't know which cars were typically parked on the street.

She went to the living room. It was a small apartment. Empty moving boxes made it smaller. She sat down on the sofa, folded her legs beneath her, and waited, hoping that the doorbell wouldn't ring.

The doorbell rang.

Gisela waited and hoped it wouldn't ring again.

It rang again. She stood up, her heart pounding, went to the kitchen, and took a knife from the drawer. The door had a peephole. She studied the man outside. The lens of the peephole made him look oddly small. She turned the lock but didn't open the door, then took two steps back and squeezed the knife, staring at the handle.

It lowered. The door swung open.

"Hello?" said a tentative male voice.

He had a voice that didn't match his face. It was deeper than she'd expected.

He peered in and saw her in the front hall with a knife in one hand, teeth clenched, tense as a bowstring, but he didn't seem surprised by what he saw.

"My name is Sven," he said. "I'm a police officer. I just came from your mother's place. She gave me your address."

She invited him into the kitchen and he took a seat. She asked if he wanted coffee. He declined and took out a small black notebook. Gisela poured herself a glass of water and sat down across from him, wondering if he wouldn't ask about the knife after all. Or maybe it was a common sight? She probably wasn't the first he'd met.

"I know this is difficult," he said. "But I'd like to talk a little about what happened a month ago."

"Okay," she said tonelessly.

Whatever hope she'd had that her attacker and Robert's killer would be caught, it was already gone.

"I'll be honest," he said, bringing his hand to his mouth and coughing violently. Afterward he looked at his palm. "Strictly speaking, I'm no longer a police officer. But I was. I retired at the end of last year. I worked with . . . I'm the one who found Stina and searched for Frida."

No last names, as though he'd known them. She wanted to ask if this went for her too, if in his head she had become just Gisela, if he thought of the two of them, her and him, as acquaintances. She said nothing.

She recognized him now. It wasn't easy—he'd changed a lot since the pictures in the paper.

"I got close once," he said dejectedly, as though he knew what she was thinking. "But I wasn't fast enough. He got away from me and ran into the forest."

"When was that?"

"Several years ago. In '88."

"If you'd gotten him, Robert would still be alive."

"Yes. That's true."

She didn't understand why he would say so. It was like confessing something; he had to know that. Maybe he wanted to make an apology. Or did he just want to be honest with her? Not without some aim in mind. Cops always had some reason for saying what they said, she had learned. She wondered what his was. This was probably the only reason she didn't throw him out.

"What did you want to talk about?"

"Hmm?"

He had lowered his gaze as if in shame. Now he looked up, confused.

"You said you wanted to talk about what happened."

"Oh, yes." He cleared his throat. "Right." He opened his notebook. His hand trembled slightly. "Did you know Stina and Frida? Or one of them?"

She shook her head.

"I knew what happened to them, of course. I was with the boy, Wille, when he said he'd seen the car. And I joined in the search for Frida, more than once. I wanted to help."

"Was Robert there too? In the search party, I mean."

She shook her head.

"He was there the first time. But that was all. He couldn't come, it was his job, he was away a lot. But no, I can't say I knew them."

His name. She thought of Robert every five, maybe ten, minutes, couldn't help bringing him up in every conversation she had, but always as *him*. She seldom said his name aloud, and when she did, it hurt. To think that so much pain could be wrapped up in a name.

"We were trying to have a baby," she said faintly.

"Sorry?" Sven said. "What was that?"

"Nothing."

"I was wondering, did you recognize him?"

"Who?"

"The man who attacked you."

"Oh." This was a question she'd been asked many times now. "I don't know. At first I thought I did, but now . . . it's hard to say. My memory has been . . . it's come back now. But I never saw him. I remember he was wearing a mask."

"What kind?"

"Like a hood, over his face. One of those . . . what's it called, the kind you wear when you're riding a motorcycle."

"A balaclava?"

"Right." She'd heard the word before, but had forgotten it. "He had one of those over his face."

"What color?"

"Green. Dark green, I think."

The questions forced her memories to surface again, but it was okay, she could control them. She was expecting them. She was prepared.

"How was his voice?"

"What do you mean?"

"I'm sorry." Sven finished jotting down a note before meeting her gaze. "Was it high, low, do you think he was from Halland or did he have a different dialect, stuff like that."

"It was the same voice as on the tape. They played it for me."

"You mean the call he made to the emergency line?"

She nodded. He made notes. It was very quiet in her apartment.

"Calls came in to your house beforehand, right? I mean, someone would call and hang up."

"Yes. I just thought they were plain old prank calls."

"You never suspected it was that guy, what's his name, who you slept with that one time?"

She was taken aback by his forwardness. "You mean Micke?"

"Right."

She hesitated. Then she shook her head. "No. No, it wasn't him."

Sven nodded and coughed again, worse this time. He didn't seem prepared. It grabbed hold of him, and, one hand held tight to his lips, he used the other to rummage in his pocket and bring out a small inhaler, from which he took deep drags. When he was finished, she glimpsed a little streak of red on the mouthpiece. She wanted to say something but didn't know what.

"Did he say anything?" he managed to ask, his words strained and muffled. "When he called, I mean."

"No. Nothing. But I think . . ." she began, hesitantly, but fell silent again.

"You think . . . ?"

"One time, this was a few years earlier, I thought I saw something outside my window. But there was no one there. Or there was no one there at the moment. I thought I had just been mistaken. But maybe I wasn't."

"Was this in 1988?"

It could have been. Little Wille, the search for Frida, the years in Risarp before the attack ruined everything, Robert's funeral, it was so strange—everything remained crystal clear for her, and yet it had all run together.

Sven nodded. He made some more notes. She thought of his inhaler. From his other pocket he produced a piece of paper, folded double. He opened it. She had expected it to be the composite sketch, but it wasn't. It was a photograph.

"Could this be the man who attacked you?"

Gisela was surprised. She recognized him. He was familiar, but she couldn't say exactly where she knew him from. That was how recognition worked, neither more nor less. No shock, no sudden flash of insight that would stick with her for the rest of her life. This must be how it was in real life, and not in the movies. Something was definitely familiar about him; she had seen him before.

"Does he live in the area? I recognize him. I think I've met him."

"I think you might have met," Sven said slowly. There was a flash of intensity in his eyes, in a way she hadn't seen before. "Is it him?"

She hesitated. Tried to recall the Tiarp Man's eyes. It was just about all she had. That and his hands, how they felt when they held her down, how heavy his body had been, how much fear he had evoked in her. But that kind of thing wasn't visible in a photograph. Or maybe it was. She studied him more closely.

Her idea of that one chillingly clear instant in which the picture of a man sent shockwaves through her memory, back into the bedroom where she had seen him when the worst was happening and the pain was sharpest, a link between then and now that made the truth appallingly clear, was just that—an idea. This was what really happened when the victim saw the perpetrator's eyes: A faint vibration ran through her body and made her gasp. His eyes were familiar.

"Yes."

Then something unexpected happened.

Sven didn't look relieved. He looked absolutely shattered.

61

That spring, there was something strange about Sven Jörgensson. Just about everyone who ran into him said so. The first days of his retirement had taken a toll, that much was clear; hell, you almost felt a little worried about the fellow. He seemed so tired and lonely at home in Marbäck. They'd seen it before: Sometimes, at the end of a career, there wasn't much left. As if someone had sucked the life from his body.

Not that he'd seemed particularly happy with his work in the past few years. Had he in fact been going downhill for quite some time? Hard to say.

Those who saw Sven thought he looked more haggard and hollow than before; physically he was probably in pretty bad shape. He coughed a lot, and strangers in the store sometimes looked at him in alarm and backed away. He seemed lonesome too; those who chatted with him heard that there wasn't much to his social life now that he was retired and all.

One of Sven's few friends, for instance, David Linder, got fed up with watching his family farm fall apart in these difficult times. He just left it all behind and moved to Sundsvall. It was probably no wonder, but it left Sven even more on his own.

One morning, Sven was even spotted in his yard, in sock feet, his eyes on a picture of some sort, maybe a photograph. The neighbor passing by on their way to work didn't have time to see what it was.

Maybe people should have worried about him more. But they didn't, because later that spring something happened with his eyes. In April and May it was as if they were gleaming—not with hunger and determination, now, but with confidence. They radiated calm. Sven seemed almost peaceful.

But why that would be, how this transformation had come about, no one knew.

62

That summer, there was a car accident on Kustvägen. Vidar and Markus were eating hot dogs near the campground in Villshärad when the comm radio crackled to life. They were less than a kilometer from the accident, and Markus was still chewing his last bite of hot dog when they arrived.

It was clear to anyone with eyes to see and the stomach to look that the accident was serious. A passenger car, a Saab, had hit a truck head-on, crumpled like a piece of paper, and ended up in the ditch. The truck sat on the side of the road, like a sad, mangled animal.

Vidar and Markus climbed out of their patrol car. People who had stopped came up to them, fear in their eyes and sweat glistening on their foreheads.

"He's breathing. But we can't wake him up. It smells like gasoline."

Markus wiped his mouth and began to run. Vidar was a step ahead. The heat burned the back of his neck.

An unconscious man was trapped in the Saab, the steering wheel on his chest and the dashboard jammed against his legs. Blood, Jesus, so much blood, tons of it. A puddle was forming on the rubber floor mat. They looked at the man's ravaged face. Shards of glass everywhere. Still, they could tell who it was, and for a moment everything stopped.

"Fuck," Markus breathed. "It's him. Should we—"

"Later," said Vidar.

No other lights and sirens yet. They were alone on the scene when the first lick of flame appeared. The heat was sharp and cruel. As the fire gained strength, it spread along the back door.

"Fuck!"

"Quick," said Vidar. "We've got to move fast."

They tried to get in, Vidar from the driver's side and Markus from the passenger's side. The smell of smoke was strong and Vidar's upper arm burned as the flames whipped up with the breeze. Markus groaned with the effort.

The steering wheel gave way, no problem, but when Vidar began to prize at the dashboard it creaked stubbornly. The flames were melting the plastic on the ceiling. It oozed down and hissed as it met the upholstery, the fabric of their uniforms. It became hard to breathe, and their lungs burned. He heard Markus gasping for air.

"There," Vidar choked. "Grab it there."

"If you can hold right here. Otherwise I can't."

"Me neither."

Panic began to creep into Vidar's brain. *He's dying,* he thought, *he's dying on us.* Only at the last second, with a strength he didn't know he possessed, did Vidar manage to pull the driver from the car.

The man fell to the ground, his limbs slack. He was bleeding profusely from his face, and his legs lay at a funny angle. His breathing was shallow. Vidar tried to examine him but it was hard; he didn't dare touch the man's body too much. Two fingers found a faint pulse at his neck. Now they were bloody. The wrecked car collapsed, creaking and popping in the heat.

"Jesus fuck." Markus stared at the body for a moment, gasping, then brought a hand to his eyes and squinted down Kustvägen. "Where the hell are they?"

Vidar turned his head.

"There."

They were coming from the other direction. Vidar saw the pearly string of blue lights getting closer. Around them, all traffic had come to a standstill. Cars crept by slowly. People stood around staring, holding their hands to their mouths. They had flip-flops on their feet and coolers and colorful towels in their arms. The sun was high in the sky. It was a warm Friday in the middle of prime vacation season, and the sky was so blue it looked unreal. He would remember that afterward.

Evy Carlén arrived in the third car. They had blocked off the road. Markus tried to talk to the truck driver, and the paramedics crouched over the man's body in the grass. They'd had to move him a bit to get him out of range of the flames.

Then she stepped out. She closed the passenger door and ran a hand through her hair, made sure everything was in place on her duty belt, and headed for the barriers.

"Hi," said Vidar. "It's bad news."

"No, I heard on the radio. We were in Tylösand, so we got here pretty quickly, thought I could provide backup if needed."

"Evy," said Markus. "That's not what we mean. It's . . ." he began, but trailed off.

Vidar looked her in the eyes.

"It's Einar."

"Einar? What, my brother Einar?"

"Yes. I'm sorry. We ran the car, too. It's his."

63

Einar Johan Bengtsson was almost twenty years younger than his big sister, an accidental late-in-life baby. His mother developed leukemia not long after Einar's birth and went back and forth between hospital stays and being home sick. Just three years later, she died.

Einar grew up with his big sister and his father. He played peewee soccer in Alet along with Janne Andersson, who would later rise through the ranks until he was head coach of the Swedish men's team. There are photos of them together, standing in front of one of the goals at Alevallen, two boys with the future ahead of them and a soccer ball at each of their feet. No information exists to suggest whether they kept in touch after their childhood. The paths of their lives diverged; Janne Andersson stayed in the soccer world, while Einar became an apprentice welder at Halmstad Welding and Mechanics, which was located at Gamletull near the Rex bike and motorcycle factory. There he had remained until the accident happened and he and Vidar crossed paths.

A month had passed since the accident on Kustvägen. The house Evy, Ronnie, and the kids lived in was in Kärleken, a quiet and lovely neighborhood full of single-family homes painted in warm colors.

Evy hugged Vidar and Markus when they arrived. It smelled like coffee in the front hall, and on the wall was a photograph of the Carlén family: Evy and Ronnie and the kids. They were all smiling at the photographer.

There was a small deck at the back of the house. The wheelchair looked unnatural there, like a foreign element in a picture that was otherwise very well coordinated: the neatly trimmed hedges, the patio furniture, the wooden decking, the quiet nature of the small things in life. Vidar saw the back of his neck, the short blond hair. It was warm out, but Einar still had a blanket covering his body.

"How is he doing?"

"Good, I'd say." Evy stood by her brother's side and bent forward. She looked awkward and stiff. "Einar. They're here."

Vidar and Markus stepped self-consciously out onto the terrace and turned to the motionless man in the wheelchair. His eyes were alert and present, but for an instant Einar was unrecognizable. He looked lifeless and empty, gaunt and pale, the skin of his neck and cheeks hanging loose. He looked twenty years older than he was, and in a moment of weakness Vidar wondered if it wouldn't have been better for him to have died.

"It was Vidar and Markus here who helped you out of the car after the accident."

They each pulled out a chair and sat down. They tried to smile and ask how he was doing. A gentle breeze blew across the deck. Einar gazed at them vacantly.

"As you know, he has a little trouble speaking. And he's still . . . Your brain is still a little swollen. So that affects your mood and reactions and so on. But I know you're glad they're here." She smiled and patted his arm gently, on top of the blanket. "I'll get the coffee."

She went into the house. Trouble speaking? According to rumors at the station, Evy's brother was mute as a stone. Vidar squirmed in his seat, and Markus looked at his hands. The sounds of the neighborhood had been absorbed into a great silence.

"Well," said Markus, mostly just to have something to say. "It's really nice out here."

Vidar turned to Einar. "Very nice. I understand why you like to sit here. Makes you want a good book to read. Evy told us you like to read. I don't know if you remember," he continued, "but we've actually met before. But on opposite sides of the field."

Markus raised an eyebrow. No reaction from Einar.

Vidar had seen him once, at home in Breared. Back then, Einar coached Alet's boys' team, and it was the day Linus Sjöö became the hero of the match in the most unpredictable way. He recounted the story and made Markus laugh.

Vidar remembered a man with blond hair and alert eyes who had cheered up his players after their loss. He'd thought he must be a good coach, the kind you recall fondly when you're older.

Evy returned with a tray, three mugs, and a glass with a straw, saying that they would have coffee but Einar preferred iced tea. She held the glass up for him; his lips found the straw and they saw the liquid in the glass sink a bit. There was no other sign of life to be found.

"How are you getting along with the kids and Ronnie and all that?" Markus asked, taking his mug from the tray. "Is it crowded?"

"Of course it is, and Einar finds that too much stimulation is hard for him right now. So we're trying to adapt a little—Ronnie took the kids to Tylösand for the afternoon. But it's going fine." She put down her brother's glass and placed a tentative hand on his shoulder. "It's only for a little while, until a spot opens up at one of the assisted living homes in town. They seem really nice, don't they, Einar? Go ahead and help yourselves to milk if you want it, it's in the jug there."

They poured and drank the coffee.

"It's good," said Vidar.

"Very," Markus agreed.

The conversation slipped into the only thing they really had in common. Work. Evy asked how the past week had gone for this colleague and that, whether they'd heard anything about the assault on

Storgatan, the attempted robbery at the restaurant on Brogatan. She was spending a lot of time at home right now, of course, so she missed quite a bit.

"How is your dad, by the way?"

"He's okay, I think. More than okay, even. When they released Christer Pettersson he stood there screaming at the TV. Seems to me that's a good sign."

"Indeed," said Evy. "In Sven's case, I suppose it is. You know, the Palme case, it really hit him hard. That they didn't capture the bastard. Incredibly hard."

"I didn't think Dad liked Palme."

"No," Evy said. "That's true. Maybe that's exactly why he took it so badly. Anyway, tell him I said hi. Like I said, it's a little hard for Einar to communicate, but both he and I want you to know we appreciate your stopping by."

Vidar looked at the man in the wheelchair. There was so much he wanted to ask about the accident, what had happened and what he had been doing beforehand, but none of that was possible now. Vidar searched for a word he'd learned during his training, something about a condition—was it called "catatonic"? A condition that left someone completely unaware, expressionless.

When they left some time later, there was an odd expression on Markus's otherwise so open, compassionate face.

"I'm not quite sure what we were doing there, to be perfectly honest. And it all upset me, shit, sometimes she talks to him like he's a child. Sometimes she doesn't."

His voice was full of distaste.

"I don't think she knows how to deal with it yet," Vidar said. "Which is no wonder."

"Damn, I never want to end up like that," Markus went on, as though he hadn't heard his colleague's words. "To have a stroke or something so all I can do is sit there sipping through a straw. Just shoot me."

The first life they'd saved, Vidar and Markus. Maybe they shouldn't have bothered. Or was this still the better outcome? Was there a fate worse than death? He thought of Evy's hand, how gently and tenderly she'd placed it on her brother's arm.

"I think in the end it's better to be alive," said Vidar.

64

One evening, the phone rang. When Vidar answered it, he heard his father's voice asking how he was doing.

"Fine," Vidar said. "I'm doing okay."

"I heard about the accident. On Kustvägen. I remember my first survivor. It was during a shift when I was in training, the summer of '58. I'd been on the job for a month or so. It was a beautiful June morning, the apple trees were in bloom, the barns were lovely and red in their meadows, and the birds were singing so sweetly. It was a young man, no more than thirty, hanging by a noose in a tree. Börje and I ran over and I remember thinking *No, no, oh my God, don't fucking let him die on us.* And wouldn't you know it, he was alive. Once we'd cut him down, he looked right at me and said, *Go to hell, you goddamn pig, just let me die.*"

Silence fell between them. Vidar tried to recall the last time his father had shared something in such detail. There'd been something different about him recently; the spring and summer had brought a fresh sort of openness in his tone when they spoke. He listened to Vidar, instead of just waiting for his turn to talk or hanging up the phone.

"It can mess with your head, something like that," he said now. "You can . . . It can be difficult to let it go. I mean, you want to understand. More than when they die, in fact."

Vidar sat down on a chair in the kitchen. His father had put words to a nebulous eeriness in his chest.

"Yeah. Why is that?"

"I don't know. But it's true. I remember feeling that way on that morning in June, how did *I* end up in that, I don't know, that *crossfire* of shit that put me in the position of saving another man's life in the middle of summer? There's almost never an answer, and you learn to live with that. But the first time it happens, it's almost unavoidable. So it . . . I don't know how you're feeling right now but I can imagine, I can understand. I just wanted to tell you that."

It sounded like he was about to hang up.

"Okay. Right. Thanks, I hope so. That it passes. How are you doing?"

"I'm just fine, actually. But how is Evy?"

"Not great, I don't think, but she'll be okay. Markus and I went to visit her and Einar last week; he's staying with them for the moment."

"We talk sometimes, her and me. She's the one who usually calls, these days." Sven chuckled. "It's really nice to be left alone, actually. But she called and mentioned the accident and that it ended badly, and I thought her voice sounded a little strained. Maybe I was just imagining it."

"Did she say anything about it? The accident and Einar, I mean."

"No." Vidar heard his father step into his clogs and walk out to the porch, sink into his chair. "Not outright," he went on, a cigarette between his lips. A lighter clicked. "Just that it was a terrible accident. And that you were the one who helped him."

"Markus and I did. The two of us."

"Of course, of course."

Sven inhaled the smoke and let out a hoarse cough.

"How are you doing?" Vidar tried, again.

"I'm just fine. I'm going to try to get rid of the mold in the bathroom this week. Nasty crap, that stuff."

Vidar waited. Sven smoked. No cough.

"Have you ever met Einar?" Vidar asked.

"No, I don't think so."

"He coached for Alet for a while. We played a match against them up at home once."

"Right," his father said, thoughtfully. "That rings a bell. But I wasn't there, was I?"

"No, you were working."

There was no accusation in his tone. Not anymore.

"How was the truck driver?" his father asked.

"He was okay. Physically, at least—how he's doing mentally, I have no idea. I've been wondering about him a lot as well. Like, he was there too."

His name was Leif Brännström; he was born in 1939 and had been driving trucks and maintaining a spotless record for thirty-two years. No complaints, no bad habits, no crime or trouble in his background. Vidar had spoken with the carrier he worked for and learned that Brännström had been on his way out of town to pick up rocks from the gravel pit, rocks that were destined for a new housing development out in Tylösand.

"What were you wondering about?" Sven asked.

Vidar gazed out the kitchen window at the late-summer evening, which rested under a warm, orange glow, the same glow his father could see from his chair on the other side of the village.

"Why it happened. Not why I was the one who . . . I mean, more like why it happened at all. But there doesn't seem to be anything off about Brännström. Or Einar, for that matter. Or his car. The witnesses say it looked like he was about to lose control right before he drifted into the oncoming lane. But why he was losing control, I don't know. What he'd been doing beforehand, where he was going, how he was feeling—no one knows any of that. And of course now we can't ask him."

"Only he knows, Vidar. That's true of a lot of things in life. Some pieces of the puzzle never fall into place. You just have to accept it. Just like," he added, more gloomily, "you know, like with Snapparp. Some things you see, you'll never forget."

They hadn't spoken about it, neither the body nor the van, nor the isolated rest stop with the children looking on. Vidar had been waiting for his father to ask about it last spring, but he never did.

"I saw your name in the case files that time," said Vidar. "When I wrote my report, afterwards."

"Yes, I'm sure I'm in there somewhere."

"In quite a few spots."

He heard his dad sigh.

"Yeah. I suppose I am. Unfortunately, I never got to the end of that case. Have you heard anything about it, by the way? How it's going? Has that composite sketch turned anything up?"

"I know they looked at Micke Håkansson. But he had an alibi for both Franzén and the Mellbergs. Besides, he wears a size forty-one shoe."

"No, no, it wasn't Håkansson, dammit." His father sounded annoyed. "Anyone can see that. But they haven't started looking at anyone else either?"

"Like who?"

"No idea. I just wondered about the sketch."

"It must be strange for you to see it," said Vidar. "After so many years. Even if it is just a picture."

"Sure, right." His father didn't say anything for a long time. "It does feel kind of tricky. It's like that sketch up in Stockholm, of the Palme killer. It could be anyone. And also not. But they're not looking at anyone right now?"

"No, not that I know of. But the case isn't down here with us, it's upstairs."

"I know. I just thought . . ." Silence. Vidar could hear his father's strained breathing. "Are you dropping by this weekend, by the way?"

"Yes, I'm coming. I'll bring pastries. But listen, how are you doing?"

"What's with all this nagging?"

"Well, all you'll say is that you're fine. What does that mean?"

"Retirement took some adjustment, that's all. But I'm feeling more at peace with it now. It's like I feel finished, through."

Vidar listened for something more in his voice, but found nothing.

"Good," he said. "I think I've noticed that in you recently, too."

"Listen, Vidar. You're going to be just fine." His dad said it as though he understood Vidar had his doubts. "It's going to be okay. You're my boy. You'll do better at this job than I did."

And if Vidar had been more attentive, maybe he would have noticed the dark undercurrent in his father's words, that he was trying to signal what he actually had in mind when he talked about the Tiarp Man and said he felt finished. That there was a story there, one about guilt and sorrow and anger, a loss that couldn't be understood unless you'd experienced it yourself. That he had resigned himself, but that this resignation came with a price he never could have imagined.

But Vidar was far too moved by his father's words to perceive anything but relief and, for the first time since the accident, hope.

"Thank you, Dad."

65

It happened one morning in November.

During the night, Sven arrived at the edge of the forest. The dawn air was very light; insects buzzed cozily nearby and the tops of the fir trees on the other side stood out against the sky, sharp and lovely. He reached a hand toward the field, which waited before him, and touched the tall grass. It was soft and thick like a horse's mane.

Sven looked down at his own body and found it transformed. Overnight he had become unnaturally old and, at the same time, very lithe and young. He now had the limbs and joints of a boy. He was wearing fine clothes, like the ones he used to wear when he and Bibbi went to church, back in the day.

Right. Sven looked around. No, he was alone. Her time hadn't come yet. That made him happy, that at least the boy would still have his mother around for a while. She wasn't finished. But he was, and a wave of relief washed through him. Everything has its time. So it was said, but how long one must bear it before it was over. So many people one had to hurt, so much one had to suffer through oneself.

When he thought about it, it was almost unbelievable that he'd managed. But he had.

A warm breeze rustled the trees and made the field bow gently. It reached his hair and nape.

He was wearing something on his head. When he raised his hand to see what it was, cautiously, as if probing for a wound, he was surprised. He took it off and looked at it, there in his palm.

His service cap.

Sven considered it for a moment before putting it back on, and as he did he thought of everyone who had stood here before him, of Mother, Father, Grandmother and Grandfather, Aunt Eva and Aunt Britt, Uncle Egon, even Aron, whom he'd only heard tales of. He could see their faces before him, all of them, and he knew they were waiting for him in the forest beyond the field, and he felt such a terrible longing to be reunited with them, felt the longing all across his skin, which pebbled with gooseflesh at the thought.

On the other side of the field, something emerged from the cool dawn light. Sven checked his cap one last time and cleared his throat. The solemnity of the moment made him straighten his back.

Yes, Sven thought, smiling faintly at the figure as it moved across the field, calmly, cautiously. *There. There you are.*

At last, you're here.

2019

66

It used to be called the airfield, Halmstad Airfield. That's what people said. Over the years, time did to it what time usually does to both places and people, and these days it went by the name Halmstad City Airport.

But everyone still called it *the airfield*.

It was located on a large expanse of land near the old coast road. When a plane took off for Stockholm, and the wind was blowing the right way, the pilots would fly out over the bay before banking north, giving the passengers a chance to view the little city by the sea from the sky, in all its verdant splendor. Only then did you notice that the airfield was sort of sunk in the valley called Vapnödalen, tucked up close below the massive ridge that was Nyårsåsen.

Once upon a time Vidar had been a cop, that was true, but after Hurricane Gudrun he left the force. It all had to do with the search for the man who had taken the life of Lovisa Markström up in Marbäck. It was a terrible crime. She had been robbed of her life in her own home on a November night in 1994, and the house had burned up. Her boyfriend was quickly apprehended and that was the end of it for ten years, until Vidar, in the fall of 2004, discovered that all was not as it should have been with the investigation. He did what he could to make it right, but failed and left the force in January 2005. Not until the summer of 2017 was the case solved. By that point, Vidar was working at the airfield as one of the ground crew.

Two years later, this was still the case. Each morning he went there. Sometimes, in the afternoons and evenings, when the sun was low in the sky, it was as if Nyårsåsen cast a heavy shadow over the area.

What happened to him began in the attic.

It was only the end of January, and the winter already seemed to be lasting forever. Slushy snow fell over Marbäck and Tofta. Flocks of winter birds sailed across the sky, impatient, as if they were waiting for spring.

His daughter, Amadia, was moving out. It was strange. It was only yesterday he'd been building her a sandbox and teaching her to ride a bike, and shortly thereafter, it seemed, she had closed herself up in her room with Hanna, Elena, and Yasha, and they played loud music and laughed, and she brought home her first boyfriend, Juha, from Östergård School. Just a month or so later, Vidar was sitting by her side at the driving school, and now, suddenly, she wasn't even going to live here anymore.

He placed a moving box on the cart in the middle of the living room floor, then another, then a third, until the cart was so heavy it would hardly budge.

"What is in these? Rocks? Stolen bars of gold?"

Amadia rolled her eyes. "Books, Dad. Books and binders."

"You should read less," he muttered, putting all his effort into steering the cart down the hall, down the front steps, and out to the waiting moving van.

When he came back, his nineteen-year-old daughter was standing there with an inscrutable expression on her face.

"Dad," she said.

He wiped his forehead with the back of his hand and put down the cart.

"Yes?"

"It's not like I'm disappearing. I'm only moving to Nyhem."

"I know that."

He tried to appear indifferent. It was a father's duty. She smiled and patted his arm.

"Okay, Dad."

"Honestly," he heard her say to her mother later that day, "what is with him and emotions? Why can't he just say how he feels?"

"I don't know, honey. But that's how he is. He's always been that way. Men are like that."

"Not all of them."

"Most of them. And your dad is no different than most."

67

That evening he sat on the living room floor, in a house that was suddenly too quiet and too big, paging through old photo albums and studying pictures of what had been their family life. Amadia ended up an only child, just like Vidar himself.

He'd taken out one of the older albums; in it, he saw himself as a child. He saw Dad, Mom. The photos were glued onto stiff paper.

Patricia sat down by his side. Her knees popped as she folded them beneath herself.

"What's wrong?"

"Do you think she felt lonely?"

She stroked his shoulders contemplatively. "Sometimes." She brought her lips tentatively to his hair. "But all children do."

"I just don't want her to have felt lonely."

"She was happy here with us, Vidar. She'll continue to be happy on Smedjegatan."

He studied a photograph of himself with his father. Sven had the bolt gun in his hands, unloaded. In the background, in the big farmyard behind the house, lay a fallen cow. The sky was pale and the tops of the fir trees tall, almost black. His mother had taken the picture. Vidar was ten, maybe eleven, and the cow had been sick. He recalled the sudden, sharp sound of the gun. The crows taking flight.

They paged on through the album, finding pictures from the late nineties. That was a peaceful time; he was a cop, had figured out what he wanted to spend his life doing, and they were expecting Amadia. Everything in its place, the path laid out.

He turned the page.

"Is that you and Markus?"

Vidar nodded.

"I remember that day." He took the photo from its sleeve. "I don't know why it's in here. It's not a happy memory."

"Why not?"

A colleague had taken the picture. They had just returned from the rest stop in Snapparp on a cold, early spring day in 1991. The memory filled him with discomfort. They kept browsing. The rest of the pictures were more cheerful, from happier times. Vidar and Patricia laughed at each other's hairstyles, clothing, how young they looked. Vidar in uniform, at a reception for the old boss Reidar Björkman when he retired, Vidar returning home from his first day with the property crimes unit.

"Do you miss it?" she asked.

"Not exactly."

It's our time now. So they had promised each other.

They went to the Tallhöjden Inn in Simlångsdalen. He drank near beer so Patricia could drink wine, and the evening sun sank between the trees the way it always had when Vidar was little, and as they made one last toast, looked each other in the eyes, and smiled, and as the last of the foamy, delicious beer slipped down and settled atop the herring, salmon, and sorbet, he told himself he felt truly contented and that was all anyone could really ask, and so he felt very fortunate.

One evening, when he was having trouble sleeping because the house was too quiet, he decided to put some of the boxes back in the attic.

They'd had to bring down a number of them to get at the ones that would be accompanying Amadia to her apartment on Smedjegatan, and they'd been sitting there along the wall ever since.

The old staircase creaked as he made his way up the attic steps with flashlight in hand. He turned on the dim ceiling light and saw their first sofa, a fat TV, some of the things Amadia had left behind when she moved.

He walked past boxes of baby clothes, the crib, a tricycle. A pang in his stomach. He'd never been good at getting rid of things.

He made sure there was room for the remaining boxes and went back down again, hauled them up one by one. Damn, they were heavy. He supposed they could just stay here until Amadia came by asking for them. He glanced at the crib. Well, sooner or later . . . maybe.

When he was finished, he picked up the flashlight and let its beam sweep over the attic. At the other end stood a heavy old cabinet. He didn't remember how they had gotten it up here—had they disassembled it before carrying it up? They must have. He opened its old doors and shined the flashlight inside. Full of boxes. Shit, had they forgotten about these? Maybe they were Amadia's.

One of the boxes was grayer than the others. It didn't look familiar. Up on top, unmarked and heavy. It was a struggle for Vidar to get it onto the floor.

He ran his palm across its lid, leaving a trail through the dust. When he opened it, the odor of stale cigarette smoke rose into the air.

Once in a while, time seemed to split open.

Dad.

68

The white beam of light swept across metal binders, document boxes, a collection of plastic folders, a few cassette tapes, and assorted junk: old pens, empty envelopes, unused stamps, a crumpled old black plastic bag.

In the plastic folders and sleeves were handwritten notes, drawings of an area Vidar soon realized was Tiarp, documents, incident reports and memos, and even minutes from a meeting.

In one of the folders waited something he recognized: the black notebook. His father had always used the same type, he recalled, the same brand, with a soft leather cover. He always bought them at the bookstore on Brogatan. Vidar wondered how many he'd gone through over the years. It must have been hundreds.

He had kept only a single one. Vidar picked it up gently, felt it, and opened to a random page. There was his father's handwriting.

Early spring, 1986. *We're searching the land around Tiarp, made a cast with V,* he wrote. *Nothing yet. The ground is frozen deep.*

V. That was him. So strange to catch sight of himself across time. He got a sudden impulse to put the notebook down. It felt too private, like barging into a secret world his father never let anyone else step into.

He could recall seeing his father from behind, puttering around the office in Vidar's childhood home. He stood, stooped over the open box, breathing heavily and filling it with work materials. Kind of like closing the books, he'd said. Must have been '91, sometime, early in the year. Vidar recalled his father sitting on the chair on the porch with a pack of cigarettes and a pile of documents on the table. A bottle of beer, from which he took sporadic sips, prevented the documents from being carried off by the evening breeze. He was gravely ill by then, his cough so terrible. Sven sat out there until late at night, reading, one piece of paper at a time, as if one of them would contain the answer to everything and therefore had to be carefully examined before he could set it aside.

He'd been allowed to keep his service weapon. It was a discreet gesture from the local police administration, who wanted to demonstrate their appreciation. He already had a license. They had withdrawn the weapon from service but hadn't scrapped it, as they usually did; instead they presented it to his father in a small ceremony during the coffee break on his last day. Vidar recalled that his father had accepted the box only with reluctance. He hadn't even opened it. Instead he'd planned to get rid of it as soon as possible, but then he never quite got around to it. He kept it in the basement along with his badge and his old service cap.

Vidar sat there with the box until the flashlight began to flicker, its batteries weak. He found his father's old badge but wondered where the weapon was. Then he recalled. They'd turned it in when Dad died.

But what about the service cap? It should be here. He searched but couldn't find it.

His father's back, heavy breathing, the stale smell of the box, old paper, and smoke. Grief grasped at Vidar like a cold and timeless hand, and he was astounded at the fact that it could be so long ago, almost thirty years in the past, and yet so close.

69

Vidar went through the motions of everyday life. He went to work, did the grocery shopping on the way home, vacuumed the house after his daughter's move, vacuumed the car too while he was at it, that needs doing once in a while, and placed the big houseplants in the bathtub to shower them off. He went to buy sidewalk salt and salted the driveway so they could walk on it, and when Patricia came home they made dinner, and later on Amadia called to ask if they wanted to come by for evening coffee. They got in the car and drove through the frozen winter landscape and into the city, to Smedjegatan.

He was biding his time, as though a decision would come to him if only he was patient.

70

"This is Markus," said Markus Danielsson on the other end of the line.

"Hi," said Vidar. "It's me. Do you have any evening coffee on over there?"

"Just finished it. Should I put on another pot?"

"Please do."

Once you've spent thousands of hours together in a patrol car, you seldom need to say much more than that. Vidar loaded the box into his car and headed south, toward Laholm.

Vidar had quit, but Markus had stayed on. He was with the criminal investigation department now, a detective in a managerial position. The wrinkles around his eyes were plentiful; the furrows bracketing his mouth had grown deep. His face was rounder; his belly too.

They hugged each other when they met, although it wasn't really their habit. Vidar went in and said hello to Hanna, who was in the kitchen.

"Are you here to make trouble for my husband again?" she said with a smile.

"As little as possible this time."

Markus took two mugs from a cabinet and poured them each some coffee. They sat down in the living room, where the TV rolled the news, on mute.

"Speaking of trouble. How's Amadia doing over in Nyhem?"

"Fine, I think."

"Is it weird?"

"So fucking weird. It's like it's so quiet. But she's doing well, and I guess that's the important thing. And we're doing okay too."

"Same here," said Markus, whose own daughter had moved out a year or so ago.

"Yes, oh my God," said Hanna. "No teenage girls occupying the bathroom all weekend, no parties when we're away, no boys blocking the driveway with their cars, we always have food left in the house, and we only have to do laundry every other week. It's hard, but we'll make it through."

Markus shrugged. "Yeah, there you go. It's unbearable."

Vidar laughed. They chatted for a while, about kids and houses and life on the force, at the airfield.

"So," Vidar said at last. "When Amadia moved out, I found something. I wasn't sure what to do with it."

Markus raised his eyebrows. "Okay?"

They put down their mugs and went out to the car. The evening air was cold and dry. Vidar opened the trunk.

"It was my dad's."

Markus opened the grayish-brown box and peered into it. Vidar had left everything inside. All he'd removed was the badge and the black notebook, in order to hold on to some sort of memory of his father.

"I'll be damned," said Markus, taking out a sheaf of documents and holding them in the compartment light so he could read them. "Stina Franzén." He flipped some pages. "Frida Östmark."

"Do you recognize these?"

"Yes, of course. The Tiarp murders. February of '86." He turned a page and squinted. "Shit, this was over thirty years ago."

"I don't know what you want to do, but I thought this box should be at headquarters instead of at my place. After all, these are investigation materials."

They stood in the dark of the driveway. A sharp north wind swept over Laholm from Veinge and Tjärby. Markus shivered.

"Sure, I'll take this. We can bring it inside, and I'll take it in with me tomorrow." He turned to Vidar, an inquisitive look on his face. "Hey, do you have time to stick around for a while? I've been meaning to call you."

Back in the living room Markus exchanged coffee for whiskey, while Vidar had a refill.

"You all still read the papers up there in Marbäck?"

"Why?"

"Do you remember the Law on Police Data?"

"To be honest, that was probably one of the first things I forgot."

Markus laughed. "We've been given new jurisdiction. Starting this year, the NFC has the authority to perform family searches. Which opens up some possibilities."

Family searches. Vidar had heard of them. They were risky, but when used judiciously could be very useful: When a case involved DNA from the perpetrator, but the perpetrator wasn't in the DNA database, the National Forensics Center could now perform a broad search to see whether their siblings, parents, or children were there. If a match turned up, it could narrow the focus of the investigation considerably.

"There'll be a backlog, naturally. In fact, there already is. The NFC follows the principle of relevance. The better the supporting evidence, the greater the relevance, it seems. They're already preparing the old Billdal case and the double murder in Linköping. My boss wanted to bring in someone who could take a look at our cases. So I'm working on that part-time now. The problem," Markus went on, suddenly looking tired, "is that I don't have the time, given all the administrative work and crap. So it would be a big help if my fifty percent could be transferred to someone else. You, for example."

"This position," said Vidar, "is it in town? Not up in Gothenburg?"

"We want someone in-house. So whoever gets the job will be working in Halmstad."

He wasn't totally averse to the thought of returning. But then he was reminded of Patricia's eyes, her graying temples, a quiet life, and, in some strange way, freedom. *This is our time now.*

"I think you'll have to find someone else."

Markus gave a weak smile. "I thought as much. But it never hurts to ask."

Such a simple thing, Vidar thought as he headed homeward. To just say no, just like that, when life opened a door to another possible path and he elected to stay where he was. To think that it was as easy as that. Once a cop, always a cop. Maybe it was true. But he was other things too.

71

The box in the attic had, for the first time in a long time, made him think of his father, of the life he had led and how it ended. We tend to see those who are no longer with us in a rosy light. Our memory smooths over imperfections, erases conflicts, and neatly bundles the past up so we can carry it with us. Surely it's the only way. We're only human, and can't always manage otherwise. It hurts to grieve the loss of someone who is also a source of pain.

Vidar was no older than twenty-three when his father died. Amadia had only ever met her grandfather as a sun-bleached gravestone at the edge of God's Field, the cemetery up in Breared.

Soon, the black notebook became part of Vidar, as necessary an object as his wallet, keys, and phone. It was scribbled so full it was hard to read in places. He began to regret having handed everything over to Markus so quickly; he should have held off, taken more time to think. That material would have been helpful in deciphering his dad's notes, which were sometimes dated, but usually not. All the notes were brief, technical, sometimes consisting of a thought or theory, a rough sketch of a location. They were about the murder of Stina Franzén in February 1986, and the suspected kidnapping and murder of Frida Östmark a few months later. The last notes were about the Mellberg couple and had been written in March 1991. His dad was too sick to work, but he still put down his ideas and tried to draw connections through time.

Vidar remembered the case of the Tiarp Man. The articles in the newspapers, the theories that were dismissed and revived. Vidar himself had been there on the periphery; so had Markus. He knew his father had been quite preoccupied with it—but this?

When he got to the last page, he noticed some cracks on the inside of the cover. More pages had once been there; you could see the small ripped edges they'd left behind. Four or five pages, maybe a few more. They'd been torn out. His father must have done it.

Perhaps he had used those pages for something else, maybe for jotting down phone numbers when he didn't have his usual address book at hand; scribbling down what Vidar's mother asked him, over the phone, to buy at Domus; writing down a date and time of a car inspection appointment; a visit from the butcher; checkups at the clinic.

Sure, maybe. There was no way to know.

And then Vidar woke up one morning in March, sat up in bed, yawned the sleep from his body, and kissed his wife's head before heading downstairs to make coffee. That was when he saw it.

The white wagtail was sitting on the windowsill, watching him whimsically with its curious face and that spot gleaming on the center of its breast. The bird cocked its little head, then flew away. Vidar watched its sleek body and long tail as it went.

Then he laughed.

That same day, he was standing in the break room at work when the phone rang. It was Markus. He thanked Vidar for his recent visit and asked how he was doing.

"Oh, I'm good, I'm at work. You?"

"Fine. Could you . . ." Markus faltered. "I wonder if you could come on in."

"What, to the station?"

"Yes, if you're able to."

"Of course. What's going on?"

"We'll talk when you get here, that'll be easier. When do you think you can come?"

He looked at the clock on the break room wall. Its face depicted an old propeller plane.

"I'm done at three today. So, three-thirty?"

"Good. That's fine. Thank you, Vidar."

72

"It's about the box," said Markus.

He sounded oddly awkward and formal.

"Right. I expected as much."

On a table in Markus's office stood Vidar's dad's grayish-brown box, with its contents unpacked; binders here, documents and folders there, all the small items that had been inside now neatly arranged and prepared, like a complicated model kit.

Dark clouds gathered outside the third-floor window, blown in from the sea by a stiff breeze. It was awfully windy outside the massive glass complex.

"I took a look at it, or rather, what was inside it. But speaking of, I wanted to ask, was there anything else in it? Anything you took out or put aside or . . . you know."

"No, I left everything there."

"Everything," Markus repeated.

"Except his old badge."

"Okay." Markus nodded. "Good. That's helpful to know."

"So, what is all this? What's the deal with the box?"

"It took some time. We've had so much else going on, you know how it is. The plan was, I would just double-check everything here against what we have in storage down in the archive, make sure it was all copies he'd made for, you know, personal use. Or whatever. Let's just say it's not like he was the only one in that regard."

He knew that Vidar, too, had once kept a box up in the attic. And not just Vidar either; it wasn't all that unusual for old cops to persist in hauling around stuff they'd never gotten a handle on. Unsolved puzzles, labyrinths. It was what it was. Some saved materials in the hopes of one day finding that missing piece of the puzzle so they could have closure; others realized it would never happen but kept materials anyway, as a reminder that it wasn't always possible to clear everything up.

"But it's not just copies," Markus went on. "And above all . . ." he began, nodding at the table where the contents of the box waited. "That plastic bag."

Vidar turned his head to look at the crumpled black plastic bag.

"Yeah, what is it?"

"Did you look inside it?"

"I thought it was empty."

"Me too. But it wasn't."

He pulled out a drawer from the filing cabinet under his desk and took out a couple of sealed plastic sleeves, the kind they used to use to gather evidence. In them were tiny pieces of fabric, hardly bigger than postage stamps, one in each sleeve.

"What are those?"

Markus looked down at a piece of paper in front of him.

"According to the records, they're blood evidence taken from Stina Franzén's car." He looked up. "Do you recognize them? I mean, did he show these to you or mention them ever, or anything?"

Vidar slowly shook his head.

"It's the only physical evidence they had," Markus added, "that was directly linked to the perpetrator. It's missing from our boxes, here at the station. I checked. It seems he took them."

A shiver went through the room. Vidar reached toward the desk and pulled the small plastic sleeves over, fingering them.

"Can you think of any reason he would have had them?"

"No, I . . . no idea."

He gingerly put them back down. It must be some sort of misunderstanding.

"They did an inventory down there in the winter of '90 and '91," Markus said, crossing one leg over the other. "You know, the kind they do to make sure everything is where it should be. It was concluded in January of '91. No irregularities. So they were removed after that."

"But by then, Dad was retired," Vidar said. "He left around the first of the year, when I started."

"Yes," Markus said. "Exactly."

So that was it. He'd been lured into a trap.

"You're joking."

"Vidar, you know how it is, I just want to—"

"You think *I* did it?"

"That's not what I'm saying at all." Markus rested his forearms on the edge of the desk. "But I have to check with you, you're the one . . . Well, the only one close to him who's still around. Who had ties to him. I thought, if you . . ." he tried, his face almost pleading. "Removing evidence, especially that sort of evidence, it's very serious. I had to ask."

"And I'm telling you that neither he nor I would have done it. I don't know what you all think is going on, but that's not it."

"But they were in his possession. You yourself handed them over to us."

"Then he must have gotten them from someone else."

"That doesn't seem very likely. But say he did. Your dad still illegally removed physical evidence from the building."

"But why would he have done it?"

"To hide something?"

A chill rose through Vidar's chest.

"What the hell is that supposed to mean?"

"Did you know there was a report filed against him as well? For manslaughter by negligence."

"What?"

Markus took a piece of paper from his pants pocket and showed him a police report. Vidar scanned the document. A preliminary investigation opened in the summer of 1988 by a Nora Selvin. He didn't recognize the name.

"This is bullshit."

"Yeah," Markus said, taking the document back and demonstratively putting it in his pocket again, as if he wanted to show that this would be treated with care, that Vidar could trust his discretion.

"Vidar."

"I don't know what the fuck you and your colleagues are up to in here," he said, standing suddenly, full of that powerful chill, "but I suggest you let it go."

His hands were trembling as he headed for the elevator. This wasn't like him. He knew that, and realized that Markus was thinking the same thing. He wasn't usually hot-tempered. But what could he do? This felt like a surprise attack.

It hadn't even been ten hours since he saw the bird.

73

Back home, he got out the Weedwacker and trimmed the weeds. He got the edges of the garden beds so Patricia could plant spring plants and flowers. After the workday, he chopped wood and cleaned out the car ahead of its inspection, scrubbed the wooden stairs and applied a fresh coat of oil. The sharp scent of it rose around him, making him long for summer. He spent time with his colleagues, chatting and laughing and discussing topics big and small. He went to the Ikea down in Helsingborg with his daughter and helped her get a new bed.

He couldn't get his departure from Markus's office out of his mind. He saw himself bolt from the chair, felt the flush in his cheeks and the weight of his steps as he left the police station. At first he thought it was just anger over being bulldozed, that maybe it was about Markus, but as the days passed he realized: All this, and he hadn't had a clue. It had all happened without his dad mentioning a word about it. Dad died in November 1991 following a collapsed lung, Mom was the one who found him, and the last notes in the notebooks were from March earlier that same year. He'd become absorbed in an old case just six months before his death, had been reported for negligent manslaughter. How had this all escaped Vidar, and how had his father managed to keep quiet about it? Why had he stubbornly dealt with it all on his own? Vidar didn't understand. And maybe he *hadn't* dealt with it alone. *Maybe Dad just didn't say anything to me. But why? Because he wanted to protect me?*

Vidar searched for answers in the notebook. He found nothing. When he closed his eyes, he saw his father before him again, leaning over the box. The case of the Tiarp Man had left its mark on his father's final years of life. In his memory, they were in the same room, just an arm's length apart.

He listened to the local news on the radio. A man had been arrested the night before on Stora Torg, under suspicion of attempted murder. The victim was taken to the hospital with stab wounds to the abdomen. A children's choir would give a spring concert in Picasso Park on Walpurgis Eve. And spring had finally come. The white wagtail had been spotted in Halland.

In time, he would be forced to examine his father in a way no child wants to: with the eyes of an inquisitor. Wasn't this what he truly feared, what he fled from during those lovely spring days that passed after he'd stormed out on his conversation with Markus and left the police station in a rage? That, and what he might find.

74

"I changed my mind," said Vidar. "Okay. I'll take it."

He could tell Markus was hesitating. There was a rustle on the line. "You mean . . ."

"The job. You offered me a job before. I'll take it."

Markus gave a heavy sigh. "You couldn't work on anything that has to do with your dad anyway. It would be conflict of interest. Not to mention, a hell of a mess."

"But . . ."

"I'm sorry it turned out the way it did. I understand why you were angry. Or whatever."

"I wasn't angry, I was . . . Can I come back or not?"

"You can come back, but you can never get close to this. And you know that. So maybe you'd like to take some more time to think it over," he added, when Vidar didn't respond.

"Then you know what, never mind," Vidar said. Before he could hang up, Markus managed to insert something that caught his attention.

"What was that?"

"I was just thinking, what if he was afraid someone else was going to take it and destroy it?" said Markus. "The blood evidence, I mean. Maybe he was trying to protect it rather than hide it, if you see what I mean."

"Oh. Sure. Maybe."

"I can't be sure, but I mean, it's possible that's what was going on."

Vidar could hear the doubt in Markus's voice. He felt doubtful too. But it would have been nice if it were true.

"Was there really a report filed against him?"

"I'm afraid so."

"I had no idea, I . . . It just came as a shock. I don't understand how that could have escaped me. What happened with it?"

"It was dismissed at the start of '89. The prosecutor didn't pursue it. Maybe I should have mentioned that from the start."

"Yeah."

"But at the same time, maybe it doesn't mean much that it was dismissed."

There was no need for Markus to elaborate. That was the usual result when a report pertained to the police, regardless of what had actually happened.

"I sent it to the NFC," he said.

"What's that?"

"The blood from the perpetrator in Stina Franzén's car. Now that we've got it, we have to try to find a match in the database. There's a good chance he's in there. But I checked with the director up there, and we're way back in line because it's such an old case."

"Will you do a family search too?"

"Not yet—it takes so much longer. We'll start with the usual inquiries, processing times are plenty long there. Listen, I . . . Seriously, Vidar. Before we wrap this up, if there's nothing else, well . . . I want to apologize. I'm really sorry. Maybe I should have been a little more . . ."

"It's fine."

Even so, once he'd hung up the phone, the rage expanded from Vidar's heart to his fingertips, a rage that made him feel lost and confused. He didn't know where it had come from or who it was for. It had no name.

He remembered the stench in the van they'd found in Snapparp, the crushed skull, the splinters of bone like shards of plastic, and he and Markus had thought of the family, those goddamn kids standing right nearby, maybe even close enough to smell it. Jesus, it was so horrid, really, was this what he was about to be dragged back . . .

His train of thought was interrupted when Patricia opened the front door, arriving home from work with sacks of groceries in her hands.

"Do you want help?" he asked, almost relieved that he could stop thinking now.

Amadia. She had never mentioned what she wanted to be. *Just not a cop*, he thought. *Anything but that.*

That night, a very gentle rain fell over Marbäck. It cooled off his emotions. Vidar stood at the kitchen window, taking in the land, as though somewhere out there, in the first green buds of spring, an enemy awaited him.

75

The Mellberg couple. It was almost the worst case of all, to the extent that gruesome crimes can be ranked. The crime had taken place in the couple's home. Surrounded by her own safe space, Gisela Mellberg had been violated, had come close to being robbed of her life, and had lost her husband.

Vidar cruised slowly down the winding highway that ran through Vapnö. Had he really been ready to come back? If Markus had only allowed him to, would he really . . . ? Probably shouldn't touch that, better to let it be. Right. Let it subside.

Yet here he was.

Vapnö was an isolated little area, not entirely unlike Marbäck, dating back to the Middle Ages. Back then, nomads passed through, and some of them decided to stay. They had erected a church.

That's the way it goes: It could be a church, a relationship, or a career. You create some sort of center point, so that you can tell yourself you have a center point.

Vidar parked the car and paged through the notebook.

The dogs had lost the trail in a nearby clearing. The man was on foot. He wore size 44 boots and went along the edge of the road, not through the forest. It seemed like a conscious choice. This way it was harder for both people and dogs to track him.

No one out.

Gisela Mellberg had been due at work at seven-thirty the next morning, was probably getting ready for bed, but it was hard to determine exactly what she was doing and where she was in the house when the man broke in. The evidence started in the kitchen, which was where he'd pried open one of the old windows.

It seemed he threw himself on top of her. The tumult indicated as much. He dragged her into the bedroom and raped her. Had he intended to kill her? They would probably never know. She survived, but possibly only because he was interrupted.

Robert, her husband, had come home. He'd been down in Malmö, delivering a truck to a carrier by the harbor. Then he drove a van home, a dark green Volkswagen, which was to be delivered to the carrier EliaExpress the next day.

Vidar stepped out of the car. Cold, weak sunlight made its way through the trees. There was no breeze. Once upon a time, a couple had lived here. Robert and Gisela. They'd been happy, if you believed what everyone said.

Vidar took a lap around the area. Dad never would have tried to destroy or withhold evidence, he thought. It's impossible. Something else must have been going on.

All at once, he felt incredibly close to his father. In his notebook, the words:

the van. why Snapparp? what is the logical conclusion?

No answer. Maybe because there wasn't one. Maybe because his father had been losing his mind toward the end, and now, years later, his son was about to take a step in that same direction.

Yes, he could see it now. He ran his fingers over the pages, felt the traces the pen left on the paper, as if they were the marks a crime left on a person. *I've seen your notes now, I know them.* And in them, Vidar saw his father better than he'd been able to see him from across the kitchen table, the other side of the sofa, or beside him in the car. Certain crimes would not rest until they were resolved. They would mark you for eternity if you failed.

What happened up here ate him alive.

Vidar turned the last page and observed the soft inside of the cover, running his fingers across the smooth surface.

Which wasn't entirely smooth. The pen had left an impression. He brought it close to study it.

1 . . . 3 . . . an eight or a six, no, an eight, 1380—the code for Halmstad. Then a K. It was a K-number, the filing number a police report was assigned when it was documented and registered at the station. His dad had jotted it down on a page he later tore out, but the impression of the pen had gone through. It was easier to make out the numbers when you knew what they stood for.

1380-K2431-85.

That was his best guess. Maybe 2437, but he thought it was 2431.

It ended in 85. That meant sometime in 1985, probably fairly late in the year since the previous number was so high. A case here in town.

It was the last thing he wrote.

76

The receptionist who greeted him was a thin man with dark hair and eyes that sat deep in his skull. He looked at Vidar as though he were some acquaintance he ought to recognize.

"You're . . ."

"Vidar Jörgensson," he said, giving the K-number.

"Right."

Vidar hadn't visited the courthouse since he'd left the force. A different era, a different life. It was strange to be back. It smelled the same.

"It took some time to unearth it. It's so old." The receptionist placed a thin sheaf of papers on the small table. "Enjoy."

"Thank you."

He took it to his car. A weak spring sun peered from behind the clouds and warmed the exterior. He sat in the driver's seat and read with the door open.

The file concerned an assault. It had taken place at nine P.M. on the evening of November 15, 1985, outside Grand Hotel, and the restaurant's bartender had been the one to call the police. One dinner guest had become upset at another, had punched him in the face, and the police had been summoned. Among other activities at the scene, they interviewed witnesses.

One of them was named Stina Franzén. Vidar clicked a pen and circled the name. She appeared twice in the investigation, in the interview on the scene and in another two days later, over the phone.

In January 1986, a man had been given a suspended sentence and ordered to pay damages, and that was the end of that.

Vidar paged through the material. He had requested both the preliminary investigation and the court ruling, and everything was there. The initial report, the incident report from the first officer on site, interrogations—a few were in the form of transcripts, but most were summaries that took up no more than half a page. He noted the names that appeared, especially of the men. Bosses, colleagues, bar regulars, the perpetrator, and the victim. None of them stood out in his mind.

Had these documents been in Dad's box? Maybe, but he doubted it.

He thought of the courthouse receptionist, the thin man with glasses. Did he know Markus? Law enforcement agencies in this town were like a little village of their own, where everyone knew everyone, talked to one another, exchanged gossip and secrets.

No point in wasting time on this; it was what it was. Vidar compiled the material and placed it on the passenger seat, closed the driver's door, and went to work.

He was in the car on the way home when the phone rang. Since he recognized the number as Markus's he didn't bother to pick up. It rang again. Vidar ignored it. He'd already made it to Skedala when Markus called a third time.

"What?" he snapped.

"Seems I'm calling at a bad time?"

"I'm in the car on my way home."

"I just have one question," said Markus. "That's all. Then I'll stop bothering you."

"Okay?"

"David Linder."

"What?"

"David Linder," Markus repeated, as if he thought Vidar hadn't heard. "Are you familiar with the name?"

"A former employee there."

After the cold streetlights of Skedala, the highway sank into darkness on the way to Marbäck and Tofta. Markus waited.

"I think he might have worked with Dad," Vidar added at last.

"Exactly. Supposedly he moved away."

"Okay," said Vidar. "What, didn't he?"

Markus didn't answer right away. "I don't know. So I wanted to check with you."

"About what?"

"Whether Sven, whether your dad, ever talked about him. Or anything else that might help me out. You said they worked together."

"Yes, I think they did."

"They did."

"What's going on? I can tell something is up."

"I can't . . ." his former colleague hesitated. "It's tricky, because I don't know yet. But there's something strange about Linder."

Vidar considered this. The name Linder rang a bell somehow. Markus kept talking, but he wasn't listening anymore. Instead he parked along the little road that led up to Marbäck from the highway. He turned on the compartment light and picked up the documents, which were still in the passenger seat, and paged through them, searching for the right page.

"Hello?" Markus's voice rang loud and clear in the quiet car. "Are you still there?"

The assault at Grand Hotel in November 1985, Stina Franzén as one of the witnesses, there was the initial report, the incident report, right.

"Yes," Vidar said, running his fingers over the paper. He hadn't noticed it before, why would he, but now. Now he saw it. "Look, I think we need to meet. But you'll have to tell me what the hell is going on."

The first officer on the scene had been David Linder.

77

Saturday was cold and clear, with bright sunlight shining on the western rest stop in Snapparp. It didn't look like it once had. Gone were the run-down sheds and buildings, the old pumps and signs. Instead, shiny, clean rental cars stood in a row along the parking lot, and the gas station's convenience store was big and bright.

Vidar sat in his car with his father's notebook. *22:30–00:30. lights out.* So it said on one page. Nothing more. He tried to make sense of it, but couldn't. The notes were out of context, cryptic, impossible to survey or rank or arrange into a pattern. The more he understood, the more what had once appeared mundane became suddenly interesting, and what had once appeared centrally important now looked like dead ends.

When Markus came out of the convenience store with two paper mugs in hand, Vidar hastily stuffed the notebook into his inner pocket. The chill between them, from their last encounter, still lingered.

"I thought this might be necessary." He handed a mug to Vidar, closed the passenger door, and put on his seatbelt. "It's the weekend, after all. Do you know the way?"

"I think so."

Markus observed the rest stop for a moment.

"Weird to be back here, isn't it?"

"Definitely. I don't think I've been here since we found the van. It's changed, to say the least."

"Like everything else. Almost everything, anyway."

"Tell me, now. What's going on with Linder?"

Markus hesitated for a long moment.

"I don't know. I've been trying to get in touch with him, but I can't find him. If I'm not mistaken, Linder made a friend while he was at the academy, an Adam Persson from Sundsvall. Persson was a cop for a while, but left to work for the family business, just like Linder himself did down here. Supposedly when the farm started going downhill, Linder turned to Persson up there for work, and ended up moving there, this would have been sometime in the spring of '91. But I talked to Persson in Sundsvall yesterday, and he hadn't heard from Linder in thirty years."

"So where did it come from, the information that he moved up there?"

"That's what I'm trying to figure out. I don't really know. It seems to have been one of those things, you know, everyone knew but no one knew quite how they knew. And I can't find any credit cards linked to him, no renewed driver's license, I don't have any address, I . . . I've got nothing. He was apparently seeing this woman we're going to meet, this Ylva Sandström down here in Genevad, shortly before he took off, so I thought we should talk to her."

Ylva Sandström lived and worked on her family's farm. Thirty years ago, she had been twenty-two. Now she ran the farm herself, had two grown children and a husband called Henrik, two cars, one tractor, a small truck, and no record except for a couple of speeding tickets.

"Where is it?"

"In the back seat."

Markus twisted around and got hold of the sheaf of paper Vidar had picked up at the courthouse the day before. While Vidar slowly guided them out of Snapparp toward Highway 15 and Genevad, Markus paged through the documents in a silence that was hard to read.

Vidar took a sip of coffee, strong and hot. "Were those in the box I gave you?" he asked.

"No. So I'm wondering how you came to have them."

"Just luck."

"Hmm. Luck."

Markus was the one who'd asked if he would consider coming along, that it might be a good idea. Vidar didn't really understand why but agreed to come anyway. What they were about to do was a job for the police, and he hadn't been a cop for a long time. *Hmm. Luck.* What was he doing here if Markus didn't trust him?

"Take a right here," said Markus.

"I know."

"So he meets Stina Franzén in 1985, in connection with an assault at her place of work. Linder is the first officer on the scene. Three months later, she's murdered and he's drawn into the investigation. He doesn't say a word to indicate they've met before. Five years later, he's supposedly moved to Sundsvall. He sells the livestock and leaves the farm, but there are no indications he was ever in Sundsvall. Instead there are unpaid, overdue bills, hundreds of them, expired credit cards, and so on." Markus closed the folder. "How are we supposed to interpret that?"

"I don't know. Is that it?"

A big farm appeared down the road.

"Yes, up here. She's expecting us."

78

Ylva Sandström was a warm, forthright woman a little over fifty, with hair that was thick and gray-brown like an old broom, little crow's feet around her eyes, and a mouth that showed crooked teeth when she smiled.

She gestured at them to have a seat on the front steps. It was cold out, but she was properly bundled up in a heavy jacket, insulated pants, and substantial boots. She had a bucket of carrots in one hand and a peeler in the other. Their conversation began tentatively; they chatted about the farm and the livestock. Vidar and Markus were from the countryside too. They recognized the tranquility and also the endless work that made up everyday rural life.

"I was thinking," Ylva said after a while, "you said this was about David Linder. It's been a long time since anyone wanted to talk about him. That's why you're here, isn't it?"

"Yes," said Markus.

"Has something happened?"

"How did you know him?"

"Oh, well. I guess we . . . you know, we were together for a while there."

"For how long?"

"Six months, maybe? From the fall of 1990 until he took off, in March of '91."

"Took off, you say."

"I didn't know it at the time, obviously."

"Can you tell us about the last time you saw him?"

"But I never did see him the last time."

Markus raised an eyebrow. "What do you mean?"

"He was supposed to come over one evening after he tended the livestock. David usually showed up around midnight, but this time he never came. And I never saw him again."

"What did you think about that?"

"What did I think? I don't know. I thought it was strange, obviously. But in one way it was a relief."

"Did you try to contact anyone about it? That he never showed up?"

"Well, yes, I called him the next day to see if he was okay and was surprised when no one answered. After I called around a little without getting hold of him, I waited a few days, then tried calling around again. That's when I heard he had moved to Sundsvall. To be honest, I wasn't surprised."

"Why not?"

"Recently he'd been . . . Well, look, I don't know. But his farm was going downhill. Everyone knew it. I think he took it awful hard, even though it wasn't his fault. He had to sell off the animals and lay off his farmhand, until he was the only one left there. I don't understand how he had time for it all. He seemed pretty worn out, and aside from me and maybe a few others he didn't have any solid ties to the area. He drank quite a bit, got pretty depressed and sort of a little unpredictable. So, why not? Really. But, look, what's this all about?"

"We're getting to that. Unpredictable, you say? How so?"

"Oh, you know . . . There was this one time he got a phone call out of the blue. It was some bad news about the farm, I think. He got really angry. Not at me; it's not like I felt threatened or anything, but . . ."

Markus cocked his head. "But, you did a little bit?"

"Yes, a little. When I asked about the call, he just got really aggressive. Not physically, but verbally. It was none of my fucking business and all that." She lowered her voice. "That time he was awful rough with me when we . . . you know." Ylva gave a laugh. "I don't know how explicit to be here."

"As explicit as you need to be."

"Well, I guess he was a little weird when we slept together too, as I recall. As if he actually wanted to be doing something else."

"How do you mean?"

She hesitated to answer.

"Just that he took his frustrations out on me. But, I mean, I don't want you to get the wrong impression. He was great. He just had some dark moments there towards the end."

"You said that in one way it was a relief that he never showed up that night. What do you mean by that?"

"We never got all that much sleep, let's put it that way. And life around here starts early. So I usually spent the whole next day feeling tired. So did he, of course."

"So that's what you did together?"

She had begun to peel the carrots. Now she blushed and looked down, staring into the pail.

"Not much else to do on a farm once all the animals are asleep. We got together other times too, of course, but not very often. Five or six times in all, maybe. I wasn't looking for much more than that, you know? I was fine on my own, and plenty busy."

"It doesn't seem like you were particularly upset that he moved," Vidar said cautiously.

"No, not exactly. Of course, I would have preferred that he mentioned it to me. But at the same time, you know . . . I had the feeling that maybe there was someone else, too."

"As in, a woman?"

"I don't know, I just had the feeling that something else was up. That he had someone else. I thought maybe he had taken off with her. Or maybe she lived in Sundsvall, who knows? No big deal, anyway, because shortly after that I met Henrik and things moved really fast with us. Love is like that. The whole David episode sort of just faded from my mind. I was mostly glad that I didn't have to think about him, to be honest, but I assumed he must be just fine, wherever he was. Although of course I thought, I mean, he could have let me know instead of ghosting me."

"So you haven't heard from him since?" Vidar asked.

"No," said Ylva. "I haven't heard a word."

"But did he ever mention Sundsvall before?" Markus asked.

"Never. That's why I was so surprised."

"Adam Persson, did he ever mention that name?"

"No idea. I don't remember."

She rose from the steps and disappeared around the corner of the house, only to return carrying a hose. She aimed it into the pail and the water spattered onto Markus.

"Oops, guess I need to watch out," he said.

"I'm sorry, did you get very wet?"

"No, it's fine. Some cops have a little trouble letting go of their job. Do you know if David was like that?"

"No, he said it was a relief to quit."

"He never brought up old cases or anything?"

"If he did, it wasn't to me. But," she added, "like I said, our relationship wasn't really that sort. If you know what I mean."

"How would you describe David as a person? I mean, based on your time together."

"Oh, you know. Aside from there at the end, when he was a little more unpredictable, he was pretty ordinary. Friendly. Stable and secure, sort of, as a former cop. Kind and generous, hardworking. Strong sense of duty. Even towards the end, when times were hard. You have to be that way, as a farmer. The animals don't care if it's Christmas or Midsummer, hot or cold, early or late. If they need you, they need you. It's not for everyone, as they say. But it suited David. And to me, that said a lot about him."

Markus's gaze shifted once more to Vidar, who was sitting still and listening.

"And yet," said Markus, "he takes off one night, possibly with a woman he's been seeing on the side, and you never hear from him again."

Markus was clever. Careful but sharp. A good voice, with discreet shifts in his tone when the conversation grew serious. Vidar imagined him digging into his dad's past. It made him feel uneasy.

"Yes . . . exactly. But you know, guys do crazy stuff when they're in love. So I assumed it was something like that. What, you think something might have happened? Is that it?"

"No," said Markus. "We actually don't know. Did he ever mention Tiarp?"

"Tiarp? Why would he have mentioned Tiarp?"

"We don't know that either," Markus said, with a gentle smile. "I was just wondering."

"No, I don't think he did, as far as I recall." She stood up and went around the corner again, turned off the hose. A fresh, earthy smell rose from the pail of carrots. "Was there anything else?"

"No. No, I think that was all."

Markus stood up. Vidar followed his lead.

"Wait, one more thing." This was Vidar. "You said you heard he'd moved to Sundsvall when you called around a second time, a few days later. Do you remember who told you that?"

Ylva raised two well-groomed eyebrows.

"No. No, I don't. It must have been someone in the village."

79

"So what do you think happened?"

Vidar posed the question in the car on the way back from Gene-vad. Markus took a deep breath.

"Maybe he was just hard to get hold of. I don't know. Or it could be that he just wanted to take off. Fly under the radar for some reason we aren't aware of but is still perfectly legitimate. Woman stuff, debt, God knows what. He could have told that lie about Persson because he had to say *something*. That, or . . . you know, or maybe he had a box full of the past up in the attic, if you know what I mean. Like you did. Like your dad."

"But then what do you think happened?"

"I think there are signs he kept up the investigation on his own, with-out anyone knowing. And that he had help. At least, it's possible to inter-pret the signs that way. Right around when Linder took off, your dad is down in the archives and . . . well. He removes some physical evidence. Ylva Sandström herself speculated that Linder was two-timing her with another woman. But maybe it wasn't a woman. You know what they always say about us. Our partners think we're unfaithful. But we're not. At least, nine times out of ten we're not, and not the way they think we are. Cops seldom cheat with other people, it's more often . . ."

"The job."

"Once a cop, always a cop."

The words struck a chord in Vidar. From the inner pocket of his jacket, Markus pulled a photograph.

"The most recent photo I could find of him," he said. "When he renewed his driver's license, in the late summer of 1989."

He had renewed his license at the police station, in the old building over on Patrikshillsvägen. He still looked young in the photo. Alert eyes gazed into the camera. He had a square face; short, blond hair; a prominent nose; a relatively narrow mouth. Vidar wondered what it had been like to work with him. He looked like a clever guy—someone who didn't give up, who was there for his colleagues when they needed him.

"I've seen his old duty logs," said Markus. "David Linder clocked a massive amount of overtime, hours he never had time to recoup as time off before he quit. Weekends, nights, holidays. Everything. So he was driven, as a cop, for as long as he was on the force. Just like your dad. Just like . . . well, like you. Maybe that's a sign, too. It's what I've got. It's all I've got. I don't know anything more."

Vidar didn't say anything for a long time. He thought of the notes in the notebook and tried to choose his words carefully to keep from rousing Markus's suspicions.

"I've got it into my head that Dad worked on that, towards the end. I don't remember very clearly, but I think he did. I know he spent time on the documents in the box, I remember that much."

Maybe they were working together, Vidar thought. Dad and his young colleague. Dad reads about Risarp in the newspaper. He suspects it's the Tiarp Man again, after five years. He catches the scent but his health won't allow him to take up the chase on his own. He needs someone who can put his ear to the rail, do the footwork.

"You don't trust me," said Vidar. "And on some level, I suppose I understand."

"What makes you say that?"

"That's why you wanted me to come along. Because it's better to keep me close now that I've gotten dragged into this. I know how you think. Just admit it."

Markus didn't respond for a long time.

"It's just . . . I'm having so much trouble putting this all together. But no. I do actually trust you." He chuckled. "I think." And then, as if to demonstrate he was telling the truth, he went on: "If we assume they were working together, Linder makes more progress than your dad does. He crosses paths with the Tiarp Man, and the Tiarp Man gets rid of him. Maybe that's why he goes missing. Because the Tiarp Man silenced him. After all, he was never reported missing, so there's no investigation to look at. To open one now—we might have to, but it's going to be fruitless. Did Sven talk about David? I mean, Sven died after he disappeared."

"Maybe once or twice. But I don't remember what he said."

Silence fell between them again.

"I wonder if they could have had a relationship," said Markus. "Linder and Franzén. Why else would he hide the fact that they'd met? Linder could have avoided saying anything because he knew how it would look. When a woman dies, who do we focus on? The men around her. And he was a young officer, new, inexperienced, smart, and hungry. Linder didn't want to risk making himself a suspect. He could have gone far as a cop, probably had his sights set on a command position. So maybe he kept quiet to protect himself. Which would also explain why he dives back into it again, along with Sven, in 1991."

And maybe that made him into the Tiarp Man's fourth murder victim.

80

The photograph of Sven and Bibbi Jörgensson hung on the living room wall and had been taken in the yard back at Vidar's childhood home. It was a spring day, must have been in the early eighties. Behind them, the new leaves had sprung forth. Mom was smiling dutifully at the camera. She was wearing jeans and a blouse and was sitting on a white wooden chair with her legs crossed. Dad stood with a hand on her shoulder, looking serious and wary, as though he didn't quite trust the photographer's intentions.

It was late at night. Vidar couldn't sleep. He was drinking whiskey. He sat at the kitchen table, taking sips from his glass and trying to form a timeline of the chain of events. He drew a line across the paper and began to put down what he knew; this always used to help him, to sort events chronologically and put them in order, say *No, first this, then this, then that.*

He wrote:

11/15/85. Franzén and Linder meet.

Was that their first point of contact? It was the first one he knew of.

2/28/86. Franzén murdered.
4/29/86. Östmark disappears. (Östmark murdered?)

He consulted his memories, Dad's notebook, what he knew from the conversation with Ylva Sandström. The entries on the timeline grew denser.

2/27/91. Attack on the Mellbergs in Risarp.
3/6/91. Robert Mellberg found in Snapparp.
3/?/91. Linder disappears.

He hesitated for a long time. Then he added:

?/?/91. Dad retrieves physical evidence from the archive.

Retrieves, a neutral word.

The pleasant rush of alcohol beneath his temples had been replaced by an intense buzzing by the time he finally went up to the bedroom. Patricia was on her stomach in bed, breathing deeply, somewhere deep in dreamland. Vidar gently placed his palm against the curve of her back. He felt her cool skin, soft and smooth against his, which was rougher. It usually brought him peace on nights when he had trouble sleeping, to hear his wife's rhythmic breathing and to simply touch her.

No peace this night.

His skin felt prickly, the way it does when you've spent too much time in the sun on a hot summer day. He cautiously got back out of bed.

"As long as you can't sleep," came Patricia's sleepy voice, "you might as well do something productive instead of just sitting at the kitchen table and brooding. Go dust and organize the bookshelf, for instance. It needs it."

"I love you."

"I know. But before you get up again, you should tell me what's going on."

And he told her that very night, even though he was reluctant. She didn't say anything for a long time.

"It must be hard, given that it has to do with him. Or your image of him. I get it."

He looked at her in the darkness.

"There was a report filed against him too. For manslaughter by negligence."

"What, on that day?"

"No, later. But because of what happened that day."

"Hey." Patricia ran a hand through his hair. "I never met your father. But I've heard stories, enough to have formed a solid picture of him. And whatever your father did, he felt exactly the same way you do, that some people shouldn't be walking around our city streets. They should be behind bars. That was what he was acting on, and you know it."

Vidar tried to find some comfort in this. But the stories she'd heard had come from him. And if he himself was wrong . . . strange that it mattered so much after so long, but it did.

He thought of his own daughter. God had been a presence in her home, but she hadn't grown up with him the way Vidar did. God might exist somewhere up there, but Amadia had never been raised to believe in something that hovered over other people's heads. For her, the question of guilt and innocence stopped with the secular world. Guilt and innocence had nowhere else to go. Only now did he realize he felt the same way.

He closed his eyes. There were a lot of things he wanted to ask his father, so many things he wondered about.

"But negligent manslaughter? Concealing evidence? The fact that, you know, I don't know what he was doing. The fact that he didn't say a word about it. That's almost the worst part. I was always so sure about him. He was so stable, sort of, so dependable. The fact that he didn't tell the police what he was doing, in the end, that worries me too. And then I think about Amadia."

"What about her?"

"That she might want to become a cop. It worries me."

Patricia laughed. "She wants to be an architect."

"What? She never said that."

She patted his chest. "You probably just weren't listening."

"But . . ."

"So don't worry about it." Patricia chuckled. "Amadia, a cop. Yeah, right. Now try to get some sleep."

"I can't."

He thought about David Linder. Had he fallen victim to the Tiarp Man? Where was he? Where was the Tiarp Man now? He'd never become much more than a figure with just a few points of reference, like glowing embers in the dark—pretty young in the year 1986, his voice, size 44 shoes, the composite sketch. It was like thinking about a shadow.

Patricia sighed in resignation and said, "The cleaner is on the counter, I used it this afternoon."

He kissed her hair, then went downstairs and sat at the kitchen table. Drank a glass of water. He debated getting out the whiskey and having more to drink; a bad idea. Instead he filled a small bucket with water and found the cleaner, grabbed a rag and walked through the house and stopped in front of the bookcase.

She hadn't been serious, he knew that. But that didn't mean it wasn't a good idea.

The books were all out of order after Amadia's move. She'd wanted to take everything that was hers, but couldn't find spots for them all in her small apartment in Nyhem. Quite a few had had to stay behind for the time being. They were shoved in here and there, stacked on top of one another; some were in piles on the floor.

Frida Östmark, Dad had scribbled in the notebook. *Where is she?* His frustration and uncertainty, his search, shone bright when you read between the lines.

Vidar took down all the books, stacked them on the floor, and began to dust the inside of the bookcase. It smelled old and comfortably familiar there in the darkness. He was still tipsy; when he moved, it felt like gentle bobbing inside his head.

It felt good to do something, to keep his hands occupied. He dipped them into the warm water and smelled the pine detergent. When he was finished, he replaced the books.

Exhaustion soon came over him. It felt good. He sat cross-legged on the floor. His back ached a bit, and his joints popped. He still felt churlish. Maybe it was just the lingering effects of the whiskey.

No, it was something else. He squinted through the darkness at the bookcase. There was something he had missed.

An old memory flickered to life—didn't it?—a flash of an image, free of context, from a very long time ago.

Vidar slowly got up and approached the bookcase, running his hand across the old spines. Like a dream, in the seconds after you wake up.

Stina Franzén died in the car on the way to the hospital. His father was driving. Gisela Mellberg survived, thanks to her husband. Vidar and Markus had found him.

Frida Östmark was never found.

Maybe the Tiarp Man got David Linder too.

Something had crept closer in recent days. He was convinced of it. Something or someone greater, older, stronger than Vidar himself, had begun to move so very close. Everything dies. That's just the way it is. But what dies may one day return.

His hand stopped at a bound book with no cover. Pretty slim. It looked grayish-blue in the darkness, but—there it was again, that memory—when Dad pulled it from the bookcase back in his childhood home, years ago, it was a deep ruby red. Vidar pulled it out.

Folk Songs of Halland. They were all there, the old songs he almost remembered, from southern Våxtorp to north of the Vallda area.

The pages were rough and dry. Toward the end of the volume was a bookmark. When he opened it to that page, he saw that the spread depicted Aron the Farmhand's encounter with Death.

It had grown perfectly silent between his temples. His fingers crackled with an invisible current between his skin and the book. The memories came back to him, and the fragments assembled into a whole. He almost couldn't breathe.

All of this. Had he forgotten?

81

One Saturday morning in the autumn of 1991, Sven picked up the phone and called Vidar.

"I need to run a few errands," he said. "But Bibbi's taking the car. I was wondering if you'd like to . . ." He coughed. It sounded harsh and painful. Seconds of silence followed before he spoke again, his voice strained: "If you could come. If we could take your car."

Vidar hadn't been there for a while, even though he lived only on the other side of the village. That's just what happens; you get too caught up in your own life. He had his house and his friends, new and old; he still hadn't completed his first year with the police. He worked a lot of overtime.

His dad looked pretty bad. Gaunt and pale, his cheeks sunken, he opened the front door and stepped out. Their car was still in the drive, which surprised Vidar. He'd assumed Mom would be gone already.

His father didn't comment on it. His hair was buzzed, just a centimeter or so long; he'd allowed a thin gray mustache to grow on his upper lip and he was wearing ill-fitting jeans, a heavy fall coat, and aviator shades with slender silver arms. He smiled slightly as he walked toward the car. Vidar opened the driver's-side door and stepped out, and was on his way around to open the passenger door when his dad waved him off in annoyance.

"No, don't get up. This isn't a damn taxi service."

"You cut off all your hair?"

"I didn't feel like dealing with it anymore."

Everything seemed a little slow and muddled, as if he had always just woken up, and sometimes he needed oxygen at the clinic. But that was really the only issue. His arms and back were still strong; he'd been chopping wood just a month or so ago. Vidar had come for a visit and asked if he wanted help, but he'd reacted the same way that time, just shook his head, waved Vidar off, muttering.

"Where are we going?" Vidar asked.

"North," said Sven. "Towards Vapnö."

It was silent in the car as they drove off.

"So where's Mom going?"

"I don't know," Sven said, facing out the window at the familiar world sweeping by outside, the fields surrounding Lake Tofta and Skedala. "Running errands."

Vidar would later learn that he was lying. Mom wasn't going anywhere. He wanted Vidar to take him, but he needed an excuse. As if he couldn't just call to say he wanted to spend time with his son.

"So how are you doing?" his dad asked. "With work and everything, I mean. Is it . . . You know, is it okay?"

"Sure. Lots to learn, of course. There's something new on basically every shift. But I'm learning."

"Good." Sven nodded thoughtfully. "That's good. You always were a fast learner. I remember that. And you're stubborn, too. When you decided to go and become a cop, no one could change your mind. And that's good, that's a credit to a fellow, you know."

"Thanks. I think. How've you been?"

"Oh, you know, not so bad. Life is calm and peaceful with your mother. Evy comes over sometimes for a cup of coffee. She asks how I'm doing, I ask how things are going with work and with Einar. And with her, of course. I think it's like last summer. From what I understand, Einar got a spot at the assisted living. I'm sure that's a help. Doesn't sound so bad to me."

"You would go crazy at an assisted living."

He chuckled. "Yes. I sure would. Vidar, I . . . You've always been so good to me. And I . . ." He fell silent and looked at his son's hand on the gear stick. Very slowly, he laid his own hand over Vidar's and squeezed it gently. "And I haven't always been so good to you. Or to Mom. I'm sorry for that."

They were approaching the city. His dad didn't move his hand.

"I don't think there's much I can teach you. But if there's anything you're curious about, or wondering about, or you want to know the best way to get someone like Björkman to cooperate, or whatever the hell it might be. You can always come to me. Even if it might not seem like it," he added. "I just wanted you to know that. That I'm here."

At last he moved his hand.

Vidar didn't say anything for a long time. Questions? He had so many. But right now he couldn't think of a single one. His dad's sudden touch had made everything go perfectly silent inside his head.

"And maybe you don't want to ask me," Sven went on. "In which case, I certainly understand. Or maybe there's nothing I can teach you; you already know more than I do. Sometimes it seems like the older I get, the less I know."

"I don't think that's true," said Vidar. "I'm sure I have tons of questions, things I've wondered about and stuff. It's its own special thing, being a cop, I've noticed."

Sven guffawed. Coughed. His airways squeaked.

"Indeed. You can say that again."

Much later, the questions would come to him. Multitudes of them, but by then it was too late. The dead can't reply, at least not the way you might prefer.

They drove past the clinic, up along Flottiljvägen. To the right waited the old white church; to the left, beyond the airfield, the expanses of Vapnödalen rested under a pale gray sky. The lovely days of September were gone. The colors of the earth had taken over:

gray, brown, dark green. Vidar found it surprisingly beautiful. No traffic as far as the eye could see, just straight strips of asphalt and fallow fields bending gently in the wind, the farms and mills visible in the distance, the massive Nyårsåsen a blue outer limit.

"Take a left down there, onto the straightaway. Then a left, up towards Tiarp. Can you slow down a little? I think I'm seeing it for . . . for the first time in a long time. Haven't been here for so many years."

Vidar hadn't heard it then. But when he thought back on it afterward, he understood. *I think I'm seeing it for the last time.* That's what Dad had been about to say. As if he knew, and was preparing himself.

82

"Didn't you have a colleague up here?" Vidar asked.

"David Linder," Sven said, a note of heaviness in his voice, as if he was reminded of a dark memory.

"Right. I heard from Evy that he moved to Sundsvall."

They cruised slowly on. Vidar took in the countryside that surrounded the car.

"Which house are we headed for?"

"Not a house. A clearing."

"A clearing?"

"Near Tiarp Farm. Go straight here, then up by a rock and to the left."

"What rock?"

But Dad didn't respond. He had sunk into his seat as though a burden had settled over him, and he fell silent. Vidar decided to wait.

After a while he saw it: a rock the size of a person, big and heavy, TIARP carved into it with rough capital letters. It was very old. In the evening it was illuminated from below, originally with burning torches. In the days before electricity, this was how you knew you had arrived home.

"It must have been here in Aron's days," Sven said suddenly. "Take a left here."

"Who?"

But Sven had returned to silence. Alongside the new, wide road they were on ran the old Tiarp Road, much narrower, built for a time when people traveled by horse or by foot. Old trees towered there, tall and thick. Sven coughed again. Vidar kept his eyes on the road, on the hollows in the land. They passed a field, then a pasture. No horses out now, just the magpies and jackdaws.

As they reached the end of the pasture, Sven said, his eyes on one of the farms, "Take a right here. Up into the trees."

Vidar had suspected that they might be on their way to the place where he and his dad had made a cast of the tire tracks, on that day five years ago. Five years. Had it been so long? Incredible.

But no, he'd never been here before. They were farther up onto Nyårsåsen now, in among the massive trees. Although it was the middle of the day, and bright, an unnatural matte gray curtain fell over them.

"I have no idea where we are."

"There's an old song," Sven said slowly. "About this place. Do you remember it? About Aron? I think you heard it as a boy."

"No."

"He was from Marbäck, Aron was. But he came west to serve as a farmhand here."

Then his dad began to sing, his voice dull and off-key, more a hum than a song, and the melody was so lonely and desolate that it seemed to become one with the rocks and the ridge, the water and the trees:

"Listen, children, and you shall hear a tale from days of yore, of a man out in Tiarp. Of how young farmhand Aron met Death one freezing night."

The deep forest had closed around them now. The light was sucked away and nature crept in through the vents, filling the car with a rich, earthy scent that felt eternal.

"You can stop here," Sven said softly. "We're here."

The trees had opened up a bit, leaving space for a clearing. It was large enough to turn a car around in; that was all. A narrow path ran farther into the forest to the right; another diagonally to the left. Vidar turned off the ignition.

"I don't recognize it," said Vidar. "That song."

"It's very old. I . . ." Sven shifted self-consciously in his seat. "I've done a lot of bad things, Vidar, I want you to know that. A lot of good things too, but you don't think about those very often. Maybe that's why I've been dwelling on it, the story of Aron. He'd been in Harplinge, on the other side of the ridge, with the farmer there, and was supposed to head home. It was nighttime. That's how the story starts."

And then he recounted it, the story of the horses and Death, and Aron, who had abandoned God and had no one to turn to up there on his wagon, with the horses. Vidar, although he was an adult man who'd seen a damn sight more than most, felt the eeriness spread through his body. When the horses came bolting down the ridge, back to the farmer in Vapnö, he was relieved that the story was over.

"Well," said Sven. "That was that. I found the song in a book. It's at home in the bookcase. I stuck a bookmark in it, it's probably still there, in case you ever want to read it."

"You have bookmarks?"

This got a laugh from his dad. "That isn't how I first heard the story, though." He was quiet for a moment. "He was your . . . let's see. Your great-great-grandfather's brother."

Vidar turned his head. "Who was?"

"Aron."

"We're related to Aron?"

"No one was more particular about the teachings of Christianity than my father. *Remember Aron,* he used to say, to scare me out of my wits. *When you allow yourself to doubt, you stand all on your own.* But I never repeated that to you." He looked at Vidar, suddenly uncertain. "Right? Or did I?"

"No, you didn't."

"I've started getting things mixed up. Having trouble remembering things. It's not easy." All of a sudden, Sven stared intently at some nearby trees, as if he'd caught a glimpse of an animal's shadow and was trying not to miss it in case it appeared again. "In order to solve it, it all has to come together. Or else it won't work. And you have to know where to look."

"Solve what, Dad?"

"Everything. It's all connected."

"What is?"

Sven turned to look at his son, his eyes oddly vacant.

"What?" Sven asked.

For a moment it looked like he might burst into tears. But nothing happened.

"It's okay," Vidar said.

Probably Dad needed to hear it. That's why he said it. But it didn't feel okay. This was awful. Vidar felt like a child again.

"I want you to know, I've been a good husband. I have. I love Bibbi more than I've ever loved any other woman on this earth. I've never even looked at another woman. But . . . you know Evy?"

"What about her?"

"I . . . it's hard to talk about."

"What, did something once happen between you?"

His father looked confused. "Happen? What do you mean, happen?"

"Well, the way you said it, it sounded like you had an affair."

"No, no. But sometimes . . . We went down to the sea a few times. That was nice. It made me feel calm. When we had an extra hour at work, or after our shifts, if we had time. And I . . . Maybe we shouldn't have done it."

"Okay, Dad. Don't worry. I know how it is."

His dad nodded contemplatively and gazed at the clearing. "Sometimes the hunters shoot animals here, even though it's outside the hunting grounds. It's a good spot for a hunter. He's got a wide-open view, and the animals have nowhere to go."

"Speaking of," Vidar said, clearing his throat.

"Hmm?"

"What are we doing here?"

"Didn't I say? It's not just moose and deer that have run into trouble here. Animals aren't all that's buried here." Sven looked through the windshield at the darkness that waited before them. The tall forest rising at the edge of the clearing, the paths leading deeper into the ridge, so deep you couldn't see where they went. "This is where it happened. This is where Aron met Death."

83

Animals aren't all that's buried here.

You have to know where to look.

Vidar recalled the ride in the car that day, almost thirty years ago; Dad's words and his slumping figure in the passenger seat. He hadn't had much time left, not even a month. Vidar hadn't understood. It had never occurred to him that it could have anything to do with the missing Frida Östmark; he hadn't even considered it. Not until now.

Doing the right thing.

That's the hard part.

How do you know what the right thing is?

Vidar looked at his hands, at how they held the steering wheel. For an instant they were much younger and smoother, it was a different car, and he wasn't alone. If he turned his head, if he just shifted his gaze slightly, he would catch a glimpse of his father in the seat next to him.

He got out of the car and looked around. The ground sloped steeply upward. The forests at home, around Marbäck, were old, but Nyårsåsen was a different story. The woods here were blacker, older, deeper. He didn't know his way around and could easily go astray. The forest was wary, as if it knew he was a stranger.

He tentatively walked in among the trees. Wondered who owned this part of the ridge.

Animals aren't all that's buried here.

Not having answers was terrible. He knew that. It had eaten at his father day and night, until the very end.

The forest closed around him. The colors began to drain away. He walked deeper into the ridge until he stood in the clearing. He got closer, studying the plants closest to the ground. The deep roots of the trees were like an intricate system of blood vessels beneath the soles of his shoes. How much could be left after thirty years?

The Tiarp Man could very well be dead.

He went back to the car, opened the trunk, and took out the bag from the hardware store, removing citric acid, ammonium molybdate, filter papers, paper, and pen.

He'd had a brainwave. He might be wrong. In which case he wanted to be on his own, which was why he hadn't mentioned this to anyone.

There were new methods these days. Scent dogs specially trained to search for human remains. Ground radar that bounces signals into the soil and absorbs them when they return, creating images of underground on a computer screen; the most recent of these could even create a 3D image. Electromagnetic induction if it's clayey soil. You can observe the world beneath your feet to a depth of several meters without a single scoop of the shovel.

But that's expensive.

Vidar drew a network of squares in his notebook; each box equaled one square meter. There wasn't much traffic down on the road. No warmth to speak of. Dark clouds were moving in from the sea. The wind was picking up. Awkwardly, uncertainly, he set to work.

Madness. Flights of fancy. A brainwave, an impulse, that's all this was. But he kept going as though urged onward by something he couldn't see, couldn't even put words to.

You wanted to tell me something that day. Show me.

Was this too much soil? No, it was probably the right amount. No, it felt like too much. The paper was sagging. No, it was okay. Shit, he dropped the citric acid. His shoes survived unscathed, but he got some on his pants. God, it smelled awful.

Out with the filter papers, soil, mix a little ammonium molybdate with some citric acid, observe the reaction. The darker the purple, the greater the variance. When he was finished with the first quadrant, he turned the filter over and marked it with a 1, the next with a 2. He pasted them on a piece of paper and slowly a rough map of the area appeared, a map for locating a grave.

Hadn't he already done this part? No, he'd started over there: one, two, three, four, five. Yes, that was right. He was here now.

They all turned out the same. No variation in color whatsoever. No, wait, a little. There. That one was darker.

Fuck, it got on his shoes.

The rain hung in the air but refused to fall. He stepped around the clearing, careful with where he set his feet. He needed all the daylight he could get. It was going faster now; he was learning. The trees of the forest rustled a warning.

He straightened up, holding a piece of filter paper in his hand. He considered his notebook, the network. He only had two squares left now, and then he would have covered the whole area. Or rather, he was out of filter paper.

In the far, far distance he could make out the glitter of the city. Sometimes the white headlights of a car rushed by out on the main road. He took the last two samples, got a flashlight from the car so he could see better; he needed it now.

He carefully began to place the filter papers in order. Purple, purple, purple everywhere, lighter and darker.

He studied it carefully.

The top right corner was noticeably darker than the others. He turned on his bright headlights, fetched a common garden shovel from the trunk, and got to work.

One to two meters. That's typical. Perpetrators have neither the energy nor the time to dig deeper.

He set the shovel to the ground and stepped on it. The soil complained. Dust whirled against the light. Slowly the ground opened into a hole. He hacked his way through thick roots. Behind him, a pile grew. He listened for steps, voices, the bark of a dog. Wondered what he would say if anyone happened by.

The headlights cast long shadows. He was hot from the hard work. His hands got dirty and his shoulders and back started to ache. Crows cawed. In the distance, the incessant glitter of the city. He'd climbed down into the hole. It was hip-deep now. Bugs and creepy-crawlies moved invisibly through the soil, across his shoes. His feet, hair, and back all felt itchy.

How long had he been at it? He took out his phone to check the time. The glow of the screen flickered across the earth.

He stopped. The light had revealed something other than soil. He took out the flashlight and aimed it into the hole.

He sank to his knees and could smell the dirt.

It was perfectly silent. Vidar could hear his own panting breaths in the dark.

He cautiously excavated around the decaying fabric. He felt dizzy, and it took some effort to focus his eyes. Steady hand now. He chopped at the soil and some was flung into his mouth. At last he could see.

The beam of the flashlight shone sharp and cold on a bundle of bones. At what had once been a human hand.

84

That was the night he went down to the pub at Lilla Torg. In the days that followed, everyone heard about the excavation, of course. The media got a tip and made their way to the ridge with cameras and microphones, unloaded all their crap and stood at a distance, trying to climb up the tall trees and insinuating themselves into the old farmlands to get a better look. One poor guy, a journalist with one of the evening papers, got so far up a tree that he couldn't get back down again and had to be rescued by the fire department. The local farmers followed the spectacle from a distance. It was almost like you could forget there was something gruesome going on.

Those working at Nyårsåsen were strictly forbidden to discuss it. You were not to talk to anyone who didn't belong there, but somehow information got out anyway. First that they had found bones and then that the bones were human remains; considering all the commotion and the broad response, this wasn't exactly unexpected news, and then it leaked that the remains were of an adult who had been there for at least ten years but probably much longer.

The newspapers listed possible cases. At the top of everyone's list was Frida Östmark, and suspicion was aimed at the perpetrator known as the Tiarp Man.

Nothing was mentioned about how the discovery had been made, just that it was *in connection with a police operation,* which could mean anything and was interpreted as such too.

Something was wrong. If that was Frida Östmark up there, and Sven had known about it, why hadn't he said anything—either to Vidar or to the police? The case of the Tiarp Man and his victims had dogged Sven until his dying day. How could he have kept it to himself? It made no sense.

How had Vidar gotten caught up in this? Once again he was in the middle of a yet-unsolved riddle, although so much time had passed. Just a few months ago he'd been preoccupied with his feelings about his daughter's move and the new era that awaited him; he'd been deeply absorbed in the business of everyday life, tasks big and small. And then, one sleepless night, something had come to him, a great and vast force that pushed him onward, into the old book of folk songs and up to the ridge. The feeling hadn't returned since, but it had left him shaken.

A great and vast force that frightened him.

Vidar wanted nothing more than to be rid of the cold feeling of free fall that had come over him in the forest. Everything else drained away—anger, relief, fear, confusion. The only constant was the case.

"Vidar," Patricia said one night as she sat next to him on the sofa. "What's *wrong*?"

"I don't know." He swallowed. "I don't know. I'm just . . ."

A heavy spring rain was falling on Marbäck, pattering against the windows. He took out his phone and called Markus again. The phone rang on the other end, but it sounded oddly echoey. Patricia raised her eyebrows, turned her head, and gazed toward the front hall.

Vidar stood up and went to open the door.

He was standing there in the dark, his hands in his coat pockets, his hair a mess and stubble on his chin, the phone ringing in his hand, and he looked at Vidar with a strange sadness in his eyes.

"Hi," said Markus. "Can I come in?"

85

The ceiling light shone down between them at the kitchen table, filling their faces with shadows. Markus looked at him, his eyes radiating serious doubt.

"I need to know one thing. How did you end up there?"

"What do you mean?"

"You know what I mean."

"No I don't."

"How did you know where to look?"

"You saw. I showed you the grid of samples in the car."

"But how did you know to take samples in that particular spot?" Markus lowered his voice. "I know how. For the same reason you removed the blood evidence from the station. What is going on with you, Vidar? What are you up to? How did you know where to look?"

"I didn't."

"For the sake of your father, Vidar. You need to tell me. About this and the blood samples. Otherwise . . . I just don't know."

"It wasn't me," Vidar said, but there was no weight to his words.

He couldn't even be angry. He had no energy left in his body.

Vidar wondered if Patricia was listening from the sofa in the living room. Probably.

"We went up there once. To the clearing. He asked me to drive him there, this was about a month before he died."

He recounted that day, concisely and reluctantly. Markus noticed, and leaned toward him. The shadows on his face shifted under the glow of the ceiling light.

"I don't know why he didn't make it more clear," said Vidar. "Why tell me all of that, and still not tell me everything? I don't get it. That she was buried there, I mean."

Markus looked confused. "Who?"

"You know, Frida. It's her, isn't it?"

"It's David Linder." Markus took a small Dictaphone from his pocket. "I think you should listen to this."

86

The old woman had a room at the Pålsbo nursing home in the neigh-borhood of Bäckagård a few kilometers from Tylösand. Markus had called ahead, and when he arrived she was sitting in her room with yesterday's *Hallandsposten* in hand, deeply absorbed in one of the articles.

"I think the text is so tiny these days," she said.

"Is it okay if I sit here?"

The woman looked up, confused.

"Yes, of course. What's going on?"

"Didn't they tell you I was coming?"

She shook her head. "But I'm not hungry anyway."

"Hungry? But I . . ."

"You can have something to drink, though, if you like."

"I'm a police officer. My name is Markus. I'm here regarding your son, David."

Long seconds of silence. The woman dropped the newspaper. "I haven't spoken to him in . . . well, my goodness. We had an argument, you know. He didn't want anything more to do with me."

"What did you argue about?"

"Why, the farm, of course. He wanted to sell it. I said that was terrible, how could he do such a thing? Then, one day, he was just gone. I never thought we would be that sort of family, but suddenly we were. Such a tragedy, when you think about it."

When Vidar listened to her through the tiny speaker on the Dicta-phone, he recognized her voice, the way she spoke: as if she still understood and carried all those old emotions, but couldn't stand them anymore so had stopped feeling them.

"That must have been a big argument you had, you and David."

"Huge. But that's just the way it is, you know, some things are practically holy. David took over when Hasse got too weak. He wasn't old when he got sick, Hasse, and it happened fast. So David took over the work. I never imagined he would do that to us, to me and to Hasse and our entire . . . But he did. But before that, he was actually a police officer, my David. Did you know that?"

"Yes," Markus replied. "I was aware of that."

"He started right before Palme died, you know. That was a differ-ent era. My son wanted to make a difference, he said. Hasse thought he could just as well do that at home on the farm, but he didn't under-stand what David meant. I'm sorry, I'm prattling on. But there aren't many others here; I don't get to talk that much these days."

"I need to ask you a question," Markus said, "if that's . . . Do you recall how he was in the days before he moved? Whether he did any-thing unusual, or something like that?"

"He was very upset about what was going on up in Tiarp," she said. "He mentioned it several times. That girl they found in a car there."

"Before he disappeared, you mean?"

"No, no. Right after it happened. That was the night they shot Palme. It was such a dark time. Everything that happened afterwards, it seems like it wouldn't have happened otherwise. At least not the same way. Maybe that's true of my David too. That's why he . . ."

Her mind was starting to wander now. One thought led to the next, which came straight to her lips.

"Right, because I'm wondering, David, do you know if anyone wanted him . . ."

"What?"

"Well, could there have been someone who wanted to hurt him? Could he have made an enemy there towards the end?"

"Hurt him? Absolutely not. Not my David. And an enemy, my goodness, no, no. Just us, if anyone. No, everyone liked David. That was because he was considerate. Like I said, that mess up in Tiarp, it hit him so hard. I was up that night, couldn't sleep. I was taking care of Hasse, you know. He had started to have such terrible nights. So I actually heard the news on the radio when it went out. About Palme, I mean. David, too, he was awake and had come home by then."

Markus's voice on the tape sounded more urgent now, and closer. "David had been working, you mean?"

"No, he had just been out."

"Do you remember when this was? That is, when did he go out, and when did he come home?"

"He went out at ten-thirty and came home around twelve-thirty."

"You sound pretty sure of that."

"Hasse usually fell asleep at ten and slept for a half hour, then he would usually wake up and have a few difficult hours before he fell asleep again. And he woke up just before the lights went out in David's cottage, I could see it from the bedroom window, you know. He still lived on the farm, but in his own house, which he and Hasse had fixed up. We called it the cottage. And the light came on again around twelve-thirty. So that's when he came home. I'm sure of that. And my goodness, that was the night they shot the prime minister, so of course I remember. Everyone remembers."

"What had he been doing, do you think? David, I mean, between ten-thirty and twelve-thirty."

"He'd been doing some side job for a friend in Tiarp, helping someone with repairs or something like that. I don't remember. I thought it seemed odd, for him to go out like that. But he said he needed it to clear his head. Working as a police officer isn't easy, I understand," she added. "I just don't know how you manage. Do you go out at night too?"

"Not very often, actually. Do you recall whether David had a car around this time?"

"Yes, of course. You have to, on the farm there. He had a good, reliable vehicle."

"Do you remember what kind?"

"One of those big ones, with a bed."

"Like a utility vehicle?"

"Yes, I think that's what they're called."

"Has anyone else talked to you about this?"

"What, today?"

"No, no. In general. Around the time when he disappeared, for instance."

"No," she said vaguely. "No, I don't think so. Or maybe one time, but that was so many years ago. It was an old colleague of his. He wanted to talk."

"About this? I mean, about David and the night Palme died?"

"I think so. But, you know . . ."

"Do you remember his name? The officer?"

"Oh, no. I sure don't. But I do remember that he used to work with David. And he had a terrible cough."

"Could his name have been Sven?"

"Yes, maybe that was it," said the old woman. "It was so peculiar, as I recall. He wanted to know my son's blood type." She laughed. "Can you imagine?"

"What is your son's blood type?"

"B. That's what it used to be, anyway, there's more to it now."

"The Rh factor? Positive or negative?"

"Right, that's it. David is B-positive."

"And you told Sven this too? The man who visited you."

"Yes, I suppose I did."

87

Vidar stared at the table.

"What . . ."

"It would explain why he was never caught. He was a cop. He knew how to avoid leaving evidence behind."

"What do you mean, he didn't leave any evidence? You were at Snapparp," said Vidar. "It was a damn mess. Evidence everywhere."

"But did we get him? No. There was nothing there." Markus shrugged. "He knew how to avoid leaving the *wrong* evidence behind. Same difference." He held out his hand and stuck out the thumb. "He has a documented link to the first victim." He stuck out his index finger. "He withholds that information." He added his middle finger. "He lies about his alibi on the night of the murder. In other words, he doesn't have one." Ring finger. "He has access to a car of the type that was observed at the scene of the crime, at the time the crime was committed." Markus unfolded his pinkie finger. "He lives right nearby. And that's not all. He has a documented link to the intended third victim, Gisela Mellberg. The murders stop when he quits the force. And: *He quits the force.* Why would he do that? Why go through all of that training just to work for a year or two and then become a farmer? I don't buy it. I think he got scared. And, not least, he has blood type B-positive. Linder has the same blood type as the perpetrator." He threw out his hands. "I almost don't have enough fingers."

Vidar didn't respond. Recalibrating, recasting a victim to a perpetrator—it wasn't easy.

"The blood," he said. "From Franzén's car."

"We haven't got a response from NFC yet. But assuming I'm right, and I'm pretty convinced I am, it won't be any help."

"Why not?"

"Because Linder doesn't have a criminal record. I checked. So that rules out his being in the DNA database. The elimination database didn't exist in his day, and even if it had, his sample would have been removed from it once he left the force."

"But the skeleton. DNA can be extracted from bone, can't it?"

"It's unlikely in this case. The skeleton is in awfully bad condition, the ground is damp, and that moisture is groundwater. Thirty years is a long time. It's too badly deteriorated."

"But you're sure he's the one I . . . that you found him?"

Markus nodded.

"Dental records. That worked, in the end."

"How did he die?"

"We don't know. Not yet. But there's one more thing. It explains why we found Robert in Snapparp. David Linder was seeing Ylva Sandström in 1990 and 1991, less than ten minutes by car from Snapparp. He could have gone to her place right after he stashed the van in Snapparp. The times fit. And I don't know . . ." Markus continued, taking a piece of paper from his back pocket. When he unfolded it, Vidar saw the composite sketch that had been published almost thirty years ago. "It certainly resembles Linder. About as much as we'd expect, from a sketch based on witness statements. And we have to keep in mind that she didn't get a very good look at him. He was wearing a mask."

Vidar cast a doubtful eye upon the sketch.

"Right," he said, without much conviction. "Sure." There was something else about what Markus had said. "He had a link to Gisela Mellberg, you said? What was that?"

"After Stina Franzén was murdered, Gisela Mellberg came across a little boy near the house where she lived and brought him home to his parents. Apparently the boy was some sort of witness to Franzén's murder. According to one note, David Linder went up there to take down Mellberg's information. So he could have had his eye on her for a while." Markus looked disgusted. "He met them through work. Makes me fucking sick."

"And Frida Östmark?"

"There's likely a link there too. We're looking in the archives now. David Linder, the Tiarp Man." Markus said it as though he was trying it out. "Damn, what a bombshell this'll be in the media. And at the station."

"But what would the motive have been?"

Markus raised his eyebrows. "Is that necessary to know, as a cop?"

"You're the cop here. Not me."

Markus rolled his eyes. "Well, have fun with that, then. It's not my job to dig through his brain, that's up to someone else. Sadistic psychopaths are everywhere."

"But was he one?" Vidar persisted. "Shouldn't there have been signs?"

"Maybe there were, but no one noticed. Who knows? We've had cases where there was a lot less than this, and we were still sure we were right. Come on, Vidar. The evidence. The blood."

"I just don't see how you can believe I took them."

"Who else would it have been?"

"Well, not me."

Vidar stared at his friend, who stared right back. At last, Markus relented. "If you say so, I believe you. That leaves that question unanswered, too."

"What's the other open question?"

"Well," said Markus, "who put Linder in the ground? It's not like he buried himself."

Vidar shook his head. He hadn't thought that far. Everything was unclear, muddled. Sharp edges had grown blurry. His mind felt sluggish.

"No idea."

"If there's anything more, you have to tell me. And you have to do it now."

"Like what?"

"I mean, your father pointed out the exact location where we, where *you*, found David Linder. What does that suggest? That he knew where he was buried. And how could he know that? Either someone told him, and I can't imagine who that could have been, or else . . ."

"Look, you don't understand. I'm the one who started digging him up. I was totally beat afterwards. Physically, I mean. And I had only, well, you saw how far I got. And look, in 1991, my dad . . ." he began, but trailed off.

It felt too private, almost shameful. Like disclosing a vulnerability you didn't want anyone else to know about.

"You don't understand how sick he was," he whispered, as the memories came back to him. He didn't want to see them, wished they would go away. "He never could have gotten a body in the ground, he wouldn't have had the strength to dig that much. His lungs couldn't have handled it. It would have been physically impossible. It wasn't him. I'm not saying that as his son, but as a former cop."

"So I guess that means he wasn't alone? He must have had help."

"But who would have helped him?"

"No idea."

At that moment, Vidar knew what he had to do. But he couldn't say so to Markus.

"Okay," Markus said instead. "I don't know if I believe you, but for the time being let's say I do." He seemed to be getting ready to leave. "Is there anything else I need to know?"

Vidar blinked. It all stood clear to him. He could see himself excusing himself, getting up, going to the front hall, putting his hand in the inner pocket of his jacket.

On the sofa, Patricia turned her head.

"Everything okay?"

"Yeah," Vidar said softly, the way you do when you've finally reached some sort of conclusion after a lot of back-and-forth. "Everything's fine."

He saw himself going back to the kitchen table, placing the black notebook, the last little shard of his father's life that had been his alone, in front of Markus.

But when he blinked again, he saw nothing more than Markus's concerned face across the table.

"Is there, Vidar?"

He shook his head.

"No. No, if there were, I would have said so."

88

I've done a lot of bad things, Vidar, I want you to know.

He'd been so relieved when he found her, not just for his own sake, but for his dad's. It was as though the son had been able to accomplish something his father hadn't managed, hadn't had time, to finish. There was a greater, deeper meaning to it, the magnitude of which he hadn't quite understood until he found those old bone remnants in the earth. As if he could exhale now. That's how it had felt.

And it was never even her. It was David Linder all along. But Vidar wasn't yet able to understand what that meant.

There was still someone he could talk to. Someone he could trust. Someone who would tell him the truth, no matter how unpleasant it was.

There were still months left before her stroke. She was chipper and lively, a frumpy woman with bushy silver hair, a raucous, loud laugh, and merry eyes; her mind was sharp. When he pulled up in her driveway, she was already on the step, watching him intently.

"If it isn't Vidar Jörgensson!" She chuckled. "What on earth would such a fine fellow be doing here?"

"I happened to be in the neighborhood."

"I haven't seen you since you were twenty-five. Get over here."

He climbed the steps to the porch.

"The spitting image of your father, I see."

Evy came up only to his chest. He bent down to give her a hug. She smelled like ancient furniture and heavy old-lady perfume; she had the hands of an old woman but the eyes of a cop.

"Don't be shy," Evy said against his shoulder. "I may be old, but I won't break, you know." She squinted. "Why, what's the matter? You look all shaken up."

"Let's go sit down before we get to that. If you've got the time?"

"Time is all I have. Time and coffee."

She showed him into the old house at Norteforsen. The walls were decorated with colorful artwork; there were photos of her grandchildren in the bookcase and hanging in tidy rows on the wall. The fridge was adorned with a to-do list and children's artwork: stick figures and cheerful watercolor flags. *To Grandma*, they read.

"I ended up with so many," she said as she prepared the coffeemaker. "Grandkids, I mean. So they paint these wonderful things for me when they come to visit. Aren't they clever?"

"Very."

This was his first time here. She used to live in Kärleken. That's where they'd visited her, him and Markus. That was almost thirty years ago now, after her brother's accident. He recalled Einar Bengtsson's motionless figure in the wheelchair, how Evy had tenderly brought a glass with a straw to his lips. Was her brother still alive? Probably not.

The coffeemaker sputtered to life. She put out milk and sugar and gestured at Vidar to have a seat on the kitchen bench, which was rough and old. Vidar waited for her to sit down across from him, but Evy remained standing and looked troubled.

"Could you . . . if I sit down, could you get the coffee when it's ready? It takes me such a long time to get back up again."

"Of course."

The old woman, who suddenly seemed much more like a very old woman than she did a cop, sank down on the short end of the table in relief. There was a deck of cards on the table. She picked it up with able hands and began to shuffle the cards, her fingers and movements still surprisingly nimble and deft. The cards swished. Vidar asked about the house, how she and Ronnie had ended up here, what her days were like now that she was a widow.

"What brings you here?" she wondered.

"My dad."

Evy lifted away a section of cards and shuffled them again.

"I've been thinking I should visit his grave sometime, when I'm in Breared. But that doesn't happen so often these days; I don't quite have the energy. It's a pain for me to take the car and so forth."

"You're probably there more than I am."

"You say that like you feel guilty about it." The sputtering of the coffeemaker ceased. "I think we could have a cup now."

Vidar stood up.

"You shouldn't feel guilty," he heard her say behind him as he poured coffee into two white mugs. "There's no reason to. The dead can manage without us. We're the ones who need them. And they're always there."

He placed a mug in front of Evy. She poured in a splash of milk, a sugar cube, and stirred.

"I'm here about Stina Franzén and Frida Östmark," he said. "You worked with Dad back then."

"Sure did. Hell, that case just about did him in." She gazed at him curiously; one white eyebrow had quirked up a little bit on her wrinkled forehead. "But you must remember that too, don't you? You must have been old enough by then."

"I wasn't home very much. We had drifted apart. It wasn't like anything in particular had happened, it just . . ."

"Yes, it just happened," Evy chimed in. "It's not uncommon."

Vidar nodded and placed a notebook on the table. He turned to a blank page, clicked his pen, and took a drink of the hot coffee.

"Do you remember what he was like then? During '88 and '89, for instance."

"Your father had a notebook, as I recall," she said, with her eyes on Vidar's notepad. "It was small and black; he usually kept it in his breast pocket. Kind of like that one, that you have. But now, you're not working for the police again, are you? I heard you had quit."

"No, I'm not. I'm asking for . . . it's for personal reasons."

"Good." Evy took a sip of her coffee. "I'm so tired of cops."

"Have they been here?"

"They certainly have. That old colleague of yours, what's his name, Magnus?"

"Markus?"

"Him and someone else. But I didn't want to talk to them."

"What did they want?"

"To ask about Tiarp and your dad, of course. I worked on that case for a while too." She adjusted her glasses, stroked the deck of cards. "Well, listen, what did you say, '88, '89 . . . that . . . I actually have kind of a hard time talking about your father. That I do. But not . . . how should I put this? I suppose it's just as well you know this. I was married to Ronnie for fifty years before he died. But in the late eighties, I was awfully enamored with your father, I want you to know. I told myself I loved him. And hey, maybe I did. But I never told anyone. Well, except for you, right now."

She said this so straightforwardly and confidently, as though she were just informing Vidar of what she planned to make for dinner, that he didn't know how to react.

"Whoa. Okay. Did he know?"

Evy shook her head.

"I never told him either. Your father didn't understand that sort of thing." She looked at the cards and turned one faceup. King of clubs. She placed it on the table. "Or maybe he did. I don't know. But it didn't matter. He had Bibbi, and I had Ronnie. Everything has its own place, you know. Everything has its time. So nothing ever came of it."

"But, nothing ever happened between you or anything?"

"Happened?" Evy looked confused. "What do you mean, happened?"

"Well," Vidar said gingerly, a rising sense of discomfort in his belly, "did you . . ."

"Oh." Evy waved her hand dismissively. "No, no. We had our own stuff going on. We went down to look at the sea sometimes, stuff like that, which was nice. But that was all."

He considered her carefully. "Nothing at all?"

"No. But it was tough. No one can help the way they feel, as I like to tell my kids and grandkids, but you can almost always help the actions you take. Whether you act on your feelings. And I never did. But what I'm saying is, working with him got tough. He just kept getting worse, too. It was difficult in a lot of ways."

"Worse, you mean . . ."

"Physically. He was sick. But, yes, in a mental sense too, absolutely. He got . . ." Evy hesitated to say the word "dark." She nodded at the memory. "Mm-hmm. Very dark. A report was filed against him, did you hear about that?"

"I did."

"It was dismissed, of course. But it still took a toll on him. Worst of all, though, was when that Linder fella moved away. After that, it was as if . . . well, it was as if Sven turned inward. He never came back out. He had stopped working shortly before that, but we still kept in touch a little. After Linder moved, we had almost none. Sven liked him—I think he missed him a lot."

Vidar sat very still. "David Linder, he was a cop, right?"

"He worked with us for a short time, yes." Evy nodded, squinting as though she were trying to catch a glimpse of the past through a thick fog. "Eighty-six, started around the new year. But then he quit. Right." She tapped a finger on the table as if in confirmation. "That's right. His father had a farm up there in Vapnö somewhere. His name was Hasse, Hasse Linder. Hasse was a folkracer when he was young, if I remember correctly, and I think he even won some competitions. But then he took over his parents' farm and had a baby. That was David, that baby, and he became a cop. Now there was a competent young man, as I recall, and a kind person too. But when Hasse got sick he couldn't take care of the farm anymore, and David had been raised to farm. He'd even worked as a lead farmhand before, I think. So he quit the force and took over the farm instead."

Whatever kind of solitaire she was playing, it didn't seem to be going anywhere. Evy dropped the cards and crossed her arms beneath her heavy bust, gazed out the window. Spring was in bloom out there. It felt hopeful.

"But he moved?" Vidar asked in a quiet voice.

"The winter of '90 and '91. Or maybe the spring of '91. He lived by himself, the fella, but he'd started seeing a gal down in Genevad. She had her own farm, with chickens and so forth, so they didn't live together. He would go see her in the evenings and so on. I've always imagined she was the one who convinced him to leave the family farm and move away, seek his fortune in the north instead. The farm wasn't doing well, not well at all. It wasn't Hasse's or David's fault, it was just a sign of the times. It wasn't easy to be a farmer in Sweden in the early nineties, with the crisis. Lots of people went under. But if I'm not mistaken, his parents were terribly angry when he said he wanted to sell. Broke off contact, they did. Can you imagine? With your own child."

"But how do you know all of this? If you didn't know him."

Evy was flustered.

"I think Sven told me."

"What did he say?"

"You know, I have such trouble remembering things. It was so long ago."

"But it's important to me that you try to recall."

His tone was quite harsh, and Evy noticed but didn't comment.

"Right, no, I don't remember."

"Do you recall," said Vidar, who maintained his composure and made a note in his notebook, "how they talked about it? Around headquarters, that is?"

"Well, there's no law against relocating." Evy shrugged. "I guess he was just sick of everything. I don't think he liked the farm life, but that's just my guess."

"What did Dad think?"

"Same as me." Evy smiled tentatively, and as she did Vidar could see a hint of what she must have looked like back then, thirty years earlier. "When your father didn't know the specifics of something, he usually felt the same way I did. I miss him so terribly sometimes. I want you to know that, Vidar."

Vidar didn't know quite what to say. He looked at his notebook. He had only two questions left. The two that would be the most painful to ask.

"It seems like a lot was happening around Dad in those last few years. I don't know if you . . . I found a box that belonged to him when my daughter moved out. I realized it had material from a preliminary investigation inside, so I handed it over to Markus. Maybe that's why he came—no, I know that's why he came here to talk to you. It seems there was material from these cases, Franzén and Östmark, in that box. Material that Dad," he concluded, "took."

"I see." Evy blinked. "And?"

"And it was never returned. And this happened after he left the force, probably in early 1991. When he no longer had access to the archive."

Evy's lips formed a little O.

"Okay."

"You didn't know about this?"

"What did you say, material from . . ."

"It's physical evidence. Blood. The only evidence that can be linked directly to the perpetrator." Vidar gazed at her expectantly. "I understand if you don't want to talk to the police. But I hope you will talk to me."

Evy mechanically ran her hand across the tablecloth, as though she were trying to smooth out a wrinkle only she could see.

"Your father was a lovely person, Vidar. And a good police officer. But . . . you have to realize, at the end there, there was such a darkness surrounding him. He was in such bad shape. I just wanted to help him. He asked if he could go down and look through those boxes one last time, and I didn't have the . . . I couldn't say no. It was wrong of me, I know that. But I . . ." She sighed. "I remember, when he left that day, he had only been down there a little while . . . and I watched him go. And I felt such a pang in my chest, not just because he was who he was. But because of what I had done."

"Did he tell you what it was all about?"

"Just that he wanted to go down and take one last look at those old documents. That was all. Sven wanted to catch that bastard more than anyone. So if he, what did you say, he took something?"

"Physical evidence."

"If he took something with him, all I can imagine is that he was trying to solve the case on his own. If there's anything you learn when you grow old, it's that sometimes it's best not to know."

He looked at her for a long time. He had one last question. The hardest one. Something about her words made him suspect he already knew the answer.

"Here's the thing," he said quietly, "Linder has been found. Up in Tiarp."

Evy's eyes went wide. "What on earth?"

"Maybe you read about it in the paper? That's him."

"My God, how awful."

Vidar's stomach sank. He cocked his head. She had surprised him.

"You must have been very good at lying once upon a time," he said cautiously. "But not anymore. You have to tell me, Evy. All of it."

She didn't say anything for a very long time. Then she spoke, and she related the story to Vidar that evening as though she'd been carrying it all her life without knowing what to do with it, and had finally found a way out. The burden had been so heavy, and the surrender of it felt so powerful, that it was as if it now belonged to him instead.

89

Evy had been at home in Kärleken. She, Ronnie, and the kids had eaten dinner, and as it got on toward nine o'clock the kids went to bed and she and her husband settled down in front of the TV. She had just called Einar and spoken to the night-shift staff at the assisted living to check in about tomorrow's visit, what time she should come by.

Ronnie had a hand on her thigh, and she was gently rubbing the back of his neck. He was always sore there after a day of work. Ronnie Carlén had been working as a truck driver out at Nordiska Filt for almost twenty years, and he intended to keep doing it for about twenty more. As long as his neck held out. He'd been in a bus accident as a child, and ever since that neck of his had been weak and temperamental.

She sat next to her husband, looking at his hand on her thigh and wishing it wasn't his. It was a painful truth, but she couldn't help it.

The phone in the kitchen rang and she went to answer it. When she heard his voice, her chest felt warm inside. She'd expected it to be Einar's assisted living, but it wasn't.

"Hello, Sven. How are you doing these days? Do you miss us?"

It was late March of 1991. He laughed. She liked that.

"Maybe a little."

"How did it go, that . . ." she began, then lowered her voice. "That thing I helped you with? Did you see what you wanted to see?"

She was referring to the documents in the archive.

"Yes," Sven said, a little evasively. "Yes, I did. It was good."

His voice was hollow in some way that she couldn't quite put into words, but he didn't sound the way he used to. He sounded weaker, depleted. He said he was doing well but might need to ask her for one last favor. *Last*, that's the way he put it. She hadn't thought anything of it at the time.

"Okay?"

"I'm sure everything will be fine. But if I haven't called you by ten-thirty, I'd like you to go to this address. Do you have a pen and paper?"

This was the first time he'd asked her to write anything down. After all these years, he knew she didn't need to do so, to remember anything. But now he was asking her anyway. This was how she first suspected it was important. She jotted down the address.

"And what should I do if . . ."

"Just wait. It's probably nothing. But in the unlikely event that I don't call, just go there. You'll understand when you arrive."

She went back to the sofa. Ronnie was about to doze off, and she didn't mention any of this to him. When he went upstairs, she stayed put and watched the clock.

It was dark outside. She had to check the address against the atlas in the bookcase. It confused her. The fact that Sven was going to see David wasn't unusual; they'd always seemed to have a special bond. But what did any of this have to do with her?

Ten-thirty arrived. No call, just silence and solitude in the house. She waited another fifteen minutes, then took the car keys from the dish in the hall and drove off, anxiety throbbing in her chest. She took the county highway toward Holm and turned off at Vapnö.

:::

This was her first visit to the Linder farm. She stopped on the edge of the road nearby and softly closed the driver's-side door. In the rural silence, away from the city, she could hear all the sounds of the forest and nature. They were obtrusive, keen and sharp.

She took the flashlight from the glove box and headed for the farm. Sven's car was there, dark and still. The hood was cool. She tried the door. Locked.

There didn't seem to be anyone home. Evy walked toward the farmhouse. The ground here was gravel and dirt. She could make out footprints leading from Sven's car to the house. Then back again. She stopped. More footprints here by the gate.

Another pair. He wasn't alone.

She peered down the road. Where had they gone? Toward Tiarp or over toward Kvibille? She bet on Tiarp and stepped through the gate, following the county highway. She turned off her flashlight and waited for her eyes to adjust to the darkness.

She passed Tiarp Farm, where the big rock stood dimly but warmly illuminated in the black night. The sound of the breeze came and went in waves, rustling the trees and humming through the fields.

Evy headed up into the forest. She was close to him now. Could almost make him out among the shadows.

She walked. She turned back, spun about, or maybe she was getting dizzy. Everything looked the same. Nyårsåsen towered ahead of her, massive and black.

Then she saw something. There, among the trees. Movement. She approached carefully. Her heart was pounding so hard that she wished she had never come, and she thought of Ronnie, asleep in their bed, Ronnie, who loved her, who was the father of her children, who didn't even know she was here.

"Sven?"

She flicked on the flashlight. He turned his head, terrified, hissing at her to *turn it off, turn it off*.

He was on his knees in the dark, an emaciated, pale figure with wide-open eyes and his hair standing on end. His breath came in gasps, his airways squeaking and rattling. Blood spatter on his face.

"Sven. Oh my God, Sven, what happened?"

"You have to help me, Evy." He was having trouble breathing. "You have to help me. I can't do it on my own. He's too heavy."

90

Adrenaline coursed through her blood. She stepped toward him, her legs trembling, and saw the remains of young David Linder lying at the edge of a fresh grave.

Sven Jörgensson had gentle eyes and hands that looked soft; he possessed a thoughtful, taciturn nature and had a crooked smile, but now he was on his knees way out in the wilderness of the Tiarp forest, and he looked so terribly alone.

Sven had paid a visit to David, who was surprised but apparently happy to see him. They took an evening walk to chat; David was rather inebriated and unsteady on his feet. Sven said he understood now, that he'd found the missing evidence: the police report about an assault at Grand Hotel, Snapparp, the fake alibi, even David's blood type. Everything would work out, it would be just fine. As long as David accompanied him into town, to see their old friends at the station. That was all he had to do; they could do it together.

But it didn't work out. Sven had maintained his composure and kept talking. He asked David why he'd done it, treated them so horribly, Stina and Frida, Gisela and Robert, and whether there were more. Where Frida Östmark was. Sven didn't even lose his cool when he told David that it was Sven's own son who had found Robert Mellberg in the van in Snapparp.

David had been taken aback: "What the fuck are you saying? That it was me? What are you doing? Stop it."

Sven reached out his hand. "Come on, David."

David said that Sven was out of his mind, had gone crazy; David would report him for slander. He was just a farmer, struggling to keep his farm from going under. In the end he was shouting, saying that he would do something stupid if Sven didn't shut up and get out of there.

Sven stood there, his hand reaching out, feeling insane for not realizing sooner. That distorted voice on the phone. His physique, even his shoe size. The geography. Everything fit. This is what all his free time had given him: perspective. The opportunity to reflect. To search for the last few pieces of the puzzle.

David stepped forward one last time, asked him to leave.

"I can't do that, David. Not now. Did you have a relationship, you and Stina?"

"Sven. I don't know how you came up with such a crazy idea, but you're saying I did it?"

There would never be enough to bring charges. The case was just like the assassination of the prime minister—nothing but witness statements, circumstantial evidence, a timeline. Sometimes that was all you had to go on. Sven had managed to learn David's blood type. That was the crucial factor. This had to be right. It didn't make sense otherwise.

Sven took out his old service weapon.

"I know it was you. You even called me. Did you want to confess? Why did you call me?"

David stared at the gun, which gleamed in the dark. "Sven. For Christ's sake. Surely you can see—"

"I just want you to stop lying to me, David. That's all. Just tell me what happened."

He raised the gun, but not as a threat. As a warning.

"For Christ's sake!" David roared. "Stop!"

He took a step forward and tried to grab the pistol, get it away from Sven. But Sven resisted. He was much weaker than his opponent, slower and feebler, and he realized he was going to be the loser. He tried to head-butt David but missed. The gun was trapped between their chests, hands grabbing for it. He could smell the alcohol on David's breath, got a spray of saliva to the face. Sven's right index finger was about to be twisted out of joint and in that instant, a shot popped off. He heard it echo through the forest and felt the body next to his lose its strength and will and sag to the ground.

With every joint and muscle in his body aching and tender, Sven sank to his knees and looked at the man who was now writhing and whimpering on his back.

"Why?" Sven roared. "That's all I want to know. Huh? Why?"

Beneath him, David gasped for air.

"Answer me!"

David blinked. Blood welled from his mouth.

"Say something, for God's sake!"

Sven clasped his hands and hit the dying killer in the face with all his might.

The betrayal burned inside him, it was all just lies and deceit, there was no truth to be found in any of it—just like the country he lived in.

Yes, the world was so heinous, so incredibly callous in the face of itself and everything it was capable of. It was unfathomable.

And then it was over.

Evy helped Sven bury him. It took half the night. Sven became short of breath a number of times and had to rest. All the while he looked around, terrified that someone would appear in the dark, a witness, and it would all be over.

When they returned at dawn, they got into their separate cars, headed home their separate ways, grieved for each other in their separate homes.

: : :

Yes, each other. That's how it felt. Sven and Evy had to bear the burden of what they'd done. They couldn't breathe a word to anyone. Not even Stina Franzén's parents, who still lived in uncertainty. Sven hadn't seen them after the investigation against him was dismissed, and he never saw them again, never got to inform them of the identity of their daughter's killer. He was ashamed; he couldn't do it. He and Evy had to bear the truth about the Tiarp Man and themselves together, yet alone.

Sven died content, peace in his heart. Evy was sure of that. But when he died, she was left behind, alone. That was how she thought of it. She had to bear the truth about Sven Jörgensson, David Linder, and the Tiarp Man all on her own, and she kept mum. She began to smoke cigarettes and drink gin at night, alone in the dark when Ronnie and the kids were asleep, and the memories returned to her like a scourge, a scourge from which she couldn't free herself.

She didn't think she would survive, but it's shocking, really, how much you can carry on your own. If you have to.

91

Everyone used to meet up at Fridhem Grill in Halmstad. That's where you would stop to grab a hot dog or hamburger from the kiosk, shoot the shit, drink, and see folks you hadn't had time to talk to all week. On weekends it was so packed it was impossible to get there by car. Some people drifted over from People's Park, others from the beaches or the dance floor at Galejan, but they all gathered at Fridhem Grill in the end. Some needed to think, others needed to eat; some people just needed a way to keep the night from ending quite yet. There was a jukebox inside, and that was the reason Sven had been summoned. An intoxicated man wanted to hear the Ronettes' "Be My Baby," and he grew more agitated with every coin he inserted into the jukebox. The machine was stuck and refused to play anything but an old folk tune by Evert Taube.

Eventually the man became violent and kicked the jukebox, prompting another guest to step forward and ask the gentleman to calm down. This had the opposite effect, and fisticuffs broke out. When Sven arrived, he could still hear the folk tune playing softly, a little distorted now that one of the speakers had been damaged in the scuffle. The two brawlers were sitting outside, on the steps of Fridhem Grill, trying to sober up with a cup of coffee and a bottle of Pucko chocolate milk each.

"So what have we here?"

"Nothing, we're fine," said one, drinking his coffee.

He had a black eye the diameter of an orange.

"He just got a little angry, is all," said the other, who was bleeding from a split eyebrow. "But it's okay now."

The man with the black eye nodded at the Grill just as Evert Taube sang *Here comes the sweet summer I promised you.*

"And this song is starting to grow on me. Pretty nice, if you listen to the words."

Sven liked it too. He recalled it from the days of his and Bibbi's youth. They'd danced to it. So he sat there with the two men, listening to the song as it started over on the jukebox. Then he wished them a pleasant evening and asked them to take it easy on the way home.

He related this story with joy in his eyes, with a smile.

It was a world he felt at home in, where he had a place and a purpose. Life was dependable and made sense, and nothing was really a problem, in the end—you could look in the mirror and be sure of who you were looking at. Later, something had rotted, becoming cold and unfamiliar.

Solving the case of the Tiarp Man meant a reconciliation not only with a perpetrator, but with the country that had produced him from deep within its heart.

Vidar understood why his father had done it. Maybe it wasn't defensible from a legal perspective. But ethically, when it came to someone who had caused as much suffering as David Linder had? Not to mention all the next of kin. Some of them had been ruined.

No, he thought. *You were right, Dad. I understand. You did the right thing, to the very end.*

And he also felt a deep sense of relief, as you might when you have escaped great danger by the skin of your teeth.

A few weeks later, they received the report from the National Forensic Center. The analysis of the blood evidence that had been collected

and recorded over thirty years ago—which had subsequently vanished, only to be rediscovered recently—did not match any individual
in the police DNA database. The same went for the skeleton at
Nyårsåsen. The bones had decayed far beyond a condition that would
allow for a forensic DNA analysis.

Just as Markus had predicted.

But why had Linder done it? There must be a reason. It wasn't
unusual for the answer to that question to remain in the shadows.
Maybe it would be forthcoming in time. That happened sometimes:
The explanation lay deep beneath the surface, obscured by memories
and silence. A vulnerable childhood, early tendencies toward violence,
isolation, a warped view of women, pornography—they hadn't seen
signs of any of this. But there were other possible signs too, ones that
seldom revealed themselves before you understood what they might
mean. Only then did they become visible.

In time, it would become clear. And if it didn't, that meant something too. No one knew anything anymore. People stopped knowing
things in 1986.

Maybe that was the truth of it, I thought as I sat in the yellow
house, trying to compile the story of Sven and Vidar. The evil on
Nyårsåsen had been unleashed by the same rot that led someone to
put a bullet in the back of the prime minister. And now that evil was
destroyed.

III

DISINTEGRATION

2019

92

That was how I viewed and believed myself to understand the two men I had placed onstage. A high-resolution image, one developed by me and those I spoke with, not least Evy. When she told me about herself and Sven and what happened up in the forest on the night David Linder met his fate, I could come up with only a single question: "Does Vidar know about this?"

"Of course he does. This is his father we're talking about. When he asked me last spring, I told him the story."

"Good," I said, because it seemed like that was what I needed to say. "That's good, Evy."

But inside me it felt like an abyss had opened. After spending night and day trying to vanish into Sven and Vidar Jörgensson, I found myself almost grieving the fact that the father had been forced to go to such lengths. And the son's anguish, all of this, *my God, all of this*. When I took a step back I was alarmed to think of how this could have been going on all around me without even the slightest suspicion on my part.

A man with a firm belief in the body he was born into and the life he lives, in the time he inhabits, in the country that's his own—and is betrayed by every one of them. That must be the worst tragedy of all. That is what befell Sven, the annihilation of the man who, in our eyes, had seemed so indestructible. At last he was allowed to rest, but that rest had come at the highest of prices.

Was this the same sorrow that had befallen his son? No, I thought. Not quite. It was different for him. His sorrow would never be as visible. Unlike his father, there was a coolness to Vidar's character. It wasn't possible to step right into him.

When I picture Sven Jörgensson, I see a man stiff with what has afflicted him, as if an incomprehensible mistake has been made.

A mistake. That was probably the catalyst of the whole story, the actions he took up there in the forests of Tiarp when he found Stina Franzén. How he shook, or perhaps didn't shake, her. I marked this as a sort of beginning, a starting point. Maybe a deep source of pain. And even if it really wasn't, this was probably how Sven saw it. That was the sort of man he was. The man we had imagined as children, the man we had looked up to, wasn't the type to deflect blame. Nor was he a man who was at a loss to explain what had happened, whatever it was that happened. If he couldn't find any other source, then it must simply be because of him. He, a man whose noble nature depended on actually being the very person he appeared to be, had to step forward and accept responsibility.

This was another route to justice. A man who neither inflated nor minimized his contributions, and who allowed himself to be placed in the blank space that demanded an explanation. It was hard to imagine a more Swedish man in a more Swedish time. This was what I had been searching for. An explanation. A key that could open the locked door. I found it in Sven himself, and, accordingly, in the country where he lived, in a time that would come to break him. Yes, I thought, this must have been the case, and every part of it—his suffering, the beauty of his beloved fields and forests that year, the great faith people dared to show each other against all odds in the wake of the murders, and how he, who had never had a part in the vast arc of Swedish history as it was written in schoolbooks, now ended up at its very center, to be cut through and destroyed by it—it almost broke my heart.

I tried to grasp the consequences of what Sven Jörgensson had done. In the end, he had taken the life of another human being because he refused to give up; he, a man who had borne the yoke of justice so proudly for so many years, had, in the end, stepped over the line to do what had to be done. Didn't this in fact bolster our image of him? The Tiarp Man had suddenly been standing in front of Sven, in the dark, the man who had brought about so much evil and suffering but had been no more than a transient shadow, was now as evident and measurable as a customer at a tailor's shop.

Right. Damn straight, it was right to shoot him! Even if it was by accident. We would have done the same ourselves, or we hoped we would have been brave enough. I felt an almost more intense bond with Sven, a barren and bitter bond, because that was the way of reality. After the shots on Sveavägen in 1986, a lot of what we felt was challenged and tested, and in the hysteria and panic that broke out, a shard of chaos tore loose and flew all the way out to Marbäck, Tofta, and Sven and Vidar Jörgensson. He had done what he had to do to restore order, to bring answers into the light. One last time, he had done exactly what was asked of him.

93

By this point, I was living on savings. Inquiries about columns and opinion pieces had been scarce all summer; everyone had been lying on the beach or watching TV in their summer cottages. It didn't matter to me. Autumn was here and I had begun to welcome the solitude my work afforded me, the silence out at the house, the opportunity to immerse myself in a Sweden that no longer existed and see what sorts of traces it had left in people whose orbits I had once moved near.

I was ten when they shot Palme; I too suffered through the heat in that strange year of 1988, and I left Halmstad in the aftershocks of the crisis of the 1990s that forced several area farms to go under. I had watched it happen but I hadn't cared, hadn't understood.

This was the root of it all, I thought. The work itself. No love affairs or friends to distract me, nor any thoughts that what I was working to uncover might one day appear in a bookstore. Maybe I should stop trying to publish? Wasn't the work sufficient on its own?

It had to be a personal crisis of some sort. I'm not crazy; I knew that much. But what was I supposed to do about that? Knowing that you're in a crisis doesn't make it any easier to deal with. Rather the opposite.

Since I didn't have a place to belong in the real world, I tried to create one inside my head by living the lives of others. I want to make that clear, because it's very important. I certainly didn't mind concentrating on myself and my work for the time being. What happened later happened because I had no choice. Anything else is a lie.

When autumn came and the temperature fell, the cold began to seep into the house. One morning, the indoor temperature was below sixty, even though the radiators were hot. The floor remained cold and the old walls couldn't keep in the heat. I stood there shivering, coffee cup in hand, considering the old woodstove in the living room and wondering if it worked. I couldn't quite remember when it had last been used. When I was a child, we had a fire in it almost every autumn and winter day. I liked the smell of it, I recalled, and the contained flames that licked at the logs Dad had chopped out in the yard, the close heat that steamed from the blazing mouth of the stove.

"Why, no," Dad said when I called, "I don't remember when we last used the stove. We bought a fan heater instead. And a portable radiator. Why, is the house cold?"

"A little," I said. "Where are the fan and the radiator?"

"Well, we took them with us. So I imagine they're here, in storage. Shall we bring them out?"

"No, I'll try to get a fire going in the stove."

"How are things over there? I've hardly seen you since summer. Rasmus says all you do is sit in there working."

"I'm fine. But yes, I've mostly been working."

"Still all about what went on up there in Tiarp?"

"Yes," I said cautiously. "That's right."

"Hell of a story," Dad said. "You know, I—"

"Dad, I'm sorry, but I need to go," I interrupted him. "I have to try to get a fire going in the stove. We'll talk soon."

It didn't go very well. Since I had no way to get kindling, I had to go up to Marbäck to buy wood from Backlund. On the way I passed Vidar and Patricia Jörgensson's house. It stood where it had always stood, its driveway neat and tidy, no car visible. They must be off at work like everyone else. Only I was alone.

Backlund recognized me, invited me in for coffee, and asked about life up in Stockholm, why I had come home—*home,* that's how he put it—and how that father of mine was doing, before he gave me the wood for free and told me to say hello from him. Then I spent the rest of the morning trying to light a fire in the stove, and when, after several attempts, I succeeded, I stepped out of the house to see if smoke was coming from the chimney.

I stood there for a moment, waiting, but saw nothing. Instead, all the smoke detectors in the house started howling like a furious choir. I squinted at the kitchen window and thought I saw smoke.

I hurtled inside, filled a bucket with water, and poured it into the stove. The flames hissed and spat and the lovely parquet living room floor was splashed with sooty black water. What should I do? Surely something other than this, but I was clueless. Dizzy and coughing, I staggered around the house opening all the windows and doors; then I stood out on the driveway, in the cold, watching the smoke escape from every opening in the house except the chimney.

I tried to climb onto the roof. I really did.

But I kept slipping on the roofing tiles and came very close to falling off, and in the end things got so bad that I accidentally kicked the ladder, which toppled to the ground. In a cold sweat, humiliated and filthy, I had to grab the gutter and wriggle down until I was dangling from it; I dropped almost two meters and hit the ground. *This never would have happened to a Jörgensson,* I thought, resigned to my fate. I contacted a chimney sweep who said he could come look at the chimney next week, and then I called Dad again to ask if I could borrow the heating fan or the radiator for a few days.

"You can have them both," he said, sounding slightly amused, as though he could just imagine the scene in the house.

94

Elsa Grave came from Skåne but moved to Vapnödalen outside of Halmstad in the mid-1950s. There she lived for forty years before she got too old and ended up in a nursing home down in Laholm, and even though she was from my old stomping grounds I heard of her only after I'd moved to Stockholm. We read Swedish poets in a course I took at university, and this was where I was introduced to her poetry.

From her farm in Vapnö, not far from Tiarp, she wrote about life around Nyårsåsen, its wildlife and nature, the mystique and anguish of love, the pain of womanhood and motherhood, the murkiness of the landscape and what it did to people:

> *You shall give me a darkness*
> *of the clawlike, benailed*
> *gothic of hands*
> *of the roiling, ray-petaled*
> *capitals of throats*

These lines come from "Darkness," a poem in which I see, now, years later, a much deeper meaning than I did before.

One of my classmates, who knew I was from Halmstad, once turned to me and said, "Does this seem familiar to you?"

My father is from Tiarp. He grew up there with a father—my

grandfather Arvid—who first worked as a quarryman and later as a builder, and a mother, Grandma Greta to me, who spent a large part of her life as the sexton of Vapnö Church. My brother and I were both christened there. Perhaps that is where our gravestones will one day be erected.

Dad moved away from Tiarp when he met Mom in the early seventies, and after a few years they bought the lot here in Tofta—on my grandfather's advice; he'd seen it was for sale and said it was good land—and built the yellow house. I don't remember spending any time in Tiarp, aside from the occasional Christmas Eve or Midsummer as a boy.

So, no, I said to my classmate. It didn't seem familiar to me.

But to others it did, and in the autumn after my homecoming I often wandered through Grave's neighborhood, from Nyårsåsen down to Risarp, where the Mellbergs had once lived.

I thought about the Tiarp Man and tried to understand what it was about a place that could engender such dark undercurrents in a person's life. There was beauty there, almost lyrical beauty. But it was a cruel, sharp beauty, full of fury.

Elsa Grave had feared the shadows of the ridge, and what lurked among them. In "Darkness" she reveals both her fascination with and her fear of her surroundings: *blaze me a sun tonight / you who shall bring me the dark*. She used two different spellings for "me," in the original Swedish, one more vernacular, and it makes me wonder. It must mean something.

The one she asks for light is also the one who will bring darkness. Like the face of Janus.

Maybe that was how he felt, Sven. As though the truth about the Tiarp Man would pass him by unless he steadfastly continued to call upon it, seek it out, chase it down. And as though, at the same time, deep down, he already knew.

: : :

Dad followed me down to the storage room and together we pulled out the fan and the radiator. He told me about the crime novel he was almost done reading and said it was good, but involved too many names.

"I get confused," he said. "I'm sure it's just that I'm old, but I read one page and then one sucker pops up there. Okay, I think, who the hell is this now? And I have to go back."

I rolled my eyes at him.

"Try *Robinson Crusoe* then. Maybe that's more your speed."

"That one's fine, until Friday shows up. Then I get all confused."

This made me laugh.

"The radiator is behind that box," Dad said, "if you move that, we can get it out."

I did as he said. We unearthed the radiator.

"Do you remember Elsa Grave?"

"Elsa?" Dad raised his eyebrows. "Hell, yes. We went to a party at her house now and then. Or maybe it was one of her daughters who threw the party. Elsa wasn't home, as I recall. That was probably why there was a party. She lived by the sporting fields in Vapnö and mostly kept to herself. I liked Elsa, even though she was a little prickly. Why?"

"Just wondering. I read one of her books recently. Her material about Nyårsåsen and Tiarp is really strong."

"Seems to me people write about every last place these days. Can't some of them be left alone? It's eerie enough, what happened up there. Damn." He picked up the fan and stepped out of the storage room. "The newspapers too, they just write and write, like there's no end in sight. Do poets have to do the same?"

"Okay," I said, straining under the weight of the radiator. "But Elsa Grave wasn't writing about—"

"I know, I know." Dad waved me off. "I just think it's so tragic. And I get all, I don't know, snippy."

"Sure. But I think, maybe," I said, my mind on the story I was personally piecing together, "there's an important story there. Despite all that's been written about it."

David Linder had become the year's most widely discussed Hallander. Suddenly he, and everyone close to him, had become public property. There was an article about him in *Hallandsposten* that day, a report that described the series of events up in Tiarp, the exhumation, and parts of the police investigation. Linder's brief stint as a police officer was mentioned, along with plenty of speculation about why he'd become a cop and why he'd quit. The reporter spun out wild, unchecked possible scenarios. I had printed out this article to save it, had put it in the pile of documents that now smelled like smoke after my failed attempt to build a fire in the woodstove.

"You know," Dad said as we stood by the car, "it sure was strange, all that."

I closed the trunk. "What's strange?"

"Well, about Linder. You'll have some coffee before you go, right?"

"Sure. But what do you mean?"

"Oh, you know, your old grandfather. He and Ma lived up there in those days."

I'd done away with a lot of my Halland accent, but since my move back it had started to return. I noticed it in the prosody of my voice, how I sometimes intoned words in a way that felt out of character but was still remarkably familiar. Dad, of course, had never lost his accent, and he spoke that type of booming, ringing Halland Swedish that men used to use in the past, a dialect that revealed his origins as the son of a quarryman. It hadn't exactly grown more subdued given his life as a car mechanic and coworker of sons of other quarrymen, farmers, and laborers. He didn't say *Mom* or *Mama*, *Dad* or *Papa*. He said *Ma* and *Pa*.

We were heading back to the front door. It was windy up in Tegelbruket, a bitingly brisk, cold autumn breeze, and we stuffed our hands in our pockets, hunching over.

"But, listen," he said tentatively. "How are you doing?"

"What?" I said. "Fine . . . ? Why do you ask?"

"Oh, I just . . . well, are you sure? That you're fine, I mean. I was thinking, with Sara and everything, you know . . ."

"I'm a little worn out," I admitted.

"But you don't look worn out. You look sick."

"Thanks."

"Too thin, sort of. And pale as a newborn calf. Your ma will be worried."

"I'm fine, Dad," I said, annoyed.

"Okay. If you say so."

Then he told me a story. And if it weren't for that story, what happened next probably never would have happened, and all of this truly would have been for nothing.

95

"So I was talking to Rasmus on the phone yesterday and he said you were doing a lot of work out there. On the house, I thought he meant, can he handle all that on his own? Then I realized that he meant you were working on what happened up in Tiarp. But it must be hard, I mean, I don't know what you usually do when you write. But you must not have many memories from those days. Right? Or do you?"

"No," I said. "No, I don't."

"I thought so. We didn't go up there much, except for when Ma and Pa had birthdays and so on. After I talked to Rasmus I tried to read my book for a while, but then all those damn names popped up, plus a new one I didn't recognize at all. So I went over to Jula and bought a new screwdriver instead. When I got home, I thought I would rest for a while, we usually do in the afternoons, just lie down in bed for an hour and close our eyes. But then I happened to think about what Rasmus had said."

We had reached the apartment. Mom was in the kitchen, car keys in hand.

"Well hello there, honey," she said. "How are you?"

"Fine."

She gave me a hug, with worry in her eyes and a small smile on her lips; she asked if I wanted coffee or something to eat, commenting that I smelled like smoke.

"I made a fire in the woodstove."

"I was just heading out to get groceries," she said. "Are you sure you don't want anything? You look so thin."

"I said the same thing," said Dad.

"It's fine, Mom."

"Are you sure?"

"Yup."

Once she'd left, Dad showed me to the kitchen table, where three thick books waited. They were my grandfather's old work journals, heavy and fine, bound in leather the color of hazelnuts.

"Pa kept track of his work in them," Dad said. "Every day, like a calendar. Dates and everything. The houses he built, the jobs he did, whether anything special happened in the neighborhood, stuff like that. You know, I remember how he would sit there with Ma each night, and they would have their evening coffee and he would write down the day's entry. She helped him with the calculations. I saved them because I thought these books were so nice." He ran his hand over them. The sound it made was cool and dry, agreeable. "I had the idea that I'd seen them when we moved and assumed they were somewhere down in the storage room. And indeed they were. So I brought up the ones from 1986. I thought maybe they would . . . Well, I just wanted," he fumbled, "to try to help you out, for once. If I could. I thought maybe there might be something in them that was, you know, interesting or something. If you needed that," he added cautiously, "because from what Rasmus said, I thought you might."

I could tell that he really didn't want to interfere. That was nice. I thought of what distance there had once been between us, the conflicts and the silence, and how not a trace of that was left. If you hadn't experienced it, it was probably hard to imagine. I sat down at the table, picked up one of the books, and opened it.

This book belongs to: and then my grandfather's full name, formally, in gorgeous, smooth handwriting. There were daily entries, I noted, just as Dad had said: about construction jobs, meetings, visitors. I could find myself in there too: *9–11:30, planning meeting with F. Jonasson at Söndrum Construction & Supply. Mats and Monica came by with the boys this afternoon.* It was the day before Midsummer's Eve, 1986.

"Okay," I said slowly, afraid I was going to disappoint him. "I've never heard of Söndrum Construction and Supply, for instance. I'm sure there could be lots of other good information here. Thank you, Dad."

"Yes, I thought so too." Dad pulled over another of the three books. "But that was before I . . ."

He opened the book and began to page through it. I noticed that it was the first book of the year; the entries were from January and February. When he found the right page, he stared at it for a moment, as though he needed to reassure himself of what he'd seen.

He looked up at me, uncertainty in his eyes.

"They say Linder committed the first murder sometime between eleven P.M. and one in the morning. Right? That's what it said in the paper, anyway."

"Yes."

"Come here and take a look."

Dad had placed his finger alongside Grandpa's notes from the evening of February 28.

11:00–12:30. D. Linder here. Helped me fix the cement mixer. Must get it to Frösakull tomorrow. (300 kronor).

"D. Linder," I read.

"Right," Dad said. "And I . . . well, I don't know. This isn't my area of expertise. But in the paper they said he met that woman outside her work, when she finished up there after eleven. But he couldn't have been there."

I looked at the open book. Ran my fingers over Grandpa's words.

"How old was Grandpa in 1986?" I asked.

"He was born in 1913. So he must have been seventy-three. But you remember him," Dad said, as if he understood what I was getting at. "His mind was clear as a spring stream before his stroke in 1990. And he was strong as an ox, too. But I remember that cement mixer; it was from the fifties and it took two to turn it over. They had the same model over at Linder's farm. I played there as a boy sometimes, with Frasse and Göran, and old man Hasse Linder kept an eye on us."

"And . . ." I began, not quite sure what to say.

"Your grandfather Arvid was a very precise man, I'm telling you," Dad said, tapping the page. "If it says Linder was there at that time, then he was. It has to be him. I don't know if we . . . There's been so much in the newspapers, but should the police be notified? A man can't be in two places at once, after all. So it's strange. Right?"

"But eleven, twelve-thirty—that's so late at night. What was he doing up?"

"Pa always took a walk around the farm at night before he went to bed. I do remember that. He made sure everything was in order for the next day. You know, it could waste time if a saw or a sander was missing, if something was out of place. I remember that once he needed a screwdriver that was missing. He was out looking for it until two-thirty in the morning, angry as a hornet. That must be what he was doing that night too, and he realized that the mixer was on the fritz. And he must have called for Linder. So he was probably there at that time. Isn't that strange?"

"Yes," I said, my voice oddly cold. "Strange. May I borrow these?"

"Sure, of course." Dad looked almost relieved, as if I had offered to lighten his load. "Just be careful with them, they're so lovely."

96

The technical investigation had taken place during the hottest weeks of summer. Since it coincided with several people's vacations, it took an extra long time and had to be completed in rounds. Now the farm was deserted, but a lone blue-and-white section of police tape had been left behind to flutter in the autumn breeze that blew across the barren fields. I shivered in the cold.

I parked nearby and walked along the edge of the farmyard. Linder's old abandoned farm was just one out of hundreds that had failed over the years in the backwater corners of Halland and now lay empty. They were a frequent sight on a drive through the countryside, in the regions where the major financial crises had hit hardest. These farms seldom recovered. People had had to leave their family land and life's work behind. But this particular farm was an unusual case. A killer had lived here, had been active here, until justice caught up with him.

I turned my head. No one around. I bent down and ducked under the police tape and onto the property.

I saw the remnants of the crime-scene technicians' investigations: impressions in the ground, old scale sticks and plastic sleeves, a forgotten purple latex glove. They hadn't bothered to clean up. I could see narrow grooves left by the ground-penetrating radar, running across the farm like parallel bicycle tracks.

I searched for an open grave. An excavation. They ought to have found her somewhere up here, a discovery that could have been protected by the technicians and investigators to such an extent that it escaped attention from the media.

Here and there they had stopped to examine the ground, dug down a little.

I spent over two hours in the vicinity of the farm, combing it for any sign that they'd found Frida Östmark. My hands and feet grew cold, until they were so frozen I had to return to my car to warm up for a bit.

My phone rang. It was Evy. It had been awhile since we spoke.

"Hi," I said. "How are you, Evy?"

"I've been having such awful dreams. And I'm hungry, but I don't have any food."

"Hasn't anyone done the shopping for you?"

I heard her shuffling along with her rollator. The fridge opened.

"Why, the fridge is full."

She sounded surprised and confused. I thought of Grandpa's work records and wanted to ask her about them, but I didn't know how to start, so I said nothing. Instead I gazed out at the farm.

"Can I ask you something?" I began, finally.

"Yes, of course."

"When you and Ronnie moved from Kärleken to Norteforsen."

"Mmm?"

"How did it feel?"

"Good. Why?"

"It's just a kilometer or so from Sven. I thought, given your history and everything."

"History?"

She sounded perplexed, and silence fell between us.

"You know," she began, "I'm not saying I didn't have any blame in it, in what happened. But there was nothing we could do. No one could."

"What happened between you and Sven, you mean?"

"No, what happened in Tiarp, what you keep asking about. The murders."

"But how would you be to blame for that? Because you helped Sven, you mean?"

There was a lengthy pause before she responded.

"You'll come over for a visit soon, won't you?"

"I'll come for a visit soon," I said. "But, Evy, do you feel like you are guilty in this? I don't think you've mentioned that before. Although I understand if you feel that way, of course, I suppose it would be stranger if you didn't."

"Well, I don't know. My head, it's all muddled. This old dolly is doing her best, but it . . ."

The sentence trailed off into silence. My sense of frustration grew. It was always like this, trying to talk to her. I tried to keep it up for a little longer, but I heard the exhaustion take over in Evy's voice. Maybe she would return to it another time. I'd learned to be patient. We brought the conversation to a close.

Fog had formed on the car windows. I stepped into the cold again and gazed around the land. It really wasn't so strange. Why would he have buried the body on his own property? If she happened to be discovered, the landowner would be the obvious suspect. Linder had known this. He'd gotten rid of her somewhere else.

I remembered my grandfather as a brawny, broad-shouldered, tall man. He almost always wore a threadbare flannel shirt and overalls, with wooden clogs on his feet. His voice was deep and warm, his laugh a low rumble, and he had once helped me build my first sandbox. He and Grandma gave me ice cream with fruit and berries when I came for a visit, and I drank lots of sugary cordial that Grandma made herself. I felt safe when I was near them, and I liked to hold Grandpa's hand.

Now, when I studied his work journals, I saw a busy, careful craftsman with a deep desire to pull his weight. Despite his advanced age, he worked nearly every day, either out at one of his building sites or at a drawing board, transforming an idea into someone's house or summer cottage. *Didn't have change for M. Jansson,* he noted. *Will have to drop by tomorrow and pay. (54.50 kronor).*

The amount of money was always in the margin and in parentheses, given down to the exact *öre.*

David Linder didn't reappear in Grandpa's work journals from 1986. The note on February 28 was the only time he was mentioned. The next day there was a note about a C-H Håkansson, who had come by with his truck to pick up the mixer. That Sunday was blank, save for a memo about the service at Vapnö Church.

Sitting at my workstation, with the heating fan beside me in the comforting solitude out at the house, I tried to ascertain what the work journal could mean, the conclusions that could be drawn from these notes. What I should do next. *Search party 9:00–1:00,* he noted one day in May. *F. Östmark.* It filled me with warmth. They had participated in the search. My grandma and grandpa had been involved, had cared and wanted to help.

When evening fell, I realized that the dishwasher had stopped working. I sighed and bent down to look for dish soap and a scrub brush. When I stood up again, I saw a shadow sweep through the dim light outside the window.

Someone had been standing there, a few steps out on the uneven lawn, observing me through the window. I was totally sure of it.

I went to the front hall, opened the cabinet by the door, and grabbed a flashlight, then stepped into the yard in my sock feet. The beam of the flashlight was sharp but shaky in my hand, and my heart was pounding in my ears.

Nothing there. I tried to collect myself and walked to the corner of the house, in the direction the shadow had moved. Above me, the sky was dark and clear, and the trees rustled in the wind.

I took a deep breath and stepped around the corner. The

flashlight's beam moved across the lawn, down to the fence and the cycling path that waited beyond.

No one. Nothing.

I must have been mistaken.

When I went back inside, I was shaking with something deeper than the evening chill.

97

I still felt shaken the next morning. I moved cautiously, I was more hesitant and uncertain as I searched for signs. But I couldn't see anything as I stood there on the lawn in my robe, with a cup of coffee in hand. It didn't mean that no one had been there.

To keep my mind off it, I put myself to work. I went out and bought a printer, installed it, and printed out the manuscript I'd been writing since summer. I placed it next to the computer in a neat pile and stared at it. There it sat, waiting, the fruit of my recent months' labor, still smelling faintly of the laser printer.

I didn't touch it. Instead I felt a peculiar resistance toward the text, or perhaps what it portrayed.

It was quite early in the day, but when I found the number I didn't hesitate to bring the phone to my ear. Elderly people get up early. After several attempts I'd been given access to the investigation and a recording of the interrogation she'd conducted of Sven Jörgensson back in 1988—exactly how this happened I can't really state here, out of consideration for the person who provided me with the material— and I thought this would be enough. In recent days, though, I'd begun to mull over what I heard on the recording, what could be read in the documents.

"Hello?"

"Is this Nora Selvin?"

"Who's asking?"

Although more than thirty years had passed, the voice was nearly identical to the one I'd heard on the tape. Just as thin and nasal, just as wary and clear. I didn't dare to tell her anything but the truth: who I was, what I was working on. That I had, at least in a geographical sense, grown up very close to Sven.

"I see. And how did you get hold of this material?"

"I can't say, exactly. But I've treated it with great caution."

"Okay." She said it as though she did not, on the whole, believe me. "And what do you want from me?"

"Actually, what I really want to know is . . ."

"Hold on." Rustling in the background. "For once I actually have a visitor here. It's my daughter; she's just going to drop a few things off. Can you call back?"

Nora Selvin was thirty-six years old when she investigated Sven Jörgensson's actions at Nyårsåsen, and she hadn't retired until the first of this year. She'd spent the latter part of her working life in Jönköping, which was where she lived now. I believe she spoke with me only because, after an intense and eventful career as a prosecutor, she now spent most of her days in boredom.

"Anyway," I said, when we spoke again a little while later. "What I'm really curious about is . . . I'm thinking of Sven. Do you remember this case?"

"Yes, of course. I remember all of them."

"What I want to know is, I've studied all of this material and I'm trying to figure out whether his actions were right or wrong."

"Right or wrong?"

"Yes."

She laughed. "You think the world is that simple?"

"No, but . . ."

"Everyone always wanted to know what really happened. Back then, when I was working as a prosecutor. People who weren't trained in law or jurisprudence often asked about the truth, about what was *true*. As if that were possible to say."

"But I'm not asking about what's true or false."

"What did you say you were writing? Is it a book?"

"I think so. Yes. I'm essentially finished."

"And you have access to the investigation materials?"

"Yes."

She didn't say anything for a long time.

"You should know, then, that it didn't go anywhere. The investigation, I mean. It's not easy to investigate your own people—and that's what happened here. He worked at the station. These days, they're better at that, but back then, in '88, you know, it was still such a sticky situation. I dismissed it, if I'm not mistaken?"

"Yes."

"Just like we dismissed almost everything else that had to do with the police."

"But in your opinion," I said, "was he a contributing factor in Stina Franzén's death?"

"Yes, he was. Absolutely."

It was strangely painful to hear, even after all I now knew about what had happened.

"Was it reasonable to investigate him because of it?" she went on. "Yes, it was. And was it reasonable that he was exonerated?" She sighed. "Hard to say, of course. But yes, actually, I would say it was, despite what I said about cops never being convicted of anything. But in this case, what choice did he really have? He was trying to save her life. Sure, he could have thought the better of it. He shook her, wasn't that it?"

"Yes, allegedly."

"But I don't know, I don't think you can . . . Like I said. In this case, he was trying to save her life. It was a strange night. I don't think we should regard him so harshly."

I considered this.

"Based on the image you had of Sven, do you think it was of significance to him?"

"What, that I dismissed the case?"

"Yes, that he was exonerated."

She didn't say anything for a long time.

"I didn't know him," she said at last. "So you're asking me to speculate. I don't like that." Silence heavy with thought. "But I remember thinking about that," she went on, "how it probably meant less to him than it would have for lots of others. The fact that I dismissed the case, I mean. Sven Jörgensson seemed so burdened by guilt and, I don't know, something deeper. As if what had happened had already taken its toll on him, and what happened to him personally, as a result, didn't matter as much. But now I'm speculating. Why?"

"No, it's nothing, I'm just trying to . . ."

"You know, it's funny," she said, "because his son called me over the summer. He asked the same question."

"Vidar? Vidar Jörgensson has been in touch with you?"

"Yes, Vidar. That was his name."

"What did he want?"

"To clear some things up about his father, he said. I answered as best I could, more or less the same answers I've given you. He seemed sort of relieved afterwards, as though he needed to hear it. I'm getting on in years now, so my ear isn't what it used to be. But still, I think I heard correctly. Was there anything else?"

I observed the lawn outside the window. Someone had been out there. Who? Who would be after me? I didn't understand.

"I suspect you've heard the news from here, about the Tiarp Man."

"That it was Linder, yes. My God. I met him a few times when I was in Halmstad. I thought he seemed like a competent police officer."

"Were you surprised?"

"I'm a prosecutor," said Nora Selvin. "I'm never surprised."

98

Later that week, I ran into Vidar again, completely by chance.

It was a sunny October day, and my brother was home from Lund. He'd come out to the house and insisted I needed to get some fresh air. Whatever I was spending my time mulling over, he claimed, I should do something else for a few hours.

"Like what?"

"Breared is playing Snöstorp Nyhem in an hour."

The thought of crowds and half-familiar faces from the past made me break out in a cold sweat. Would the shadow from the yard be among them? Reluctantly, I went along with him.

When you turned onto the county highway, you first went past the wooded area around Marbäck. There the trees grew so tall that they bent over the road, heavy with moisture after a summer rain, as though they wanted to offer protection to the people zooming by down there. Today they were bare and stiff, all in a row. Beyond Marbäck was a long stretch of highway. The sign for Skärkered. We used to ride bikes there as kids. I could almost smell the odors rising from asphalt and earth. Beyond Skärkered waited Simlångsdalen with its small houses and old workshops. There had once been an outdoor adventure shop in town there, and when we were little we thought it was a place you could literally buy an adventure.

Rasmus laughed when I reminded him of that.

We parked at the sporting fields. The bleachers were full of people. They smiled and shook hands, hugged. It smelled like coffee, and smoke rose from the grill. Out on the pitch, the teams were warming up. Puffs of steam escaped their mouths.

As we walked from the car, I took it all in and felt hesitation rising in my legs. My brother didn't notice my anxiety. Instead he told me about an injured player from Snöstorp Nyhem, I don't remember who anymore, who was still bedridden, and he claimed this meant the day looked promising for Breared. That was when I caught sight of him, for the first time since that night in the bar. It was weird, seeing him again: All of a sudden he was just standing there, the man who had been something of a starting point for my tale, and whom I had forced, without his authorization or knowledge, onto the stage alongside his dead father.

He and Patricia were talking to someone I didn't recognize. Vidar looked younger than he had in the bar, his face was rounder and his movements easier; there were no dark circles under his eyes, and his gaze was steady and open. He looked like he was right where he wanted to be. That was the thought that struck me. Here, we were far from violence, grief, and painful memories. Instead it was just a Sunday full of cold October sun, people you hadn't seen in a long time, old Per Gessle music on the loudspeakers, the business and concerns of a small world. Ove's combine had broken and he'd need a new one next spring; Johansson's garage had had to close; the kids wanted new ice skates for winter; there were a few vacation days left to take and that was a blessing, but what about today? Breared was looking strong.

We headed for the bleachers to find a spot. The teams began to gather on the pitch. Vidar said something to his wife and took off for the kiosk.

"I'll get some coffee," I said, "if you'll find us some spots?"

My brother watched, perplexed, as I headed for the kiosk. I don't know why I did it. I just did it.

I ended up behind him in line. He was holding a folded bill and only then did I realize I didn't have any cash on me.

"Do you know if they take Swish?"

"Oh, hello there, Moth. What are you doing here?"

Vidar had turned around. He observed me with big green eyes, warm and clear.

"My brother dragged me along."

"That's good, soccer is important stuff. I try to tell Patricia as much, but she's not convinced."

"Yet," I added. "Not convinced *yet*. Is what my brother tells me."

This got a laugh from Vidar.

"Exactly. Your brother's right. And yes, I think they take Swish."

"How are things with you?"

"Great, actually." And then, as if the memory had only just come to him: "Better than last time I saw you."

"That's nice."

"And you?"

"More or less the same as last time, to be honest," I said, and we both smiled, the way you do when you don't know what to say. "You mentioned your dad, as I recall. That you'd been thinking about him."

"Oh. Yeah, I had quite a bit on my mind last spring."

He hadn't wanted to talk about it that time, and he was sending clear signals that the same went for today. Yet I pressed on, as if something were pulling it out of me: "I've been . . . well, to be honest, I've actually been thinking a lot about it since we ran into each other."

Vidar raised his eyebrows. "You have?"

"I was thinking, if you can spare the time sometime, about what happened up there, you know, I've been reading the papers, of course, there's something I'd like to show you."

"What about?"

"I recently got to take a look at my grandfather's work journals. You know, his records. There's an unusual note in one of them."

"Oh?"

Vidar turned his head to check on the line to the kiosk. It would be his turn next.

"Yes, and I talked to Evy Carlén."

This put him off balance. "Evy Carlén?"

"Yes. She said—"

"I'm sorry, Moth," he interrupted, regaining his composure, "but I just want to watch soccer and spend time with my wife, if you'll excuse me."

"Of course. Definitely."

It was Vidar's turn. He ordered two cups of coffee.

"See you, Moth."

I turned my head to look for my brother. People were starting to settle on the bleachers. The teams were preparing for kickoff. I raised my hand toward my brother, who smiled. I was about to smile back when I froze in my tracks.

Something had come to me, a cursory, split-second image, like when you suddenly recall a snippet of a nightmare from the night before in the middle of an ordinary day. One second it's there, the memory, sharp and clear and baring its teeth like a monster, and the next it's gone again.

Was it the shadow from yesterday? No. No, this was something else. I looked around. Something here, I thought. Something that made me think of Stina Franzén. What was it?

I stood stock-still, as if the memory would come back to me if I was only patient. It didn't. I paid by Swish, and Breared lost 1–3.

99

Maybe it was the image of Vidar and Patricia at the sporting fields of Breared, smiling side by side, content just before the match began, that made me reflect upon my own life in an unexpected way. I, a person who had always been running away from something, stood there observing a man who had never felt the impulse to flee. A man without relationships observing a man who seemed to be defined by relationships more than anything else: the strong bonds to his home-town, to his wife, to his maxims.

One late-summer day in 1994, I left the town where I'd grown up to pursue a degree in literature at Stockholm University. At this point, Sven Jörgensson had been dead for almost three years.

I had thought about them then too, Sven and Vidar. Leaving had been necessary but not simple at all. Few people from Tofta had taken off for anywhere farther afield than a few kilometers west—into Halm-stad. The sons of craftsmen became craftsmen, farmers became farm-ers, the son of a cop had himself gone and become a cop. There was something lovely and meaningful about this sort of inheritance, and I'm sure it was painful for my parents when they realized it wouldn't be the case for us. By that point Dad and I in particular had trouble talking to each other. It would get better in time; with distance between us we would spend years seeking our way back to each other, and eventually we would succeed. But in 1994 our relationship was in bad shape. I, who had always been Daddy's rather than Mommy's boy, was so far away from him.

"Can't you just . . ." he said one time that summer. "I mean, what's wrong with staying here? Is your life so terrible?"

"No. But . . ."

"Look at everyone else around here. They're content, they're satisfied. Look at Bengt and Örjan up the bend, look at Vidar Jörgensson. There's not a damn thing wrong with them, they're all fine. And this is enough for them. Why can't it be enough for you? Why can't you be satisfied?"

When I try to remember my youth, I can't think of any other instance in which he was this frank.

"It's not that, Dad. It's not about how I'm doing or what's good enough. I just want to see something else."

"But what? What do you want to see? What do you think will be so much better in Stockholm?"

"Well, I don't *know* yet."

Sitting opposite Dad on that summer day, I wondered if Vidar, too, had entertained the thought of moving away, but put it out of his mind. It seemed impossible, almost absurd. How could uprooting himself be in the cards for someone who had always felt at home? To be at peace, to be satisfied. That was what Vidar seemed to want from his life, all you could ask. It was everything *I* wanted to escape.

I've always felt a need to defend my emotions and the way they drove me when I was young. It had nothing to do with my parents: They loved me and my brother to the best of their ability. They worked a lot and were often tired and worn out when they got home, because they struggled to keep a handle on our everyday life with food, laundry, water leaks, getting the cars inspected, and life with each other. We didn't spend very much time together, and they might have wished they could have more time with me and Rasmus, that we were closer and had stronger bonds. I'm sure I would have appreciated that too, but I wasn't negatively affected when that wasn't how it turned out. In fact, I sometimes find myself astonished at how much time the children of today spend with their parents, and how much the children know about them. Maybe more than is good for any of them, really.

In time I would hear about them, of course, the tragedies big and small that befell my home region. Poor harvests, Göransson's stolen tractor, Nilsson's wife who got sick and died. The terrible house fire in Tolarp, where a young woman was found dead, took place just a few months after I moved away, and I understood that Vidar was involved somehow but I wasn't sure exactly how. I remembered Lovisa Markström, of course, had met her a number of times.

I'd ended up renting a room in an apartment in Vasastan in the city center of Stockholm, and I would take the two metro stops into T-Centralen, wide-eyed and still afraid of taking the wrong train, to pick up a copy of *Hallandsposten* at the big Pressbyrån convenience store in the departure hall. This was the day after Sweden voted on the EU. In Stockholm, Europe was all anyone talked about.

When I saw the pictures in the paper, I was struck by how wide the gulf had become, the gap between me and the village described in the centerfold, the place that had once been my entire world. I wasn't one of them anymore, I thought. Instead I was brimming with the excitement of living in the center of everything in the capital city. I felt no shame, only relief. How could I ever move back? Everything I had been lacking in Tofta was here.

That was how I saw them, all of them, as if from a great distance. Vidar; his mother, Bibbi; even my parents; the memory of Sven, Lovisa, and everyone else who was no longer there: Even when I returned for short visits, Christmas Eve or Easter, I thought of them all as parts of what I'd left and would never miss.

In those days, it seemed to me as though time stood still in my home region, that everything stayed the same. I recognized all the faces, concerns, and hopes as soon as I set foot on Halland ground.

That was more or less when my existence became a whirlwind. I had a short story published in a newspaper, and then another, a third, and after that a publisher called to ask whether I'd thought about writing something longer. Two years later, the year I turned twenty-six, my debut novel, *Prerequisites for Dreamers,* came out—a novel that to date has sold exactly 656 copies, not an insignificant number of which can be attributed to my parents, who bought the book to have something to give away to relatives and friends as presents. It wasn't until my fourth novel, *The Freedom Game,* came out in 2010 that things really got moving. I appeared on talk shows, was interviewed for the culture pages, and was invited to write columns, plays, and screenplays for television. By this point I was thirty-five, had met Sara, and was making enough that I could stop working a second job at the register at my local ICA grocery store.

Sara and I had a good life. She worked at the firm, read books, worked out at the neighborhood gym, and ate dinners out with her friends, while I rented a desk in an open office in Södermalm, went to events to mingle, visited bookstores and libraries, and met up with friends for a beer now and then. I appeared interested when I spoke with our neighbors, I polished the windows of our apartment, I did dishes, and I worked.

Sara didn't seem to have any problem living with an author, or at least that's what she said, and she seemed happy. We took vacations sometimes, we paid the bills, we did weekly grocery shops when necessary, went to the movies, bought insurance, and renovated the bathroom; we planted seeds in little boxes on the balcony and courted each other in that semi-romantic way adults do when they're trying to live with each other.

The restlessness I felt as a seventeen-year-old on the streets of Halmstad hadn't cropped up for a long time, possibly because I was far too busy to identify it.

Toward the end of our marriage I started walking around with a peculiar feeling in my body. I didn't know what it was; it had no name. Sometimes, at odd moments charged with electricity like the air right before a thunderstorm, I looked around and had no idea where I was. Which street I was standing on, how old I was, what kind of life I was living. Brief moments of absolute weightlessness, or lack of oxygen, as if everything around me was frozen in strange, gray ice. I had nothing behind me and nothing waiting ahead of me either.

Then, as though someone had snapped their fingers in my ear, I was right side up again and returned to the present with an impression of, I don't know, a sensation like loss in my chest.

Somewhere around there is when I started dreaming of the house in Tofta again.

Construction had begun in early 1979. I was two years old at the time. The house was built by Dad, his brother, and my grandfather Arvid. It was a sturdy house, a work of family. I think of it as being full of love.

The house was finished near the end of the year, and we moved in. When I started dreaming about it almost forty years later, I hadn't been there in a long time.

Many people who had once visited that house were no longer around: All four of my grandparents, my maternal uncle, and all the other faces I can see only in photographs these days.

I myself had traveled far, become an author and almost a different person. That's how it felt.

But I had returned in my dreams; I stood in the driveway in the twilight, and those who were no longer alive had only gone to fetch something. *Wow,* I thought in my dream, feeling the urge to laugh, *what a misunderstanding! That must be it.* When I stepped into the kitchen, I could almost hear them, distantly, and it occurred to me that I missed them something awful.

: : :

It was around then, when I started having the dream about the house in Tofta, that Sara said to me for the first time that I had become so oddly empty.

But I didn't feel empty. Not then.

Instead I felt, very strongly, that something was coming to a close and something else was about to begin, but I could not for the life of me understand what these somethings might be.

100

I had put off contacting Gisela Mellberg and hesitated for a long time. In the end I realized it was only a matter of time, that sooner or later I would simply do it, and I picked up the phone. There was some information only she could give me.

To my surprise, she agreed to see me. Gisela lived in a lovely one-story house in Furet, and that's where we met, just over two months ago now. I recognized her from old pictures in the paper, taken before the attack and published shortly thereafter. I was surprised at how little she'd changed. I'd expected that the life Gisela Mellberg had ended up living would have left its mark on her face more than it apparently had.

Her home in Furet was tidy and tastefully decorated, but there were still signs of the teenagers who lived there. We sat in a comfortable furniture set in the living room, and I listened to her story, which began with what it was like in Tiarp immediately after Stina Franzén was found, about the search for Frida Östmark, and Sweden in 1986. Only later did I venture to ask about her own experiences, about Robert and the time that followed. We sat there for hours, until one of her sons came barging in with his practice bag over his shoulder, and she looked at the clock in surprise.

"Oh God, time flies. I have to get dinner started."

I think at first she spoke to me because I had no connection to her.

Everyone else around Gisela was, in one way or another, drawn into or linked to the tragedies that had marked her life. Not me. She could speak to me freely, as freely as she liked. Furthermore, I felt a sort of chemistry between us, not in a sexual way exactly, but something like it. Maybe it was trust. She felt, she said, as though I understood her, which I did. Sometimes that's all a person wants.

"That," she said, "and to reach a point in life where our past can no longer explain who we are and where we're going. That's all anyone wants."

Even so, I was hesitant to contact her again—even more hesitant this time, if that was possible. Eventually I went to see her.

"Oh, it's you again!"

She opened the door a little wider, took a step forward, and shook my hand in a firm, cool grip. She had clear, alert eyes that held mine in a steady gaze.

"I know I should have called first," I said, "but I was in the neighborhood, and I'm hoping to talk about what happened one more time."

What happened. That's how I had decided to refer to it this time too, even though the words sounded contrived. She gazed at me for a long time.

"Why?"

I held up the heavy canvas tote I'd brought.

"It has to do with my father."

She studied me, curious. "Why? Who's your father?"

"He's the son of Arvid and Greta Carlsson from Tiarp."

I hadn't mentioned this last time. It hadn't seemed important.

"He is?"

"I hope you can help me. Or, well, him. Us." I tried to look apologetic. "Can I come in? It won't take long. Or should I come back another day?"

Something was happening in Gisela's eyes. Thoughts swirling. I wondered what they were. Then she took a step back and moved aside.

We sat where we had the first time, in the living room, in the expanses of the deep furniture set. She drank tea; I had water. She'd asked about coffee and I declined, afraid that in the time it took to brew it she might change her mind.

"You know," she said after a while, "thinking back on it now, it's so strange. So many years have passed. I've lived with it longer than without it. But sometimes I have, like . . . well, almost like distorted thoughts."

"How so?"

"I haven't been alive for fifty-five years, but twenty-eight. The Gisela who existed back then, before all of this happened, it's like she doesn't count. That was someone else. The woman who lived with Robert in Risarp. That wasn't me. Do you know what I mean? It must sound pretty weird, right? And kind of sad. I've gone to those crime-victim support groups and stuff too, I've read about lots of people who kind of let their victimhood define them. Women, of course, almost always women, and it's always violence perpetrated by men, one way or another. I don't think I've ever understood it, how people see themselves as crushed. You can't go to such and such place, because he might be there, you can't visit a certain store because he might shop there, you walk around terrified of running into him on the street, or pulling up next to him at a red light. I thought it was . . . well, weak. Even though I understood, I still thought that. But, you know, what about *me*? My God, I didn't even *exist* before this. The person I am today was born at the hospital when they came in and told me what had happened to Robert. That they'd found him. The woman who existed before that, well . . . where is she? Who the hell knows? Dead, I guess. It's probably that simple. And really, that's worse than letting it define you. Right?"

"Sure," I said cautiously, "or maybe it's the same thing?"

"It might sound strange to you, I assume it does. But, you know, it's . . . In some ways what happened that night isn't something I carry with me, or suffer from or have nightmares about. It settled deeper than that. I'm sure that's why I can still live my life and be happy, not full of fear, with my kids and husband and everything. When the pain is that deep, maybe it's not even pain anymore. It's a way of being. And that allows you to move on."

She spoke like a person who was used to expressing herself verbally, almost with a poetic or academic ring to it. I wanted to ask if she was a reader. If she'd read my books. Presumably not.

"Do you know when I realized this?" she asked. "That I had started to move on, as impossible as that may sound?"

"No."

"The first time I heard someone say 'dolly' afterward, I think it was in a movie, and I didn't react to it. And how could I have reacted, anyway? He didn't say that to *me*. He said it to the woman who lived before me. That's how I felt."

"That's right," I said slowly. "Because, dolly, he said . . ."

"Lie still now, dolly."

Right. I jotted it down.

"Did you follow the events of last spring and summer?"

"I didn't have to. The police called."

"They did?"

"Of course they did. Partly because they wanted to tell me, of course. But they wanted me to identify him too. That is," she added, "they showed me pictures of him."

"Of David Linder?"

"Yes. The police were very kind, honestly. I got to pick the time and place and everything, and they brought a psychologist with them. It didn't help all that much, but, you know, I appreciated the effort."

Beyond the picture window in the living room, the tranquillity was somewhat disturbed by a cargo truck cruising by slowly.

"And it was him?"

"Well, you know, in my case I never saw him. He was wearing a mask. All I saw were his eyes and part of his nose. But I told you that last time, didn't I? Was that what you wanted to ask?"

I took the tote bag from the floor and placed it next to me on the sofa, pulled out the heavy work journal.

"What I wanted to ask you was really just . . . here."

I opened the journal and told her about my grandfather's records, *D. Linder,* about the mixer and how my father had gotten out these old books because he thought they might help me in my work.

"And, I mean," I said, "if I'm not mistaken, well . . . the times can't be right. Or maybe they can? Maybe it's just that I don't understand."

Gisela looked up from the journal, looking grim and stiff. "Are you going to include this in what you're writing?"

"I . . . It's not that simple. I just want to understand why my grandfather wrote this. But I understand if you feel . . ." I didn't finish my sentence, because I had no idea what she might be feeling and didn't dare to guess, either. Instead I held up my hands. "I can leave, if you want."

Gisela looked at the open journal again.

Looking back, in my mind, I would see her sit up straighter in the easy chair, sort of bracing herself. But she probably didn't, really. What I do recall is that she said: "I remember this."

Her index finger rested on Grandpa's note from the following day, March 1.

C-H Håkansson came by with his truck, he had written. *Picked up the mixer. Broken beyond repair.*

"I was on my way home," she said, her finger still on the page, as though the memory would fade unless she were touching the paper. "After taking Wille home. That's when I ran into him."

"Håkansson?"

"He was a scrap hauler in Tiarp. All kinds of stuff, mostly car parts, but other things too. He took it all to the junkyard in town, where they sold it on. His name was Carl-Henrik Håkansson, that's what 'C-H' stands for. He had been up to see Arvid and Greta on the ridge when I ran into him. This makes sense." She tapped the page. "He had a cement mixer in the truck bed."

I wished I had thought this through more carefully, that I had been better prepared. Should I have recorded this conversation?

Now she quickly pulled her hand away from the page, as if it had burned her.

"A cement mixer," I said. "Are you sure of it?"

"Yes."

Outside, a line of birds flew across the pale sky, sharp and black like malicious strokes of ink.

"But then, given my grandfather's note here . . . what you're saying seems to suggest he was right. Or am I misunderstanding?"

Gisela considered the journal.

"I remember that. But what it means, I don't know. Maybe the times are wrong? Either your grandfather's, or the times the police gave for Stina. Maybe the murder took place later or earlier."

"That's what I thought at first, too. But it couldn't have been earlier, because she left work at eleven. The perpetrator was waiting for her, assuming he was the one standing outside, but I think we do have to make that assumption. And it couldn't have been later, either, because when she was declared dead at the hospital her wounds weren't fresh, they were a few hours old. So it must have happened right around then, the same time Linder was at my grandfather's place."

The time estimate for her wounds was an important fact. I'd been lucky to get hold of it by way of the investigation into Sven; the times were included there because they were part of the supporting documentation in the report that was filed against him and investigated by Nora Selvin.

Gisela cocked her head.

"What about your grandfather? Could he have been mistaken?"

I hesitated before responding.

"I don't know. I don't think so."

101

I hoped Sven had been right. That he'd done the right thing. I needed that to be the case. If he was wrong, that made him seem out of context for me, cloven. But it was a real possibility that David Linder was at my grandparents' farm that night. Which ruled him out as Stina Franzén's killer.

How could it be possible? How had this happened? Even as I understood everything, I understood nothing.

I knew it was approaching, the moment I would have to see Vidar again and talk to him. Our brief conversation at the soccer match hadn't exactly made me feel more optimistic about how it would go. Even now I could picture his reaction, his protests and objections in the face of the story I had produced during the summer and fall:

"No, no, *no*, Moth, for Christ's sake. That's not what happened at all. Dad's and my relationship wasn't nearly as complicated as you imagine. He wasn't nearly as, hell, I don't know, as *unstable* as you make him out to be. You describe him as a fucking mental case. As if he came that close to strangling an innocent man in a café in town? And Evy, to suggest that she and Dad . . . how dare you. Are you crazy? And *me*. It never crossed my mind that Einar would have been better off dead in that accident, what the hell kind of person do you think I am? And worst of all was Dad's death. For starters, where the fuck do you get off, writing about a real person's death? Not only that, you also describe it like it was straight out of some old rural legend. It's not a fucking saga. My father died on the bathroom floor with his mouth full of blood and vomit, suffocated by his own lungs while Mom was in town running errands. He had shit his pants and his face was the color of an unripe banana. What the fuck do you think you're doing?"

Yes. That's exactly what would happen. He would glare accusingly at me and conclude with: "You got none of this right, Moth. Not a thing. Chuck it."

And if I were to ask him to tell me how it really happened, the truth, the events as they seemed to him, he would just shake his head indifferently, possibly because he'd moved on but possibly in an attempt to protect himself. I couldn't blame him, I mean, I understood.

I returned home disarmed and thus ill prepared, mentally, for what I saw through the kitchen window: the light above the counter. The fluorescent tube emitted a cold, desolate glow in the dark. I stepped out of the car and walked slowly to the front door.

I'd turned the light on this morning when it was still dark out and I was doing yesterday's dishes. Hadn't I turned it off when I was done? I was almost certain I had.

I gingerly stepped onto the porch and peered through the window, put the key in the lock, and turned it. The canopy of trees rustled around me and the darkness drifted closer, like smoke. I held my breath and felt a peculiar fear in my belly, like when you become aware of a great danger.

What scared me were the edges. As I looked around, shapes around me began to dissolve. Was this how Sven had felt? Obsession was like a poison, making you uncertain which shadows were real and which were imagined.

"Hello?" I said loudly as I stepped into the hall, my heart beating hard against my rib cage.

The house responded with mere silence.

I turned on my phone flashlight and aimed it at the floor. Hoping to see what, footprints?

I didn't know. I knew nothing.

Instead I took a deep breath and strode with firm, loud steps into the kitchen, where I turned on the warm overhead light and went over to the counter to turn off the fluorescent light. I looked around. Everything was just where I'd left it, everything was just where it should be, yet I couldn't quite shake the feeling that someone else had been there.

102

One former police officer, Sven Jörgensson, had taken the life of another, David Linder, a man who had turned out to be the apparition that had struck fear into the people of Nyårsåsen in the latter half of the 1980s. It had been written up in the papers, discussed in debates and on TV. The anchors of the news programs had asked the usual questions. *How could this happen? Is this more common than you'd think within law enforcement? What should be done about it? Should the police undergo greater scrutiny?*

But there was also the opposite point of view. A killer had been put out of commission for good. People could appreciate that, in the end.

The scrutiny lasted all summer, and the police must have been under immense pressure for a while there; I often saw Markus Danielsson looking grim in front of a microphone or against the wall of a building in a hastily snapped photo in the paper. At one point, they'd even managed to get the national chief of police to give a statement, but by the time autumn rolled around things had calmed down. Only the local news channels and a couple of rabidly opinionated folks on social media were still pushing the story.

Now I went back to the clips, watched the interviews on SVT and TV4. The names of the individual officers were never mentioned, but a quick search online would certainly provide answers for anyone who cared to look. There was already a long thread on Flashback Forum about David Linder. Sven and Vidar were mentioned in it too.

The author in me had been awakened, and because I didn't know how to move forward I started digging where I stood. I tried to contact someone who'd worked at Halmstad Welding and Mechanics so I could add another couple lines about that company, to bring fullness and color to my description. I spent a whole day trying to find out what kind of cement mixer my grandfather had owned. I read about the marl holes and searched for details about Aron, the man who, it was said, was taken by the devil up on the ridge. All I could find was a note in one of the old parish registers. He was listed there, recorded as an unmarried farmhand. I visited the city library; contacted *Hallandsposten* and looked through their photo archive for pictures of Halmstad from autumn 1985 and onward. I saw pictures from Nyårsåsen that year, from the area around Vapnö, from the search parties and the hunt for Frida Östmark. I filled my bag with photocopies.

There was something she'd said, Gisela. Something that was pestering me, but I couldn't get a fix on what it was.

I was interrupted by my phone. It was Dad calling.

"Hi," he said. "How are you?"

"Fine," I said, and they came back to me: the shadow outside my window and the light on in the kitchen. The feeling that someone had been in my house. "I'm just not getting enough sleep."

"You spend a lot of time inside your head," said Dad. "Don't you miss . . ."

"What?"

"I don't know. Other people?"

"Sure. But I'll be okay. I've got you and Mom and Rasmus, after all."

"Do you think you'll ever get married again?"

Given the awkward way he said it, it was almost as though he was reading the question off a piece of paper. For an instant, I experienced something that usually ever happened only in Stockholm: I had opened the kitchen window for some fresh air and now I smelled an odor I couldn't identify. That never happened down here. All the smells, sounds, and impressions were familiar and recognizable. The house, the land, the nature, the road, the cars and trucks, the farm equipment—it was all clear and obvious, and none of it demanded an explanation.

It was a different story in the big apartment buildings in the capital city. When you stood on the balcony on an oddly hot August night, you might suddenly catch a whiff of some grilling going on nearby, the scent of detergent from freshly washed clothes on a line a few balconies away; you might hear laughter or scolding, declarations of love or breakups, from people you never saw. That was one of the things I loved about the capital city, these events great and small that played out around you but had nothing to do with you.

Down here, you were a part of everything. Even now. I recognized the odor, of course, it just took me a moment to identify it. It was diesel. Sure enough, when I went to the kitchen window, the phone to my ear, and looked at the pull-off on the other side of the highway, there was a truck idling there. A driver scratched his head in concern and knelt down to inspect the undercarriage of his truck. Sometimes the wind carried the odors of the pull-off over to the house.

"I don't know," I said to Dad.

"If you met the right person, would you want to get married again?"

Definitely, I wanted to say. Of course. If I met the right person, sure. But what I actually said was closer to the truth.

"I don't know if I could survive it one more time."

Dad laughed. "Listen," he said. "I've been married to your ma for forty years. With love, you can survive anything."

103

"Yes, hello. Is this Bernt Olofsson?"

I heard crackling, as though he were rubbing the phone against his shirt to clean it. Then his voice returned, gruff and flat.

"Yes, that's me. Who is this?"

I told him my name and that I was working on a book about what happened up in Tiarp. I didn't have to say more. By this point, I was starting to learn how to make a snap judgment of the person I was talking to, whether it was best to reveal as little as possible or if I could just be blunt. Lots of people I talked to at first had closed themselves off, but a number of them had also been eager to share their own ideas, even though they might not be of much importance.

"Right, sure. Damn shame, all of that."

I listened to him for a while, this man approaching retirement, his weekends passing far too slowly and with far too little to fill them up. He shared his views on criminals, politics, and immigrants, and then he was silent.

"What I wanted to ask you was, you worked at Halmstad Welding and Mechanics until they closed in '94, right?"

"Sure did," said Bernt.

"And you were there back in the eighties too?"

"Damn straight I was. I was there for over twenty years. From '74 to '94 when they closed up shop, it was because of that fucking Social Democrat, what the fuck was his name . . ."

"What I'm wondering," I continued, "is what it was like working there."

"Oh, it was fine, I guess. Hard, heavy work, of course, but a hell of a lot of fun too. I like machines, y'know? And we had good stuff there. Fun to work with; we had lots of vehicles."

"You had your own fleet, then?"

"Hell yes. Back then we had just about everything. But mostly we had trucks. I'm thinking they were Fords. Yeah, I think they were Fords, one of those classic flatbed types, you know. Those are the ones we took out most often. Powerful as hell, they had V8s, you know."

"Did you do that often? Take them out? What does that entail, to take one out?"

"Well, you know, we had regular customers, like. Where things broke down a lot." Bernt laughed. "You know how it is. Things aren't built to last, but to break. That's what makes the world go round. People fixing what's broken."

"What sorts of things?"

"We dealt with all kinds of stuff over there at Welding and Mechanics. We weren't just welders, you know, we were mechanics too. So we went out to all sorts of jobs. Anything from machines in restaurants to huge fucking machinery at construction sites, car washes. I even went to one of these gyms once. We did it all."

I looked at my notes. "One of these gyms." He said it like he had visited another planet.

"You said you had regular customers. Who were they?"

"Like I said, anyone. All around town, or nearby. Steninge, I remember, there was a fleet of heavy machinery we maintained there. A factory in Trönninge, I went there myself pretty frequently. Even down in Snapparp. Yeah, and Eldsberga, Åled, we—"

"What was that? Snapparp?"

"There was a rest stop there with a gas station. They had a car wash that was always on the fritz. One of our guys went out there often. What the hell was his name . . ."

I didn't move a muscle.

"It was a fucking terrible car wash, by the way," Bernt went on. "I would never wash my car there. They came out looking like you'd gone at them with an electric whisk. Fuck."

Lie still now, dolly.

That's what the Tiarp Man had said to Gisela, and Evy's words had come back to me. *This old dolly is doing her best.*

Such an innocent word; maybe it had been a term their parents used, and the kids picked it up.

Dolly.

I almost couldn't breathe.

I contacted Alevallen, the sporting fields where Alet had played and continued to play their home matches. I reached an answering machine and had a hard time getting any further, but eventually I got my hands on the number to a woman who lived in Frösakull and took care of the association's administrative work now and then.

She met me in the parking lot that same afternoon, a short woman in a burgundy coat, with dark hair and lively eyes.

"So you're writing a book about soccer? Is that right?"

"Not exactly, but soccer is a part of it."

"Exciting. Well, there's plenty of material in here, I'll tell you that." From her coat pocket she took a bunch of keys on a ring and looked for the right one. "Let's see. Here it is."

The clubhouse was a squat wooden building. It smelled like old lumber and stale air. The office was at the back, and it was small and full of furniture from the seventies. There was a copy machine in one corner, the walls were adorned with team photos, a narrow display case boasted trophies, and along the wall closest to the desk towered a heavy bookcase full of binders. I looked at the wall of team photos, the rows of young men and women in pictures that looked old and new.

"These are nice," I said, "but surely not every year is here?"

"No, no. I hear they used to put them all up, but over the years it got to be too many. These ones are just the memorable teams. But listen." She patted the bookcase full of binders. "It should be in here. Unfortunately, I can't allow you to take anything with you. But you're welcome to snap some pictures if you like, unless you find some sensitive information. But I don't think there's much of that here."

"Thank you. That's very kind of you."

"I'll just take a walk around the fields in the meantime, since it's a Monday. Sometimes people party here on weekends and leave a hell of a mess."

I stood in front of the shelves of binders. They seemed neatly organized. I opened some, studying lists and plans for training camps, away trips, and end-of-season celebrations. There were team rosters, schedules, inventories. I took out my phone and photographed the old documents. I looked for pictures, but didn't find any. I was leaning over the desk, and when my back began to ache I replaced a binder on the shelf and stood up straight. No member lists yet. I went over to the framed team pictures on the walls. There were about twenty of them, some of them very old, others almost new. I found the 1985 team, but not 1986. Maybe that was because they'd lost to Breared. At least, I told myself that was it.

I took out another binder. From the autumn of 1985, a letter addressed to the club president at the time. The letter had been written on a typewriter; it was very short and riddled with errors:

> *Greetings.*
> *I want to bring it to the clubs attension that some coaches are socializing improperly with the girls on there teams. I witnessed this myself at last weeks practis (9/22/85) when I came to pick up my dauter. This doesnt look good. This girl is of age and maybe this kind of thing happens all the time but it made me uncomfterble. It could also cause unecesary conflict among the team. Since I dont know if this was already something you were aware of I wanted to let the club know.*

I looked for a written response from the club but found none; maybe the letter hadn't prompted any reaction, which wouldn't surprise me, or maybe it had been dealt with verbally. The only signature on this note was "a parent."

I considered the date mentioned in the letter. It took me a while to find, near the end of another binder, the schedule for September 1985. Only two of Alet's teams had practice that day: the peewee boys, and the sixteen-plus women.

I opened a binder, found a tab labeled LIST OF MEMBERS & COACHES, and flipped to it. Now here was something.

Yes, I thought, *exactly, it might be here.* I paged through the documents and found a list for 1985 and 1986, and photographed the names. Placing my index finger on the page, I ran down the list to see if I recognized any. There she was, Stina Franzén. She had played for Alet in the fall of 1985.

Her name wasn't the only one I recognized. I knew the coach, too. When I understood why, my body tensed up as though I'd just heard a thunderclap. I wasn't wrong. It was just as I'd thought as I stood up on the sporting fields at Breared—something about this was awfully familiar.

Einar Bengtsson had been Stina Franzén's coach.

106

In the midst of the summer doldrums, Death had appeared, had come very close to taking someone with him; maybe it was just a coincidence that he had been forced to turn back empty-handed.

The images from the accident were of good quality, I noticed as I sat in the archives of the city library, finally finding them in the newspaper after hours of browsing. There they were, two of them, in *Hallandsposten*, under a headline about a serious car accident that happened one July day in 1991. *A man was gravely injured in a traffic accident on Kustvägen on Thursday*, the article began. *The man's vehicle collided head-on with a truck and caught fire. The man was transported to the hospital with life-threatening injuries.*

Evy had told me about the accident, but I'd never seen the pictures. I studied them carefully. One had been taken at close range and captured the wrecked Saab close up. The other had been taken from a distance and was angled slightly downward, as though the photographer had sought out a high vantage point from which to survey the scene. It was a chaotic image; the still summer day in the background, the truck in the foreground, and, farther in the distance, the police tape, a crowd of onlookers, the mangled car, the emergency vehicles so hastily parked, and the asphalt, badly scorched by the fire.

There was something off about the picture, but for a long time I couldn't quite figure out what it was. Then I saw the issue. I squinted and bent closer.

Clearly the truck had braked hard; the tire tracks were dark on the sun-bleached asphalt. But from the Saab—nothing. As if he hadn't even tried to stop.

Strange that no one had noticed this back then. Or had they? There was no mention of it in the article, but of course it might have been part of the investigation. Maybe he hadn't had time to slow down; that was one possibility. Or maybe something had happened inside the car that rendered him unable. Or maybe he had tried but it didn't work; maybe the brakes failed. There were countless possible scenarios.

None of them made me feel more at ease.

It was dark out, and an icy wind blew across the Nissan River and whistled around the corner as I stepped out of the city library and walked to the parking lot. As I drove, my eyes kept going to the rear-view mirror, and it took me a while to figure out why.

I was checking to see if I was being followed.

No one was there. No one at all.

So I told myself.

When I returned home, I turned on the lights and tried to get a handle on the intricate mess my workspace had become. That's when I found the family photo again, under a pile of old newspapers. It was the picture Evy had given me as a memento, a gift I'd found remarkably touching. I had excused myself to go to the bathroom. There it was, the picture of her and Ronnie and their kids, Ronnie's mother, and Einar.

I stared for a long time at the young blond man who was smiling at the camera. I wondered who had taken the picture; I'd forgotten to ask.

I was reminded of something else and kept digging. It took a while to find it, but eventually I pulled it out of a green plastic folder that was half-buried under old newspaper clippings: a bundle of photographs from the human chain that had moved toward the sea in the spring of 1986, as they searched for Frida Östmark.

The pictures had been taken along the edges of the search area; temporary cordons had been put up and taken down as the search party progressed. The photographer had been standing on the other side, capturing those involved: men and women walking in an uneven line, their expressions serious; many had their eyes trained on the ground but a number of them were looking up, ahead, or in the direction of the photographer. Along the edges were glimpses of anxious and curious onlookers who were standing around shivering, improperly dressed in the chilly spring sunshine. I noticed a lot of details in those pictures now, nuances I'd overlooked before. Not just the peculiar fashions, the hairstyles and shoes and high-waisted jeans. It was a different Sweden I saw, a time shortly after the shots on Sveavägen, when trauma and sorrow were extremely fresh and fear was expanding, but there was still hope to be found.

There he was, at the very edge of the image. His stance was casual, his hands in his pockets, his face a little turned away. He matched the man from my memories, the young coach I'd seen encouraging his team after they lost to Breared. I took out the family photo and tried to compare the two.

Here, I thought, looking at the pictures from the search party. *This is where you found her. Gisela.*

107

The address. His address, where had he lived back then, before the accident? I searched through my materials. Didn't I have it somewhere?

Here it was. Fammarpsvägen. Fammarp was a geographically broad township with a population of about a hundred. It was seldom mentioned in the history books except as something in the way. It most commonly arose in the context of the Halmstad coastline. It's incredibly beautiful, people would say, and long. And if it weren't for Fammarp, you could see the sea from all the way up in Heagård.

I searched for it on my phone, studied the map that appeared, and printed it out. Standing at the kitchen table, I got out a marker and made two *X* marks at Tiarp and Ringenäs. I ran my finger along the roads, observing the distances, and drew a circle around Fammarp, which was right in between them.

His center point.

I had started glancing over my shoulder, sensing shadows everywhere. I woke up at night and made a circuit of the house, staring into the darkness because I thought someone might be waiting for me out there, someone who wished me harm. The walls of my house had grown paper-thin, brittle as a wafer, and the ceiling hung low;

sometimes I thought I heard a ticking sound; I walked around the rooms as if the floor were covered in water. A pipe had burst somewhere but there was no handyperson to call. It was all driving me closer and closer to the edge, and I didn't know quite what to do to make it stop, if that was even possible.

108

One evening, while I was still going back and forth about what I should do, two bright headlights flashed across the driveway and I heard gravel spitting and crunching under tires. Unsure of what was happening, I stepped onto the porch and squinted into the darkness. A car door slammed.

"Hi," came a voice.

She sounded much younger than she was, and I thought of what she'd said, that she wasn't actually that old. That she had died and been reborn as someone new, almost thirty years ago.

Gisela Mellberg wondered if this was a bad time; after all, it was quite late.

"Not at all, come in," I said, taking a step out into the dark. "That is," I amended, "would you like to come in?"

She had stepped into the warm light that shone across the porch from the window and front hall. She smiled, but it was a cool smile—the kind I sometimes noticed in women, the kind that could mean both openness and distance, wariness.

"Yes, just for a little bit. I want . . . I have some questions, after our last conversation."

That was understandable. She stepped into the hall. I asked if she wanted some coffee. She declined, saying instead, "What a cozy house."

"I don't know if I'd say that. But thanks. I haven't lived here very long."

"When did you move in?"

"It was . . ." I began, before realizing, "almost a year ago."

She smiled the same smile.

"Maybe you've had more important things to worry about."

"Yes, in one way."

"That's what I wanted to ask about."

She spotted my desk and approached it, eyeing the computer as you might study a weapon. She rested a hand on the stack of paper that lay there.

"What's this?"

"Just a misunderstanding, maybe. Or a mistake."

She looked confused.

"What? You mean, a draft? Of your book?"

"It's . . . We'll see. Maybe."

I didn't know quite what to say. An account? A record, of sorts? What happened and when, who and why. Or was it just an attempt to remember? An explanation, sure, maybe, at least to myself, an explanation of what must have happened to Sven Jörgensson and his nearly grown Vidar, to the country that belonged to them.

Or so I had thought, at least.

I showed her to the kitchen, which was lit by the muted glow of a small table lamp I'd found in Mom and Dad's storage area earlier that fall.

She said she wanted to know what was actually going to come of all this. The first time we spoke, she'd gotten the idea that it was just for a book, but after the second time she wasn't so sure.

I told her the same thing as when we'd met earlier, but this time my words meant more. I hadn't gone searching for the story of the Tiarp Man; rather, it had come to me. This wasn't entirely true, but it was, at least, what I tried to tell myself. I had returned, and things had happened. It was a story in which I, the author, carried no blame. There's a recklessness in those of us who write, one that's not always easy to grapple with. We need to rationalize, justify. So I told her I simply wanted to understand, although perhaps, in truth, I was the one who had placed myself at the center of all this disintegration.

"Okay," she said when I was finished. "I get it."

"I'm sorry if I . . ."

"It's fine. I get it now. It's mostly that I didn't . . . I was so taken aback last time, is all, and I didn't quite understand."

"I apologize for that."

She looked at the manuscript on the table again. "What did you mean by 'mistake'? Do you regret writing it?"

"Yes . . . or no. Maybe I was wrong. I don't know."

"What were you wrong about?"

I hesitated. Here she was again. *What should I do?* I thought, but although I didn't want to, I realized I had no choice. If I didn't do it now, I would do it later.

"As long as you're here, may I show you a picture?"

"What kind of picture?"

"Of a person."

The copies were on my computer; I'd cropped close-up shots of him to make his face as prominent and isolated as possible.

I went to get the computer, browsed through my growing image archive, and after a moment of hesitation I showed her.

She had told me before about being shown the picture of David Linder. It was a hesitant sort of recognition; she'd described a vibration that went through her body. No shockwave, no sudden flash of insight. I had quoted her on this, because it was impossible to express with any greater precision. Nor did I dare to try, I must admit.

I studied Gisela carefully, watched as she drew up her shoulders and went stiff, a glimmer of perception and fear in her clear eyes.

"Who is that?"

"I don't know," I lied. "Do you?"

How did I feel in that moment? How did I experience it, was I shocked? Maybe I should have been shocked, or even afraid, because as I looked around I was in such deep water that I didn't even know what "the bottom" could mean. But none of this happened. Instead, I just thought, once more: *Here she is. The woman who survived, although she has claimed that she died.*

She stared at the screen. Gulped.

"I didn't think it would be like this." She was whispering. "So perfectly obvious. Once I saw them."

"Last time we spoke, you said you recognized Linder."

She nodded, grim.

"I was wrong. Maybe I got mixed up . . . after all, I met him once. Linder. Maybe those times blended together, I don't know, it was . . . It was . . ."

"Gisela? Gisela, are you okay?"

"His eyes," she said tonelessly, as though the face in the picture had bewitched her. "I remember his eyes."

109

For a brief moment, in the instant between climbing the steps in Marbäck and knocking on his door, I had the sense of getting very close to
them, being so near, an unexpected link between me and the two men
who had suffered so mightily. And here I was—forced to make it even
worse.

A chilly rain was falling, and it felt like a long way to Christmas, to
the light, to rest. A single bulb cast a yellow glow over the steps. When
Vidar opened the door, he looked surprised.

"Moth?"

"Hi," I said. "Do you have a moment? We need to talk."

"What about?"

"Tiarp."

Vidar rolled his eyes.

"Moth, I . . ."

"Vidar."

There must have been an odd tone in my voice. He moved aside
and let me in. I stepped out of my shoes and took off my jacket.

"Is Patricia home?"

"No, she's at a staff meeting or something. What's wrong with
you?"

"Could we sit down?"

"Only if you tell me what the hell is going on."

I took a seat on the sofa and set the canvas tote on the floor beside me. Vidar sank into the closest easy chair. He had a glass of whiskey before him, and he scrutinized me as he picked it up to take a sip.

I didn't know quite where to begin. So I simply started talking.

"Do you recall whether Frida Östmark had any siblings?"

Vidar raised his eyebrows. "Why?"

"I didn't think she had any."

"No, she did. A little brother. Sören Östmark. Things didn't go so great for him; we brought him in for drunkenness and mischief more than once."

I nodded slowly. From my bag I took a copy of a yellowed sheet of paper.

"This is a team roster," I said. "Alet, 1986. I visited their archives and found it myself."

Listed as center back was one *S. Östmark*. The coach's name was at the top of the page.

I set out another sheet of paper.

"This," I said quietly, "is the team roster for Alet's women's team the season before."

I could tell when his eyes landed on *S. Franzén*. When he saw the same coach listed. With each second of silence that ticked by on the old wall clock above his head, I grew more tense. I had found it. The connection.

"They had a relationship, I think." I handed him a copy of the letter from *A parent*. "It doesn't explicitly say that it's talking about Stina Franzén, but that's how I interpret it."

"I don't understand what this is," he said at last. "Is this . . . What is this all about? What does it have to do with Tiarp?"

I had seen him. Einar coached Frida Östmark's little brother, Sören, and he had been Stina's coach just six months earlier. Stina had left the team because she didn't have time for it, didn't want to play, couldn't play—what did I know. It didn't matter. He was the one Stina had been seeing. But it was questionable—a coach and a former player.

That was why she kept it to herself. But her mother had suspected something. What had she said, according to the investigation? I'd read it in the newspaper. *I had gotten this idea that something was up. Recently, maybe in the last month or so. I thought maybe she had met someone.* Mothers always knew.

"And Gisela Mellberg," I went on, producing a picture from *Hallandsposten,* "he finds here. During the search for Frida Östmark. She participated in the human chain and he's standing right there. See? That was how he chose her."

"'That was how he chose her'? What are you talking about, are you writing about this?" Vidar didn't even look at the picture. "Is that what you're doing over there in Tofta? If so, then for the record, it was David Linder."

"But how can you be so sure? Did they ever find Frida Östmark's remains?"

"No, but—"

"I've been up there, to his farm. I saw how meticulously they searched it. The body wasn't there. If it was him, why wouldn't it be there?"

"Because it's too close!" Vidar exclaimed, throwing up his hands.

"I thought the same thing at first," I said, "but how easy is it to move somebody like that, without attracting attention? Without leaving evidence behind?"

"Maybe he never even brought her to the farm. It would be too risky. She could be anywhere. This doesn't prove anything. And Snapparp, why would Einar . . ."

"Einar worked at Halmstad Welding and Mechanics. One of their regular customers was the gas station in Snapparp, the car wash there." I took out another piece of paper. "Einar was frequently there to repair it. He would have known it was a good spot to ditch the van, maybe the only spot he could think of in the heat of the moment. After all, as far as we know, it was the one time he was almost caught, so maybe he panicked."

Vidar gaped at me.

"Tracks from a utility vehicle were found at the scene of the crime. Einar Bengtsson drove a crappy little Saab, not a utility vehicle. Linder had one, though."

It was tough, but I steeled myself. I had been working on this for so long, and all I wanted was to bring it to a close. And something, I'm not sure what, had convinced me.

"Einar drove one for work. He even lived in Fammarp." I took out my phone and showed him the picture of Einar. "Gisela Mellberg identified him as the man who attacked her."

"She said that to you? She identified him in front of you?"

"Yes."

"For Christ's sake, Moth."

"I didn't tell her who he was, or anything. I haven't . . ." I began, but paused. "I didn't quite know what I should do."

And in a cold, clear voice, completely unaffected by the whiskey, Vidar leaned toward me and said: "Forget it. Just leave it be."

110

I don't know what I was expecting. Maybe exactly this—but not quite. Right? It's not always easy to identify the differences in what you believe and what you hope. It was quiet in the house, and the walls were closing in. I sat in front of him, perfectly still, eyeing the whiskey and fervently longing for a glass of my own.

"You must have suspected it yourself," I said.

"Suspected what?"

"That it was Bengtsson."

"It wasn't him."

"And yet you lingered around him after his accident. You went to his house. Why?"

Vidar turned up his palms. "I was invited. And it wasn't just me; Markus was there too. I couldn't refuse."

"Was that all?" I pressed.

"He'd been in an accident. It was the first time I'd saved anyone's life, and it came as a shock. I suppose I just had a little trouble letting it go."

"Because of the skid marks?"

"What about the skid marks?"

"There weren't any. Not that I could see, at least."

This caught him off guard, and, I noticed, for the first time he seemed worried, as though he had only just realized that he had no idea how much I knew.

"I don't know. There are tons of possible reasons why marks on the asphalt might not have been visible there. But I sure as hell never thought it could have been him, because it wasn't." I caught a whiff of the whiskey on his breath. "The murders stopped when Linder died," he went on.

"Or when Einar had his accident."

Vidar shook his head. "The accident happened months later."

"But there was a long time between murders. And," I added, "Linder has an alibi. At least for the murder of Franzén."

Vidar snorted. "And what's that supposed to be?"

I pulled my grandfather's work journal onto my lap and opened it to the right page.

"I found this."

I turned the book so Vidar could see. Frowning, he took in my grandfather's note from February 28, 1986:

11:00–12:30. D. Linder here. Helped me fix the cement mixer. Must get it to Frösakull tomorrow. (300 kronor).

He considered the note for a long time. I watched for signs in his face, fresh tension or uncertainty, but I couldn't discern any.

"This isn't an alibi, Moth. A journal entry is no alibi."

"Gisela Mellberg says she ran into Håkansson the next day. That's in here too. Håkansson was up to my grandpa's farm to pick up the mixer. She confirmed it. Vidar, couldn't it all be wrong?"

"No," he said coolly. "It can't. He did the right thing."

I looked at him in confusion.

"Who did the right thing?"

"Have you gone to the police with this?"

"No. I didn't know what I should do."

"What did you think would happen, Moth, huh? Even if it's true, this is just one of a number of crimes. Does he have an alibi for the others?"

"I don't know, but they're all connected."

"Just drop it, Moth."

"But isn't there more to suggest it was Bengtsson rather than Linder? For instance, no connection was ever found between Linder and Östmark. Was there? Gisela Mellberg is still alive. Stina Franzén's parents are still alive. There are still next of kin who—"

Vidar rose from his chair so suddenly that it was shoved backward and scraped against the floor. He looked down at me with a combination of disgust and fear, as though he was afraid I was going to do something terrible.

"So you're going to go to the police and say that a former officer took the law into his own hands and killed another former officer who you now believe was innocent? Do you think they're going to want to even touch this? Don't you see how it would look? And all to finger a man who can't even be punished in any meaningful way. Einar Bengtsson is a goddamn vegetable in a wheelchair. He can't move, can't talk, who the fuck even knows if he can think? Everyone wants answers, everyone wants to find meaning, an explanation. What the hell kind of explanation would this be?"

"Vidar," I said. "Why are you so angry?"

"Why the fuck do you think? This isn't a game."

"I know that. Believe me. I just want," I said, and even as the words left my mouth I could hear how naïve and simple they sounded, "to figure out the truth."

"The truth?" Vidar spat. "*What* truth? *Whose* truth? Yours? Everyone in the world walks around thinking they know the truth about themselves, their neighbors; they think they understand each other. But you have no idea. There is no limit to what we don't know. And now you think you know how things stand. But truth means consequences. What do you honestly think would happen? And up here! My father's name, my name, what would happen to us? What are you going to do, Moth? Huh?"

Maybe he was right.

The pursuit of the truth could go on forever, or until all the survivors forgot there was any truth to be found. The truth was a fantasy. The truth never ended. Just like the lies and misconceptions, the smoke and mirrors. I was struck by everything I didn't know. Everything I told myself I knew, when in fact I had only assumed.

"What the hell are you up to? Chasing after me, after Dad. Just like the old days—I remember the way you looked at us. Your own life up there in that house is so fucking mundane that you have to make up stories. That's exactly what you told me—you have no life, so you live the lives of others. You sit there at your computer like a fucking desk detective. You don't have any demons of your own, but you need some, so you feed on mine and my dad's. And the others, and their families. That's what you're doing, that's what you've done."

I started to say something but fell silent. In one sense, this was a reasonable accusation. I had regarded Vidar and his dad with both wonder and envy, and to some extent I still did—maybe more than ever. I needed a story where everything made sense, one I could piece together neatly. A monument to Sven and Vidar.

"I want to believe your dad too. I want to believe what he did was right. He believed it was. But it was wrong. I want to believe you too, but it wasn't Linder. I don't know what to do. That's why I'm here."

I was talking to his back. Whiskey glass in hand, Vidar had turned around to stare at the wall. It took me a moment to realize he was looking at a photograph of his parents.

He turned around again and looked right at me, and in that instant I could see Vidar Jörgensson, I could see straight into him, and it stung like a painful memory.

"I've been thinking about what happened around here a few years ago," I said. "When Lovisa Markström was murdered. I wasn't here then, but I've heard stories. I know you did everything you could that time, to right wrongs. To get the right man convicted. And you succeeded. Maybe you're thinking that's what happened this time too, with Linder. It would be no wonder."

"You have no idea what you're talking about. I'm no—"

"Listen to me," I said. It was the first time I had interrupted Vidar, but there was a force to my words that made him obey. "Even if you think you've put things to rights, even if that was your only intention, it turned out wrong."

"You don't know that."

"When it came to Lovisa Markström, you dug through the mistakes the police made without batting an eye. And I know it's different when it's your own father, that he's the one who . . . but Vidar, he didn't know. He believed he was doing the right thing, just like you. If he *had* known, what would he have done? Have you thought about that?"

Vidar blinked. When he didn't respond, I continued, almost pleading: "Your father gave you everything you need to do the right thing this time. You know that. If he'd been aware that he made a mistake, he wouldn't rest until he—"

"He would have killed himself! Don't you see that? He never would have been able to stand it! Some things can't be undone. He never would have forgiven himself."

"And you won't be able to, either. You know that."

"He would have killed himself, Moth."

"But he's already dead!"

Vidar looked as though I had slapped him.

"He's no longer with us," I went on, more gently. "Sven was a good man who made a mistake. It's possible to be a good person and still make mistakes. And he's gone. But we—*you*—are still here."

"Do you even have any idea what you're doing, what you're asking of me? Huh?" He stared at me. "Do you even understand?"

"Yes. I understand."

He dropped his gaze to the glass of whiskey in his hand. He was short of breath after his outburst.

There were others around us, a collection of ghosts only he could see.

Without a word, he hurled the glass at the wall.

111

He wanted me to leave. I had nothing more to say and didn't resist. It was over, whatever "it" was. I got in the car and cruised out of Marbäck, down to the highway that would take me back to Tofta. I took out my phone and listened to it ring on the other end.

"Yes, this is Gisela."

Before we'd taken leave I had promised to get in touch if and when I found out who the man in the photograph was. I told her that now I knew. That it was him. I had already known this, of course, but had held off on telling her in the hope that Vidar would react differently when I spoke to him. I would have preferred to go to the police along with Vidar, and then, side by side, we could have told Gisela.

After I said his name, she was quiet for a long time. I wondered what she was thinking, what emotions were rising inside her, whether she *was* thinking, whether she felt anything at all.

"Is he still alive?"

"Yes. He's alive. I'm going to go to the police with this. But I wanted to tell you first."

"I truly appreciate it. Thank you."

"I'm sure they'll be calling you, possibly even tomorrow. Just so you know, so you're prepared in case they get in touch."

"Of course. Thank you. I have to get back to dinner, we're just about to eat here."

She sounded oddly mechanical. Which was really no wonder; it must have been a shock.

I drove home. The headlights shone desolate and white over the highway. Did I blame Vidar? I didn't. It was probably asking something superhuman of him, my hope that he wouldn't try to deflect.

When I got home, I turned on the porch light and stared at the front door. There was something off about it. As I pulled the handle down I understood what that was.

It was unlocked.

The door was old, its flaking paint in the wood around the lock full of little scratches and marks that had accumulated over the years. I myself had caused several of them, coming home drunk as a teenager and fumbling with my keys in the dark. Impossible to say whether there were any fresh ones.

I cautiously opened the door. The only potential weapon I had was my keys, so I squeezed them tight between my fingers and I searched the house, my phone in the other hand, the emergency number ready to go if I needed it.

My heart was pounding in my ears, making it hard to hear anything.

No one was there. I was alone.

My legs trembling, I sat down at my desk and called Dad. It was like something had gotten caught in my throat, so as the phone rang I tried to clear it, practiced saying "Hi, it's me" aloud into the silent house, to hear how it sounded.

"Hello?" he said.

"Hi, it's me."

"Why, hello there."

"Is this a bad time?"

"Your ma and I are watching the news, is all. I'll turn it off."

I looked at the clock.

"The news is on now?"

"No, we recorded it. How are you?"

"I'm fine. I just wanted to let you know that . . . tomorrow. I'm going to the police tomorrow."

"Okay . . . ?" Dad sounded anxious. "What's wrong, is, what—did something happen? You sound really strange."

I thought of the shadow outside the window, the light on in the kitchen, the unlocked door. Was it me? Maybe I'd just forgotten. Maybe I was looking for patterns where there weren't any. I couldn't figure out who would be after me.

"No, no."

I looked toward the living room. There was a picture of us, Dad and me. I think I was six, maybe seven. Dad has a full head of hair and is younger than I am now. We're sitting on the sofa together, deeply absorbed in a comic book. Our heads are propped together. He has a hand on my shoulder.

"Should I . . ." Dad began. "Should I come with you or anything? Should we go together?"

"No, I can do it on my own. It's fine, Dad. But I'm sure they'll be calling you soon too. Since you're the one who found the work journals."

"So Pa was right?"

"Pa was right."

"Damn right he was," Dad said.

That night I wrote, as though surrounded by shadows real and imagined. I was still working when the phone rang several hours later. I recognized the number.

"Vidar?" I said.

"You've talked to Evy, right?"

Vidar's voice was sluggish. He'd kept drinking.

"Yes." I'd mentioned it to him when we saw each other at the soccer match, but he must not have filed it away in his memory. Maybe he hadn't even heard me. "Lots of times. But only about David and Sven. Not Einar. I held off on that. I haven't told anyone but you. And Mellberg."

"Mellberg? You talked to her again?"

"I had promised her I would call."

There was a fresh drop of fear in Vidar's voice. "When? What did you say to her? Did you say it was him?"

"I . . ." I began. "Yes, this evening. A few hours ago."

"For Christ's sake, Moth!" I heard rapid steps, heard him start to throw on his coat. "You'll have to drive, I've had too much to drink. Come pick me up."

"Now?"

"Now, for Christ's sake, now!"

He hung up, and only then did I realize what I'd done.

112

"Pass them."

I veered out a little bit. The center line of the county road rumbled beneath the tires. Two bright headlights screeched through the darkness.

"I can't, there's a car coming."

"Pass them."

"Sure, then neither of us will get there; that's a great plan."

"Then honk."

"It's a truck, what's he going to do, stop?"

The oncoming car sailed by. I downshifted and passed the truck. We were approaching Brogård, the fields and pastures giving way to houses and side streets. When I glanced away from the road for a moment and turned my head, Vidar looked grim and aged; the dim light inside the car made his many furrows and wrinkles look even deeper.

"Shit, Moth. Ancient team rosters? Notes in a work journal from the eighties? What got into you? It's senseless. Totally senseless."

He stank of whiskey. I didn't say anything. I had nothing to say. All I could think about was what we would find when we arrived.

"I'm too drunk for this." He squeezed his eyes shut and brought his fingertips to them, pressing in. "I went to see her once. Evy. It was last spring, after we found Linder. She told me about Dad, David, all of it.

How she helped him, up there on the ridge. I hadn't expected she would dare to tell me. She looked so sad, so full of regret, and yet . . . she acted as though there was no alternative. So fucking . . . I don't know. Genuine. I believed her, of course. Anyone would have. She revealed things about herself, about Dad, misconduct she committed for his sake. If what you're saying is true, she lied straight to my face. I can't believe it."

I couldn't either. Evy had told me the same story, of course. That sense of surreality, that I could have been betrayed like that, and by *her*—I felt the sting of it too.

"Your dad did what he thought was right. It wasn't, but that doesn't change anything."

"Doesn't it?"

Vidar turned to look at me. That's when I realized: He would have to live with a riddle he might never be able to solve.

According to the information I'd found in recent days, Einar Bengtsson lived in an assisted living facility near Tylösand. He had made it to the age of fifty-eight, but aside from that, nothing much had happened in his life since 1991. He was still unable to speak and used a wheelchair. In recent years he'd gotten a dog, which he and the staff took for a walk each morning and evening. That was all.

The building was in a nice location; you could smell the sea. It looked like an ordinary apartment building, two stories high, dark brick. On the ground floor were signs for a treatment area, a small cafeteria that was closed for the evening, and two elevators alongside a staircase. It smelled like a hospital inside.

Vidar stopped at the resident directory and gazed at it for a moment, then headed for the stairs to the second floor. His body was large and heavy. The sound of his steps and movements echoed off the walls. I could feel my pulse in my cheeks and ears, fear as vibrations.

The door to his room wasn't locked; she hadn't even bothered with that much. Vidar pushed down the handle and hurried in ahead of me.

The apartment included a set of furniture arranged in front of a television, and this was where Gisela sat, her elbows on her knees, facing the door as if she'd been waiting for us.

Einar was on his back in the wheelchair, on the floor in front of her. She had struck him so hard he tipped over. His face was a mask of meat; he was no longer recognizable. In the midst of all that red, one eye was wide open and darting around in panic. I didn't know what had happened to the other eye, but I couldn't see it. A pool of blood was spreading beneath his head. There was a rasping sound as he exhaled, bubbles of blood escaping his mouth. Next to him lay a shaggy little dog, whining and trembling, trying to lick his face.

I wanted to throw up. But I couldn't. I couldn't do a thing. It was my fault, it was all my fault, I was frozen in place and couldn't—

"Moth, call an ambulance. And get the dog out of here. Run down and get the staff, someone must be fucking working here."

Vidar had knelt down by the man.

"They're having coffee downstairs." This was Gisela. Her gaze was fixed on an invisible spot somewhere between her feet and Einar's body. "I didn't know he had a dog. I couldn't . . . It just lay there whining. I had to stop." She looked at me. What I saw in her eyes frightened me. "I met him once. He was one of the bystanders when we were searching for Frida. He asked what we were doing, if he could help. That must be how he found me." Blood dripped from her hands. She didn't seem to care. She stood up. "And now I found him. I didn't do this for me. I did it for Robert."

"What did you do to him?"

She slowly walked past me, toward the hall.

"I don't know."

Photographs on the wall; I recognized the people in them: his parents, Evy, Evy's children and grandchildren. I imagine Evy was the one who had hung them up.

The body on the floor began to shake violently, as though a current were running through it. The dog howled.

"Moth," Vidar roared. "Moth! Call right fucking now, before he dies!"

113

There was a wintry chill and it was hours before dawn, but I don't remember the cold, don't remember shivering, nothing.

Blue lights flashed rhythmically around us. I could hear waves; I turned my head and caught a glimpse of the sea between the buildings and trees, the dark sky meeting an even darker surface. He'd lived a pleasant life here for thirty years. What a remarkable thought.

I looked at the sea and could see a hint of the shore. In summertime it would be teeming with tourists and families, children laughing, bad buskers, the air hot and heavy, the stink of beer and sunscreen. Now it was deserted. The waves grew louder, becoming powerful and threatening and vast.

"What is it?" Vidar asked.

"I kept thinking I'd seen someone. Outside my window. That someone had been in my house, that someone was following me. I don't know, I . . . now I think I was seeing a pattern that wasn't there."

It scared me. Not the thought that someone could have been watching me through the window, that someone could have been right outside the walls that make up the safest place I've ever known, or that the light was on and the door unlocked.

There had never been anyone there. No one had been following me; no one had been there in the house but me. I had made it all up. That was the worst part. That I had acted on impulse, had imagined it was a possibility. Just as Sven had done when he watched David Linder, I saw something that was never there. I never thought it would end up like this. It doesn't take much to lose yourself, and I shared much more than soil and origins with Sven Jörgensson.

"I guess I was hoping that the same was true here," I said. "With Einar. That it was like you said, it was all a figment of my imagination."

Vidar didn't respond.

We watched them carry him out. The attendants were bustling, focused, exchanging curt words. *Here he is*, I thought. The body, the man who caused others such incredible suffering. For so long he was no more than a shadow, a horror in the night, a nightmare. Now he was finally a whole person, someone who could live and die. Here he was. Just a human being like any other.

"I wonder," Vidar said softly, "if you could give me a ride."

"Home?"

He shook his head.

"No. Not home." He looked at me. "What's wrong?"

I turned to look at the water.

"This is the first time since I came home that I've been near the sea."

We set off for Tofta. On the way he called and woke her up. No one had had time to contact her yet, and Vidar didn't tell her what was going on, just that they needed to talk.

"How did she sound?" I asked.

"Tired."

"You know she had a stroke in August."

"Yes, I heard."

She met us at the door, one hand keeping a tight grip on her burgundy rollator. She had wrapped her big, round body in a robe, and the warm scent of coffee wafted out to us, in the cold.

"Hi, Evy. I'm so sorry to bother you like this."

"Hi." She looked at me in confusion. "Him too?"

"Yes."

I gave her a gentle hug. From behind her glasses, Evy aimed an unusually sharp squint at Vidar.

"Have you been drinking?" Only now did she notice his hands. In the dim light, the blood looked unnaturally dark. "Oh my God, what happened?"

"Can we come in?"

We sat down on the sofa. Vidar washed his hands, and then we had coffee. Evy sat on her rollator, resting her forearms on its handles and folding her hands over her belly. She looked oddly absentminded, the way she used to when she was in the middle of a story, heading into a memory she couldn't quite feel the shape of. Her robe gaped, and I could see the deep varicose veins just above her knees and on her lower legs.

"Here's what happened," Vidar said slowly.

And he told her.

"Okay," she said weakly when he was done. "Is she . . . where is she now? Gisela?"

"Down at the station. They took her into custody shortly after it happened. She didn't get very far, nor did she seem to try."

Evy nodded slowly. She looked at her hands.

"Okay," she said again.

"You had your suspicions," I said tentatively, "didn't you?"

She startled, as though she had forgotten I was sitting there.

"Yes," she said firmly. "Yes, I did." She sighed. "Lies have their time. The truth must have its own too."

It had been up to me to ask the question. I did it because Vidar couldn't. I could hardly bear to do it myself. I thought of everything she had told me, in fragments and incoherent stories, tiny moments and scenes I'd had to piece together myself when her own memory wouldn't allow. The story of what had happened between her and

Sven, between Sven and David Linder. None of it appeared, now, as given, as true. Everything, I realized, might be a lie. I had wanted something from her, a story. And that's what I got.

Lies have their time; the truth has its own.

But which is which?

"It was that summer there, '91, just before the accident. I confronted Einar. I got the idea that that's why he . . . I don't know. That that's why he did it. Crashed, I mean. He must have been trying to end it." She took a little packet of tissues from the pocket of her robe, pulled one out, fiddled with it. "I suppose I should have done something. Said something. I knew I should. But of course I couldn't be certain, and as injured as he was after the accident, I knew he could never hurt anyone again. And he would never be able to plead his case either; he couldn't defend himself. So I didn't do anything. I did nothing."

"But you confronted him," Vidar said. "So you must have had some reason to suspect it was him. What was it?"

She hesitated to reply.

"I saw him in a picture in the newspaper, from the search party. I asked what he was doing there, because he should have been at work, and he couldn't give me a good answer. That was enough for me. He never could lie to me."

"Speaking of lies. You lied to me, and I understand that. But to Dad?"

"I didn't lie," she said. "I didn't lie to him."

"But you suspected something. You said so."

"But not—"

"You actually said so to me too, Evy," I said. "Right? *There was nothing we could do. No one could.* That's what you said. Remember that?"

"I . . . yes . . . no, I . . ."

"I don't understand how you could lie to Dad like that. Don't you see, it drove him to . . ."

He trailed off as she began to cry. It's so uncomfortable when old people cry. You always assume that because they've lived so long and seen so much they don't need to cry anymore.

"I know," she said, once she'd collected herself a bit. "I know. But my God, we're all only human."

As though that was any sort of explanation. Although it was, of course; I'd thought the same thing a number of times myself. Vidar too, and maybe even Sven. There is a limit to what a person can handle, and once in a while we are forced to grapple with something beyond that limit. Which means loss—in one way or another.

But isn't it also the case that, when this happens, we are forgiven precisely *because* we are human? As though—even though we don't deserve it, and simply by virtue of being born human—we have per-mission to do wrong and then ask forgiveness from others? It's not an excuse; it's a way to say that you're probably not to blame for every-thing in the end. To say you're only human is also to say *so you should forgive me.* To be human is to be able to escape guilt.

Maybe not responsibility, but guilt. I glanced at Vidar. He hadn't inherited his father's guilt, but the responsibility for the truth sur-rounding it rested with him. The responsibility to make it right. That was the case, wasn't it? Because it wasn't my responsibility, was it?

"You believed Sven was doing the right thing when you helped him up there in the forest, Evy," I said. "Didn't you? That David Linder was actually the guilty one?"

She nodded vehemently.

"Yes, of course. The idea . . . I mean, my brother, the thought that it could have been him . . . I only started to suspect when summer came around. Right before the accident."

"But Dad died in November of that year," Vidar said. "Almost six months after the accident. By that point, you must have realized it was Einar. And still you said nothing to him, even though you could have."

"But we're talking about my brother!" she exclaimed. "There was no way I could, or wanted to, believe he was that terrible. He isn't that terrible. If I told Sven about it, it would be like admitting it was true. And, besides, well, I . . . I was thinking of Sven, too. I wanted to spare him. He felt awful that David died, if it had come out that David was innocent, on top of that . . ."

"But he was innocent," I said coldly. "And Sven was alive. Didn't he deserve to know?"

"Dad never would have been able to handle it." Vidar hung his head and stared at the floor between his shoes. "He would have gone to his old colleagues and told them. It would have gotten out." When he looked up again, it was straight at Evy. "And you would have lost your brother."

He waited for her to say something, but no words escaped Evy's mouth. I could tell she was thinking about something and asked what it was.

"Oh, I just . . . it's all so terrible."

"I know," I said.

"Einar was, or he is, a man of faith, did you know that? He used to say that evil can take root in the least of the world's creatures. But people are different. When God created us, the devil must have been right close by."

"He used to say that?" I asked.

"Sometimes. When he saw something awful on TV, or read it in the paper, you know."

"What do you think he meant?"

"I don't know." She shuddered, as if from a sudden chill. "I really don't know."

"Do you think he was talking about himself?"

Or something inside him, I thought. *Something he saw or felt, and feared.*

"No. He was so kind, you see. Einar is so kind. He wants to help people, not hurt them."

"Was he ever convicted of anything, Evy?" I asked instead. "Einar? I mean, not for these crimes, but in general. Does he have a record?"

"No, God no. Einar has no criminal record."

That was why the blood spatter didn't turn up a DNA match for him either. I wished I had some paper to write on; I was afraid the shock and exhaustion would make it hard for me to remember this conversation later.

"Then was he sick or anything?"

"Sick? What do you mean, sick?"

"I don't know, just . . . just sick. Before the accident, I mean."

She shook her head.

"He was never depressed or anything? Did he take pills, or . . ."

"No."

"Did he have . . . do you remember whether he had . . ."

Vidar had been sitting there quietly, and now he turned to me with curiosity in his eyes. I wanted to ask Evy if her brother had been into porn. Sex clubs, violence, whether she'd ever found any written fantasies about taking control over women. What I was looking for was an explanation, based on the preconceptions I had of men who committed the sorts of crimes her brother was guilty of. I needed some way to make it all make sense.

"He was just kind of wild when he was younger," she said. "I was the only one he would listen to. But he was really lovely. A great coach, stable and warm and considerate. There was nothing . . . I never saw anything mean in him."

And now he had nearly been beaten to death.

I spent the better part of each day inside my head, in a world I dreamed up myself, a world made of fantasies. The line between fiction and reality had never been more blurry and yet so icily clear. What had I done, in making that call? I hadn't thought it through. I hadn't understood.

"Did they have a relationship, Evy?" This was Vidar. "Stina and Einar, I mean."

"I think so. But I don't know for sure."

"They often have some sort of bond with the first one," Vidar went on. "That's why I'm asking. It's not necessarily planned; it just happens. Maybe that was the case for him? Then they realize that they want to or need to experience it again, and start searching for their next victim more actively."

"Yes," Evy said faintly. "Yes, maybe. He said he liked one of his players. I think that was Stina."

She couldn't say more. I'm sure it was too difficult.

Yes, I thought, *maybe that was it*. They embark on a relationship in the fall of 1985. It doesn't look good, in other people's eyes. There's a lot of gossip and whispers in Alet circles. She stops playing so they can continue to see each other. And the gas station receipt Sven and David found in her car. He meets up with her outside Grand Hotel when she gets off work at eleven that night. She wants to fill up the tank before the next day, if that's how their night is going to go. They keep driving, out to Vapnödalen. They might have been on their way to his place. Then something happens—an argument? Maybe it just happens. Or is it deliberate?

Or: They embark on a relationship in the fall of '85, but she wants to end it; he sends signals she doesn't like, signals that scare her? Maybe she just doesn't like him. She has to quit soccer and they stop seeing each other, but he can't stop thinking about Stina. Einar calls her house, tracks her down outside Grand Hotel. He wants to talk. She is hesitant, but eventually she says she can give him a ride home to Fammarp, but she wants to get gas first. She goes by way of Tiarp.

Vidar started to speak again, but I jumped in ahead of him.

"Evy," I said. "They're going to look for Frida Östmark. They're starting tomorrow already, on the farm where Einar lived. Is that the right place?"

She nodded, breathing hard, and blew her nose again. "I think so."

"Do you know where? Where on the farm, I mean?"

She shook her head. Her frizzy silver hair moved in waves. When

I looked at her, I could see her face for what it was. Cloven, steeped in the moral pain caused by the many years—or maybe it was no choice of her own, I don't know, maybe you don't always have a choice, in the end—of wearing a Janus face.

Perhaps Evy said more that night, I don't recall. I was so tired. There's just one more thing I remember.

"I suppose I was expecting you to show up one day, Vidar. You are your father's son, after all. Anything else would be out of character for a Jörgensson. But still, I had hoped I would have time to die before you came."

115

The dogs found her at dawn. She was behind a toolshed in the corner of the property that had once belonged to Einar Bengtsson. Frida Östmark was dressed in the same clothes she'd been wearing the day she was reported missing. They had been searching for two days.

A few weeks later, following a prosecutorial order, the National Forensic Center ran a comparative analysis of the blood from Stina Franzén's car and a sample of Einar Bengtsson's saliva, taken as he lay half beaten to death in a hospital bed.

The two DNA tests were a grade +4 match, putting them in the highest category on the NFC scale. *The result,* according to the analyst who handled the sample, *strongly indicates that the DNA in the sample belongs to Einar Bengtsson.*

One of the major papers published, one day, a long article about the case of the Tiarp Man. I was asked if I wanted to be quoted in it, but declined. The piece centered on David Linder's innocence and Einar Bengtsson's guilt, and above all it highlighted suspicions against "the then-fifty-four-year-old former police officer who is suspected of taking the law into his own hands in the spring of 1991." Everyone knew whom the article was referring to. The police authority was taken to task and Markus Danielsson had to make another statement, now that there was an even more remarkable development in the case. He handled it well, as far as I could tell. He made it sound as if he was the one who had contacted the media, rather than the other way around, that he wanted the truth about the Tiarp Man to be made public rather than that he must be held accountable for it.

I watched unfamiliar cars head up to Marbäck and Norteforsen. People wanted to talk to Vidar and Evy. I wondered whether they responded. It was starting to creep into the newspaper, names and fragments of what had happened. I kept to myself even as I suspected that, in time, those cars would appear in my driveway as well.

There must have been something in Einar. An explanation. I just hadn't managed to find it yet. A childhood trauma, an obsession, a tendency. I thought of the coach, slim and well dressed, open and smiling, I'd once seen from my spot in the bleachers across the soccer pitch. There was nothing there. Nothing at all. Aside from the opportunity, maybe, and the fact that he was a man. What kind of explanation was that? As though a series of crimes of that magnitude doesn't need to be explained by a corresponding and equally powerful origin.

Sven was a perpetrator of sorts. It had taken time to understand, but I realized it now: He had made himself guilty of the gravest of crimes. Even so, I could explain Sven; the author in me found him comprehensible. But Einar? I could find no inroad from which to comprehend Einar Bengtsson. He did what he did. What happens happens. It's not always possible to understand. Evil can take root in the smallest of earth's creatures; according to Evy, Einar had said so himself. Was it true, and if so, was it that simple?

I thought of the terrible things we sometimes do to each other, the injustices and lies, the tragedies big and small that befall us. It's natural to ascribe meaning to them, to want them to make sense.

I suppose that, unless the darkness in some of us is kept in check, it can well forth like a monster. That was an answer of sorts. If you could call it an answer. One way to solve a riddle is for the riddle itself to dissolve; something that seemed to be stable becomes volatile and goes up in smoke.

Yes, I thought, *maybe that was it.* The Swedish crimes that took place in those long-ago years have taught us the bleakest truth life has to offer: There is no meaning.

An early March morning in 2020, clear weather. The air is so light. I'm standing at the window in my office, with a view of Lake Tofta. I can see it approaching, a black silhouette against all the blue. Wings like silver.

Everything has its place. Everything has its time.

Winter has its time, and spring has its own.

It's quite small, the bird. It cuts a slim, sharp figure. It alights on one of the heavily pruned fir trees that line the cycling path. I squint at its silhouette, but I can't tell whether it's looking at me or not; it's too far away.

I've started to consider how I want to live the rest of my life.

I've come a long way now.

It's been more difficult than I expected. Should I, perhaps, have let Sven remain a hero? I think he still is a hero to me, but to Vidar? I don't know. Even heroes can make mistakes. The dream of a spotless past is, after all, only a dream. No one makes it through unmarked. We have to learn to live with it. If we can.

Maybe that's it. I feel very close to an answer now; I don't know if I can get any closer. But who would we be if we didn't try?

Not long after I wrote the words on the previous page, I received two pieces of news. The first was a death notice. It had happened peacefully during the night. She fell asleep and never woke up. Sometime after midnight, Death descended over Norteforsen 195 and took Evy Carlén to the other side. I received this news alone in the yellow house and realized I had never gotten the chance to say goodbye. However such a farewell would have looked.

The other piece of news was about Vidar Jörgensson. I heard that he had called up his old friend and colleague and asked to come back, to start working as a cop again.

When this news reached me, I thought about all the things we don't know. All the things we never will know. It's surprising, really. Even more remarkable is everything we think we know that we later find out is wrong. The results can be devastating. Since there is no escaping this possibility, I do exactly the same thing as everyone else. I invent, imagine, ascribe, fill in. That's what I do. It's my job.

I haven't investigated the matter, and I probably never will, but if you go down to the highway in the morning, you can probably catch a glimpse of Vidar now, just like we used to see his father. I know what kind of car he has, after all. He must come driving by from up in Marbäck, as if time is standing still, on his way into the city, to the police station, to start the workday more or less at the same time as everyone else in the village.

ACKNOWLEDGMENTS

I'd like to thank Ida Maria Kim, my strange and wonderful travel companion through life; my son, Stig; my Swedish editor, Daniel Sandström, and all the great people at Albert Bonniers Förlag; my amazing agents Christine and Astri over at Ahlander Agency; my parents and my brother; my wonderful translator, Rachel Willson-Broyles; and last but not least, David Ebershoff and Darryl Oliver at Random House/Hogarth, for being such generous and kind people, fierce readers, and great craftsmen. Without you, *Blaze Me a Sun* would never have seen the light of day.

C.C.

ABOUT THE AUTHOR

CHRISTOFFER CARLSSON was born in 1986 in Marbäck, on the west coast of Sweden. He holds a PhD in criminology from the University of Stockholm and is one of Sweden's leading crime experts. Carlsson is the youngest winner of the Best Swedish Crime Novel of the Year, voted by the Swedish Crime Writers' Academy, and has been a finalist for the prestigious Glass Key Award, given to the best Scandinavian crime novel of the year. A number one bestseller in Sweden, *Blaze Me a Sun* marks Carlsson's American debut.